HONOR IS AS HONOR DOES

Honor leaned across the table toward the ambassador. "Shut your cowardly mouth. You disgust me."

"I'll have your commission!" Houseman gobbled. "I have friends in high places, and I'll—"

She put all the strength of her Sphinx-bred muscles into a backhand blow that catapulted Houseman back from the table as blood burst from his nostrils and pulped lips. She grabbed the end of the heavy conference table and hurled it out of her way. As she advanced on Houseman, the bloody-mouthed diplomat's hands scrabbled frantically at the floor as he propelled himself away from her.

Fortunately he had within him not a scrap of physical courage; she didn't know what she would have done next if he'd shown fight. She never would know, for as she loomed above him she heard him actually *sobbing* in his terror, and the sound stopped her dead.

Her raw fury slunk back in the caves of her mind, still flexing its claws and snarling, but no longer in control, and her voice was cold and distant . . . and cruel.

"Your entire purpose here was to conclude an alliance with Yeltsin's Star. To show these people an alliance with Manticore could *help* them. That was a commitment from our Kingdom. The Queen's *honor* is at stake here. The honor of the entire Kingdom of Manticore. If we cut and run, if we abandon Grayson, it will be a blot on Her Majesty's honor *nothing* can ever erase. If you can't see it any other way, consider the impact on every other alliance we ever try to conclude! If you think you can get your 'friends in high places' to cashier me for doing my duty, you go right ahead and try. In the meantime, those of us who aren't cowards will just have to muddle through as best we can without you!"

BAEN BOOKS by DAVID WEBER

HONOR HARRINGTON
The Honor Of The Queen

DAVID WEBER

BAEN

Copyright © 1993 by David Weber

A Baen Books Original

Baen Publishing Enterprises
P.O. Box 1403
Riverdale, NY 10471
www.baen.com

ISBN: 0-7434-3572-9

Cover art by David Mattingly
Map by Eleanor Kostyk

First paperback printing, June 1993
Eighth printing, August 2002

Distributed by Simon & Schuster
1230 Avenue of the Americas
New York, NY 10020

Printed in the United States of America

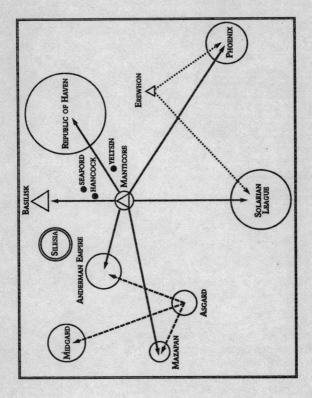

• CHAPTER ONE

The cutter passed from sunlit brilliance to soot-black shadow with the knife-edge suddenness possible only in space, and the tall, broad-shouldered woman in the black and gold of the Royal Manticoran Navy gazed out the armorplast port at the battle-steel beauty of her command and frowned.

The six-limbed cream-and-gray treecat on her shoulder shifted his balance as she raised her right hand and pointed.

"I thought we'd discussed replacing Beta Fourteen with Commander Antrim, Andy," she said, and the short, dapper lieutenant commander beside her winced at her soprano voice's total lack of inflection.

"Yes, Ma'am. We did." He tapped keys on his memo pad and checked the display. "We discussed it on the sixteenth, Skipper, before you went on leave, and he promised to get back to us."

"Which he never did," Captain Honor Harrington observed, and Lieutenant Commander Venizelos nodded.

"Which he never did. Sorry, Ma'am. I should've kept after him."

"You've had a lot of other things on your plate, too," she said, and Andreas Venizelos hid another—and much more painful—wince. Honor Harrington seldom rapped her officers in the teeth, but he would almost have preferred to have her hand him his head. Her quiet, understanding tone sounded entirely too much as if she were finding excuses for him.

"Maybe so, Ma'am, but I still should've kept after him," he said. "We both know how these yard types hate node replacements." He tapped a note into his pad. "I'll com him as soon as we get back aboard *Vulcan*."

"Good, Andy." She turned her head and smiled at him, her strong-boned face almost impish. "If he starts giving you a song and dance, let me know. I'm having lunch with Admiral Thayer. I may not have my official orders yet, but you can bet she's got an idea what they're going to be."

Venizelos grinned back in understanding, for he and his captain both knew Antrim had been playing an old yard trick that usually worked. When you didn't want to carry out some irksome bit of refit, you just dragged your feet until you "ran out of time," on the theory that a ship's captain would rather get back into space than incur Their Lordships' displeasure with a tardy departure date. Unfortunately for Commander Antrim, success depended on a skipper who was willing to let a yard dog get away with it. This one wasn't, and while it wasn't official yet, the grapevine said the First Space Lord had plans for HMS *Fearless*. Which meant this time someone *else* was going to buy a rocket from the Admiralty if she was late, and Venizelos rather suspected the CO of Her Majesty's Space Station *Vulcan* would be less than pleased if she had to explain the hold-up to Admiral Danvers. The Third Space Lord had a notoriously short fuse and a readiness to collect scalps.

"Yes, Ma'am. Ah, would you mind if I just happened to let slip to Antrim that you're lunching with the Admiral, Skipper?"

"Now, now, Andy. Don't be nasty—unless he looks like giving you problems, of course."

"Of course, Ma'am."

Honor smiled again and turned back to the view port.

Fearless's running lights blinked the green and white of a moored starship, clear and gem-like without the diffraction of atmosphere, and she felt a familiar throb of pride. The heavy cruiser's white skin gleamed in reflected sunlight above the ruler-straight line of shadow running down her double-ended, twelve-hundred-meter, three-hundred-thousand-ton hull. Brilliant light spilled from the oval of an open weapon bay a hundred and fifty meters forward of the after impeller ring, and Honor watched skinsuited yard techs crawling over the ominous bulk of Number Five Graser. She'd thought the intermittent glitch was in the on-mount software, but *Vulcan's* people insisted it was in the emitter assembly itself.

She twitched her shoulders, and Nimitz scolded gently as he dug his claws deeper into the padded shoulder of her tunic for balance. She clicked her teeth and rubbed his ears in wordless apology, but she never took her eyes from the view port as the cutter continued its slow tour of *Fearless's* exterior.

Half a dozen work parties paused and looked up as the cutter ghosted past them. She couldn't make out expressions through their visors, but she could imagine the combination of exasperation and wariness some of them would wear. Yard dogs hated to have a captain peering over their shoulders while they worked on her ship . . . almost as much as captains hated turning their ships over to the yard dogs in the first place.

She swallowed a chuckle at the thought, because while she had no intention of telling them so, she was impressed by how much *Vulcan*—and Venizelos—had accomplished during her two-week absence, despite Antrim's passive resistance to the node change. Replacing an impeller node was a major pain, and Antrim obviously hoped he could skate out of it, but that ambition was doomed to failure. Beta Fourteen had been a headache almost since *Fearless's* acceptance trials, and Honor and her engineers had put up with it long enough. It wasn't as crucial as an alpha node, of course, and *Fearless* could easily maintain eighty-percent of max acceleration without it. Then, too, there was the little matter of the price tag for a replacement—something like five million dollars—which Antrim would have to sign off on. All of which no doubt helped explain his reluctance to pull it, but Commander Antrim wouldn't be aboard the next time HMS *Fearless* had to redline her drive.

The cutter curled back up over the hull, crossing

diagonally above the after port missile battery and the geometric precision of Radar Six. The long, slender blades of the cruiser's main gravitic sensors passed out of sight under the lower lip of the view port, and Honor nodded in satisfaction as her chocolate-dark eyes noted the replacement elements in the array.

All in all, she was more than pleased with how *Fearless* had performed over the last two and half T-years. She was a relatively new ship, and her builders had done her proud in most respects. It wasn't their fault someone had slipped them a faulty beta node, and she'd stood up well to an arduous first commission. Not that anti-piracy patrols were Honor's first choice for assignments. It had been nice to be on her own, and the prize money from picking off that Silesian "privateer" squadron hadn't done her bank balance a bit of harm. For that matter, the rescue of that passenger liner had been a piece of work anyone could be proud of, but the moments of excitement had been few and far between. Mostly it had been hard work and more than a little boring once she got over the sheer excitement of commanding her first heavy cruiser—and a brand spanking new one, to boot.

She made a mental note of a scuffed patch of paint above Graser Three and felt a tiny smile tugging at her lips as she contemplated the rumors about her next assignment, for the alacrity with which Admiral Courvosier had accepted his invitation to the traditional recommissioning party suggested there was more than a bit of truth to them. That was good. She hadn't seen the Admiral, much less served under him, in far too long, and if diplomats and politicians were normally a lower order of life than pirates, it should at least be an interesting change of pace.

"You know, that young man has a really nice ass for a round-eye," Dr. Allison Chou Harrington observed. "I bet you could have some fun chasing *him* around the command deck, dear."

"*Mother!*" Honor stepped on an unfilial urge to throttle

her parent and looked around quickly. But no one seemed to have overheard, and, for the first time in her memory, she was grateful for the chatter of other voices.

"Now, Honor," Dr. Harrington looked up at her with a deadly gleam in those almondine eyes so much like Honor's own, "all I said was—"

"I *know* what you said, but that 'young man' is my executive officer!"

"Well, of course he is," her mother said comfortably. "That's what makes it so convenient. And he certainly is a *handsome* fellow, isn't he? I'll bet he has to beat them off with a stick." She sighed. "Assuming he wants to," she added thoughtfully. "Just look at those eyes! He looks just like Nimitz in mating season, doesn't he?"

Honor hovered on the brink of apoplexy, and Nimitz cocked his head reprovingly at Dr. Harrington. It wasn't that he objected to her comments on his sexual prowess, but the empathic 'cat was only too well aware of how much his person's mother enjoyed teasing her.

"Commander Venizelos is *not* a treecat, and I do *not* have the least intention of chasing him with a club," Honor said firmly.

"No, dear, I know. You never have had very good judgment where men are concerned."

"Mother—!"

"Now, Honor, you know I'd never dream of criticizing," the twinkle in Allison Harrington's eyes was devilish, yet there was a trace of seriousness under the loving malice, "but a Navy captain—a *senior-grade* captain, at that— ought to get over those silly inhibitions of yours."

"I'm not 'inhibited,' " Honor said with all the dignity she could muster.

"Whatever you say, darling. But in that case, you're letting that delicious young man go sadly to waste, executive officer or not."

"Mother, just because you were born on an uncivilized and licentious planet like Beowulf is no reason for you to make eyes at my exec! Besides, what would Daddy think?"

"What would I think about what?" Surgeon Commander Alfred Harrington (retired) demanded.

"Oh, there you are." Honor and her father stood eye to eye, towering over her diminutive mother, and she jerked a thumb downward. "Mother's casting hungry looks at my exec again," she complained.

"Not to worry," her father replied. "She looks a lot, but she's never had any reason to roam."

"You're as bad as *she* is!"

"Meow," Allison said, and Honor fought back a grin.

For as long as she could remember, her mother had delighted in scandalizing the more conservative members of Manticoran society. She considered the entire kingdom hopelessly prudish, and her pungent observations to that effect drove certain society dames absolutely berserk. And her beauty, and the fact that she doted on her husband and never actually did the least thing for which they could ostracize her, only made it worse.

Of course, if she *had* been inclined to follow the mores of her birth world, she could have assembled a drooling male harem any time she cared to. She was a tiny thing, little more than two-thirds Honor's own height and of almost pure Old Earth Oriental extraction. The strong, sharply carved bone structure which had always made Honor feel plain and unfinished was muted into exotic beauty in her mother's face, and the prolong process had frozen her biological age at no more than thirty T-years. She really was like a treecat herself, Honor thought—delicate but strong, graceful and fascinating, with just a hint of the predator, and the fact that she was one of the most brilliant genetic surgeons in the Kingdom didn't hurt.

She was also, Honor knew, genuinely concerned about her only child's lack of a sex life. Well, sometimes *Honor* was a bit worried about it, but it wasn't as if she had all that many opportunities. A starship's captain simply could not dally with a member of her crew, even if she had the desire to, and Honor was none too sure she did. Her sexual experience was virtually nil—aside from a single *extremely* unpleasant Academy episode and one adolescent infatuation that had trickled off in dreary unhappiness—because she'd simply never met a man she cared to become involved with.

Not that she was interested in women; she just didn't seem particularly interested in *anyone*—which might be just as well. It avoided all sorts of potential professional difficulties . . . and she rather doubted an overgrown horse like her would provoke much reciprocal interest, anyway. That reflection bothered her a bit. No, she thought, be honest; it bothered her a *lot*, and there were times her mother's version of a sense of humor was less than amusing. But this wasn't one of them, and she surprised them both by putting an arm around her and squeezing in a rare public display of affection.

"Trying to bribe me into being good, huh?" Dr. Harrington teased, and Honor shook her head.

"I never try to do the impossible, Mother."

"That's one for your side," her father observed, then held out his hand to his wife. "Come along, Alley. Honor ought to be circulating—you can go make someone else's life miserable for a while."

"You Navy types can be a real pain in the . . . posterior," Allison replied with a wickedly demure glance at her daughter, and Honor watched fondly as her parents vanished into the crowd. She didn't get to see them as often as she would have liked, which was one reason she'd been so happy when *Fearless* was sent to *Vulcan* for refit, instead of *Hephaestus*. *Vulcan* orbited Honor's own homeworld of Sphinx, ten light-minutes further out than the capital planet of Manticore, and she'd taken shameless advantage of the fact to spend time at home, wallowing in her father's cooking.

But Alfred Harrington was quite right about her responsibilities as a hostess, and Honor squared her shoulders for the plunge back into the festivities.

A rather proprietary smile touched Admiral of the Green Raoul Courvosier's mouth as he watched Captain Harrington mix confidently with her guests and

remembered the gangling midshipman, all knees and
elbows and sharp, angular face, he'd first met sixteen
Manticoran years—over twenty-seven T-years—ago. She
really had been a piece of work, he reflected affec-
tionately. Absolutely dedicated, shy to the point of
speechlessness and determined not to show it, terrified
of math courses, and one of the most brilliant intuitive
shiphandlers and tacticians he'd ever met. She'd also
been one of the most frustrating. All that promise and
potential, and she'd near as nothing flunked out on
him before he could convince her to use that same
intuition on her math tests! But once she'd gotten her
feet under her, nothing could stop her.

Courvosier was a childless bachelor. He knew he'd
invested so much of his life in his students at the
Academy as compensation, yet few of them had made
him as proud as Honor. Too many officers simply wore
the uniform; Honor *lived* it. And it became her well, he
thought.

He watched her chatting with the husband of
Vulcan's commanding officer and wondered where that
awkward midshipman had gone. He knew she still disliked parties, still thought of herself as the ugly
duckling, but she never let it show. And one of these
days, he thought fondly, she would wake up to the fact
that the duckling had become a swan. One of the draw-
backs of the prolong treatment, especially in its later,
more effective versions, was that it stretched out the
"awkward periods" in physical development, and Honor,
he admitted, really had been on the homely side as a
girl—at first glance, at least. She'd always had the cat-
quick reflexes of her 1.35-gravity homeworld, but the
grace of her carriage had been something else, something that went beyond her high-gee birth environment.
Even as a first-form middy, she'd had that elegance in
motion which drew second glances from eyes which had
dismissed her unprepossessing surface too quickly, and
hers was a face that improved with age. Yet she truly
didn't realize, even now, how the too-sharp edges had
smoothed into character, how her mother's huge eyes

lent her triangular face an intriguing, exotic air. He supposed it wasn't all that surprising, given how long the prolong-slowed smoothing process had taken, and it was true she would never be "pretty"—only beautiful . . . once she realized it.

Which only added to his present concerns. He frowned down into his drink, then checked his chrono and sighed. *Fearless*'s recommissioning party was an outstanding success. It looked like lasting for hours yet, and he didn't have hours. There were too many details that needed clearing up back on Manticore, which meant he was going to have to drag her away from her guests—not that he expected that to bother her unduly!

He made his way casually through the crowd, and she turned towards him as her internal radar sensed his approach. Courvosier wasn't much taller than her mother, and he smiled up at her.

"Quite a bash, Captain," he said, and she smiled back a bit sourly.

"It is, isn't it, Sir? And noisy, too," she added with a grimace.

"Yes, it is." Courvosier glanced around, then back up at her. "I'm afraid I'm going to have to catch the shuttle back to *Hephaestus* in another hour, Honor, and we need to talk before I leave. Can you get away?"

Her eyes narrowed at his unexpectedly serious tone, and she, too, glanced around the crowded wardroom.

"I really shouldn't. . ." she said, but there was an almost wistful note in her voice. Courvosier smothered a grin as he watched temptation war with her sense of duty. It was an unfair contest, especially with curiosity weighing in on temptation's side, and her lips tightened in decision. She raised her hand, and Chief Steward's Mate James MacGuiness materialized out of the crowd as if by magic.

"Mac, would you please escort Admiral Courvosier to my day cabin?" She pitched her voice low enough to be lost in the crowd noise.

"Of course, Ma'am," her steward replied.

"Thank you." She looked back at Courvosier. "I'll join

you there as soon as I find Andy and warn him he's on
his own as host, Sir."

"Thank you, Captain. I appreciate it."

"Oh, so do I, Sir," she admitted with a grin. "So do I!"

Courvosier turned from the cabin view port as the
hatch slid quietly open and Honor stepped through it.

"I know you're not fond of parties, Honor," he said,
"but I really am sorry to call you away from one that
seems to be going so well."

"At the rate it's going, I'll have plenty of time to get
back to it, Sir." She shook her head. "I don't even know
half of them, anyway! A lot more planet-side guests
accepted their invitations than I'd expected."

"Of course they did," Courvosier said. "You're one of
their own, and they're proud of you."

Honor waved her hand, and her cheekbones heated.

"You're going to have to get over that blush reaction,
Honor," her old mentor told her severely. "Modesty is
all very well, but after Basilisk Station, you're a marked
woman."

"I was lucky," she protested.

"Of course you were," he agreed so promptly she
gave him a very sharp look indeed. Then he grinned,
and she grinned back at how easily she'd risen to his
bait. "Seriously, if I haven't gotten around to mentioning
it before, you did us all proud."

"Thank you," she said quietly. "That means a lot,
coming from you."

"Really?" His smile was a bit crooked as he looked
down at the gold rings on his own space-black sleeve.
"You know, I'm really going to hate giving up the
uniform," he sighed.

"It's only temporary, Sir. They're not going to leave
you on the beach for long. In fact," Honor frowned, "I
still don't understand why the Foreign Office wanted
you in the first place."

"Oh?" He cocked his head and his eyes glinted at
her. "Are you saying an old crock like me can't be
trusted with a diplomatic mission?"

"Of course not! I'm just saying you're far more valuable at the Advanced Tactical Course than fooling around at diplomatic soirees." Her mouth curled in distaste. "If the Admiralty had a lick of sense, they'd have told the FO to take a flying leap through the Junction and given you a task force, Sir!"

"There are more things in life than running ATC—or a task force," he disagreed. "In fact, politics and diplomacy are probably more important, when you come right down to it." Honor snorted, and he frowned. "You don't agree?"

"Admiral, I don't like politics," she said frankly. "Every time you get involved in them, things go all gray and murky on you. 'Politics' were what created the mess in Basilisk in the first place, and they darn near got my entire crew killed!" She shook her head. "No, Sir. I don't like politics, I don't understand them, and I don't *want* to understand them!"

"Then you'd better change your mind, Captain." There was bite in Courvosier's suddenly chill voice. Honor blinked in surprise, and Nimitz raised his head on her shoulder, bending his own grass-green gaze on the cherubic little admiral. "Honor, what you do in your sex life is up to you, but *no* captain in Her Majesty's service can be a virgin where politics are concerned—and especially not where *diplomacy* is concerned."

She blushed again, much more darkly, but she also felt her shoulders straighten just as they had at the Academy when then-Captain Courvosier had laid down the law. They were both a long way from Saganami Island, but some things never changed, she realized.

"I beg your pardon, Sir," she said a bit stiffly. "I only meant that politicians seem more concerned with payoffs and empire-building than with their jobs."

"Somehow I don't think the Duke of Cromarty would appreciate that characterization. Nor does it suit him." Courvosier waved a gentle hand as Honor opened her mouth again. "No, I know you weren't referring to the PM. And I understand your reaction after what happened to your last ship. But diplomacy is absolutely critical to the Kingdom's survival just now, Honor. That's why I agreed to the FO's request when they needed someone for Yeltsin's Star."

"I can understand that, Sir. And I suppose I was a bit petulant sounding, wasn't I?"

"Just a bit," Courvosier agreed with a small smile.

"Well, maybe more than a bit. Then again, I haven't really had much to do with diplomacy. My experience has been more with domestic politicos—you know, the slimy sort."

"A fair enough estimation, I suppose. But this is far more important, and that's why I wanted to talk to you." He rubbed one eyebrow and frowned. "Frankly, Honor, I'm a little surprised the Admiralty assigned you to it."

"You are?" She tried to hide her hurt. Did the Admiral think she'd do less than her best—especially for him—just because she didn't like politics? Surely he knew her better than that!

"Oh, not because I don't think you're up to it." His quick response eased her hurt, and he shook his head. "It's just— Well, how much do you know about the Yeltsin situation?"

"Not a lot," she admitted. "I haven't gotten my official orders or download yet, so all I know is what I read in the papers. I've checked *The Royal Encyclopedia*, but it hasn't been much help, and their navy's not even listed in *Jane's*. I gather Yeltsin doesn't have much to pique our interest, aside from its location."

"I assume from that last remark that you at least know why we want the system in our camp?" Courvosier made the statement a question, and she nodded. Yeltsin's Star lay less than thirty light-years to galactic northeast of the Manticore binary system. It also lay between the Kingdom of Manticore and the conquest-bloated People's Republic of Haven, and only an idiot—or a member of the Liberal or Progressive Party—could believe war with Haven wasn't coming. The diplomatic confrontation between the two powers had grown increasingly vicious in the two and a half

T-years since the PRH's brazen attempt to seize the Basilisk System, and both of them were jockeying for position before the inevitable open clash.

That was what made Yeltsin's Star so important. It and the nearby Endicott System had the only inhabited worlds in a volume twenty light-years across, squarely between the two adversaries. Allies, or (perhaps even more importantly) an advanced fleet base, in the area would be invaluable.

"What you may not realize," Courvosier went on, "is that more is involved here than just strategic real estate. The Cromarty government is trying to build a fire break against Haven, Honor. We're rich enough to stand up to the Peeps, probably, and we've got the technical edge, but we can't begin to match their manpower. We need allies, but, even more, we need to be seen as a creditable player, someone with the guts and will to face Haven down. There are still a lot of neutrals out there; there probably still will be when the shooting starts, and we need to influence as many as possible of them to be 'neutral' in our favor."

"I can see that, Sir."

"Good. But the reason I'm surprised the Admiralty assigned you to this particular effort is that you're a woman." Honor blinked in complete surprise, and Courvosier laughed without humor at her expression.

"I'm afraid I don't follow that, Sir."

"You will when you get your download," Courvosier promised sourly. "In the meantime, let me just give you the high points. Have a seat, Captain."

Honor sank into a chair and lifted Nimitz from her shoulder to her lap as she regarded her superior. He seemed genuinely concerned, and for the life of her, she couldn't see what her gender had to do with her suitability for command.

"You have to understand that Yeltsin's Star has been settled far longer than Mantioore," Courvosier began in his best Saganami lecturer's voice. "The first colonists landed on Grayson, Yeltsin's single habitable planet, in 988 P.D., almost five hundred years before we arrived

on the scene." Honor's eyes narrowed in surprise, and
he nodded. "That's right. In fact, Yeltsin hadn't even
been surveyed when they left Sol. For that matter, the
entire cryo-process had been available for less than ten
years when they shipped out."

"But why in God's name come way out *here*?" Honor
demanded. "They must've had better astro data on systems closer to Sol!"

"They did, indeed, but you've already hit their
motivation." She frowned, and he smiled thinly. "'In
God's name,' Honor. They were religious zealots looking for a home so far away no one would ever bother
them. I guess they figured five hundred-plus light-years
was about far enough in an era before hyper travel
had even been hypothesized. At any rate, the 'Church
of Humanity Unchained' set out on a leap of faith,
with absolutely no idea what they were going to find
at the other end."

"Lord." Honor sounded shaken, and she was. She was
a professional naval officer, and the mere thought of all
the hideous ways those colonists could have died was
enough to turn her stomach.

"Precisely. But the really interesting thing is why they
did it." Honor quirked an eyebrow, and Courvosier
shrugged. "They wanted to get away from 'the corrupt-
ing, soul-destroying effect of technology,'" he said, and
she stared at him in disbelief.

"They used a *starship* to get away from *technology*?
That's—that's insane, Sir!"

"No, not really." Courvosier leaned back against a
table and folded his arms. "Mind you, that was my own
first thought when the FO handed me the background
on the system, but it actually made sense, in a crazy
sort of way. Remember, this was way back in the early
fourth century of the Diaspora, when Old Earth was
finally getting a real handle on pollution, resource
depletion, and overcrowding. Actually, things had been
getting better for at least two hundred years, despite
the eco-nuts' and 'Earth First' groups' efforts to kill the
various space initiatives. The Earth-Firsters probably

had a better case, given the resource demands STL colony ships made on Sol's economy, but at least they recognized the spinoff advantages. Deep-space industry, asteroid mining operations, orbital power collectors—all of them were on line at last, and the quality of life was climbing system-wide. Most people were delighted, and the Earth-Firsters' only real complaint was that it could have climbed even faster if people would only stop building interstellar colony ships.

"On the other hand, there were still crackpot groups—particularly the extreme 'Greens' and the Neo-Luddites—who didn't distinguish between the colonizing efforts and any other space activity. They insisted, each for their own reasons, that the only *real* solution was to throw technology out on its ear and 'live the way man was intended to live.'" Honor snorted in derision, and he chuckled.

"I know. They'd have looked pretty sick if they'd tried it, especially with a system population of over twelve billion to feed and house, but most of the idiots were from more developed nations. Extremists tend to grow more extreme, not less, as problems get closer to solutions, you know, and these extremists didn't have any real concept of what a planet without technology would be like, because they'd never experienced it. Besides, after three centuries of preaching the evils of technology—and their own societies' 'greedy, exploitative guilt'—the 'Greens' were techno-illiterates with no real relevance to the world about them, and most of the Neo-Luddites' job skills had been made redundant by new technologies. Neither background really qualified them to understand what was happening, and sweeping, simplistic solutions to complicated problems are much more appealing than tackling the real thought that might actually solve them.

"At any rate, the Church of Humanity Unchained was the product of a fellow named Austin Grayson—the Reverend Austin Grayson from someplace called the State of Idaho. According to the Foreign Office, there were hordes of lunatic fringe groups running around at the time, and Grayson was a 'back to the Bible' type who got caught up in the ban-the-machine movement. The only things that made him different from other crackpots and bomb-throwers were his charisma, his determination, and his talent for attracting converts with real ability. He actually managed to assemble a colony expedition and fund it to the tune of several billion dollars, all to take his followers away to the New Zion and its wonderful, technology-free Garden of Eden. It was really a rather elegant concept, you know, using technology to get away from technology."

"Elegant," Honor snorted, and the Admiral chuckled again.

"Unfortunately, they got a nasty surprise at journey's end. Grayson's a pretty nice place in many ways, but it's a high-density world with unusual concentrations of heavy metals, and there isn't a single native plant or animal that won't kill any human who eats it for very long. Which meant, of course—"

"That they couldn't abandon technology and survive," Honor finished for him, and he nodded.

"Exactly. Not that they were willing to admit it. In fact, Grayson never *did* admit it. He lived another ten T-years after their arrival, and every year the end of technology was just around the corner, but there was a fellow named Mayhew who saw the writing on the wall a lot sooner. According to what I can dig out of the records, he more or less allied with another man, a Captain Yanakov, who'd commanded the colony ship, and the two of them pulled off a sort of doctrinal revolution after Grayson's death. Technology itself wasn't evil, just the way it had been *used* on Old Earth. What mattered wasn't the machine but the ungodly lifestyle machine-age humanity had embraced."

He rocked on his heels in silent thought for a moment, then shrugged.

"At any rate, they abandoned the anti-machine portion of Grayson's theology and concentrated on creating a society in strict accordance with God's Holy Word. Which—" he darted a quick glance at Honor from under lowered brows "—included the theory that 'Man is the head of Woman.'"

It was Honor's turn to frown, and he sighed.

"Damn it, Honor, you're too Manticoran! And," he added with a sudden genuine laugh, "God help us all if your *mother* ever ended up on Grayson!"

"I'm afraid I still don't quite understand, Sir."

"Of course you don't," Courvoisier sighed. "But, you see, women on Grayson have no legal rights, Honor—none at all."

"*What?!*" Honor jerked upright in her chair. Nimitz chittered in alarm as her lap shifted under him, and she winced as one centimeter-long claw dug a bit deeper than he'd intended, but her conscious mind hardly noticed.

"Precisely. They can't vote, can't own property, can't sit on juries, and—especially!—can't serve in the military."

"But that's . . . that's *barbaric*!"

"Oh, I don't know," Courvoisier said with a lurking grin. "Might be a bit restful, now and then."

Honor glared at him, and his grin faded.

"That wasn't quite as funny as I thought it would be. But the situation's even less funny. You see, Masada, the habitable planet of the Endicott System, was settled from Grayson, and not exactly voluntarily. What started as a schism over the retention of technology turned down other paths once it became clear they couldn't survive without it. The original pro-Tech faction became 'Moderates,' and the anti-Techies became 'the Faithful.' Once the Faithful were forced to accept that they couldn't get rid of the machines, they turned to creating the *perfect* godly society, and if you think the present government of Grayson is a bit backward, you should see what *they* came up with! Dietary laws, ritual cleansing for every imaginable sin—law codes that made any deviation from the True Way punishable by *stoning*, for God's sake!

"In the end, it came to open fighting, and it took the Moderates more than five years to beat the Faithful.

Unfortunately, the Faithful had built themselves a doomsday weapon; if they couldn't have a godly society, then they'd blow up the whole planet—in, of course, exact accordance with the obvious Will of God."

The Admiral snorted in pure disgust and shook his head, then sighed.

"Anyway, the Grayson government—the Moderates—cut a deal with them and exiled them lock, stock, and whipping post to Masada, where they set about creating the society God Had Intended. It saved Grayson, but the Faithful have grown more intolerant, not less. There are a lot of points about their so-called religion that I can't get definitive information on, but I do know they've chopped the entire New Testament out of their Bibles because if Christ had really been the Messiah, technology never would have arisen on Old Earth, *they* wouldn't have been kicked off Grayson, and Woman would have been put in her proper place throughout the human community."

Honor looked at him, too bemused to disbelieve any longer, and he shook his head once more.

"Unfortunately, they also seem to believe God expects them to fix all the things that are wrong with the universe, and they're still set on making *Grayson* toe their doctrinal line. Neither system has, you should pardon the expression, a pot to piss in, economically speaking, but they're too close together, and they've fought several wars over the centuries, complete with the occasional nuclear strike. Which, of course creates the opening both we and Haven are trying to exploit. It's also why the Foreign Minister convinced me that we need a fairly well known military type—like your humble servant—to head our delegation. The Graysons are only too well aware of the threat Masada presents to them, and they're going to want to know the person they're negotiating with is aware of it, too."

He shook his head and pursed his lips.

"It's a hell of a mess, Honor, and I'm afraid our own motives aren't as pure as the driven snow. We need a forward base in that area. Even more importantly, we need to keep Haven from securing one that close to us. Those factors are going to be as obvious to the locals as they are to us, so we're bound to get involved in the local conflict, in a peacekeeping role at the very least. If *I* were the Grayson government, that would certainly be the point *I'd* insist on, because the basic credo of Masadan theology is that someday they will return to Grayson in triumph and cast down the heirs of the ungodly who exiled their forefathers from their rightful home. Which means Grayson can really use a powerful outside ally—and that as soon as we started courting *them*, the Peeps started sucking up to *Masada*. Mind you, they'd probably prefer Grayson to Masada, too, but the Graysons seem a bit more aware of just how fatal it can be to become a 'friend' of the People's Republic.

"And that, Honor, is why you need to know exactly what's going on, diplomatically speaking, on this little jaunt. You're going to be very, very visible, and the fact that the Kingdom is sending a woman to command the *military* side of the mission, well—"

He broke off with a shrug, and Honor nodded slowly, still trying to grapple with the idea of a modern-day Dark Age culture.

"I see, Sir," she said softly. "I see, indeed."

• CHAPTER TWO

Honor released the hanging rings and whipped through a flashing, somersault dismount. She was far from a professional-quality gymnast, but she landed almost perfectly and bowed with extravagant grace to her audience—who regarded her with a tolerant eye from his comfortable perch on the parallel bars. She inhaled deeply, using her hands to strip sweat from her dripping, two-centimeter hair, then scrubbed her face vigorously with her towel before she draped it around her neck and gave him a severe look.

"A little workout wouldn't hurt *you*, either," she panted.

Nimitz responded with an airy flirt of his fluffy, prehensile tail, then sighed in relief as she padded across to the wall-mounted grav controls. She reset the gym to the regulation one-gee maintained aboard all RMN ships, and the 'cat swarmed down from the bars. He'd never been able to understand why she insisted on cranking the gym's gravity clear up to the 1.35-gees she'd been born to. It wasn't that Nimitz was *lazy*, but in his uncomplicated view exertion was something to be endured, not chased after. He regarded the lower standard shipboard gravity as the greatest invention since celery, and if she *had* to exercise, she might as well do something *he* enjoyed, as well.

He scampered into the dressing room, and Honor heard her locker door rattle. Then he reappeared with a happy "Bleek!" and her hand shot up just in time to snatch a hurtling plastic disk out of the air in front of her face.

"Why, you little creep!" she laughed, and he chittered in delight, dancing from side to side on his mid and rearmost limbs while he spread his true-hands wide.

She laughed again and tossed the ancient frisbee back. There was too little space for the kinds of intricate flight paths she could manage on a planet, but Nimitz buzzed with gusto. He'd been a frisbee freak ever since the day he saw a much younger Honor's father playing the same game with his golden retriever, and, unlike a dog, he had hands.

Honor caught a sizzling return and grinned, then feinted a high, looping curve and sent the actual toss streaking out at knee-level . . . which brought it right to chin height on Nimitz. He snagged it adroitly and skittered around in a circle, using both true-feet and his hand-paws to build momentum like a discus-thrower before he released it.

Honor's palms stung with the force of the catch, and she shook her head as she tossed it back. After all these years, she'd still never managed to fool him. No one knew precisely how treecats' empathic senses worked, but the little devil *always* knew when she was trying to put something over on him.

Which was more than she could say about him. His next throw carried wicked terminal English and came curving in like a boomerang. She missed her catch, ducking barely in time as it hissed past her head and bounced across the decksole, and Nimitz dashed over to it. He leapt into the air and landed directly on top of the frisbee, bleeking his triumph as he executed an impromptu victory dance.

Honor straightened and shook her head, then laughed.

"All right, you won," she told him, propping her hands on her hips. "I suppose you want your usual forfeit?" Nimitz nodded complacently, and she sighed. "All right—two celery sticks with lunch tomorrow. But only two!"

The treecat considered for a moment, then flipped the tip of his tail in agreement and rose to his full sixty-centimeters on his true-feet, hugging her knee with his mid-limb hand-paws and patting her thigh with his true-hands. Nimitz was incapable of speech, despite an intelligence humans were sadly prone to underestimate, but she knew what he wanted. He patted again, harder, and she grinned down at him as she plucked her sweat-soaked unitard away from her breasts with one hand and fanned her cheeks with the other.

"Oh, no, you don't, stinker! I'm not about to trust your claws when I'm wearing something this thin."

He sniffed, managing to look simultaneously disdainful, trustworthy, pitiful, and neglected, then broke into a loud, buzzing purr as she relented and gathered him in her arms. She knew better than to lift him to his normal position on her shoulder, but he twisted onto his back, waving his two rear sets of limbs in the air (his true-hands clutched his frisbee, instead) as she cuddled him.

"Lord, but you are one spoiled beastie," she told him, nuzzling her nose into his cream-colored belly fur, and he bleeked in cheerful agreement as she headed for the showers.

Honor had the gym to herself, for it was late in *Fearless*'s official night, and most of the cruiser's off-watch crew were snug in their beds. She ought to be there herself, but she was spending too much time behind a desk, and there never seemed to be enough hours for her to steal exercise time during the "day." Besides, working out late let her reset the grav field without inconveniencing anyone else, though her present heavy breathing and a slight muscle quiver of overexertion told her she hadn't been putting in enough hours here at night, either.

She stepped into the dressing room, set Nimitz down, and made a mental note to *make* more gym time as she peeled off her unitard. The treecat tucked his frisbee neatly back into her locker and gave her a disgusted look as she dropped the sweaty garment untidily on the deck and stepped into the showers.

The hot water sluiced deliciously over her, and she turned her face up to the spray as she reached for the soap dispenser. Yes, she definitely needed to get in more gym time. And, while she was thinking about it, it was past time she found another sparring partner, too. Lieutenant Wisner had been pretty good, but he'd been transferred out as part of the routine personnel rotation during *Fearless*'s refit, and Honor knew she'd been putting off finding a replacement on the score that she had no time for it.

She frowned up into the shower, working up a lather in her short, curly hair. Sergeant Major Babcock, the Marine detachment's senior noncom, might be a good bet. Maybe too good. It had been a long, long time since Honor was on the Academy unarmed combat team, and judging from her personnel jacket, Iris Babcock could probably tie her up in knots without breaking a sweat. Which embarrassing fate, Honor reflected as she gave herself one last rinse and turned off the shower, would no doubt inspire her to recover the top of her own form quickly.

She dripped her way back into the dressing room and reached for a fresh towel. Nimitz curled up on a bench and waited patiently while she dried herself, climbed back into her uniform, and settled the white beret of a starship commander on her still-damp hair, but he was more than ready to hop up onto the specially padded shoulder of her tunic once she was dressed.

She lifted him into place and headed for her quarters. She really ought to turn in, but there were still a few items of paperwork to deal with, so she turned into her day cabin, instead.

She palmed the lights up and crossed to her desk, resolutely refusing to let the knee-to-ceiling view port distract her until she finished her chores. She did allow herself to pause and check the treecat-sized life-support module clamped to the bulkhead beside her desk. It was the latest model, with all sorts of whistles and bells, increased endurance, and added safety features, yet it was also new. She'd made regular checks on its readouts a part of her daily routine, but until she felt completely familiar with all its features, she intended to check it every time she passed it, as well.

Nimitz made a soft sound of agreement on her shoulder. He knew what—and who—that module was for, and personal experience made him a firm supporter of her conscientiousness. She grinned at his sound, then straightened a heat-warped golden wall plaque minutely and seated herself behind her desk.

She'd barely brought her terminal alive when Mac-Guiness appeared with a steaming mug, and she wondered yet again if he had a power meter on her computer circuits. He always seemed to appear, as if by magic, the instant she booted the system, and this late at night he could be counted upon to ply her with the rich, sweet cocoa she loved while she worked.

"Thank you, Mac," she said as she took the cup.

"You're welcome, Ma'am." MacGuiness completed the ritual with a smile. The chief steward had followed her from her last command, and they'd settled into a comfortable routine over the past twenty-seven months. He was a bit too inclined to fuss over her, but Honor had discovered (somewhat guiltily) that she had no particular objection to being spoiled.

He vanished back into his pantry, and Honor returned to her screen. Officially, she wasn't here expressly to support Admiral Courvosier's mission. Instead, she was senior officer of the escort assigned to a convoy whose ultimate goal was the Casca System, twenty-two light-years beyond Yeltsin's Star. Neither Yeltsin nor Casca were in a particularly good galactic neighborhood, for the single-star policies out here tended to be hard-scrabble propositions. Many had bitter personal experience of piratical raids, and there'd always been a temptation to better their lots with a little piracy of their own against the passing commerce of wealthier star systems. The situation had gotten far worse of late, and Honor (and the Office of Naval Intelligence) more than suspected that Haven's interest in the region helped account for that—a suspicion which, in turn, explained why the Admiralty had provided the convoy with an escort of two cruisers and a pair of destroyers.

Honor nodded as status reports scrolled across her

screen. They looked good—as she'd expected. This was her first opportunity to command what was, for all intents and purposes, her own squadron, but if every captain in the Navy were as good as *her* COs, squadron command would be a breeze.

She finished the last report and leaned back, sipping her cocoa while Nimitz curled on his bulkhead-mounted perch. She wasn't particularly impressed with one or two members of Admiral Courvosier's staff of Foreign Office experts, but so far she had nothing to complain about where her own duties were concerned, aside from the chunks of time her new job was eating up. And that, she told herself yet again, was her own fault. Andreas was perfectly capable of running the ship without her, and she felt fairly certain she was spending too much time worrying over the convoy's day-to-day operations. Delegating had always been the hardest thing for her to do, yet she knew there was another factor this time. Keeping her hands off while Andreas managed *Fearless* and freed her to worry about the rest of the squadron was precisely what she *ought* to be doing, and she didn't want to. Not because she distrusted his competence, but because she was afraid of losing the thing every Navy captain most craved—the active exercise of her authority and responsibility as mistress after God in one of Her Majesty's starships.

She snorted tiredly at herself and finished the cocoa. MacGuiness knew exactly how to make it, and its rich, smooth calories were another reason to put in more gym time, she thought with a grin. Then she rose and crossed to the view port to stare out into the weird, shifting splendor of hyper space.

That view port was one of the things Honor most treasured about her ship. Her quarters aboard her last ship, the elderly light cruiser which had bequeathed her name and battle honors to the present *Fearless*, hadn't had one, and it gave Honor an ever-renewed sense of the vastness of the universe. It offered both relaxing contemplation and a sense of perspective—an awareness of how small any human being truly was against the enormity of creation—that was almost a challenge, and she stretched her long body out on the padded couch beneath it with a sigh.

Fearless and the ships of her convoy rode the twisted currents of a grav wave which had never attained the dignity of a name, only a catalog number. Honor's cabin was barely a hundred meters forward of *Fearless*'s after impeller nodes, and the immaterial, three-hundred-kilometer disk of the cruiser's after Warshawski sail flickered and flashed like frozen heat lightning, dominating the view port with its soft glory as it harnessed the grav wave's power. Its grab factor was adjusted to a tiny, almost immeasurable fraction of its full efficiency, providing a minuscule acceleration which was exactly offset by the forward sail's deceleration to hold *Fearless* at fifty percent of light-speed. The cruiser could have sustained a velocity twenty percent higher, but the hyper bands' heavier particle densities would have overcome the freighters' weaker radiation shielding long before that.

Honor's brown eyes were rapt as she watched the sail, fascinated as always by its flowing-ice beauty. She could have shut down her ship's sails and let momentum take its course, but those sails balanced *Fearless* delicately between them like exquisitely counterpoised fulcrums that lent the cruiser an instant responsiveness. Their current grav wave was barely a half light-month deep and a light-month wide, a mere rivulet beside titans like the Roaring Deeps, yet its power was enough to send her ship leaping to an effective five thousand gravities' acceleration in less than two seconds. And should *Fearless*'s gravity detectors pick up unexpected wave turbulence ahead of her, she might have to do just that.

Honor shook herself and let her eyes rove further out. The sail cut off all view of anything astern of *Fearless*, but the bottomless sweep of hyper space stretched out ahead and abeam. The nearest freighter was a thousand kilometers away, giving both vessels' sails ample clearance from one another, and even a five-megaton freighter was an invisible mote to unaided vision at that distance. But Honor's trained eye picked out the glittering disks of the ship's Warshawski sails, like flaws of strange, focused permanence against the gorgeous chaos of hyper space, and astern of her was the gleam of yet another stupendous merchantman.

Her merchantmen, she told herself. Her charges— slow, fat, clumsy, the smallest of them six times more massive than *Fearless*'s three hundred thousand tons but totally defenseless, and stuffed with cargoes whose combined value was literally beyond comprehension. Over a hundred and fifty *billion* Manticoran dollars' worth of it headed for Yeltsin's Star alone. Medical equipment, teaching materials, heavy machinery, precision tools, and molycirc computers and software to update and modernize the Graysons' out-of-date industrial base—every penny of it paid for by Crown "loans" which amounted to outright gifts. It was a sobering indication of how high Queen Elizabeth's government was willing to bid for the alliance Admiral Courvosier sought, and it was Honor's responsibility to see it safely delivered.

She leaned further back into the cushioned couch, reclining to savor the melting muscular relaxation in the wake of her exercise, and her brown eyes were heavy. No Navy skipper enjoyed convoy duty. Freighters lacked warships' powerful Warshawski sails and inertial compensators, and without them they dared not venture much above the delta bands of hyper space, whereas warships ranged as high as the eta or even theta bands. At the moment, for example, Honor's convoy was cruising along in the mid-delta bands, which translated their .5 C true velocity into an *effective* velocity of just over a thousand times light-speed. At that rate, the thirty-one light-year voyage to Yeltsin's Star would require ten days—just under nine, by their shipboard clocks. Left to herself, *Fearless* could have made the same crossing in less than four.

But that was all right, Honor thought drowsily as Nimitz hopped up onto her chest with his soft, buzzing purr. He curled down and rested his chin between her breasts, and she stroked his ears gently. Four days or ten, it didn't matter. She didn't need to set any records. She *did* need to deliver her charges safely, and commerce protection was one of the purposes for which cruisers were specifically designed and built.

She yawned, sliding still further down on the couch, and considered getting up and taking herself off to bed, but her sleepy gaze clung to the wavering gray and black and pulsing purple and green of hyper space. It glowed and throbbed, beckoning to her, starless and shifting and infinitely, beautifully variable, and her eyes slipped shut and Nimitz's purr was a soft, affectionate lullaby in the background of her brain.

Captain Honor Harrington didn't even twitch when Chief Steward MacGuiness tiptoed into her cabin and tucked a blanket over her. He stood a moment, smiling down at her, then left as quietly as he had come, and the cabin lights dimmed into darkness behind him.

• CHAPTER THREE

White table linens glowed, silver and china gleamed, and conversation hummed as the stewards removed the dessert dishes. MacGuiness moved quietly around the table, personally pouring the wine, and Honor watched the lights glitter deep in the ruby heart of her glass.

Fearless was young, one of the Royal Manticoran Navy's newest and most powerful heavy cruisers. The *Star Knight* class often served as squadron or flotilla flagships, and BuShips had borne that in mind when they designed their accommodations. Admiral Courvosier's flag cabin was even more splendid than Honor's, and the captain's dining cabin was downright huge by Navy standards. If it wasn't big enough to seat all of Honor's officers—a heavy cruiser *was* a warship, and no warship had mass to waste—it was more than large enough to accommodate her senior officers and Courvosier's delegation.

MacGuiness finished pouring, and Honor glanced around the long table. The Admiral—who, true to his newly acquired status, had exchanged his uniform for formal civilian dress—sat at her right hand. Andreas Venizelos faced him at her left; from there, her guests ran down the sides of the table in descending order of seniority, military and civilian, to Ensign Carolyn Wolcott at its foot. This was Wolcott's first cruise after graduation, and she looked almost like a schoolgirl dressed up in her mother's uniform. Tonight was also the first time she'd joined her new captain for dinner, and her anxiety had been obvious in her over-controlled table manners. But the RMN believed the proper place for an officer to learn her duties, social as well as professional, was in space, and Honor caught the ensign's eye and touched the side of her glass.

Wolcott blushed, reminded of her responsibility as junior officer present, and rose. The rest of the guests fell silent, and her spine straightened as all eyes turned to her.

"Ladies and Gentlemen," she raised her wine, her voice deeper and more melodious—and confident—than Honor had expected, "the Queen!"

"The Queen!" The response rumbled back to her, glasses rose, and Wolcott slipped back into her chair with obvious relief as the formality was completed. She glanced up the table at her captain, and her face relaxed as she saw Honor's approving expression.

"You know," Courvosier murmured in Honor's ear, "I still remember the first time it was *my* turn to do that. Odd how terrifying it can be, isn't it?"

"All things are relative, Sir," Honor replied with a smile, "and I suppose it does us good. Weren't you the one who was telling me a Queen's officer has to understand diplomacy as well as tactics?"

"Now that, Captain, is a very true statement," another voice said, and Honor suppressed a grimace. "In fact, I only wish more Navy officers could realize that diplomacy is even *more* important than tactics and strategy," the Honorable Reginald Houseman continued in his deep, cultured baritone.

"I don't believe I can quite agree with that, Sir," Honor said quietly, hoping her irritation at his intrusion into a private conversation didn't show. "At least, not from the Navy's viewpoint. Important, yes, but it's our job to step in after diplomacy breaks down."

"Indeed?" Houseman smiled the superior smile Honor loathed. "I realize military people often lack the time for the study of history, but an ancient Old Earth soldier got it exactly right when he said war was simply the continuation of diplomacy by non-diplomatic means."

"That's something of a paraphrase, and that 'simply' understates the case a bit, but I'll grant that it sums up the sense of General Clausewitz's remark." Houseman's eyes narrowed as Honor supplied Clausewitz's name and rank, and other conversations flagged as eyes turned toward them. "Of course, Clausewitz came out of the Napoleonic Era on Old Earth, heading into the Final Age of Western Imperialism, and *On War* isn't really about politics or diplomacy, except inasmuch as they and warfare are all instruments of state policy. Actually, Sun Tzu made the same point over two thousand T-years earlier." A hint of red tinged Houseman's jowls, and Honor smiled pleasantly. "Still, neither of them had a monopoly on the concept, did they? Tanakov said much the same thing in his *Tenets of War* just after the Warshawski sail made interstellar warfare possible, and Gustav Anderman certainly demonstrated the way in which diplomatic and military means can be used to reinforce one another when he took over New Berlin and built it into the Anderman Empire in the sixteenth century. Have you read his *Sternenkrieg*, Mr. Houseman? It's an interesting distillation of most of the earlier theorists with a few genuine twists of his own, probably from his personal background as a mercenary. I think Admiral White Haven's translation is probably the best available."

"Ah, no, I'm afraid I haven't," Houseman said, and Courvosier blotted his lips with his napkin to hide a grin. "My *point*, however," the diplomat continued doggedly, "is that properly conducted diplomacy renders military strategy irrelevant by precluding the need for war." He sniffed and swirled his wine gently, and his superior smile reasserted itself.

"Reasonable people negotiating in good faith can always reach reasonable compromises, Captain. Take our situation here, for example. Neither Yeltsin's Star nor the Endicott System have any real resources to attract interstellar commerce, but they each have an inhabited world, with almost nine billion people between them, and they lie less than two days apart for a hyper freighter. That gives them ample opportunity to create local prosperity, yet both economies are at best borderline . . . which is why it's so absurd that they've been at one another's throats for so long over some silly religious difference! They should be trading with one another, building a mutually supported, secure economic future, not wasting resources on an *arms* race." He shook his head sorrowfully. "Once they discover the advantages of peaceful trade—once they each realize their prosperity depends on the *other's*—the situation will defuse itself without all this saber rattling."

Honor managed not to stare at him in disbelief, but if she hadn't known the Admiral so well, she would have assumed someone had failed to brief Houseman. It would certainly be nice to make peace between Masada and Grayson, but her own reading of the download accompanying her orders had confirmed everything the Admiral had said about their long-term hostility. And nice as it would be to put that enmity to rest, Manticore's fundamental purpose was to secure an ally against Haven, not engage in a peacemaking effort that was almost certainly doomed to failure.

"I'm sure that would be a desirable outcome, Mr. Houseman," she said after a moment, "but I don't know how realistic it is."

"Indeed?" Houseman bristled.

"They've been enemies for more than six hundred T-years," she pointed out as gently as she could, "and religious hatreds are among the most virulent known to man."

"That's why they need a fresh viewpoint, a third party from outside the basic equation who can bring them together."

"Excuse me, Sir, but I was under the impression our primary goals are to secure an ally and Fleet base rights and to prevent Haven from penetrating the region instead of us."

"Well, of course they are, Captain." Houseman's tone was just short of impatient. "But the best way to do that is to settle the locals' differences. The potential for instability and Havenite interference will remain as long as their hostility does, whatever else we may accomplish. Once we bring them together, however, we'll have *two* friends in the region, and there won't be any temptation for either of them to invite Haven in for military advantage. The best diplomatic glue is common interest, not simply a common enemy. Indeed," Houseman sipped his wine, "our entire involvement in this region stems from our own failure to find a common interest with the People's Republic, and it *is* a failure. There's always some way to avoid confrontation if one only looks deep enough and remembers that, in the long run, violence never solves anything. That's why we have diplomats, Captain Harrington—and why a resort to brute force is an indication of failed diplomacy, nothing more and nothing less."

Major Tomas Ramirez, commander of *Fearless*'s Marine detachment, stared at Houseman in disbelief from further down the table. The heavyset, almost squat Marine had been twelve years old when Haven conquered his native Trevor's Star. He, his mother, and his sisters had escaped to Manticore in the last refugee convoy through the Manticore Wormhole Junction; his father had stayed behind, on one of the warships that died to cover the retreat. Now his jaw tightened ominously as Houseman smiled at Honor, but Lieutenant Commander Higgins, *Fearless*'s chief engineer, touched his forearm and jerked a tiny headshake. The little scene wasn't lost on Honor, and she sipped her own wine deliberately, then lowered her glass.

"I see," she said, and wondered how the Admiral tolerated such a nincompoop as his second in command. Houseman had a reputation as a brilliant economist and, given Grayson's backward economy, sending him made sense, but he was also an ivory-tower intellectual who'd been plucked from a tenured position in Mannheim University's College of Economics for government service. Mannheim wasn't called "Socialist U" for nothing, and Houseman's prominent family was a vocal supporter of the Liberal Party. Neither of those facts were calculated to endear him to Captain Honor Harrington, and his simplistic notion of how to approach the Grayson-Masada hostility was downright frightening.

"I'm afraid I can't quite agree with you, Sir," she said at last, setting her glass down precisely and keeping her voice as pleasant as humanly possible. "Your argument assumes all negotiators are reasonable, first, and second, that they can always agree on what represents a 'reasonable compromise,' but if history demonstrates one thing quite clearly, it's that they aren't and they can't. If you can see the advantage of peaceful trade between these people, then surely it ought to be evident to *them*, but the record indicates no one on either side has ever even discussed the possibility. That suggests a degree of hostility that makes economic self-interest immaterial, which, in turn, suggests that what we consider rationalism may not play a particularly prominent part in their thinking. Even if it did, mistakes happen, Mr. Houseman, and that's where the people in uniform come in."

"'Mistakes,' as you put it," Houseman said more coolly, "often happen because 'the people in uniform' act hastily or ill advisedly."

"Of course they do," Honor agreed, and he blinked at her in surprise. "In fact, the *final* mistake is almost always made by someone in uniform—either because she gave the wrong advice to her own superiors when they were the aggressors or because she squeezed the trigger too quickly when an enemy made an unexpected move. Sometimes we even make the mistake of projecting threats and responses in too much detail and lock ourselves into war plans we can't break free of, just as Clausewitz's own disciples did. But, Mr. Houseman," her dark eyes met his suddenly across the snowy tablecloth, "the situations which make military mistakes critical, even possible, grow out of political and diplomatic maneuvers which preceded them."

"Indeed?" Houseman regarded her with grudging respect and marked distaste. "Then wars are primarily the fault of the civilians, Captain, and not the pure-hearted military protectors of the realm?"

"I wouldn't go quite that far," Honor said, and a grin lit her face briefly. "I've known quite a few 'military protectors,' and I'm sorry to say all too few of them were 'pure-hearted'!" Her grin vanished. "On the other hand, I'd have to point out that in any society in which the military is controlled by duly constituted civilian authorities—like ours—the ultimate responsibility has to lie with the civilians who make policy between the wars. I don't mean to suggest that those civilians are stupid or incompetent—" after all, she thought, one must be polite "—or that the military gives them unfailingly good advice, but mutually contradictory national goals can present insoluble dilemmas, however much good faith there may be on both sides. And when one side *doesn't* negotiate in good faith—" She shrugged.

"It was also Clausewitz who said 'Politics is the womb in which war is developed,' Mr. Houseman. My own view is a bit simpler than that. War may represent the failure of diplomacy, but even the best diplomats operate on credit. Sooner or later someone who's less reasonable than you are is going to call you, and if your military can't cover your I.O.U.s, you lose."

"Well," Houseman twitched his own shoulders, "the object of *this* mission is to avoid being called, isn't it?" He smiled thinly. "I trust you won't object to our avoiding a war if we can?"

Honor started to retort sharply, then made herself shake her head with a smile. She really shouldn't let Houseman get under her skin this way, she scolded herself. It wasn't his fault he'd been reared in a nice, safe, civilized society that protected him from the harsh reality of an older and grimmer set of imperatives. And foolish as she might think he was outside his own undoubted area of expertise, it wasn't as if he were in charge of the mission. That was Admiral Courvosier's responsibility, and she felt no qualms about *his* judgment.

Venizelos stepped into the brief lull, tactfully engaging Houseman in a discussion of the government's new taxation policies, and she turned her own head to speak to Lieutenant Commander DuMorne.

A rustle of movement swept the briefing room as Admiral Courvosier followed Honor into the compartment and her officers rose. The two of them walked to their chairs at the head of the table, then sat, followed a moment later by the others, and Honor let her eyes sweep the assembled faces.

Andreas Venizelos and Stephen DuMorne, her own exec and second lieutenant, represented *Fearless*. Honor's second in command, Commander Alice Truman of the light cruiser *Apollo*, sat beside Lieutenant Commander Lady Ellen Prevost, *Apollo's* exec, both of them as golden-haired as Honor was dark, and Commander Jason Alvarez of the destroyer *Madrigal* sat facing them, accompanied by *his* exec, Lieutenant Commander Mercedes Brigham. After Admiral Courvosier, Brigham was the oldest person in the compartment, and just as dark and weathered—and competent—looking as Honor remembered her. The escort force's most junior CO sat facing her from the end of the table: Commander Alistair McKeon of the destroyer *Troubadour* and his exec, Lieutenant Mason Haskins.

None of the Admiral's civil service associates were present.

"All right, people," she said. "Thank you all for coming. I'll try not to use up any more of your time than I have to, but, as you all know, we'll be translating back into n-space for Yeltsin's Star tomorrow, and I wanted one last chance to meet with all of you and the Admiral before we do."

Heads nodded, though one or two of Honor's officers had been a bit taken aback initially by her taste for face-to-face meetings. Most senior officers preferred the convenience of electronic conferences, but Honor believed in personal contact. Even the best com conference, in her view, distanced the participants from one another. People sitting around the same table were more likely to feel part of the same unit, to be aware of one another, and spark the sorts of ideas and responses that made a command team more than the sum of its parts.

Or, she thought dryly, it seemed that way to *her*, anyway.

"In light of the fact that your mission is the primary one, Admiral," she went on, turning to Courvosier, "perhaps you'd care to begin?"

"Thank you, Captain." Courvosier looked around the table and smiled. "I'm sure by this time you're almost depressingly familiar with my mission brief, but I'd like to hit the high points one more time.

"First, of course, is the absolute importance of securing our relationship with Grayson. The government hopes we'll come home with a formal alliance, but they'll settle for anything that brings the Yeltsin System more fully into our sphere of influence and *decreases* Haven's access here.

"Second, remember that anything we say to the Grayson government will be filtered through their perception of the Masadan threat. Their navy and population are both smaller than Masada's, and whatever certain members of my own delegation may think—" a soft chuckle ran around the table "—*they* have no doubt that Masadan rhetoric about returning to their planet as conquerors is completely serious. It hasn't been that long since their last shooting war, and the current situation is very, very tense.

"Third, and in conjunction with the military balance of power in the region, remember your single small squadron masses seventy percent as much as the entire Grayson Navy. Given the relative backwardness of their technology, *Fearless*, alone, could annihilate everything they have in a stand-up battle. They're going to realize that, whether they want to admit it or not, but it's essential that we not rub their noses in their 'inferiority.' Make them aware of how useful we could be as allies, by all means, but *don't* let yourself or any of your people condescend to them."

He held them with level blue eyes, every centimeter the admiral despite his temporary civilian status, and his cherub face was deadly serious until heads nodded around the table.

"Good. And remember this—these people aren't from the same societal matrix as we are. They don't even come close. I know you've all studied your downloads, but be certain your crews are as aware of the differences as *you* are. In particular, our female personnel are going to have to be extremely careful in any contacts with the Graysons." Commander Truman grimaced, and Courvosier nodded. "I know, and if it seems foolish to us, imagine how much more foolish it's going to seem to some of your junior officers and ratings. But foolish or not, it's the way things are here, and we're the visitors. We must conduct ourselves as guests, and while I don't want anyone acting a millimeter less than fully professional at all times, regardless of gender, the mere fact that we have women in uniform—far less *officers'* uniforms—is going to be hard for them to accept."

Heads nodded once more, and he sat back in his chair.

"That just about covers it, Captain," he told Honor, "at least until I meet their representatives and have more of a feel for the situation."

"Thank you, Sir." Honor leaned forward and folded her hands on the table. "Aside from endorsing everything Admiral Courvosier just said, I have only one thing to say about Grayson. We're going to have to play things by ear, but our responsibility is to contribute to the Admiral's success, not to make waves. If there are problems with any representative of the Grayson government, or even a private Grayson citizen, I want to hear about it immediately—and *not* from the locals. There's no room here for prejudice from our side, however merited it may seem, and I'd better not hear about any. Is that clear?"

A quiet murmur of agreement answered, and she nodded.

"Good." She rubbed her left forefinger lightly across

the back of her right hand and nodded. "All right, then, let's turn to our own schedule.

"We've got four *Mandrake*-class freighters to drop off at Yeltsin's Star, but we're not supposed to actually turn their cargoes over to Grayson until Admiral Courvosier's people have begun negotiations and released them. I don't anticipate any problem in that regard, but that means they'll remain our responsibility until we *do* hand them over, and that means we're going to have to leave at least some of the escort to keep an eye on them. In addition, of course, we're supposed to be a show of force, a sort of pointed reminder to the Grayson government of just how valuable the Navy can be to their security vis-a-vis Masada—or, for that matter, the Peeps.

"On the other hand, we've got five more ships going on to Casca. We'll have to send along a reasonable escort, given the reports of increased 'pirate' activity in the area, so my present thought is to keep *Fearless* here, as our most impressive unit, and send you and *Apollo* on to Casca in company with *Troubadour*, Alice." Commander Truman nodded. "With Alistair to scout for you, you should be able to handle anything you run into, and that will give me Jason and *Madrigal* to support *Fearless*. It'll take you a bit over a T-week to get there, but I want you back here ASAP. You won't have any freighters to slow you down on the return voyage, so I'll expect you back in eleven days.

"In the meantime, Jason," she moved her eyes to Alvarez, "you and I will operate on the theory that the Graysons know what they're talking about where Masada is concerned. It wouldn't be very bright of them to try anything against us, but unlike certain members of the Admiral's delegation, we're not going to take their rationality for granted." Another ripple of amusement flowed around the table. "I want our impellers hot at all times, and assuming we can arrange local leave, I don't want more than ten percent of our people dirt-side at any one time."

"Understood, Ma'am."

"All right, then. Does anyone else have anything to add?"

"I do, Skipper," McKeon said, and Honor cocked her head with a smile. "It just occurred to me to wonder, Ma'am—did anyone ever expressly *tell* the Graysons that, well, that our senior officer is a woman?"

"I don't know," Honor said, and the admission surprised her, for she hadn't even considered it. She turned to Courvosier. "Admiral?"

"No, we haven't," Courvosier replied with a frown. "Ambassador Langtry's been on Grayson for over three local years, and his advice was that making a point of explaining that we have female military personnel might be counterproductive. They're a proud, touchy lot—not least, I suspect, because, scared as they are of Masada, they know the real balance of power between them and the Kingdom as well as we do and resent their weakness. They don't want to be our supplicants, and they go out of their way to refuse to admit they may be. At any rate, Sir Anthony felt they might see it as some sort of slur, as if we were pointedly telling them how uncivilized we consider them. On the other hand, we transmitted a list of our ships and their COs to them, and their colonists came predominately from Old Earth's Western Hemisphere, just as our original settlers did. They certainly ought to recognize feminine names when they see them."

"I see." McKeon frowned, and Honor watched his face carefully. She knew Alistair well enough to see that something about the situation bothered him, but he chose to say nothing more, and she looked around the table again.

"Anything else?" she asked, and heads shook. "Very well, then, ladies and gentlemen, let's be about it."

She and Courvosier stood and led the way to the boat bay to see their visitors to their pinnaces and back to their own ships.

• CHAPTER FOUR

Sword of the Faithful Matthew Simonds stumped angrily down the passage aboard his new flagship and reminded himself not to speak to Captain Yu like the heathen he was. He had no doubt Yu was going to be displeased by what he was about to hear, and though the captain was always exquisitely polite, he couldn't quite hide his feeling of superiority. That was particularly maddening in a man from such an ungodly culture, but the Church needed Yu, for a time, at least. Yet that wouldn't always be true, Simonds promised himself. The time would come when God delivered their true enemies into their hand at last. On that day infidel outsiders would no longer be necessary . . . and if these godless foreigners could create the conditions for Maccabeus to succeed, that day might come far sooner than they suspected.

The bridge hatch opened before him, and he summoned up a smile and made his irritated pace slow as he stepped through it.

Captain Alfredo Yu rose from the chair at the center of the magnificent command deck. He was a tall, slender man, overtopping Simonds by at least fifteen centimeters, comfortable and elegant in the scarlet and gold of the Navy of Masada, yet there was something subtly wrong with the way he came to attention. Not disrespectful or insolent, but simply *different*, as if he'd learned his military courtesy somewhere else.

Which, of course, was exactly what he *had* done.

"Good morning, Sir. This is an unexpected honor. How may I serve you?"

"Come into my briefing room, please," Simonds

41

replied, somewhat mollified, despite himself, by Yu's unfailing courtesy.

"Of course, Sir. Commander Manning, you have the watch."

"Aye, Sir," the commander—*not*, Simonds noted with fresh grumpiness, a Masadan—acknowledged crisply, and Yu followed Simonds into the briefing room and turned an attentive countenance to him as the hatch closed behind them.

Simonds studied that bland, waiting expression and wondered, not for the first time, what the mind behind those dark eyes thought. Yu had to know how critical he and his ship were to Masada's plans—or, at least, to the plans he *knew* about—and a third of *Thunder of God's* crew were still heathens filling the specialist roles no Masadan could. They looked to Yu for their orders, not Simonds, and not simply because he was the captain of their ship. Simonds had survived thirty years of internecine political and doctrinal warfare within Masada's theocracy, and he knew perfectly well Yu had his own superiors and his own agenda. So far, that agenda had marched side-by-side with the Faith's, yet what would happen on the day that was no longer true? It wasn't something Simonds liked to contemplate, but it was also something he had no choice but to ponder—and the reason it was so critical to handle Yu perfectly. When the time came for their ways to part, it must be on the Faithful's terms, not theirs.

He cleared his throat, banishing his moody thoughts, and waved at a chair.

"Sit, sit, Captain!"

Yu waited with punctilious courtesy until Simonds had taken his own seat, then dropped neatly into the indicated chair, and the Sword swallowed the bitter bile of envy at how easily Yu moved. The captain was ten years older than Simonds and looked half his age. Looked? Yu *was* half Simonds' age, physically, at least, for his people were so lost to God they saw no evil in tampering with His plan for their species. They used the prolong process liberally, among their military and ruling families, at least, and Simonds was disturbed by how much he envied them. The temptation to drink from that spring of youth was a deadly one. Perhaps it was as well Masada's medical community was incapable of duplicating it, even if that inability was one more galling indication of the things these infidels could do and the Faithful couldn't.

"We have a problem, Captain," he said at length.

"A problem, Sir?" Yu's foreign accent, with its longer vowels and sharper consonants, still fell strangely on Simonds' ear.

"Yes. Our agents on Grayson have just discovered that the convoy will arrive with a powerful escort."

"How powerful, Sir?" Yu asked, sitting straighter, and Simonds smiled sourly.

"We don't know yet—only that it will be 'powerful.'" He snorted. "We should have anticipated it, I suppose. Their bitch of a queen will guard her thirty pieces of silver well until Mayhew sells Grayson to her."

Alfredo Yu nodded, carefully concealing his reaction to the savagery of Simonds' voice. The mere idea of a *woman* as a head of state appalled Masada—didn't the Bible itself say it was Eve's corruption which had tainted all humanity with sin?—and Simonds' disgust at the thought that even *Grayson* might consider allying itself with such a vile and unnatural regime was clear. Yet it probably gave him a certain horrified satisfaction, as well, for it must pander to his own sense of superiority as one more indication of Grayson's apostasy beside the uncorrupted fidelity of the Faithful. But Masadan bigotry was less important at the moment than the information that the convoy had a real escort to worry about, and the captain frowned in thought.

"Have you been able to discover anything about this escort's orders, Sir?"

"How can we?" the Sword grumbled in a deliberately sour voice. "It's hard enough to discover what the *Apostate* are up to! But we have to assume the Manticorans won't sit idly by while we eliminate their potential ally."

"They might, depending on their orders, Sir."

Simonds' eyes flashed, and the captain shrugged. "I didn't say it was likely, Sir, only that it was possible—and I sincerely hope it *is* the case, under the circumstances."

Yu's quiet tone held a carefully measured bite, and Simonds flushed. Yu and his superiors had pressed the Council of Elders for weeks—respectfully, but strongly—to move forward on Operation Jericho. Simonds was more than a little frightened of taking the plunge himself, but he knew Yu had been right from a purely military viewpoint, and he'd said so. Not that it had mattered. The Council as a whole had been determined to wait until after the Manticoran bribe was delivered to Grayson. Their own ally, unable to match the efficiency of Manticoran industry, would have been hard pressed to provide the same sort of infrastructure boost, and the Elders, intent on gathering in that largess for Masada's benefit, had delayed too long.

Or perhaps not. Not even the majority of the Council of Elders knew everything, and the inner circle had its own reasons to delay. Of course, it was always possible that *they*'d waited too long, as well, but they had more than one way to their end. And even if it came down to the operation everyone else expected, the escorts would withdraw with their unloaded freighters once the clique ruling Grayson had sold what was left of their souls as the vassals of infidels who let themselves be ruled by women. There would be a window, however brief, between the signing of the draft treaty and its ratification. If the Faithful struck then, before the treaty was formalized, and eliminated the government which would have ratified it . . .

"The Council of Elders is unanimous on this, Captain." The Sword made himself sound pleasant. "Until and unless we can confirm that the Manticoran escort commander has orders not to intervene, we will postpone Jericho."

"With all due respect, Sir, their escort would have to be *very* powerful to offset *Thunder*'s presence in our own order of battle. Particularly when they don't know we have her."

"But if they intervene, Jericho will result in a shooting confrontation with Manticore, and we can't possibly stand off the Royal Manticoran Navy."

"Not alone, no, Sir," Yu agreed, and Simonds bared his teeth in a tight grin of understanding. He knew where Yu was headed—and he had no intention of following him there. The Council of Elders wouldn't thank the Sword for creating a situation in which their continued existence depended upon Yu's true masters dispatching a powerful fleet to "protect" them! They would become little more than prisoners under house arrest if they allowed that to happen—which would no doubt suit their "ally's" purposes perfectly. Not that he could say that to Yu.

"There's too much room for error in precipitate action, Captain," he said instead. "Manticore is much closer than your friends are. If it came to open combat and *any* of their ships escaped, their reinforcements would get here before yours could. Under those circumstances, even a victory would be a disaster. And, of course," he added, "it's much too late for us to preposition Republican naval units here before we launch Jericho."

"I see." Yu leaned back in his chair and folded his arms. "What does the Council want to do instead, then?"

"We'll proceed with the planning and initial deployments for Jericho, but we won't mount the actual operation until the Manticoran escort withdraws."

"And if it *doesn't* withdraw, Sir? Or if they replace it with a regular picket force before it does?"

"We believe that to be unlikely—and the risk of precipitating open war with Manticore outweighs the possibility." It was Simonds' turn to lean back. While there were things it would never do for the captain to learn, it was time for a few unambiguous, if carefully chosen, words, he decided.

"Captain Yu, your superiors' objectives and ours are not identical. We both know that, and much as we appreciate your help, the Council isn't blind to the fact that you're helping us because it suits your own purposes."

Simonds paused while Yu cocked his head. Then he nodded, and the Sword's smile turned more genuine. Infidel or not, there was a core of frankness in the captain, and Simonds appreciated it.

"Very well, then," he continued. "We know your fundamental objective is to keep Manticore out of the region, and we're willing to guarantee that outcome after our victory. We are not, however, prepared to risk the survival of the True Faith in pursuit of it. We've waited over six centuries to crush the Apostate; if we must, we can wait another six, because unlike you, if you'll forgive my frankness, we know God is on our side."

"I see." Yu pursed his lips, then shrugged. "Sir, my orders are to support your decisions, but I'm also charged with advising you on the best use of *Thunder* and *Principality* in pursuit of our common goals. Obviously, that includes giving you my honest opinion of the best timing for Jericho, and frankly, the *best* timing has already escaped us. I hope my saying that doesn't offend you, but I'm a military man, not a diplomat. As such, my first concern must be avoiding misunderstandings, not the formal nuances of courtesy."

"I realize that, Captain, and I appreciate it," Simonds said, and, in fact, he did. He might worry about his blood pressure when Yu disagreed too bluntly with him, and keeping him ignorant of Maccabeus made things much harder all around, but it was far better to hear the man out, heathen or no, than drive him into working behind Simonds' back.

"Within those limitations, then," Yu continued, "I must respectfully argue that God helps those who help themselves. This 'escort force' may not withdraw at all, at least until it's time to convey Manticore's diplomats home, and even a draft treaty of alliance might very well bring the Manticorans in against you if you hit Grayson after their delegation leaves. I believe the probability that a binding alliance between them will make any future action far more dangerous must be balanced against the possibility that the escort's current orders are simply to protect the convoy and their own representatives."

"You may be correct, Captain," Simonds admitted, "but that supposes that we act openly at all. The Council believes—rightly, I think—that even if they sign their cursed treaty it will be primarily defensive. Without a Manticoran guarantee to support offensive action, the Apostate won't dare attack us alone, and one thing the Faithful have learned is patience. We would prefer to be your friends and to strike now, but if doing so jeopardizes the security of the Faith, we're prepared to wait. Sooner or later you and Manticore will settle your differences, one way or the other, and Manticore's interest in this region will wane. Either way, our chance will come in time."

"Perhaps, Sir—and perhaps not. As you say, you've waited six centuries, but those have been six centuries of relative peace in this region. The odds are very high that that peace will soon be a thing of the past. My superiors hope and believe that any war with Manticore will be short, but we can't positively guarantee that, and Endicott and Yeltsin's Star will be caught squarely between us when the shooting starts. If Manticore secures base rights in Yeltsin, that shooting is almost certain to move right onto your doorstep, with consequences no one can predict."

Simonds tasted the distant tang of iron in the captain's measured words. Yu was being careful not to say that one of those consequences might well be the annexation of both star systems by Masada's present "ally," but they both knew what he meant.

"Under the circumstances, Sir," Yu went on quietly, "it's my opinion that any operation which promises a significant chance of victory *now* is well worth a few risks. From our perspective, it relieves us of the necessity of dealing with an advanced enemy base squarely in our path to Manticore; from your perspective, it avoids the high probability that your star system will be caught in the crossfire at a later date."

"There's a great deal of truth in that, Captain," Simonds conceded, "and I'll certainly bear it in mind when next I speak with the Council. On the other hand, some of the Elders may feel your victory over Manticore is less assured than you seem to believe."

"Nothing is ever assured in war, Sir, but we're far bigger than they are, with a much larger fleet. And, as you yourself have pointed out, Manticore is weak and degenerate enough to allow a woman to hold the reins of power."

Simonds twitched, face flushing, and Yu hid a smile. The Sword would undoubtedly recognize the manipulation of that last sentence, but it appealed too strongly to the man's intolerance for him to simply shrug it off as someone from a more civilized culture might.

Simonds swallowed a harsh remark and looked long and hard at the captain, sensing the smile behind those courteous eyes. He knew Yu didn't believe his own dismissal of Manticore's degeneracy . . . but, then, Yu himself sprang from a degenerate society. The People's Republic of Haven was even more corrupt than most foreigners, yet the Faithful were willing to use any tool that was offered for God's Work. And when one used a tool, one need not tell it of all of one's *other* tools. Especially not when the object was to use one of them to displace another at the proper time, and Haven's cynical ambition was too barefaced, and far too voracious, for anyone to trust. That was the very reason anything Yu said, however professional and reasonable, must be examined again and again before it was accepted.

"Your point is well taken, Captain," the Sword said after a moment, "and, as I say, the Elders and I will consider it carefully. I believe the decision to wait until the Manticoran escort withdraws will stand, but I also feel certain God will guide us to the correct decision in the end."

"As you say, Sir," Yu replied. "My superiors may not

share your religion, Sword Simonds, but we respect your beliefs."

"We're aware of that, Captain." Simonds said, though he didn't for a moment believe Yu's superiors respected the Faith. But that was acceptable. Masada was accustomed to dealing with unbelievers, and if Yu was sincere, if Haven did, indeed, believe in the religious tolerance it prated about, then their society was even more degenerate than Simonds had believed.

There could be no compromise with those who rejected one's own beliefs, for compromise and coexistence only opened the door to schism. A people or a faith divided against itself became the sum of its weaknesses, not its strengths, and anyone who didn't know that was doomed.

• CHAPTER FIVE

Hyper space's rippling energy fluxes and flurries of charged particles hashed any sensor beyond a twenty-light-minute radius, but the convoy's clustered light codes were clear and sharp and gratifyingly tight on Honor's maneuvering display as it approached the hyper limit of Yeltsin's Star at a comfortable third of light-speed.

The translation from n-space to hyper was speed critical—at anything above .3 C, dimensional shear would tear a ship apart—but the reverse wasn't true. Which didn't make high-speed downward translations pleasant. The energy bleed as the convoy crossed each hyper wall would slow them to a crawl long before they reached the alpha bands, and shear wasn't a factor as far as hardware was concerned, but the effect on *humans* was something else again. Naval crews were trained for crash translations, yet there was a limit to what training could do to offset the physical distress and violent nausea, and there was no point in putting anyone—especially her merchant crews—through that.

"Ready to begin translation in forty-one seconds, Ma'am," Lieutenant Commander DuMorne reported from Astrogation.

"Very well, Mr. DuMorne. The con is yours."

"Aye, aye, Ma'am. I have the con. Helm, prepare for initial translation on my mark."

"Ready for translation, aye," Chief Killian replied, and the helmsman's hand hovered over the manual override, just in case the astrogator's computers dropped the ball, while Honor leaned back to watch.

"Mark!" DuMorne said crisply, and the normally

inaudible hum of *Fearless*'s hyper generator became a basso growl.

Honor swallowed against a sudden ripple of nausea as the visual display altered abruptly. The endlessly shifting patterns of hyper space were no longer slow; they *flickered*, jumping about like poorly executed animation, and her readouts flashed steadily downward as the entire convoy plummeted "down" the hyper space gradient.

Fearless hit the gamma wall, and her Warshawski sails bled transit energy like an azure forest fire. Her velocity dropped almost instantly from .3 *C* to a mere nine percent of light-speed, and Honor's stomach heaved as her inner ear rebelled against a speed loss the rest of her senses couldn't even detect. DuMorne's calculations had allowed for the energy bleed, and their translation gradient steepened even further as their velocity fell. They hit the beta wall four minutes later, and Honor winced again—less violently this time—as their velocity bled down to less than two percent of light-speed. The visual display was a fierce chaos of heaving light as the convoy fell straight "down" across a "distance" which had no physical existence, and then they hit the alpha bands and flashed across them to the n-space wall like a comet.

Her readouts stopped blinking. The visual display was suddenly still, filled once more with the unwinking pinpricks of normal-space stars, the sense of nausea faded almost as quickly as it had come, and HMS *Fearless*'s velocity had dropped in less than ten minutes from ninety thousand kilometers per second to a bare hundred and forty.

Honor drew a deep breath and suppressed the automatic urge to shake her head in relief. One or two people around the bridge were doing just that, but the old hands were as purposely blasé about it as she herself. It was silly, of course, but there were appearances to maintain.

Her lips twitched at the familiar thought, and she glanced at her astrogation repeater. Stephen had done his usual bang-up job, and *Fearless* and her charges floated twenty-four light-minutes from Yeltsin's Star, just outside the F6's hyper limit. Even the best hyper log was subject to some error, and the nature of hyper space precluded any observations to correct, but the voyage had been relatively short and DuMorne had shaved his safety margin with an expert touch.

She pressed a com stud on her chair arm while he took normal-space fixes to refine their position, and the voice of her chief engineer answered.

"Engineering, Commander Higgins."

"Reconfigure to impeller drive, please, Mr. Higgins."

"Aye, aye, Ma'am. Reconfiguring now," Higgins acknowledged, and *Fearless* folded her Warshawski sails into her impeller wedge.

There was no internal sign of the change, but Honor's engineering readouts and visual display told the tale. Unlike Warshawski sails, which were invisible in normal space except for the brief moment in which they radiated the energy bleed of a translation, the stressed gravity bands of an impeller drive were almost painfully obvious. Now they sprang into existence above and below *Fearless*, angled towards one another in a wedge open both ahead and astern, and stars red-shifted as a gravity differential of a hundred thousand MPS^2 grabbed at their photons. The cruiser floated within her wedge, like a surfer poised in the curl of a wave which hadn't yet begun to move, and Honor watched her communications officer.

Lieutenant Metzinger pressed the fingers of her right hand gently against her earbug, then looked up.

"All ships report reconfigured to impeller, Ma'am."

"Thank you, Joyce." Honor's eyes moved to the blue-green light code of the planet Grayson, ten and a half light-minutes further in-system, and then to DuMorne. "May I assume, Mr. DuMorne, that, with your usual efficiency, you now have a course worked out for Grayson?"

"You, may, Ma'am." DuMorne returned her smile. "Course is one-one-five by—" he double-checked his position and tapped a minute correction into his computers "—zero-zero-four-point-zero-niner.

Acceleration is two-zero-zero gravities with turnover in approximately two-point-seven hours."

"Lay it in, Chief Killian."

"Aye, aye, Ma'am. Coming to one-one-five, zero-zero-four-point-zero-niner."

"Thank you. Com, pass our course to all ships, please."

"Aye, aye, Ma'am." Metzinger dumped figures from DuMorne's computers to the rest of the convoy. "Course acknowledged and validated by all units," she reported a moment later. "Convoy ready to proceed."

"Very good. Are *we* ready, Helm?"

"Yes, Ma'am. Standing by for two-zero-zero gravities."

"Then let's be on our way, Chief."

"Aye, aye, Ma'am. Underway."

There was no discernible sense of movement as *Fearless* gathered speed at just under two kilometers per second per second, for her inertial compensator allowed her to cheat Newton shamelessly.

Two hundred gravities was a leisurely lope for *Fearless*, less than half of what she could have turned out even at the eighty percent "max" power settings the Manticoran Navy normally used, but it was the highest safe acceleration for Honor's freighters. Merchantmen were far larger yet had much weaker impeller drives than warships, with proportionately less powerful compensators.

She looked back at Metzinger.

"Hail Grayson Traffic Control, please, Joyce."

"Aye, aye, Ma'am. Transmitting now."

"Thank you." Honor leaned back in her command chair, propped her elbows on its arms, and steepled her fingers under her pointed chin. It would take her hail over ten minutes to reach Grayson, and as she watched the distant, gleaming marble swell with infinitesimal speed in the visual display, she wondered how much of a problem her gender would actually be.

High Admiral Bernard Yanakov looked up from his reader as his aide rapped gently on the frame of the open door.

"Yes, Jason?"

"Tracking just picked up a hyper footprint right on the limit, Sir. We don't have impeller confirmation yet, but I thought you'd want to know."

"You thought correctly." Yanakov switched off the reader and rose, twitched his blue tunic straight, and picked up his peaked cap. Lieutenant Andrews moved out of his way, then fell in beside and slightly behind him as he strode briskly towards Command Central.

The chatter of voices and old-fashioned impact printers met them as they stepped through the soundproofed door, and Yanakov hid a grimace, for the clattering printers were even more primitive than those the original colonists had brought from Old Earth. They did the job, but they were one more indication of how far Grayson's technology had backslid. It wasn't something that usually bothered the Admiral, but today wasn't usual. That footprint almost had to be the Manticoran convoy, and his planet's backwardness would be embarrassingly apparent to their visitors.

Crimson status lights caught his eye, and he nodded in satisfaction. Until they knew for certain that that footprint was the convoy, the Grayson Navy would assume it was a Masadan attack force. The unscheduled drill would do all hands good . . . and given the current levels of tension, Yanakov had no intention of taking any chances with his home world's security.

Commodore Brentworth looked up as Yanakov crossed to him.

"Passive sensors just registered incoming impeller drives, Admiral," he said briskly, and a light glowed on the master system display behind him. Tiny letters and numerals beside it detailed numbers and accelerations, and Yanakov grunted softly as he studied them.

"Numbers and formation match the Manticoran convoy, Sir. Of course, we only have them on gravitics now, not light-speed sensors. We won't hear anything from the com for another eight minutes or so."

"Understood, Walt." Yanakov watched the board a moment longer, then glanced at his aide. "Alert my cutter for immediate liftoff, Jason, and inform *Grayson* I'll be arriving aboard shortly."

"Yes, Sir." Andrews vanished, and Yanakov turned back to the board. *Austin Grayson* would be small and antiquated beside the *Star Knight* cruiser heading the Manticoran escort, but she was still the flagship of the Grayson Navy, and he would greet their guests from his flag deck, where he belonged.

Grayson looked oddly patchy in the visual display as *Fearless* and her brood settled into their parking orbit, and Honor had been amazed on the trip in-system by the scale of Grayson's spaceborne industry. For a technically backward system, Yeltsin's Star boasted an amazing number of bulk carriers and processing ships. None of them appeared hyper capable, and the largest massed barely a million tons, but they were *everywhere*, and some of the orbital structures circling Grayson itself were at least a third the size of *Hephaestus* or *Vulcan* back home. No doubt the scale of the orbital construction projects also explained the plethora of energy sources and drive signatures plying between Grayson and the local asteroid belt, but the sheer numbers of them still came as a shock.

Fearless cut her wedge as Chief Killian signaled "done with engines" and station-keeping thrusters took over, and Honor frowned over her displays while a corner of her mind monitored the flow of communications between the planetary authorities and Admiral Courvosier's staff on the heavy cruiser's flag bridge. Everything she saw only seemed to underscore the strange—to Manticoran eyes, at least—dichotomy between the almost incredible energy of Grayson's activities and the crudity with which they were carried out.

Old-fashioned electric arc and laser welders glared and sputtered, despite the wastefulness of such primitive, energy-intensive techniques compared to modern chem-catalyst welders. Hard-suited construction crews heaved massive frame members around, overcoming mass and momentum by brute muscle power without the tractor/counter-grav exo-suits Manticoran workers would have used as a matter of course, and it took her a while to realize (and even longer to accept) that some of them were using *rivet guns*. The local orbital power receptors were huge and clumsy and looked none too efficient, and her sensors said at least half the structures out there were using *fission* power plants! Fission plants weren't just old-fashioned; they were dangerous technical antiques, and their presence baffled her. The original Church of Humanity's colony ship had used fusion power, so why were the colonists' descendants using fission power nine hundred years later?

She shook her head and turned her attention to the nearest complete habitat. It rotated slowly about its central axis, but it obviously boasted internal grav generators, for the spin was far too slow to produce anything like a useful gravity. In fact, there was something peculiar about that leisurely, almost trickling movement. Could it be that—?

She punched a query into her tactical display, and her puzzlement grew as CIC confirmed her suspicion. That structure was spinning on its axis exactly once per local planetary day, which seemed very odd, and it glittered like a huge, faceted gem as Yeltsin's light bounced off unusually vast stretches of transparent hull. She frowned and leaned closer to her visual display, zooming in on an enormous surface dome, a blister of transparency over a kilometer across, and her eyes widened. The designers had used something like old-fashioned Venetian blinds, not the self-polarizing anti-rad armorplast Honor was used to; now the "blinds" were half-open on the nearer side of the dome as it rotated its way towards "evening," and she stared at the image for a long, disbelieving moment.

That wasn't an orbital habitat after all. Or, rather, it wasn't a habitat for *people*. She watched the herd of cattle graze across a knee-high meadow on what had to be one of the most expensive "farms" in the explored galaxy, then shook her head again—this time with slowly dawning comprehension. So *that* was why they were building so many orbital installations!

She turned back to the planet, and the peculiar splotchiness of its coloration really registered for the first time. Grayson's land surface was the life-breathing green of chlorophyll, with very few patches of desert, but most of it was a rich, blue-toned green, darker than anything Honor was used to seeing. Lighter patches, with suspiciously neat and regular boundaries, broke the darkness up, but the lighter areas were centered on what were obviously cities and towns, and all of those habitations were well inland. Grayson's seas were a deep and sparkling blue, painfully similar to those of Honor's native Sphinx, yet there were no cities along those bright, white beaches, and she nodded to herself as she realized why.

Grayson was, as Admiral Courvosier had said, a lovely planet. Its colors had a rich, jewel-like tone rare even among life-bearing worlds, and despite its thirteen and a half light-minute orbital radius, its brilliant star and minimal axial tilt gave it surface temperatures and weather patterns any resort planet might envy. But beautiful as it was, Grayson had never been intended as a home for man. It was considerably smaller than Old Earth, yet its mass was almost Earth Standard, for it was rich in heavy elements. Dangerously rich. So rich its plant life fixed arsenic and cadmium, mercury and lead, and passed those same elements on to the herbivores who ate it. So rich its seas weren't merely "salt" but a brew of naturally occurring toxins that made merely swimming in them potentially lethal. No wonder Grayson's people lived inland, and Honor hated even to think of the unremitting struggle they must face to "decontaminate" the soil that supported those lighter green patches of terrestrial food crops.

Honor's parents were doctors, and she shuddered at the potential for neural and genetic damage Grayson's environment offered. It must be like living in a chemical waste dump, and these people had lived here for nine *centuries*. No wonder they built farms in outer space—if she'd been they, she would have moved her entire *population* into orbit! The sheer beauty of their planet must make its dangers even harder to endure . . . and a still more bitter cosmic joke. Austin Grayson's followers had come five hundred and thirty light-years to escape the technology they believed polluted their birth world and racial soul only to find this poisonous jewel of a planet at journey's end.

She shuddered and turned away from that gorgeous, deadly view to concentrate on her tactical display. The local naval units which had come out to greet them had decelerated to match vectors with the convoy; now they shared *Fearless's* orbit, and she knew she was studying them to avoid looking at their homeworld until she could come to terms with its reality.

Most of them were light attack craft, purely sublight intrasystem vessels, the largest massing barely eleven thousand tons. The LACs were dwarfed by their light cruiser flagship, yet however large she might be beside her diminutive consorts, the cruiser was only a little over ninety thousand tons, barely two-thirds the size of Alice Truman's *Apollo*. She was also thirty years old, but Honor's last command had been even smaller and older, and she could only approve of the crisp deft way the Graysons had maneuvered to rendezvous with her own command. Those ships might be old and technically inferior, but their crews knew what they were doing.

She sighed and leaned back, glancing around her bridge once more. Admiral Courvosier's staff had handled all message traffic, but she'd monitored it at his invitation, and she'd been relieved by the genuine welcome in Admiral Yanakov's voice. Maybe this wasn't going to be as bad as she'd feared—and even if it was, her new insight into the environment from whence these people sprang should certainly temper her own reaction.

"Admiral Yanakov will arrive in six minutes, Skipper," Lieutenant Metzinger said suddenly, and Honor nodded. She pressed a button, and her command chair displays folded into their storage positions.

"I think it's time you and I got down to the boat bay to join the Admiral and greet our guests, Exec."

"Yes, Ma'am." Andreas Venizelos climbed out of his own chair and joined her as she headed for the bridge lift.

"Mr. DuMorne, you have the watch."

"Aye, aye, Ma'am. I have the watch," DuMorne replied, and moved from his station to the command chair as the lift door slid shut behind her.

High Admiral Yanakov tasted pure, undiluted envy as HMS *Fearless* swelled before him. Now *that* was a warship, he thought, drinking in the sleek, double-ended spindle appreciatively. The big, powerful ship hung against the bottomless stars, gleaming with reflected sunlight, and she was the most beautiful thing he'd ever seen. Her impeller wedge and defensive sidewalls were down, displaying her arrogant grace to the naked eye, and her midships section swelled smoothly between the bands of her fore and aft impeller rings, bristling with state-of-the-art radar and gravitic arrays and passive sensor systems. Her hull number—CA 286—stood out boldly against the white hull just aft of her forward impeller nodes, and weapon bays ran down her armored flank like watching eyes.

His cutter shivered as one of the cruiser's tractors locked on, and his pilot cut his thrusters as they slid into the bright cavern of *Fearless*'s boat bay. The tractor deposited the small craft neatly in a cradle, the docking collar nestled into place, and the pressure signal buzzed, indicating a solid seal.

Lieutenant Andrews and his staff fell in behind him as the Admiral swam down the access tube, and he smiled as he saw the Manticoran rating stationed diplomatically by the scarlet-hued grab bar just short of the tube's end. The rating started to speak, but stopped himself as he saw Yanakov already reaching for the bar. The Grayson Navy used green, not scarlet, but the Admiral recognized the meaning of the color code and swung himself nimbly across the interface into the cruiser's internal gravity. He stepped out of the way, moving forward to make room for his staff, and the shrill of the bosun's pipes greeted him as he cleared the tube hatch.

The boat bay gallery was huge compared to the one he'd left behind aboard *Grayson*, but it seemed absolutely filled with people. The Marine honor guard snapped to attention in its green-and-black dress uniforms, naval personnel in the black and gold of the Royal Manticoran Navy saluted sharply, and Yanakov blinked in surprise.

The damned ship was crewed by *children*! The oldest person in sight couldn't be over thirty T-years old, and most of them looked like they were barely out of high school!

Trained reflex took his hand through an answering salute even as the thought flashed through his mind, and then he kicked himself. Of course they weren't children; he'd forgotten the prolong treatment was universally available to Manticorans. But what did he do now? He wasn't *that* familiar with Manticoran naval insignia, and how did he pick the senior officers out of this morass of juvenile delinquents?

Part of the problem answered itself as a small, round-faced man in civilian clothing stepped forward. Logic suggested he had to be the delegation head, and that meant he was Admiral Raoul Courvosier. At least he looked like an adult—there was even gray in his hair—but he was far less impressive than Yanakov had anticipated. He'd read every article and lecture of Courvosier's he could find, and this smiling man looked more like an elf than the brilliant, sharp-eyed strategist the Admiral had anticipated, but—

"Welcome aboard, High Admiral," Courvosier said, clasping Yanakov's hand firmly, and his deep voice, unlike his face, was *exactly* what Yanakov had envisioned. The crisp accent sounded odd—Grayson's long isolation had produced one which was much softer and slower paced—but its very oddness was somehow right and fitting.

"Thank you, Admiral Courvosier, and allow me, in the name of my government and people, to welcome you to our system."

Yanakov returned the handclasp while his staff assembled itself behind him. Then he glanced around the crowded gallery once more and stiffened. He'd known Manticore allowed women to serve in its military, but it had been an intellectual thing. Now he realized almost half the people around him—even some of the Marines!—were female. He'd tried to prepare himself for the alien concept, but the deep, visceral shock echoing deep inside him told him he'd failed. It wasn't just alien, it was *unnatural*, and he tried to hide his instinctive repugnance as he dragged his eyes back to Courvosier's face.

"On behalf of my Queen, I thank you," his host said, and Yanakov managed to bow pleasantly despite the reminder that a woman ruled Manticore. "I hope my visit will bring our two nations still closer together," Courvosier continued, "and I'd like to present my staff to you. But first, permit me to introduce *Fearless*'s captain and our escort commander."

Someone stepped up beside Courvosier, and Yanakov turned to extend his hand, then froze. He felt his smile congeal as he saw the strong, beautiful, *young* face under the white beret and the tight-curled fuzz of silky brown hair. Yanakov was unusually tall for a Grayson, but the officer before him was at least twelve centimeters taller than he was, and that made it irrationally worse. He fought his sense of shock as he stared into the Manticoran captain's dark, almond eyes, furious that no one had warned him, knowing he was gaping and embarrassed by his own frozen immobility—and perversely angry with himself *because* of his embarrassment.

"High Admiral Yanakov, allow me to present Captain Honor Harrington," Courvosier said, and Yanakov heard the hissing gasp of his staff's utter disbelief behind him.

• CHAPTER SIX

"I don't like it. I don't like it at all, Mr. Ambassador."

Leonard Masterman, the Havenite ambassador to Grayson, looked up and frowned. Captain Michaels was seldom this vocal, and his expression was uneasy.

"Why in hell did they have to send *her?*" The senior military attache paced back and forth across the ambassador's carpet. "Of all the officers in the Manticoran Navy, they had to stick us with *Harrington!* God, it's like history repeating itself!" he said bitterly, and Masterman's frown deepened.

"I don't quite understand your concern, Captain. This isn't the Basilisk System, after all."

Michaels didn't reply at once, for Masterman was an anachronism. The scion of a prominent Legislaturist family, he was also a career diplomat who believed in the rules of diplomacy, and Special Ops had decided he shouldn't know about Jericho, Captain Yu, or *Thunder of God* on the theory that he could play his role far more convincingly if they never told him it *was* a role.

"No, of course it's not Basilisk," the captain said finally. "But if any Manticoran officer has reason to hate us, it's her, and she gave us a hell of a black eye over Basilisk, Mr. Ambassador. The Graysons must have heard about it. If Courvosier uses her presence to play up the 'Havenite threat' to their own system—"

"You let me worry about that, Captain," Masterman responded with a slight smile. "Believe me, the situation's under control."

"Really, Sir?" Michaels regarded the ambassador dubiously.

"Absolutely." Masterman tipped his chair back and crossed his legs. "In fact, I can't think of a Manticoran officer I'd rather see out here. I'm astonished their foreign ministry let their admiralty send her."

"I beg your pardon?" Michaels' eyebrows rose, and Masterman chuckled.

"Look at it from the Graysons' viewpoint. She's a woman, and no one even warned them she was coming. However good her reputation may be, it's not good enough to offset that. Graysons aren't Masadans, but their bureaucrats still have trouble with the fact that they're dealing with *Queen* Elizabeth's government, and now Manticore's rubbed their noses in the cultural differences between them."

The ambassador nodded at Michaels' suddenly thoughtful expression.

"Exactly. And as for the Basilisk operation—" Masterman frowned, then shrugged. "I think it was a mistake, and it was certainly execrably executed, but, contrary to your fears, it can be made to work *for* us if we play our cards right."

The captain's puzzlement was obvious, and Masterman sighed.

"Grayson doesn't *know* what happened in Basilisk. They've heard our side and they've heard Manticore's, but they know each of us has an axe to grind. That means they're going to take both versions with more than a grain of salt, Captain, but their own prejudices against women in uniform will work in our favor. They'll *want* to believe the worst about her, if only to validate their own bias, and the fact that *we* don't have any female officers will be a factor in their thinking."

"But we do have female officers," Michaels protested.

"Of course we do," Masterman said patiently, "but we've carefully not assigned any to this system. And, unlike Manticore—which probably didn't have any choice, given that their head of state is a woman—we haven't told the locals we even have any. We haven't told them we *don't*, either, but their sexism cuts so deep they're ready to assume that unless we prove differently. So at the moment, they're thinking of us as a good, old-fashioned patriarchal society. Our foreign policy makes them nervous, but our *social* policies are much less threatening than Manticore's."

"All right, I can see that," Michaels agreed. "It hadn't occurred to me that they might assume we don't *have* any female personnel—I thought they'd just assume we were being tactful—but I see what you're driving at."

"Good. But you may not realize just how vulnerable Harrington really is. Bad enough she's a woman in a man's role, but she's also a convicted murderer," the ambassador said, and Michaels blinked in astonishment.

"Sir, with all due respect, no one's going to believe that. Hell, I don't like her a bit, but I know damned well that was pure propaganda."

"Of course you do, and so do I, but the Graysons don't. I'm quite aware the entire thing was a show trial purely for foreign consumption, and to be perfectly honest, I don't like it. But it's done, so we may as well use it. All any Grayson knows is that a Haven court found Captain Harrington guilty of the murder of an entire freighter's crew. Of course Manticore insists the 'freighter' was actually a Q-ship caught red-handed in an act of war—what else *can* they say?—but the fact that a court pronounced her guilty will predispose a certain percentage of people to believe she must have *been* guilty, particularly since she's a woman. All we have to do is point out her 'proven guilt' more in sorrow than in anger, as the natural result of the sort of catastrophe which results when you put someone with all of a woman's frailties in command of a ship of war."

Michaels nodded slowly. He felt a twinge of guilt, which surprised him, but Masterman was right, and the locals' prejudices would make them far more likely to accept a story no civilized planet would believe for a moment.

"You see, Captain?" Masterman said quietly. "This will let us change the entire focus of the internal Grayson debate over Manticore's overtures from a cold-blooded consideration of advantages to an emotional rejection based on their own bigotry. And if I've learned one thing over the years, it's that when it comes down to raw emotion against reason, emotion wins."

" . . . and this is our combat information center, gentlemen." Andreas Venizelos was short by Manticoran standards, but he stood centimeters taller than the Grayson officers in the compartment as he gestured about himself at the shining efficiency.

Admiral Yanakov managed not to gawk, but his palms itched as he took in the superb instrumentation. The holo tank was over three meters across, and the flat-screen displays around him showed every ship within ten light-minutes of Grayson. Not with single, annotated light codes for groups of vessels, but as individual units with graphic representations of mass and vector.

He stepped closer to one of the ratings and peered over his shoulder. The young—or, young-*looking*, anyway—man didn't even twitch at his presence, and Yanakov turned back to Venizelos.

"Could you bring up the holo tank, Commander?"

Venizelos regarded him for a moment, then looked past him.

"Captain?"

Yanakov felt his expression try to freeze, then turned. Captain Harrington stood behind him, her strongly carved face showing no emotion at all, and he made himself meet her eyes. The sense of the alien grew greater, not less, every time he saw her uniform, and he suspected she'd delegated the task of spokesman to her executive officer because she felt it, too.

"Would you object to our observing the holo display in operation . . . Captain?" Yanakov's voice sounded strained even in his own ears, and he cursed himself for the slight hesitation he gave her title.

"Of course not, Admiral." Her musical soprano only increased his feeling of unreality. It sounded almost exactly like his third wife's, and the thought of *Anna* in uniform appalled him.

"Bring up the tank, please, Chief Waters," she said.

"Aye, aye, Ma'am," a petty officer responded with a

crispness that seemed odd addressed to a woman. But, Yanakov thought almost despairingly, it didn't sound a bit odd addressed to an *officer*. Damn it, the very concept of a female officer was an oxymoron!

The holo tank blinked to life, extending its upper edge almost to the deckhead, and the clustered Grayson officers made a soft noise of approval and delight. Small light codes drifted beside every dot: arrows denoting headings, dotted lines projecting vectors, numerals and letters defining drive strength, acceleration, and active sensor emissions. It was how God Himself must see the stars, and pure envy for this ship's capabilities tingled in Yanakov's brain.

"As you can see, Admiral," Harrington raised a hand to gesture gracefully at the holo, "we proj—"

She broke off as Commander Harris, Yanakov's operations officer, stepped between her and the tank in search of a closer look at one of the symbols. Her hand hovered a moment, and then her lips firmed.

"Excuse me, Commander," she said, her tone devoid of all emotion, "I was just about to point something out to Admiral Yanakov."

Harris turned, and Yanakov flushed at his cold-eyed, contemptuous expression. Yanakov was having trouble enough with the concept of a senior female officer, but Harris was a hardline conservative. He started to open his mouth, then snapped it shut at a tiny gesture from his admiral. His lips tightened further, but he stepped back, every line of his body a silent expression of resentment, for Harrington to proceed.

"As you can see, Admiral," she continued in that same, even voice, "we project the probable weapons range for each warship. Of course, a display with this much detail can be a liability for actual tactical control, so we use smaller ones on the bridge to avoid information overflow. CIC, however, is responsible for deciding which threats we need to see, and—"

Her voice went on, showing no sign of anger at Harris's insulting behavior, and Yanakov listened attentively even while he wondered if he should have dressed Harris down. Certainly he'd have to have a long talk with him in private, but should he have made the point now? It would have humiliated his ops officer in front of his fellows, but how would the Manticorans react to his own restraint?

He glanced up and caught Andreas Venizelos unawares, and the anger in the Manticoran officer's eyes answered his question.

"I know they're different, Bernard, but we just have to make allowances." Benjamin Mayhew IX, Planetary Protector of Grayson, snipped another rose and laid it in the servant's basket, then turned to regard his naval commander in chief sternly. "You knew they had women in uniform. Surely you realized we'd have to deal with that sooner or later."

"Of course I did!" Admiral Yanakov glowered at the basket, not bothering to hide his conviction that flower arrangement wasn't precisely the most manly art his head of state might have pursued. He was one of the few who made no secret of his feelings, but then, he was also Protector Benjamin's fifth cousin, with very clear memories of an infant who'd still been making puddles on the palace carpet when he himself was already in uniform.

"Then I don't quite understand your vehemence." Mayhew gestured, and the servant withdrew. "It's not like you to carry on this way."

"I'm not speaking for myself," Yanakov said a bit stiffly. "All I said was that *my officers* don't like it, and they don't. In fact, 'don't like' is putting it far too mildly, Ben. They *hate* it, and there are some ugly rumors about her competence."

"Her *competence*? Good God, Bernard! The woman holds the Manticore Cross!" Yanakov looked at him in some confusion, and Mayhew sighed. "You'd better bone up on foreign decorations, cousin mine. For your information, the Manticore Cross is about one notch lower than the Star of Grayson—and it can only be earned for heroism under fire."

"The Star of Grayson?" Yanakov blinked as he digested that thought. It didn't seem possible someone as good looking and young—

He stopped himself with a mental curse. Damn it, the woman *wasn't* as "young" as he kept thinking! In fact, she was forty-three T-years old, barely twelve years younger than Yanakov himself, but still . . .

"All right, so she's got guts," he growled. "But I'll bet she won that medal in Basilisk, didn't she?" The Protector nodded, and Yanakov shrugged. "Then it's only going to make the officers who don't trust her more suspicious, not less." He flushed at his cousin's expression but plowed on stubbornly. "You know I'm right, Ben. They're going to think exactly what the Havenites are going to say out loud: decorating her was part of a deliberate propaganda effort to cover up what really happened when she lost it—probably because it was her time of month!—and blew away an unarmed merchantman." His teeth grated in fresh frustration. "Damn it, if they *had* to send us a woman, couldn't they at least have sent us one who isn't rumored to be a murderer?!"

"Oh, that's bullshit, Bernard!" Mayhew led the way across the domed terrace into the palace, followed by his blank-faced personal Security man. "You've heard Manticore's version of Basilisk, and you know as well as I do what Haven wants in this region. Who do *you* think is telling us the truth?"

"Manticore, of course. But what you or I believe isn't the issue. Most of my people are only too ready to see any woman as potentially dangerous in a command slot. Those who don't automatically assume they must be loose warheads are horrified by the thought of exposing women to combat, and real conservatives, like Garret and his crowd, are reacting on pure emotion, not reason. *They* see her as a calculated insult to our way of life—and if you think I'm making that up, you should have heard a little conversation I had with my ops officer! Under the circumstances, Haven's version of what happened only validates all three groups' concerns.

And don't come down too heavily on *my* people, either!
Some of your civilian types are even worse than
anybody in the military, and you know it. Hell, what
about Jared?"

"Dear, sweet cousin Jared." Mayhew sounded as disgusted as he looked, then waved his hands in the air.
"Oh, you're right—you're right! And old Clinkscales is
even worse, though at least *he's* not second in line for
the protectorship." The Protector sank into an over-
stuffed armchair. "But we can't afford to see this thing
go down the tubes over something as stupid as cultural
prejudice, Bernie. Manticore can do a lot more for us
than Haven can: they're closer, their technology's better,
and they're a hell of a lot less likely to absentmindedly
gobble us up one fine day."

"Then I suggest you tell your negotiators that,"
Yanakov sighed.

"I have, but you're the historian. You know how the
Council's cut back the Protector's constitutional authority
over the last century. Prestwick is a decent sort as
Chancellor, but he doesn't really want to open the door
to resumption of direct rule by Yours Truly. I happen to
think we need a stronger executive to deal with all that's
about to come down on us, but I may be a bit biased
by who I am, and whatever I'd *like* to have, the fact is
that I'm pretty much reduced to the power of prestige.
Admittedly, the Mayhew Clan still boasts a fair amount
of that, but a disproportionate share of it's with the conservatives—and the conservatives, as you yourself just
pointed out, think accepting *any* outside help 'will
threaten the Grayson way of life'! I've got the Council
in line so far, and I think I've got a majority in the
Chamber, but it's slim—very slim—and if the military
doesn't sign on, I'll lose it. You've *got* to get your
people to see reason about this."

"Ben," Yanakov said slowly, "I'll try, but I don't know
that you fully grasp just what you're asking for."
Mayhew straightened in his chair, but the Admiral went
on speaking. "I've known you since you were a kid, but
I've always known you were smarter than I am. If you

say we need the Manticoran alliance, I believe you. But sometimes I think your grandfather made a mistake having you and your father educated off-world. Oh, I know all about the advantages, but somewhere along the way you sort of lost touch with how most of our people feel about some issues, and that's dangerous. You talk about the conservatives in the Chamber, but, Ben, most of them are *less* conservative than the population as a whole!"

"I realize that," Mayhew said quietly. "Contrary to what you may think, having a different perspective actually makes it easier to see some things—like how difficult it really is to change entrenched attitudes—and the Mayhews have no more desire to be Grayson's Pahlavis than its Romanovs. I'm not proposing to overturn society overnight, but what we're talking about is the survival of our planet, Bernie. We're talking about an alliance that can bring us modern industry and a permanent Manticoran fleet presence Simonds and his fanatics won't dare screw around with. And whether we sign up with Manticore or not, we're not going to be able to sit this one out. I give the Havenites another T-year at the outside before they move openly against Manticore, and when they do, they'll come straight through us unless there's something here to stop them. We're in the way, Bernie, and you know that even better than I do."

"Yes," Yanakov sighed. "Yes, I do. And I'll try, Ben. I really will. But I wish to hell Manticore had been smart enough not to stick us with a situation like this, because I will be *damned* if I think I can pull it off."

• CHAPTER SEVEN

Sergeant Major Babcock smiled as Honor stepped onto the mat.

Babcock was from Gryphon, Manticore-B V. Gryphon's gravity was only five percent above Terran Standard, less than eighty percent that of Honor's native Sphinx, and Babcock was a good twenty centimeters shorter, with a much shorter reach, to boot. She was also just over twice Honor's age, and like Admiral Courvosier, she was first-generation prolong. The original treatment had stopped the aging process at a much later point than current techniques, and there were strands of gray in her red hair and crows-feet around her eyes.

None of which had kept her from throwing Honor around the salle with embarrassing ease.

Honor was taller and stronger, with better reaction speed and hand-eye coordination, but that, as Ms. Midshipman Harrington had learned long ago on Saganami Island, didn't necessarily mean a thing. Babcock was in at least as good a shape as she was, and she'd been doing this forty T-years longer. She knew moves her CO hadn't even thought of yet, and Honor suspected the sergeant major was delighted by the opportunity (one couldn't exactly call it an *excuse*) to kick the stuffing out of a senior Navy officer.

On the other hand, Honor was getting back into the groove herself, and she wasn't in the mood to be humiliated today.

They met at the center of the mat and fell into guard positions, and there was no smile on Honor's lips. Her face was still and calm, her background anger and frustration—not at Babcock, but nonetheless real—

71

leashed and channeled, and only those who knew her very well would have noted the hardness in her eyes.

They circled slowly, hands weaving in deceptively gentle, graceful patterns. Both were black belt in *coup de vitesse*, the martial art developed to combine Oriental and Western forms on Nouveau Dijon eight centuries before, and a hush enveloped the gym as other exercisers turned to watch them.

Honor felt her audience, but only distantly as her senses focused on Babcock with crystal, cat-like concentration. *Coup de vitesse* was a primarily offensive "hard" style, a combination of cool self-control and go-for-broke ferocity designed to take advantage of "Westerners'" larger size and longer reach. It wasn't too proud to borrow from any technique—from *savate* to *t'ai chi*—but it was less concerned with form and more with concentrated violence. It made far less effort to use an opponent's strength against her than most Oriental forms did and laid proportionately more emphasis on the attack, even at the occasional expense of centering and defense.

A classmate from the Academy unarmed combat team who preferred the elegance of *judo* to the *coup* had once likened it to fencing with two-handed swords, but it worked for Honor. And, like any of the martial arts, it wasn't something one thought through in the midst of a bout. You simply *did* it, responding with attacks and counters which were so deeply trained into you that *you* didn't know what you were doing—not consciously—until you'd already done it. So she didn't try to think, didn't try to anticipate. Babcock was too fast for that, and this was a full contact bout. She who let herself become distracted would pay a bruising price.

The sergeant major moved suddenly, feinting with her left hand, and Honor swayed backward, right hand slapping Babcock's right ankle aside to block the flashing side-kick. Her left palm intercepted the elbow strike follow up, and Babcock whirled on her left foot, using the momentum of Honor's block to turn still faster. She slammed the ball of her right foot onto the mat and her left foot came up in a lightning-fast back-kick, but Honor wasn't there. She slipped inside the striking foot, and Babcock grunted as a rock-hard fist drove home just above her kidneys. Honor's other hand darted forward, snaking around the noncom for the throw, but Babcock dropped like a string-cut puppet, pivoted out of Honor's grip, and kicked up through an instant backward somersault. Her feet caught Honor's shoulders, driving her back, and Babcock bounced up like a rubber ball—only to find herself flying away as hands like steel clamps flung her through the air.

She hit the mat, rolled, vaulted to her feet, and recovered her stance before Honor could reach her, and it was the captain's turn to grunt as stiff fingers rammed into her midriff. She buckled over the blow, but her left arm rose instinctively, blocking the second half of the combination and carrying through in an elbow strike to Babcock's ribs that rocked the sergeant major on her heels, and a fierce exultation filled her. She pressed her attack, using her longer reach and greater strength ruthlessly, but the sergeant major had a few tricks of her own.

Honor was never certain precisely how she found herself airborne, but then the mat slammed into her chin, and she tasted blood. She hit rolling, bouncing away from Babcock's follow-through, and rocked up on her knees to catch an incoming kick on her crossed wrists and upend her opponent. Both of them surged upright, and this time they were both smiling as they moved into one another with a vengeance.

"I trust you feel better now?"

Honor's smile was a bit puffy as her tongue explored a cut on the inside of her lower lip, and she wrapped the towel around her neck as she met Admiral Courvosier's quizzical eyes. She should have worn a mouth protector, but despite what promised to be an amazing array of bruises, she felt good. She felt *very* good, for she'd taken Babcock three falls out of four.

"As a matter of fact, I do, Sir." She leaned back against the lockers, playing with the ends of her towel, and Nimitz hopped up on the bench beside her and rubbed his head against her thigh, purring more loudly than he had in days. The empathic treecat was always sensitive to her moods, and she grinned as she freed one hand from the towel to stroke his spine.

"I'm glad." Courvosier wore a faded sweatsuit and handball gloves, and he sank onto a facing bench with a wry grimace. "But I wonder if the Sergeant Major realizes how many frustrations you were working out on her."

Honor looked at him more closely, then sighed.

"I never could fool you, could I, Sir?"

"I wouldn't go quite that far. Let's just say I know you well enough to know what you're thinking about our hosts."

Honor wrinkled her nose in acknowledgment and sat beside Nimitz while she dabbed absently at the small, fresh blood spots on her *gi*.

The situation hadn't gotten better, especially since the Havenite embassy had hit its stride. There was no way to eliminate the courtesy calls between her ships' companies and their hosts, and she knew the Graysons' special discomfort with her was spilling over onto her other female personnel.

Nimitz stopped purring and gave her a disgusted look as he picked up the direction of her emotions. Honor spent entirely too much time worrying over things, in his opinion, and he leaned up to nip her admonishingly on the earlobe. But Honor knew him as well as he knew her, and her hand intercepted him and scooped him into her lap to protect her ear.

"I'm sorry, Sir. I know how important it is that we all hang onto our tempers—Lord knows I've laid it all out for everyone else often enough!—but I hadn't counted on how infuriated I'd be. They're so—so—"

"Pigheaded?" Courvosier suggested. "Bigoted?"

"Both," Honor sighed. "Sir, all I have to do is walk into a room, and they clam up like they've been freeze-dried!"

"Would you say that's quite fair where Admiral Yanakov is concerned?" her old mentor asked gently, and Honor shrugged irritably.

"No, probably not," she admitted, "but he's almost worse than the others. They look at me like some unsavory microbe, but *he* tries so hard to act naturally that it only makes his discomfort even more evident. And the fact that not even the example of their commander in chief can get through to the others makes me so mad I could strangle them all!"

Her shoulders slumped, and she sighed again, more heavily. "I think maybe you had a point about the Admiralty's choice of senior officers for this operation, Sir. The fact that I'm a woman seems to get right up their noses and choke them."

"Maybe." Courvosier leaned back and folded his arms. "But whether it does or not, you're a Queen's officer. They're going to have to face senior female officers sometime; it's part of our mission description to teach them that, and they might as well get used to it now and spare us all grief later. That was the FO's opinion, and though I might have gone about things a bit differently, overall I have to agree with their assessment."

"I don't think *I* do," Honor said slowly. She played with Nimitz's ears and frowned down at her hands. "It might have been better to spare them the shock until after the treaty was a *fait accompli*, Sir."

"Bushwah!" Courvosier snorted. "You mean it might have been better if Ambassador Langtry had let us go ahead and warn them you were a woman!"

"Would it?" Honor shook her head. "I'm not so sure, Sir. I think maybe it was a no-win situation—and the fact is that the Admiralty was wrong to pick *me*. To hear Haven tell it, I'm the most bloodthirsty maniac since Vlad the Impaler. I can't imagine anyone we could have sent who would've been more vulnerable to that kind of attack after Basilisk."

She stared down at her hands, caressing Nimitz's fluffy fur, and Courvosier gazed at the crown of her head in silence. Then he shrugged.

"Actually, Basilisk is precisely why the Admiralty chose you, Honor." She looked up in surprise, and he nodded. "You know I had my own reservations, but Their Lordships believed—and the FO agreed—that Grayson would see what happened there as a warning of what could happen here. And just as they tapped me because I've got a reputation for strategy, they picked you because you've got one for tactics and guts . . . and because you're a woman. You were meant to be a living, breathing symbol of just how ruthless Haven can be, on the one hand, and how good our female officers can be, on the other."

"Well," Honor squirmed at the thought that she might have a "reputation" outside her own service, "I think they made the wrong call, Sir. Or, rather, Haven's turned it around on them. I'm a liability to you. These people can't get past *who* I am to think logically about *what* I am."

"I believe that will change," Courvosier said quietly. "It may take time, but no one gave me a time limit when we shipped out."

"I know they didn't." Honor rolled Nimitz onto his back to stroke his belly fur, then sat straight, planted both feet on the floor, and met the admiral's eyes levelly. "Nonetheless, I think I should remove myself from the equation, Sir. At least until you get the ball rolling in the right direction."

"You do?" Courvosier arched his eyebrows, and she nodded.

"I do. In fact, I sort of thought that might be wiser from the moment Yanakov and his people came on board *Fearless* to greet you. That's why I didn't go ahead and send Alice and Alistair straight on to Casca as I'd originally planned."

"I thought that might be the case." The admiral considered her soberly. "You're thinking about taking the other merchies to Casca yourself?" She nodded. "I'm not sure that's a good idea, Honor. The Graysons may see it as running out, as proof a 'mere woman' can't take the heat."

"Maybe. But I don't see how it could create any more negative reactions than my *presence* seems to be generating. If I take *Apollo* to Casca with me, it'll leave Jason Alvarez as SO. He doesn't seem to be having any problems with his opposite numbers—except for the ones who think he must be some kind of sissy for taking orders from a woman. Maybe by the time I come back, you'll have made enough progress with these people that my mere presence won't queer the deal for you."

"I don't know. . . ." Courvosier plucked at his lower lip. "If you take *Fearless* and *Apollo* out of here, our 'show of force' will get a lot weaker. Have you considered that?"

"Yes, Sir, but they've already seen both ships, and they'll know we're coming back. That should be sufficient, I'd think. And I'm not the only woman stuck in their craws right now. Alice is my second in command—*two* women, both senior to any of our male officers." She shook her head. "Better to get both of us out of the way for a while, Sir."

Courvosier was unconvinced, but she met his gaze almost pleadingly, and he saw the desperate unhappiness behind her brown eyes. He knew how deeply the Graysons' treatment hurt, not least because it was so utterly unjust. He'd watched her swallowing her anger, sitting on her temper, forcing herself to be pleasant to people who regarded her—at best—as some sort of freak. And, he knew, she was truly convinced her mere presence was undermining his own position. She might even be right, but what mattered most was that she *believed* it, and the thought of being responsible, however innocently, for the loss of a treaty her kingdom needed so badly, was tearing her up inside. She was angry, resentful, and even closer to despair than he'd realized, and he closed his eyes, weighing her proposal as carefully as he could.

He still thought it was the wrong move. He was a naval officer, not a trained diplomat, yet he knew how preconceptions shaped perceptions, and what she saw as a reasonable tactical withdrawal might be seen as something entirely different by the Graysons. There were too many implications, too many possibilities for misinterpretation, for him to know who was right.

But then he looked at her again, and he suddenly realized rightness or wrongness didn't matter to him just now. It could be argued either way, yet *she* thought she was right, and if she stayed and the treaty negotiations failed, she would always blame herself, rightly or wrongly, for that failure.

"Still planning to take *Troubadour* with you?" he asked at last.

"I don't know. . . ." Honor rubbed her nose. "I was thinking I should at least leave both tin-cans to show the flag if I pull the cruisers out, Sir."

"I don't think a single destroyer would make much difference in that regard. And you were right originally; you are going to need someone to do your scouting if the reports of pirate activity are accurate."

"I could use *Apollo* for that—" Honor began, but he shook his head.

"You could, but it might be just a bit too pointed to pull both ships with female skippers and leave both ships with men in command, don't you think?"

Honor cocked her head, considering his question, then nodded.

"You may be right." She drew a deep breath, her hands motionless on Nimitz's fur as she met his eyes again. "Do I have your permission, then, Sir?"

"All right, Honor," he sighed, and smiled sadly at her. "Go ahead. Get out of here—but I don't want you dilly-dallying around to delay your return, young lady! You be back in eleven days and not one minute longer. If I can't sort these bigoted barbarians out in that much time, the hell with them!"

"Yes, Sir!" Honor smiled at him, her relief evident, then looked back down at Nimitz. "And . . . thank you, Sir," she said very, very softly.

"Take a look at this, Sir."

Commander Theisman laid his memo board in his lap

and turned his command chair to face his executive officer, and a mobile eyebrow arched as he saw the impeller drive sources glowing in the main tactical display.

"Fascinating, Allen." He climbed out of his chair and crossed to stand beside his executive officer. "Have we got a firm ID on who's who?"

"Not absolutely, but we've been tracking them for about three hours, and they just passed turnover for the belt. That far out from Grayson, and on that heading with that acceleration, Tracking's pretty confident they aren't headed anywhere in *this* system, so they must be the convoy. And if they are, these—" five light codes glowed green "—are almost certainly the freighters, which means these—" three more dots glowed crimson in a triangle about the first five "—are the escorts. And if there're three of them, they're probably the cruisers and one of the tin-cans."

"Um." Theisman rubbed his chin. "All you've got is drive sources, not any indication of mass. That could be both of the cans and the light cruiser," he pointed out in his best devil's advocate's voice. "Harrington could be holding her own ship on station and sending the others off."

"I don't think that's very likely, Sir. You know how terrible the pirates have been out this way." Their eyes met with a shared flicker of amusement, but Theisman shook his head.

"The Manticorans are *good* at commerce protection, Al. One of their light cruisers, especially with a couple of destroyers to back her, would make mincemeat out of any of the 'outlaw raiders' out here."

"I still think this one—" one of the crimson lights flashed "—is *Fearless*, Sir. They're too far away for decent mass readings, but the impeller signature looks heavier than either of the other warships. I think she's got one tin-can out front and the cruisers closed up to cover the merchies' flanks." The exec paused, tugging at the lobe of one ear. "We could move in closer, take a little peek at the planetary orbital traffic to see who's left, Sir," he suggested slowly.

"Forget that shit right now, Al," his skipper said sternly. "We look, we listen, and we *don't* get any closer to Grayson. Their sensors are crap, but they could get lucky. And there's still at least one Manticoran around."

The exec nodded unhappily. One thing the People's Navy had learned since Basilisk was that Manticore's electronics were better than theirs. How *much* better was a topic of lively wardroom debate, but given that Captain Honor Harrington's eighty-five thousand-ton light cruiser had taken out a seven-point-five *million*-ton Q-ship, prudence suggested that Haven err on the side of pessimism. At least that way any surprises would be pleasant ones.

"So what do we do, Sir?" he asked finally.

"An excellent question," Theisman murmured. "Well, we know *some* of them are out of the way. And if they're going on to Casca, they can't be back here for ten or twelve days." He tapped on his teeth for a moment. "That gives us a window, assuming these turkeys know what to do with it. Wake up Engineering, Al."

"Yes, Sir. Will we be heading for Endicott or Blackbird, Sir?"

"Endicott. We need to tell Captain Yu—and Sword Simonds, of course—about this. A Masadan courier would take too long getting home, so I think we'll just take this news ourselves."

"Yes, Sir."

Theisman returned to his command chair and leaned back, watching the outgoing impeller traces crawl across the display under two hundred gravities of acceleration. Readiness reports flowed in, and he acknowledged them, but there was no rush, and he wanted to be certain one of those crimson dots wasn't going to turn around and head back to Grayson. He waited almost three more hours, until the light codes' velocity had reached 44,000 KPS, and they crossed the hyper limit and vanished from his gravitic sensors.

"All right, Al. Take us out of here," he said then, and

the seventy-five thousand-ton Masadan destroyer *Principality*, whose wardroom crest still proclaimed her to be the PNS *Breslau*, crept carefully away from the asteroid in whose lee she had lain hidden.

Passive sensors probed before her like sensitive cat's whiskers while Theisman made himself sit relaxed in his command chair, projecting an air of calm, and the truth was that *Principality* herself was safe enough. There wasn't a ship in the Grayson Navy capable of catching or engaging her, and despite the belt's bustling mining activity, the extraction ships tended to cluster in the areas where the asteroids themselves clustered. *Principality* avoided those spots like the plague and crept along under a fraction of her maximum power, for if the locals' sensor nets were crude and short-ranged, there was at least one modern warship in Grayson orbit, and Theisman had no intention of being spotted by her. Detection could be catastrophic to Haven's plans . . . not to mention the more immediate problem that Captain Yu would no doubt string his testicles on a necklace if he let that happen.

It took long, wearing hours, but at last his ship was far enough from Grayson to increase power and curve away from the asteroid belt. *Principality*'s gravitics would detect any civilian vessel far out of radar range and long before she was seen herself, with plenty of time to kill her drive, and her velocity climbed steeply as she headed out-system. She needed to be at least thirty light-minutes from the planet before she translated into hyper, far enough for her hyper footprint to be undetectable, and Theisman relaxed with a quiet sigh as he realized he'd gotten cleanly away once more.

Now it only remained to be seen what Captain Yu—and Sword Simonds, of course—would do with his data.

• CHAPTER EIGHT

"Thank you for coming, Admiral Courvosier."

High Admiral Yanakov stood to greet his guest, and Courvosier's eyebrows twitched as he saw the two women at the table, for the richness of their clothing and jewelry proclaimed that they were two of Yanakov's wives. It was almost unheard of for a Grayson wife to appear at even a private dinner unless the guests were among her husband's closest friends, and Yanakov knew Courvosier knew that . . . which made their presence a message.

"Thank you for inviting me," Courvosier replied, ignoring, as etiquette demanded, the women's presence, for no one had introduced them. But then—

"Allow me to present my wives," Yanakov continued. "Rachel, my first wife." The woman to his right smiled, meeting Courvosier's eyes with a frankness which surprised the Manticoran. "Rachel, Admiral Raoul Courvosier."

"Welcome to our home, Admiral." Rachel's voice was like her smile, soft but self-assured, and she extended a hand. Courvosier hadn't been briefed on how one greeted a high-ranking Grayson wife, but he hadn't spent a lifetime in the service of his Queen for nothing. He bowed over the offered hand and brushed it with his lips.

"Thank you, Madam Yanakov. I'm honored to be here."

Her eyes widened as he kissed her hand, but she neither pulled away nor showed any sign of discomfort. Indeed, she smiled again as he released her, and then laid her hand on the other woman's shoulder.

"May I present Anna, Bernard's third wife." Anna

looked up with a smile of her own and held out her hand to be kissed in turn. "My sister Esther asked me to extend her regrets, Admiral," Rachel continued, and Courvosier almost blinked before he remembered that all wives of a Grayson household referred to one another as sisters. "She's come down with a bug, and Dr. Howard ordered her into bed." Rachel's gracious smile turned into something suspiciously like a grin this time. "I assure you, but for that, she would have been here. Like all of us, she's been most eager to meet you."

Courvosier wondered if it would be proper to express a desire to meet Esther some other time. It seemed harmless enough, but Grayson men were jealous of their wives. Better to settle for something with less *faux pas* potential.

"Please tell her I'm very sorry her illness kept her away."

"I will," Rachel replied, and waved gracefully at the fourth chair.

She rang a small bell as Courvosier sat, and silent, efficient serving women—girls, really, he thought, reminding himself that these people didn't have access to prolong—bustled in with trays of food.

"Please don't be afraid to eat freely, Admiral," Yanakov said as a plate was set before his guest. "All these foods are from the orbital farms. Their metal levels are as low as anything grown on Manticore or Sphinx."

Courvosier nodded, but he knew better than to dig straight in. He waited until the servants had withdrawn, then bowed his head respectfully as Yanakov recited a brief blessing over the food.

Grayson cuisine reminded Courvosier of a cross between Old Earth Oriental and something he might have encountered in New Toscana on Manticore, and this meal was excellent. Yanakov's chef would have rated a full five stars even at Cosmo's, and the table conversation was nothing like what he'd imagined it would be. Yanakov and his officers—*all* Graysons, in fact—had been so stiff and unnatural—or half-openly contemptuous—in the presence of his own female officers that he'd developed a mental picture of a dour, humorless home life in which women were rarely seen and never heard, but Rachel and Anna Yanakov were lively and eloquent. Their affection for their husband was unmistakable, and Yanakov himself was a totally different man, out from behind the barriers of formality at last, comfortable and confident in his own setting. Courvosier had no doubt the evening was intended, in part at least, to show him the more human side of Grayson, yet he felt himself relaxing in the genuine aura of welcome.

Soft music played while they ate. It wasn't the sort of music Courvosier was used to—Grayson's classical music was based on something called "Country and Western"—but it was curiously lively, despite an undertone of sadness. The dining room was large, even by Manticoran planetary standards, with a high, arched ceiling and rich, tapestry-like wall hangings and old-style oil paintings. Religious themes predominated, but not exclusively, and the landscapes among them had a haunting, bittersweet beauty. There was a sense of the lost about them, like windows into Elfland, as if the loveliness they showed could never be wholly home to the humans who lived upon this world and yet could never be anything *but* home, either.

And between two of those yearning landscapes was a huge bay window . . . double-paned and sealed hermetically into its frame, with an air filtration intake under it.

Courvosier shivered somewhere deep inside. The scenery through that window was breathtaking, a sweep of rugged, snow-capped mountains, their shoulders clothed in lush, rich greenery that almost begged him to kick off his boots and run barefoot through the blue-green grass to meet them, yet the window was sealed forever against it, and the Embassy-issue filtration mask hung in its discreet case at his hip. He wouldn't need it, the ambassador had told him, as long as he limited his stay dirt-side . . . unless the atmospheric dust count rose. And his host's family had lived here for nine centuries, in an environment which, in many ways, was far more dangerous than any space habitat.

He made himself turn from the window and sip his wine, and when he looked up again, Yanakov's eyes were dark and thoughtful as they met his.

The meal ended, Rachel and Anna withdrew with graceful farewells, and another servant—this one a man—poured imported brandy into delicate snifters.

"I trust you enjoyed your supper, Admiral?" Yanakov said, passing his brandy back and forth under his nose.

"It was exquisite, Admiral Yanakov, as was the company." Courvosier smiled. "As, I am sure, the company was *intended* to be," he added gently.

"*Touché,*" Yanakov murmured with an answering smile, then set his snifter aside with a sigh. "In fact, Admiral, I invited you here by way of something of an apology," he admitted. "We've treated you poorly, especially your female officers." He got the word "female" out with only the barest hesitation, Courvosier noted. "I wanted you to see that we're not entirely barbarians. And that we don't keep our wives locked in cages."

Courvosier's lips twitched at the other's dry tone, but he sampled his own brandy before he replied, and his voice was level when he did.

"I appreciate that, Admiral Yanakov. But in all frankness, I'm not the one to whom you owe an apology."

Yanakov blushed, but he also nodded.

"I realize that, yet you must understand that we're still feeling our way into the proper modes. Under Grayson custom, it would be the height of impropriety for me to invite any woman into my home without her protector." His blush deepened at Courvosier's quirked eyebrow. "Of course, I realize your women don't *have* 'protectors' in the sense that our own do. On the other hand, I have to be conscious of how my own people— my subordinates and the Chamber delegates—would react if I violated custom so radically. Not just how they might react to *me*, but how they might regard your own people for *accepting* the invitation. And so I invited you, who my people see in some ways as the protector of all your female personnel."

"I see." Courvosier sipped more brandy. "I see, indeed, and I truly appreciate the gesture. I'll also be delighted to convey your apology, discreetly, of course, to my officers."

"Thank you." Yanakov's relief and gratitude were obvious. "There are people on this planet who oppose any thought of an alliance with Manticore. Some fear outside contamination, others fear an alliance will attract Haven's hostility, not guard us against it. Protector Benjamin and I are not among them. We're too well aware of what an alliance could mean to us, and not just militarily. Yet it seems whatever we've done since your arrival has been wrong. It's driven wedges between us, and Ambassador Masterman has been quick to hammer those wedges deep. I regret that deeply, Admiral Courvosier, and so does Protector Benjamin. In fact, he specifically charged me to express his regrets, both personal and as Grayson's head of state, to you."

"I see," Courvosier repeated much more softly, and a tingle went through him. This was the frankest avowal of interest yet, an opening he knew was meant to be taken, but it left a sour, angry taste in his mouth, as well. It was his duty to pursue the treaty, and he wanted to. He *liked* most of the Graysons he'd met—not all, certainly, but most—despite their reserved natures and prickly social codes. Yet grateful as he was for the overture, he couldn't forget that Honor had been out of the way less than one day when it was issued.

"Admiral Yanakov," he said finally, "please tell Protector Benjamin I deeply appreciate his message and, on behalf of my Queen, look forward to securing the alliance we all hope for. But I must also tell you, Sir, that your subordinates' treatment of Captain Harrington has been inexcusable in Manticore's eyes."

Yanakov's flush returned, darker than ever, yet he sat motionless, clearly inviting his guest to continue, and Courvosier leaned towards him across the table.

"I am in no sense Captain Harrington's 'protector,' Admiral. She doesn't need one, and, frankly she'd be insulted at the suggestion that she did. She is, in fact, one of the most dedicated and courageous officers it has ever been my pleasure to know, and her rank—at what is a very young age for a person from our Kingdom—is an indication of how highly she's thought of by her service. But while she needs no one's protection, she's also my friend. My very dear friend, a student I regard very much as the daughter I never had, and the way in which she's been treated is an insult to our entire Navy. She hasn't responded to it only because of her professionalism and discipline, but I tell you now, Sir, that unless your people—at the very least your military personnel—can treat her as the Queen's officer she is, not some sort of prize exhibit in a freak show, the chances of genuine cooperation between Grayson and Manticore are very, very poor. Captain Harrington happens to be one of the best we have, but she isn't our only female officer."

"I know." Yanakov's reply was almost a whisper, and he held his brandy snifter tightly. "I realized that even before you arrived, and I thought we were ready to deal with it. I thought *I* was ready. But we weren't, and Captain Harrington's departure shames me deeply. I realize our behavior was responsible for it, whatever the official story may be. That's what . . . galvanized me into inviting you tonight."

He inhaled deeply and met Courvosier's eyes.

"I won't try to refute anything you've just said, Admiral. I accept it, and I give you my personal word that I'll work to resolve it to the very best of my ability. But I also have to tell you it won't be easy."

"I know it won't."

"Yes, but you may not fully understand *why*." Yanakov gestured out the window at the darkening mountains. The setting sun dyed the snowy peaks the color of blood, and the blue-green trees were black.

"This world isn't kind to its women," he said quietly. "When we arrived here, there were four women for every adult male, because the Church of Humanity has always practiced polygyny . . . and it was as well we did."

He paused and sipped at his brandy, then sighed.

"We've had almost a thousand years to adapt to our environment, and my tolerance for heavy metals like arsenic and cadmium is far higher than your own, but look at us. We're small and wiry, with bad teeth, fragile bones, and a life expectancy of barely seventy years. We monitor the toxicity of our farmland daily, we distill every drop of water we drink, and still we suffer massive levels of neural damage, mental retardation, and birth defects. Even the air we breathe is our enemy; our third most common cause of death is lung cancer—*lung cancer*, seventeen centuries after Lao Than perfected his vaccine! And we face all of that, Admiral, all those health hazards and consequences, despite nine hundred years—almost a *millennium*—of adaptation. Can you truly imagine what it was like for the first generation? Or the second?"

He shook his head sadly, staring down into his brandy.

"Our first generation averaged one live birth in three. Of the babies born living, half were too badly damaged to survive infancy, and our survival was so precarious there was no possible way to divert resources to keep them alive. So we practiced euthanasia, instead, and 'sent them home to God.'"

He looked up, his face wrung with pain.

"That haunts us still, and it hasn't been that many generations since the custom of euthanizing defectives, even those with minor, correctable flaws, stopped. I can show you the cemeteries, the rows and rows of children's names, the plaques with no names at all, only dates, but there are no graves. Even today there are none. The traditions of our founding die too hard for that, and the first generations had too desperate a need for soil which would support terrestrial food crops." He smiled, and some of the pain eased. "Our customs are different from yours, of course, but today our dead give life to gardens of remembrance, not potatoes and beans and corn. Someday I'll show you the Yanakov Garden. It's a very . . . peaceful place.

"But it wasn't that way for our founders, and the emotional cost to women who lost baby after baby, who saw child after child sicken and die, yet had no choice but to bear and bear and bear, even at the cost of their own lives, if the colony was to survive—" He shook his head again.

"It might have been different if we hadn't been such a patriarchal society, but our religion told us men were to care for and guide women, that women were weaker and less able to endure, and we couldn't protect them. We couldn't protect *ourselves*, but the price they paid was so much more terrible than ours, and it was we who had *brought* them here."

The Grayson leaned back and waved a hand vaguely before him. No lights had been turned on, and Courvosier heard the pain in his voice through the gathering dimness.

"We were religious zealots, Admiral Courvosier, or we wouldn't have been here. Some of us still are, though I suspect the fire has dimmed—or mellowed, perhaps—in most of us. But we were certainly zealots then, and some of the Founding Fathers blamed their women for what was happening, because, I think, it was so much easier to do that than to bleed for them. And, of course, there was their own pain when their sons and daughters died. It wasn't a pain they could admit, or they would simply have given in and died themselves, so they locked it deep inside, and it turned into anger— anger they couldn't direct at God, which left only one other place it could go."

"At their wives," Courvosier murmured.

"Exactly," Yanakov sighed. "Understand me, Admiral. The Founding Fathers weren't monsters, nor am I trying to excuse my people for being what they are. We're no less the product of our past than your own people are. This is the only culture, the only society, we've ever known, and we seldom question it. I pride myself on my knowledge of history, yet truth to tell, *I* never thought this deeply about it until I was forced up against the differences between us and you, and I suspect few Graysons ever really delve deep enough to understand how and why we became what we are. Is it different for Manticorans?"

"No. No, it's not."

"I thought not. But those early days were terrible ones for us. Even before Reverend Grayson's death, women were already becoming not wives but chattels. The mortality rate was high among men, too, and there'd been fewer of them to begin with, and biology played another trick on us. Our female births outnumber male by three to one—if we were to sustain a viable population, every potential father had to begin begetting children as soon as possible and spread his genes as widely as he could before Grayson killed him, so our households grew. And as they grew, family became everything and the patriarch's authority became absolute. It was a survival trait which tied in only too well with our religious beliefs. After a century, women weren't even people—not really. They were property. Bearers of children. The promise of a man's physical continuation in a world which offered him a life expectancy of less than forty years of backbreaking toil, and our efforts to create a godly society institutionalized that."

Yanakov fell silent again, and Courvosier studied his profile against the fading, bloody sunset. This was a side of Grayson he'd never even imagined, and he was ashamed. He'd condemned their parochialism and congratulated himself on his cosmopolitan tolerance, yet his view of them had been as two-dimensional as their view of him. He didn't need anyone to tell him Bernard Yanakov was an extraordinary representative of his society, that all too many Grayson men would never dream of questioning their God-given ascendancy over the mere females about them. But Yanakov was just as real as those others, and Courvosier suspected it was Yanakov who spoke for Grayson's soul.

God knew there were enough Manticorans not worth the pressure to blow them out the lock, but they weren't the *real* Manticore. People like Honor Harrington were the real Manticore. People who made the Kingdom be better than it dreamed it could, made it live up to its ideals whether it wanted to or not, because they *believed* in those ideals and made others believe with them. And perhaps, he thought, people like Bernard Yanakov were the real Grayson.

Yanakov straightened finally, then waved a hand over a rheostat. Lights came up, driving back the darkness, and he turned to face his guest.

"After the first three centuries, things had changed. We'd lost an enormous amount of our technology, of course. Reverend Grayson and his First Elders had planned for that to happen—that was the entire point of making the journey—and they'd deliberately left behind the teachers and text books, the essential machinery that might have supported the physical sciences. We were fortunate the Church hadn't regarded the life sciences with the same distrust, but even there we were desperately short of the specialists we needed. Unlike Manticore, no one even knew where we were, or cared, and because they didn't, no Warshawski sail ship called here until barely two hundred years ago. Our colony ship left Old Earth five hundred years before Manticore's founders, so our starting point was five centuries cruder than yours, and no one came to teach us the new technologies that might have saved us. The fact that we survived at all is the clearest possible evidence that there truly is a God, Admiral Courvosier, but we'd been smashed down to bedrock. We had only bits and pieces, and when we began to build upon them we found ourselves face to face with the worst danger of all: schism."

"The Faithful and the Moderates," Courvosier said quietly.

"Precisely. The Faithful, who clung to the original doctrines of the Church and regarded technology as anathema." Yanakov laughed mirthlessly. "It's hard for *me* to understand how anyone could have felt that way—I don't imagine it's even possible for an outsider! I grew to manhood depending on technology, crude though it may be compared to your own, for my very survival. How in the name of God could people so much closer to extinction believe He expected them to survive without it?

"But they did—at first, at least. The Moderates, on the other hand, believed our situation here had been our own Faith's Deluge, a disaster to make God's true Will clear at last. What He wanted from us was the development of a way of life in which technology was used as He had intended—not as Man's master, but as his servant.

"Even the Faithful accepted that at last, but the hostilities already existed, and the factions grew even further apart. Not over technology, now, but over what constituted godliness, and the Faithful went beyond conservatism. They became reactionary radicals, chopping and pruning at Church doctrine to suit their own prejudices. You think the way we treat our women is backward . . . have you ever heard of the Doctrine of the Second Fall?"

Courvosier shook his head, and Yanakov sighed.

"It came out of the Faithful's search for God's Will, Admiral. You know they regard the entire New Testament as heretical because the rise of technology on Old Earth 'proves' Christ couldn't have been the true Messiah?"

This time Courvosier nodded, and Yanakov's face was grim.

"Well, they went even further than that. According to their theology, the first Fall, that from Eden on Old Earth, had been the fault of Eve's sin, and we'd created a society here that made women property. The Moderates might interpret what had happened to us as our Deluge, might have believed—as we of Grayson believe today—that it was part of God's Test, but the Faithful believe God never intended us to face Grayson's environment. That He would have transformed it into a New Eden, had we not sinned after our arrival. And as the first sin was Eve's, so this sin, the cause of our Second Fall, was committed by Eve's *daughters*. It justified the way they treated their own wives and daughters, and they demanded that all of us accept that, just as they demanded we accept their dietary laws and stonings.

"The Moderates refused, of course, and the hatred between the factions grew worse and worse until, as you know, it ended in open civil war.

"That war was terrible, Admiral Courvosier. The Faithful were the minority, and their hardcore zealots were only a small percentage of their total number, but those zealots were completely ruthless. They *knew* God was on their side. Anything they did was done in His name, and anyone who opposed them must therefore be vile and evil, with no right to live. We were still far from having rebuilt an advanced tech base, but we could produce guns and tanks and napalm—and, of course, the Faithful built their doomsday weapon as a last resort. We didn't even know of its existence until Barbara Bancroft, the wife of their most fanatical leader, decided the Moderates *had* to know. She escaped to us—turned against all the Faithful believed—to warn us, but her courage had its cost in fresh tragedy as well."

Yanakov stared down into his brandy glass.

"Barbara Bancroft is—well, I suppose you could call her our 'token heroine.' Our planet owes her its very life. She's our Joan of Arc, our Lady of the Lake, with all the virtues we treasure in our women: love, caring, the willingness to risk her life to save her children's. But she's also an ideal, a figure out of myth whose courage and toughness are too much to expect from 'ordinary' women. We've forced her into the frame of our own prejudices, yet to the *Faithful*, the woman we call The Mother of Grayson is the very symbol of the Second Fall, the proof of all women's inherent corruption. They may have rejected the New Testament, but they retain their version of the Antichrist, and they call her The Harlot of Satan.

"But because of Barbara Bancroft, we were prepared when the Faithful threatened to destroy us all. We knew the only possible answer was to cast out the madmen, and that, Admiral—that was when the universe played its cruelest trick of all on Grayson, for there was a way we could do that."

He sighed and sank back in his chair.

"My own ancestor, Hugh Yanakov, commanded our colony ship, and he tried to hang onto at least a limited space capability, but the First Elders had smashed the cryo installations immediately after we planeted. It was their equivalent of burning their boats behind them, committing themselves and their descendants to their new home. I doubt they would have done it if they'd been more scientifically educated, but they weren't. And since the ship couldn't take us away, our desperate straits left us no choice but to cannibalize it.

"So we were here to live or die, and somehow, we'd lived. Yet by the time of the Civil War, we'd reached the point where we could once more build crude, chem-fueled sublight ships. They were far less advanced than the one which had brought us here, with no cryo capability, but they could make the round trip to Endicott in twelve or fifteen years. We'd even sent an expedition there and discovered what today is Masada.

"Masada has an axial inclination of over forty degrees, and its weather is incredibly severe compared to Grayson, but humans can eat its plants and animals. They can live without worrying about lead and mercury poisoning from simply breathing its dust. Most of our people would have given all they owned to move there, and they couldn't. We didn't have the capability to move that many people. But when the Civil War ended with a handful of fanatics threatening to blow up the entire planet, we could move *them* to Masada."

He laughed again, harshly and more mirthlessly even than before.

"Think about it, Admiral. We had to cast them out, and the only place to which we could banish them was infinitely better than where all the rest of us had to remain! There were barely fifty thousand of them, and under the peace settlement's terms, we equipped them as lavishly as we could and sent them off, and then the rest of us turned to making the best we could of Grayson."

"I think you've done quite well, all things considered," Courvoisier said quietly.

"Oh, we have. In fact, I love my world. It does its best to kill me every single day, and someday it will succeed, but I love it. It's my home. Yet it also makes us what we are, because we *did* survive, and we did it without losing our faith. We still believe in God, still believe this is all part of a testing, purifying process. I suppose you think that's irrational?"

The question could have been caustic, but it was almost gentle.

"No," Courvoisier said after a moment. "Not irrational. I'm not certain I could share your faith after all your people have been through, but, then, I suppose a Grayson might find *my* faith incomprehensible. We are what our lives—and God—have made us, Admiral Yanakov, and that's as true of Manticorans as Graysons."

"That's a very tolerant view," Yanakov said quietly. "One I'm quite confident a great many, perhaps most, of my people would find difficult to accept. For myself, I believe you're correct, yet it's still our Faith which dictates how we regard our own women. Oh, we've changed over the centuries—our ancestors didn't call themselves 'Moderates' for nothing!—but we remain what we are. Women are no longer property, and we've evolved elaborate codes of behavior to protect and cherish them, partly, I suspect, in reaction against the Faithful. I know many men abuse their privileges—and their wives and daughters—but the man who publicly insults a Grayson woman will probably be lynched on the spot, if he's lucky, and they're infinitely better treated than Masadan women. Yet they're still legally and religiously inferior. Despite The Mother of Grayson, we tell ourselves it's because they're weaker, because they bear too many other burdens to be forced to vote,

to own property . . . to serve in the military." He met
Courvosier's eyes with a slight, strained smile. "And
that's why your Captain Harrington frightens us so. She
terrifies us, because she's a woman and, deep down
inside, most of us know Haven's lied about what happened in Basilisk. Can you imagine what a threat that is
to us?"

"Not completely, no. I can see some of the implications, of course, but my culture is too different to see
them all."

"Then understand this much, Admiral, please. If Captain Harrington is as outstanding an officer as you
believe—as *I* believe—she invalidates all our concepts
of womanhood. She means we're *wrong*, that our
religion is wrong. She means we've spent nine *centuries*
being wrong. The idea that we may have been in error
isn't quite as devastating to us as you may think—after
all, we've spent those same nine centuries accepting
that our Founding Fathers were wrong, or at least not
completely correct. I think we can admit our error, in
time. Not easily, not without dealing with our current
equivalent of the Faithful, but I have to believe we can
do it.

"Yet if we do, what happens to Grayson? You've met
two of my wives. I love all three of them dearly—I
would die to protect them—but your Captain Harrington, just by existing, tells me I've made them less
than they could have been. And the truth is that they
are less than Captain Harrington. Less capable of her
independence, her ability to accept responsibility and
risk. Just as I, they're products of a civilization and
Faith that *tells* them they're less capable in those
respects. So what do I do, Admiral? Do I tell them to
stop deferring to my judgment? To enter the work
force? To demand their rights and put on the same
uniform I wear? How do I know where my doubts over
their capability stop being genuine love and concern?
When my belief that they must be reeducated before
they can become my equal stops being a realistic
appreciation of the limitations they've been taught and

becomes sophistry to bolster the status quo and protect my own rights and privileges?"

He paused again, and Courvosier frowned.

"I . . . don't know. No one can but you, I suppose. Or them."

"Exactly." Yanakov took a long swallow of brandy, then set the glass very precisely on the table. "No one can know—but Pandora's Box is open now. Just a crack, so far, yet if we sign this treaty, if we bind ourselves to a military and economic ally who treats women as the full equals of men, we'll have to learn to know. All of us, women as well as men, because the one certain thing in life is that no one can make the truth *un*true simply because it hurts. Whatever happens to us where Masada or Haven is concerned, our treaty with you will destroy us, Admiral Courvosier. I don't know if even the Protector realizes that fully. Perhaps he does. He was educated off-world, so perhaps he sees this as the opening wedge to forcing us to accept your truth. No, not *your* truth, *the* truth."

He laughed again, more easily this time, and toyed with his snifter.

"I thought this conversation would be much more difficult, you know," he said.

"You mean it wasn't difficult?" Courvosier asked wryly, and Yanakov chuckled.

"Oh, it was, Admiral, *indeed* it was! But I expected it to be even worse." The Grayson inhaled deeply and straightened in his chair, then spoke more briskly. "At any rate, that's why we've reacted the way we have. I promised the Protector I'd try to overcome my prejudices and those of my officers and men, and I take my duty to my Protector as seriously as I'm certain you take yours to your Queen. I swear we'll make the effort, but please bear in mind that I'm better educated and far more experienced than most of my officers. Our lives are shorter than yours—perhaps your people gain wisdom while you're still young enough for it to be of use to you?"

"Not really." Courvosier surprised himself with a

chuckle. "Knowledge, yes, but wisdom *does* seem to come a little harder, doesn't it?"

"Yes, it does. But it does come, even to stiff-necked, conservative people like mine. Be as patient with us as you can, please—and please tell Captain Harrington, when she returns, that I would be honored if she would be my guest for supper."

"With a 'protector'?" Courvosier teased gently, and Yanakov smiled.

"With or without, as she pleases. I owe her a personal apology, and I suppose the best way to teach my officers to treat her as she deserves is to learn how to do it myself."

• CHAPTER NINE

The K4 star called Endicott burned in the view port, and the planet Masada basked in its warmth. Endicott was far cooler than the F6 furnace at the heart of the Yeltsin System, but then, Masada's orbital radius was barely a quarter that of Grayson's.

Captain Yu sat with folded arms, chin on his chest, contemplating the planet and star, and wished the government had found someone else for this assignment. He disliked clandestine ops on principle, and the superiors who'd explained how this was supposed to work had either totally underestimated the narrowminded hesitancy of the Masadans or else lied when they briefed him. He was inclined to believe it was the former, yet one could never be entirely certain of that. Not in the People's Republic.

The outside galaxy saw only the huge sphere Haven had conquered. It didn't realize how fragile the Republic's economy truly was or how imperative that fragility made it that Haven *continue* to expand. Or just how calculating and cynically manipulative the PRH's leaders had become, even with their own subordinates, under the pressure of that imperative.

Yu did. He had more sense of history than most officers of the People's Navy—more of it than his superiors would have preferred. He'd almost been expelled from the Academy when one of his instructors discovered the secret cache of proscribed history texts written when the People's Republic was still simply the Republic of Haven. He'd managed to create enough uncertainty over who actually owned the offensive tapes to avoid expulsion, yet it had been one of the more terrifying episodes of his life—and he'd been careful to conceal his innermost thoughts ever since. The sophistry he practiced bothered him, at times, but not enough to change it, for he had too much to lose.

Yu's family had been Dolists for over a century. The captain had clawed his way out of prole housing and off the Basic Living Stipend by sheer guts and ability in a society where those qualities had become increasingly irrelevant, and if he had no illusions about the People's Republic, he had even less desire to return to the life he had escaped.

He sighed and checked his chrono. Simonds was late—again. That was another thing Yu hated about this assignment. He was a punctual, precise man, and it irked him immensely that his nominal commander came from a culture where superiors habitually kept juniors waiting for the express purpose of underlining their own superiority.

Not that Haven didn't have its own warts, he reflected, falling back into the dispassionate reverie whose Social Dysfunction Indicators would have horrified the Mental Hygiene Police. Two centuries of deficit spending to curry favor with the mob had wrecked not only the People's Republic's economy but any vestige of responsibility among the families who ruled it. Yu despised the mob as only someone who had fought his way clear of it could, but at least its members were honest. Ignorant, uneducated, unproductive leeches, yes, but honest. The Legislaturists who mouthed all the politically correct platitudes for the benefit of the rest of the galaxy and the Dolist Managers who controlled the prole voting blocs were better educated and *dis*honest, and that, in Captain Alfredo Yu's considered opinion, was the only way they differed from the mob.

He snorted and shifted in his chair, staring out the view port, and wished he could respect his own government. A man ought to be able to feel his country was worth fighting for, but Haven wasn't, and it wouldn't be. Not in his lifetime, anyway. Yet corrupt and cynical or not, it *was* his country. He hadn't asked for it, but it was the one he'd drawn, and he would serve it to the best of his ability because it was the only game in town. And because serving as its sword arm and succeeding despite its flaws was the only way to prove he was better than the system which had created him.

He growled to himself and rose to pace the briefing room. Damn it, sitting around and waiting like this *always* turned his mind down these gloomy, worn out pathways, and that was hardly what he needed at a time like—

The briefing room hatch opened, and he turned, then came to attention as Sword of the Faithful Simonds walked in. He was alone, and Yu's spirits rose a bit. If Simonds had intended simply to stonewall, he would have brought along a few of the Masadan Navy's plethora of flag officers to trap Yu in the formal channels of military courtesy and prevent him from pushing hard.

Simonds nodded a wordless greeting and found a chair much more briskly than usual, then punched the button that popped the data terminal up out of the table top and keyed the terminal on line. There'd been a time, Yu remembered, when he wouldn't have had the least idea how to go about even that simple task, but he'd learned a lot from Haven—and not just about the workings of *Thunder of God's* information systems.

Yu took a chair facing the Sword and waited while Simonds quickly reread the report from *Bres*—

The captain caught himself. He never thought of *Thunder of God* as *Saladin* these days, and he had to stop thinking of *Principality* as *Breslau*. Not just because of the fiction that Masada had "bought" them from Haven, either. Anyone who could count on his fingers and toes would realize the two warships represented over eighty percent of the Endicott System's annual GSP, but their formal transfer to the Masadan Navy put Haven at a safe remove, legally (or at least technically), from whatever Masada did with them. It also made it important for Yu to prevent the Masadan officer corps from suspecting he and his fellow "immigrants" regarded them as a collection of half-assed, bigoted, superstition-ridden incompetents. Especially when he *did* think of them that way and couldn't make himself stop, however hard he tried.

"I've taken your proposals to the Council of Elders, Captain," Simonds said at last, leaning back in his chair, "but before deciding, Chief Elder Simonds wishes to hear your reasoning from your own mouth, as it were. For that reason, with your permission, I intend to record our conversation."

He looked at Yu, and the captain suppressed a frown before it reached his mouth. So it was *his* proposal, was it? Well, that wasn't too surprising. The Sword badly wanted to become Chief Elder himself when his older brother shuffled off, yet he seemed unable to grasp that decisiveness was more likely than timidity to win him the council chair he craved.

On the other hand, if the responsibility was going to be Yu's, then so was at least a share of the credit, and it couldn't hurt to enhance his own power base—to the extent any "heathen" could have one with these fruitcakes.

"Of course I don't object, Sir," he said courteously.

"Thank you." Simonds switched on the recorders. "In that case, suppose you simply begin at the beginning, Captain."

"Certainly, Sir." Yu tipped his chair back and folded his arms once more. "In essence, Sword Simonds, my belief is that the departure of three-quarters of the Manticoran escort gives us a window to activate Jericho with a high probability of success. It's possible they've moved on permanently, though I think it likely that they'll be returning in the not too distant future. In either case, however, I believe that, if we act promptly, your government will be able to suppress the current regime on Grayson and regain possession of the planet." Although, the Captain thought, only a batch of certifiable lunatics would *want* Grayson when they already had a much nicer planet all their own.

"At this time," he continued in the same level voice, "there is only one Manticoran warship in Yeltsin space, probably a destroyer. That vessel's primary responsibility is undoubtedly the protection of Manticoran nationals, and I estimate that its secondary mission priority will be to protect the freighters which have yet to be unloaded. Under the circumstances, I would expect its commander to adopt a wait and see attitude, at least initially, if we attack Grayson. Obviously I can't guarantee that, but Grayson should assume they can defeat our 'raids' themselves, and if the commander of the remaining Manticoran ship shares that belief, he'll almost certainly remain in Grayson orbit until it's too late. Once we've destroyed the bulk of the Grayson Navy, he'll be faced with a manifestly hopeless situation and may well withdraw entirely, taking his diplomats with him."

"And if he doesn't withdraw? Or, even worse, doesn't simply sit out our attack?" Simonds asked expressionlessly.

"Neither possibility will have any bearing on the military situation, Sir. His firepower can make no realistic difference to subsequent operations, and should he participate actively in Grayson's initial defensive actions, he won't be around to withdraw."

Yu smiled thinly.

"I realize your government feels anxious over the possibility of a clash with Manticore. The People's Republic, however, under the terms of your existing treaty, is prepared to defend the Endicott System and any territories added to it, and we're both well aware that Manticore's entire interest in this region stems from its desire to head off or at least delay open war against the Republic. My considered opinion is that the risk of Manticoran interference in Jericho is acceptable, since it's unlikely *Queen* Elizabeth—" he stressed the title slightly but deliberately and saw Simonds' nostrils flare "—will have the political and military will to commit her navy in a situation which is so obviously beyond retrieval. Even if that ship is destroyed, her government will probably grit its teeth and take it rather than provoke a major war now."

The captain forbore—again—to mention that if the

Masadans had been willing to provide Haven with basing rights the reinforcements needed to back them would already be in place. Of course, the chance of a premature war with Manticore would also be proportionately greater, so perhaps these fanatics' xenophobia was worth the other pains in the ass it created after all.

"You sound confident, Captain, but what if this single remaining vessel should prove to be the heavy cruiser and not a destroyer?"

"Her class is irrelevant, Sir." Simonds' nostrils twitched again, and Yu kicked himself. Habits of speech died hard, and he'd used the feminine gender without remembering that no Masadan would dream of regarding a warship as anything but masculine. But he allowed no sign of his slight chagrin to show as he continued. "Should this ship be *Fearless* and intervene in the initial operation, *Thunder* will more than suffice to assure his destruction. Should *Fearless* choose *not* to intervene at the outset, he won't be powerful enough to mount a credible defense by himself later."

"I see." Simonds scratched his chin. "I'm afraid we're not quite as confident Manticore won't respond in overwhelming force, Captain," he said slowly, and it took considerable self-control for Yu to school his flash of disappointment into an attentive expression, "but, at the same time, you do have a point about the window of opportunity. Psychologically, at least, a single warship, particularly one who's seen all of his consorts withdraw, is more likely to be aware of his responsibilities to his own government than to someone who isn't yet even a formal ally."

"Precisely, Sword Simonds," Yu said respectfully.

"How much time do we have?" Simonds asked—for, Yu knew, the benefit of the Council of Elders; he and the Sword had been over the numbers only too often in the past twenty hours.

"A minimum of eleven days from their departure, Sir, or approximately nine days from right now. Depending on their orders, we might have somewhat longer, but I certainly wouldn't count on that."

"And the time required to complete Jericho?"

"We could be ready to launch the first attack in forty-eight hours. I can't say precisely how quickly things will move after that, since so much will depend on the speed with which Grayson reacts. On the other hand, we'll still have almost seven days before any other escorts can return, which will give them plenty of time to mount their counterattack. And I suspect they'll want to strike back as quickly as possible, if only to protect their position in the treaty negotiations by avoiding an appearance of weakness."

"I know you can't be precise, but the Council would appreciate your best estimate."

"I see, Sir." Yu narrowed his eyes to hide the contempt in them. Simonds was a naval officer. He ought to know as well as Yu that any estimate would be little more than an educated guess. In fact, he probably *did* know. He simply wanted to be sure any blame for a wrong guess fell on someone else's shoulders, and Yu's contempt eased into wry humor as he realized how much alike Havenite politicos and Masadan theocrats truly were under the skin.

"Very well, Sword. Allowing for normal Grayson readiness states, and with the proviso that any estimate can be *only* an estimate, I'd say we could expect them to counterattack our second or third raid. By the widest stretch of the imagination, I can't believe it would take them more than a T-day or two to spot our 'raiding' patterns and respond."

"And you're confident of your ability to crush them when they do?"

"As confident as anyone can be about a military action. It's highly unlikely they—or even the Manticorans, should their warship intervene—will realize what they're up against in time to save themselves. It's not impossible, of course, but the possibility is slight, and even if they break off instantly, their losses should still be near total."

"*Near* total?"

"Sir, we're talking about a deep-space engagement

between impeller drive vessels, and we can't predict their exact approach vector," Yu said patiently. "Unless they come in exactly where we want them, *Thunder* will get in only a few broadsides. Their losses will still be high in that case, but it will be up to our locally-built units to mop them up, and it's highly probable at least some of them will escape. As I've already pointed out, however, they have nowhere to escape *to*. Any survivors can only fall back on Grayson, and they'll have no choice but to offer action when we advance against the planet itself. Disengaging won't be an option under those circumstances, and *Thunder* can wipe out their entire navy in an afternoon if they stand and fight."

"Um." Simonds rubbed his chin harder and frowned, then shrugged. "Very well, Captain Yu. Thank you for your time and your very clear arguments. I'll return to the Council with the recording." He pressed the stud a second time, turning off the recorders, and continued in a more natural voice. "I imagine we'll have a decision within another hour or two, Captain."

"I'm glad to hear that, Sir." Yu cocked an eyebrow. "May I ask if you have any feeling for what that decision will be?"

"I think it's going to be close, but I suspect they'll agree. Elder Huggins is all for it, and while he represents a fairly small group, it's a powerful one. Elder O'Donnal is more hesitant, but several of his adherents are leaning towards Huggins on this one."

"And Chief Elder Simonds?" Yu asked in a neutral tone.

"My brother also favors proceeding," Simonds said flatly. "He'll have to spend a few past favors to bring the waverers around, but I believe he'll pull it off." The Sword allowed himself a humorless smile. "He usually does."

"In that case, Sir, I'd like to go ahead and issue the preparatory orders. We can always stand the fleet down if the Council decides differently."

"Yes." Simonds rubbed his chin again, then nodded. "Go ahead, Captain. But bear this in mind. If the Chief

Elder commits his own prestige to this and it fails, heads will roll. Mine may be among them; yours certainly will be, at least as far as your future service to the Faithful is concerned."

"I understand, Sir," Yu said with a sudden unwilling sympathy for the Sword's waffling. Yu himself faced nothing worse than being banished back to Haven in disgrace, assuming ONI and the government bought the Masadans' insistence (which he had no doubt would be *very* insistent) that any disaster had been entirely his fault. That would be humiliating and quite possibly disastrous to his career, but in Sword Simonds' case, "heads will roll" was all too likely to be literally true, since the sentence for treason against the Faith was beheading . . . after other, much nastier, experiences.

"I'm sure you do, Captain." Simonds sighed, then stood. "Well, I'd best be getting back." Yu rose to escort him out, but the Sword waved him back. "Don't bother. I can find my own way, and I'll pick up a chip of the recording from Communications on my way out. You've got things of your own to do here."

Sword of the Faithful Simonds turned and stepped through the opening hatch, leaving Yu alone with the gorgeous panorama of Masada and its sun, and the captain smiled. Simonds might be walking like a man who expected a pulser dart any moment, but he was committed at last. This time Jericho would really be launched, and once Grayson's walls came tumbling down, Captain Alfredo Yu could shake the dust of this loathsome system from his sandals and go *home*.

• CHAPTER TEN

Ensign Wolcott nibbled a fingernail and considered the officers at the next table. Lieutenant (JG) Tremaine had come aboard *Fearless* as Commander McKeon's pilot—now he sat chatting with Lieutenant Cardones and Lieutenant Commander Venizelos, and Wolcott envied his ease with such exalted personages.

Of course, Tremaine had been with the Captain in Basilisk, too. Both the Captain and the Exec were careful about never letting that color their official relations with anyone, but everyone knew there was an inner circle.

The problem was that Wolcott needed to talk to someone from inside that circle—and not Venizelos or Cardones. They were both approachable to their juniors, but she was afraid of how the Exec might react if he thought she was criticizing the Captain. And Cardones's reaction would probably be even worse . . . not to mention the fact that anyone who wore the Order of Gallantry *and* the blood-red sleeve stripe of the Monarch's Thanks was more than a little daunting to anyone fresh from Saganami Island, even if she was his junior tactical officer. But Lieutenant Tremaine was young enough—and junior enough—to feel less threatening. He knew the Captain, too, and he was assigned to a different ship, so if she made a fool of herself, or pissed him off, she wouldn't have to see him every day.

She nibbled her finger harder, nursing her coffee, then sighed in relief as Venizelos and Cardones rose.

Cardones said something to Tremaine and they all laughed. Then the exec and tactical officer disappeared into the officers' mess lift, and the ensign picked up her coffeecup, stiffened her nerve, and crossed to Tremaine's table as casually as she could.

He was just starting to tidy his tray when she cleared her throat. He looked up with a smile—a very *nice*

108

smile—and Wolcott suddenly found herself wondering if perhaps there weren't other reasons to make his acquaintance. After all, he was assigned to *Troubadour*, so the prohibitions against involvements with people in the same chain of command wouldn't apply. . . .

She felt herself blush at her thoughts, especially in light of what she wanted to talk to him about, and gave herself an internal shake.

"Excuse me, Sir," she said. "I wonder if I might have a moment of your time?"

"Of course, Ms.—?" He cocked his eyebrows, and she sat at his gesture.

"Wolcott, Sir. Carolyn Wolcott, Class of '81."

"Ah. First deployment?" he asked pleasantly.

"Yes, Sir."

"What can I do for you, Ms. Wolcott?"

"Well, it's just—" She swallowed. This was going to be just as hard as she'd expected, despite his charm, and she drew a deep breath. "Sir, you were with Captain Harrington in Basilisk, and I, well, I needed to discuss something with someone who knows her."

"Oh?" Mobile eyebrows swooped downward, and his tone was suddenly cool.

"Yes, Sir," she hurried on desperately. "It's just that, well, something happened in—in Yeltsin, and I don't know if I should . . . ." She swallowed again, but something softened in his eyes.

"Had a run in with the Graysons, did you?" His voice was much gentler, and her face flamed. "Well, why didn't you take it to Commander Venizelos, then?" he asked reasonably.

"I—" She wiggled in her chair, feeling younger—and more awkward— than in years. "I didn't know how he might react—or the Captain. I mean, the awful way they treated *her*, and she never said a word to them. . . . She might have thought I was being silly or . . . or something," she finished lamely.

"I doubt that." Tremaine poured fresh coffee for himself and poised the pot interrogatively above Wolcott's cup. She nodded gratefully, and he poured, then sat back nursing his cup. "Why do I have the feeling it's the 'or something' that worries you, Ms. Wolcott?"

Her face flamed still darker, and she stared down into her coffee.

"Sir, I don't *know* the Captain the way . . . the way you do."

"The way *I* do?" Tremaine smiled wryly. "Ms. Wolcott, I was an ensign myself the last time I served under Captain Harrington—and that wasn't all that long ago. I'd hardly claim to 'know' her especially well. I respect her, and I admire her tremendously, but I don't *know* her."

"But you were in Basilisk with her."

"So were several hundred other people, and I was as wet behind the ears as they come. If you want someone who really knows her," Tremaine added, frowning as he ran through a mental list of *Fearless*'s officers, "your best bet is probably Rafe Cardones."

"I *couldn't* ask him!" Wolcott gasped, and Tremaine laughed out loud.

"Ms. Wolcott, Lieutenant Cardones was a JG then himself, and just between you, me, and the bulkhead, he was all thumbs, too. Of course, he got over that—thanks to the skipper." He smiled at her, then sobered. "On the other hand, you've gotten yourself in deep enough now. You may as well go ahead and ask me whatever it is you don't want to ask Rafe or Commander Venizelos." She twisted her cup, and he grinned. "Go ahead—trot it out! Everyone expects an ensign to put a foot in his or her mouth sometime, you know."

"Well, it's just— Sir, is the Captain running away from Grayson?"

The question came out in a rush, and her heart plummeted as Tremaine's face went absolutely expressionless.

"Perhaps you'd care to explain that question, Ensign." His voice was very, very cold.

"Sir, it's just that . . . Commander Venizelos sent me down to Grayson to drop off Admiral Courvosier's baggage," she said miserably. She hadn't meant for it to come out that way, and she knew she'd been stupid to ask *anyone* a question which might be taken as a criticism of her CO. "I was supposed to meet someone from the Embassy, but there was this . . . Grayson officer." Her face burned again, but this time it was with humiliated memory. "He told me I couldn't land there—it was the pad I'd been cleared for, Sir, but he told me *I* couldn't land there. That . . . that I didn't have any business pretending to be an officer and I should . . . go home and play with my dolls, Sir."

"And you didn't tell the Exec?" Tremaine's cold, ominous tone was not, she was relieved to realize, directed at her this time.

"No, Sir," she said in a tiny voice.

"What else did he have to say?" the Lieutenant demanded.

"He—" Wolcott drew a deep breath. "I'd rather not say, Sir. But I showed him my clearance and orders, and he just laughed. He said they didn't matter. They were only from the Captain, not a *real* officer, and he called her—" She stopped and her hands clenched on her coffee cup. "Then he said it was about time we 'bitches' got out of Yeltsin, and he—" she looked away from the table and bit her lip "—he tried to put his hand inside my tunic, Sir."

"He *what?!*"

Tremaine half stood, and heads turned all over the dining room. Wolcott darted an agonized look around, and he sat back down, staring at her. She made herself nod, and his eyes narrowed.

"Why didn't you report him?" His voice was lower but still harsh. "You know the Captain's orders about things like that!"

"But . . ." Wolcott hesitated, then met his eyes. "Sir, we were pulling out, and the Grayson—he seemed to think it was because the Captain was . . . running away from how badly they've treated her. I didn't know whether he was right or not, Sir," she said almost desperately, "and even if he wasn't, we were scheduled to break orbit in an hour. Nothing like that ever happened to me before, Sir. If I'd been at home, I would've— But out *here* I didn't know what to do, and if—if I told the Captain what he'd said about *her*—!"

She broke off, biting her lip harder, and Tremaine inhaled deeply.

"All right, Ms. Wolcott. I understand. But here's what you're going to do. As soon as the Exec comes off watch, you're going to tell him exactly what happened, word-for-word to the best of your memory, but you are *not* going to tell him you ever even considered that the Captain might be 'running away.'"

Her eyes were confused—and unhappy—and he touched her arm gently.

"Listen to me. I don't think Captain Harrington knows *how* to run away. Oh, sure, she's making a tactical withdrawal right now, but not because the Graysons ran her off, whatever *they* may think. If you even suggest to Commander Venizelos that you thought that might be what was happening, he'll probably hand you your head."

"That's what I was afraid of," she admitted. "But I just didn't know. And . . . and if they were right, I didn't want to make things even worse for her, and the things he said about her were so terrible, I just didn't—"

"Ms. Wolcott," Tremaine said gently, "the one thing the skipper will never do is blame you for someone else's actions, and she feels very strongly about harassment. I think it has to do with—" He stopped and shook his head. "Never mind. Tell the Exec, and if he asks why you waited so long, tell him you figured we were leaving so soon they couldn't have done anything about it till we got back anyway. That's true enough, isn't it?"

She nodded, and he patted her arm.

"Good. I promise you'll get support, not a reaming." He leaned back again, then smiled. "Actually, I think what you really need is someone to ask for advice when you don't want to stick your neck out with one of the officers, so finish your coffee. I've got someone I want you to meet."

"Who's that, Sir?" Wolcott asked curiously.

"Well, he's not exactly someone your folks would *want* me to introduce you to," Tremaine said with a wry smile, "but he certainly straightened *me* out on my first cruise." Wolcott drained her cup, and the lieutenant rose. "I think you'll like Chief Harkness," he told her. "And—" his eyes glinted wickedly "—if anyone aboard *Fearless* knows a way to deal with scumbags like that Grayson without involving anyone else, he will!"

Commander Alistair McKeon watched Nimitz work his way through yet another rabbit quarter. For some reason known only to God, the terrestrial rabbit had adapted amazingly well to the planet Sphinx. Sphinx's year was over five T-years long, which, coupled with the local gravity and a fourteen-degree axial tilt, produced some . . . impressive flora and fauna and a climate most off-worlders loved during spring and fall—well, early fall, anyway—and detested at all other times. Under the circumstances, one might have expected something as inherently stupid as a rabbit to perish miserably; instead, they'd thrived. Probably, McKeon reflected, thanks to their birthrate.

Nimitz removed flesh from a bone with surgeon-like precision, laid it neatly on his plate, and picked up another in his delicate-looking true-hands, and McKeon grinned. Rabbits might thrive on Sphinx, but they hadn't gotten noticeably brighter and, just as humans could eat most Sphinxian animal life, Sphinx's predators could eat bunnies. And did—with gusto.

"He really likes rabbit, doesn't he?" McKeon observed, and Honor smiled.

"Not all 'cats do, but Nimitz certainly does. It's not like celery— *every* 'cat loves that—but Nimitz is an epicure. He likes variety, and 'cats are arboreals, so he never had a chance to taste rabbit until he adopted me." She chuckled. "You should have seen him the *first* time I offered him some."

"What happened? Did our cultured friend's table manners desert him?"

"He didn't *have* any table manners at the time, and he practically wallowed in his plate."

Nimitz looked up from his rabbit, and it was McKeon's turn to chuckle at his disdainful expression. Few treecats ever left Sphinx, and off-worlders persistently underestimated those who did, but McKeon had known Nimitz long enough to learn better. 'Cats outpointed Old Earth's dolphins on the sentience scale, and the commander sometimes suspected they were even more intelligent than they chose to let people know.

Nimitz held Honor's gaze a moment, then sniffed and returned to his meal.

"Take *that*, Captain Harrington," McKeon murmured, and grinned at Honor's laugh, for he hadn't heard many from her in Yeltsin. Of course, he was her junior CO, and unlike too many RMN officers, who saw patronage and family interest as a natural part of a military career, she detested even the appearance of favoritism, so there'd been no invitations to private dinners since he'd joined her command. In fact, she'd invited Commander Truman to join them tonight, but Truman had planned an unscheduled drill for her crew's surprise evening entertainment.

McKeon was as glad she had. He liked Alice Truman, but however much Honor's other skippers might respect her, he knew damned well none of them would push her on any subject she didn't open herself. He also knew, from personal experience, that she would never dream of sharing her own pain with any of her own ship's company—and that she was less impervious to strain and self-doubt than she believed she ought to be.

He finished his peach cobbler and leaned back with a sigh of content as MacGuiness poured fresh coffee into his cup.

"Thank you, Mac," he said, then grimaced as the chief steward filled Honor's mug with cocoa.

"I don't see how you can drink that stuff," he complained as MacGuiness retired. "Especially not after something as sweet and sticky as dessert!"

"Fair enough," Honor replied, sipping with a grin. "I've never understood how *any* of you can swill up coffee. Yecch!" She shuddered. "It smells nice, but I wouldn't use it for a lubricant."

"It's not as bad as all that," McKeon protested.

"All I can say is that it must be an acquired taste I, for one, have no interest in acquiring."

"At least it's not gooey and sticky."

"Which, aside from its smell, is probably its only virtue." Honor's dark eyes danced. "It certainly wouldn't keep you alive through a Sphinx winter. That takes a *real* hot drink!"

"I'm not too sure I'd be interested in surviving a Sphinx winter."

"That's because you're an effete Manticoran. You call what you get there *weather?*" She sniffed. "You're all so spoiled you think a measly meter or so of snow is a blizzard!"

"Oh? I don't see *you* moving to Gryphon."

"The fact that I like weather doesn't make me a masochist."

"I don't imagine Commander DuMorne would appreciate that implied aspersion on his home world's climate," McKeon grinned.

"I doubt Steve's been back to visit Gryphon more than twice since the Academy, and if you think what I have to say about Gryphon weather is bad, you should hear him. Saganami Island made a true believer out of him, and he resettled his entire family around Jason Bay years ago."

"I see." McKeon toyed with his coffee cup a moment, then looked up with an expression that was half smile and half frown. "Speaking of true believers, what do you think of Grayson?"

Some of the humor vanished from Honor's eyes. She took another sip of cocoa, as if to buy time, but McKeon waited patiently. He'd been trying to work the conversation around to Grayson all evening, and he wasn't going to let her off the hook now. He might be her junior officer, but he was also her friend.

"I try *not* to think about them," she said finally, her tone a tacit acceptance of his persistence. "They're provincial, narrow, and bigoted, and if the Admiral hadn't let me get away from them, I would've started breaking heads."

"Not the most diplomatic method of communication, Ma'am," McKeon murmured, and her lips twitched in an unwilling smile.

"I wasn't *feeling* particularly diplomatic. And, frankly, I wasn't all that concerned with communicating with them, either."

"Then you were wrong," McKeon said very quietly. Her mouth tightened with a stubbornness he knew well, but he continued in that same quiet voice. "Once upon a time, you had a real jerk of an exec who let his feelings get in the way of his duty." He watched her eyes flicker as his words struck home. "Don't let anything push you into doing the same thing, Honor."

Silence hovered between them, and Nimitz thumped down from his chair to hop up into Honor's lap. He stood on his rearmost limbs, planting the other four firmly on the table, and looked back and forth between them.

"You've been headed for this all evening, haven't you?" she asked finally.

"More or less. You could have flushed my career down the toilet—Lord knows you had reason to—and I don't want to see you making mistakes for the same reason I did."

"Mistakes?" There was an edge to her voice, but he nodded.

"Mistakes." He waved a hand over the table. "I know you'd never let Admiral Courvosier down like I let *you* down, but some day you're going to have to learn to handle people in a diplomatic context. This isn't Basilisk Station, and we're not talking about enforcing the commerce regulations or running down smugglers. We're talking about interacting with the officers of a sovereign star system with a radically different culture, and the rules are different."

"I seem to recall that you also objected to my decision to enforce the com regs," Honor half-snapped, and McKeon winced. He started to reply, but her hand rose before he opened his mouth. "I shouldn't have said that—and I know you're trying to help, but I'm just not cut out to be a diplomat, Alistair. Not if that means putting up with people like the Graysons!"

"You don't have a lot of choice," McKeon said as gently as he could. "You're Admiral Courvosier's ranking military officer. Whether you like the Graysons or detest them—and whether they like *you* or not—you can't change that, and this treaty is as important to the Kingdom as any naval engagement. You're not just Honor Harrington to these people. You're a Queen's officer, the senior Queen's officer in their system, and—"

"And you think I was wrong to leave," Honor interrupted.

"Yes, I do." McKeon met her eyes unflinchingly. "I realize that, as a man, my contacts with their officers must have been a lot less stressful than yours, and some of them are genuine bastards, potential allies or no. But some of the ones who aren't let their guard down with me a time or two. They were curious—more than curious—and what they really wanted to know was how I could stomach having a woman as my commanding officer." He shrugged. "They knew better than to come right out and ask, but the question was there."

"How did you answer it?"

"I didn't, in so many words, but I expect I said what Jason Alvarez or any of our other male personnel would've said—that we don't worry about people's plumbing, only how well they do their jobs, and that you do yours better than anyone else I know."

Honor blushed, but McKeon continued without a trace of sycophancy.

"That shook them up, but some of them went away to think about it. So what concerns me now is that the ones who did have to know there was no real need for *Fearless* to convoy these freighters to Casca—not when you could've sent *Apollo* and *Troubadour*. For the real idiots, that may not make any difference, but what about the ones who aren't total assholes? They're going to figure the real reason was to get you and Commander Truman 'out of sight, out of mind,' and it doesn't matter whether it was your idea or the Admiral's. Except . . . if it was *your* idea, they're going to wonder why you wanted out. Because you felt your presence was hampering the negotiations? Or because you're a woman and, whatever we said, you couldn't take the pressure?"

"You mean they'll think I cut and ran," Honor said flatly.

"I mean they may."

"No, you mean they will." She leaned back and studied his face. "Do you think that, Alistair?"

"No. Or maybe I do, a little. Not because you were scared of a fight, but because you didn't want to face this one. Because this time you didn't know how to fight back, maybe."

"Maybe I *did* cut and run." She turned her cocoa mug on its saucer, and Nimitz nuzzled her elbow. "But it seemed to me—still seems to me—that I was only getting in the Admiral's way, and—" She paused, then sighed. "Damn it, Alistair, I *don't* know how to fight it!"

McKeon grimaced at the oath, mild as it was, for he'd never before heard her swear, not even when their ship was being blown apart around them.

"Then you'll just have to figure out how." She looked back up at him, and he shrugged. "I know—easy for me to say. After all, I've got gonads. But they're still going to be there when we get back from Casca, and you're going to have to deal with them then. *You're* going to have to, whatever the Admiral may have achieved in our absence, and not just for yourself. You're our senior officer. What you do and say—what you let them do or say *to* you—reflects on the Queen's honor, not just yours, and there are other women serving under your command. Even if there weren't, more women are going to follow you in Yeltsin sooner or later, and the pattern you establish is the one they'll have to deal with, too. You know that."

"Yes." Honor gathered Nimitz up and hugged him to her breasts. "But what do I do, Alistair? How do I convince them to treat me as a Queen's officer when all they see is a woman who shouldn't *be* an officer?"

"Hey, I'm just a commander!" McKeon said, and grinned at her fleeting smile. "On the other hand, maybe you just put your finger on the mistake you've been making ever since Admiral Yanakov's staff crapped their shorts when they realized you were SO. You're talking about what *they* see, not what you see or what you are."

"What do you mean?"

"I mean you've been playing by their rules, not yours."

"Didn't you just tell me I needed to be diplomatic?"

"No, I said you had to *understand* diplomacy. There's a difference. If you really did pull out of Yeltsin because of the way they reacted to you, then you let their prejudices put you in a box. You let them run you out of town when you should have spit in their eye and dared them to prove there was some reason you shouldn't be an officer."

"You mean I took the easy way out."

"I guess I do, and that's probably why you feel like you ran. There are two sides to every dialogue, but if you accept the other side's terms without demanding equal time for your own, then they control the debate and its outcome."

"Um." Honor buried her nose in Nimitz's fur for a moment and felt his rumbling, subsonic purr. He clearly approved of McKeon's argument—or at least of the emotions that went with it. And, she thought, Alistair was right. The Havenite ambassador had played his cards well in his efforts to discredit her, but she'd let him. She'd actually helped him by walking on eggs and trying to hide her hurt and anger instead of demanding the respect her rank and achievements were due when Grayson eyes dismissed her as a mere female.

She pressed her face deeper into Nimitz's warm fur and realized the Admiral had been right, as well. Perhaps not entirely—she still thought her absence would help him get a toe in the door—but mostly. She'd run away from a fight and left him to face the Graysons and their prejudices without the support he had a right to expect from his senior uniformed subordinate.

"You're right, Alistair," she sighed at last, raising her head to look at him. "I blew it."

"Oh, I don't think it's quite that bad. You just need to spend the rest of this trip getting your thoughts straightened out and deciding what you're going to do to the *next* sexist twit." She grinned appreciatively, and he chuckled. "You and the Admiral can hit 'em high, and the rest of us will hit 'em right around the ankles, Ma'am. If they want a treaty with Manticore, then they'd better start figuring out that a Queen's officer is a Queen's officer, however he—or she—is built. If they can't get that through their heads, this thing is never going to work."

"Maybe." Her grin softened into a smile. "And thanks. I needed someone to kick me in the posterior."

"What are friends for? Besides, I remember someone who kicked *my* ass when I needed it." He smiled back, then finished his coffee and rose.

"And now, Captain Harrington, if you'll excuse me, I need to get back to my ship. Thank you for a marvelous dinner."

"You're welcome." Honor escorted McKeon to the hatch, then stopped and held out her hand. "I'll let you find your own way to the boat bay, Commander McKeon. I've got some things to think about before I turn in."

"Yes, Ma'am." He shook her hand firmly. "Good night, Ma'am."

"Good night, Commander." The hatch slid shut behind him, and she smiled at it. "Good night, indeed," she murmured softly.

• CHAPTER ELEVEN

"Hello, Bernard," Courvosier said as he ran into Yanakov just outside the conference room door. "Got a minute?"

"Certainly, Raoul."

Sir Anthony Langtry, the Manticoran Ambassador, smoothly diverted the rest of Yanakov's own party, and the Grayson smiled. He and Courvosier had come to understand one another far better than anyone else might suspect over the past three days, and he knew this slickly-managed, unscheduled encounter was far from coincidental.

"Thanks." Courvosier waited while Langtry shepherded the other Graysons through the door, then smiled a bit apologetically. "I just wanted to warn you to watch your blood pressure today."

"My blood pressure?" Yanakov had become accustomed to the fact that this man who looked two-thirds his age was actually forty years older. If Courvosier wanted to warn him, he was certainly ready to listen.

"Yes." Courvosier grimaced. "Since the question of economic aid is on today's agenda, you're going to have to put up with the Honorable Reginald Houseman."

"Ah. Should I assume Mr. Houseman is going to be a problem?"

"Yes and no. I've laid down the law to him, and I'm pretty sure he'll play by my rules when it comes to actual policy drafting, but he thinks of me as a naval officer, whereas *he's* a Great Statesman." Courvosier grimaced again. "He's also a patronizing son-of-a-bitch who thinks all us military types want to solve problems with a gun in either hand and a knife between our teeth."

121

"I see. We're not completely unfamiliar with the type here," Yanakov said, but Courvosier shook his head.

"Not his type, believe me. He's part of the domestic group that wants to hold down our own Fleet expenditures to keep from 'provoking' Haven, and he genuinely believes we could avoid war with them if the military only stopped terrifying Parliament with scare stories about Havenite preparations. Worse, he thinks of himself as a student of military history." Courvosier's lips twitched with amusement at some recollection, then he shrugged.

"The point is, he's not one of my greater admirers, and he's not at all pleased with the military cooperation agreements you and I initialed yesterday. He's got all sorts of reasons, but what it comes down to is that his 'study of the problem' convinces him our assumption of Masada's fundamental hostility to your planet is 'unduly pessimistic.'" Yanakov blinked, and Courvosier nodded. "You've got it. He believes in peaceful coexistence, and he can't quite grasp that a cragsheep can coexist with a hexapuma only from the inside. As I say, he even thinks *we* should be looking for ways to coexist with Haven."

"You're joking . . . aren't you?"

"I wish I were. Anyway, I suspect he's going to see your Chancellor's presence as his last chance to salvage the situation from us warmongers. I told him to watch his step, but I'm not really with the Foreign Office. I doubt he's too worried about any complaints I may file with his superiors, and from the way he looked last night, I figure he's got his Statesman Hat on. He's just likely to start preaching to you about the virtues of economic cooperation with Masada as a way to resolve your 'minor' religious differences."

Yanakov stared at him, then shook his head and grinned.

"Well, maybe it's a relief to know you've got people on your team with bean curd for brains, too. All right, Raoul. Thanks for the warning. I'll have a word with the Chancellor and try to sit on our people if he does."

"Good." Courvosier squeezed his arm with an

answering grin, and the two admirals walked into the conference room side by side.

" . . . so our greatest need, Admiral," Chancellor Prestwick finished his initial statement, "is for general industrial aid and, specifically, whatever assistance we can secure for our orbital construction projects. Particularly, under the circumstances, for naval expansion."

"I see." Courvosier exchanged glances with Yanakov, then nodded to Houseman. "Mr. Houseman? Perhaps you'd care to respond to that."

"Of course, Admiral." Reginald Houseman turned to the Grayson with a smile. "Mr. Chancellor, I appreciate the clarity with which you've sketched out your needs, and the Kingdom will give every consideration to meeting them. If I may, however, I'd like to take your points in reverse order."

Prestwick leaned back slightly and nodded agreement.

"Thank you. As far as naval expansion is concerned, my government, as Admiral Courvosier has already agreed in principle with High Admiral Yanakov, is prepared to provide a permanent security detachment for Yeltsin in return for basing rights here. In addition, we will be establishing our own service and repair facilities, and I see no difficulty in sharing them with you."

Houseman glanced sideways at Courvosier, then continued quickly.

"I think, however, that there are other, nonmilitary considerations which have not yet been given their full weight." Yanakov saw Courvosier stiffen, and the two admirals' eyes met across the table, but then Courvosier sat back with a resigned expression as Prestwick spoke.

"Nonmilitary considerations, Mr. Houseman?"

"Indeed. While no one could overlook or ignore the military threat your planet faces, it may be that there are *non*military ways to reduce it."

"Indeed?" Prestwick glanced at Yanakov, and the high admiral made a "go easy" gesture under cover of the table. "What ways might those be, Mr. Houseman?" the Chancellor asked slowly.

"Well, I realize I'm only an economist," Houseman's voice dripped self-deprecation, and Ambassador Langtry covered his eyes with one hand, "but it occurs to me that naval expansion can only divert materials and labor from your other projects. Given the necessity of your orbital farms to your growing population, I have to wonder, as an economist, if it wouldn't be more efficient to find some means besides warships to secure peace with Masada."

"I see." Prestwick's eyes narrowed, but Yanakov's repeated braking gesture restrained his instant, incredulous response. "And those means are?"

"Self-interest, Sir." Houseman made it sound like a concept he'd just invented. "Despite the population imbalance between your planet and Masada, you have a considerably greater industrial capacity than they. They have to be aware of that. And while neither of your systems presently have any commodities to attract large volumes of interstellar trade, your mutual proximity makes you a natural market area. Transport times—and costs—between your systems would be very low, which means the possibility exists for you to enter into an extremely profitable commercial relationship."

"With *Masada?*" someone blurted, and Langtry's other hand rose to join its fellow over his eyes. Houseman's head twitched as if to turn in the direction of the question, but he didn't—quite—though his smile took on a slightly fixed air while Prestwick took the time to frame his response.

"That's a very interesting suggestion, Sir, but I'm afraid the fundamental hostility between Grayson and Masada makes it . . . impractical."

"Mr. Chancellor," Houseman said earnestly, carefully avoiding looking at Courvosier, "I'm an economist, not a politician, and what matters to an economist is the bottom line, the cold, hard figures of the balance sheet. And the bottom line is always higher when potentially hostile groups recognize their deeper mutual self-interest and act intelligently to maximize it.

"Now, in this instance, what we have is two neighboring star systems, each, if you'll pardon my frankness, with marginal economies. Under the circumstances, an arms race between them makes no economic sense at all, so it seems to me that any move which can reduce your military competition is highly desirable. I'm aware that overcoming the legacy of centuries of distrust won't be easy, but surely any reasonable person can see the profit to all sides in making a successful effort to do so?"

He paused to smile at Prestwick, and Courvosier sat on his temper. Like most ideologues, Houseman was convinced the purity of his ends justified his means—whatever means those were—which meant his promise not to open this can of worms meant absolutely nothing to him beside his calling to end six centuries of silly squabbling. He was going to have his say, and the only way Courvosier could have stopped him would have been to banish him from the discussions. That wasn't practical, given his position as the second ranking member of the delegation and connections back home, until he got blatantly out of line, so the only solution was to let him make his case and then cut him off at the ankles.

"Masada is badly over-populated in terms of its productive capacity," Houseman went on, "and Grayson requires additional infusions of capital for industrial expansion. If you opened markets in the Endicott System, you could secure a nearby planetary source for foodstuffs and sufficient capital to meet your own needs by supplying Masada with the goods and services it requires for its population. The boon to your economy is obvious, even in the short term. In the long term, a commercial relationship which serves both your needs could only lessen—perhaps even eliminate—the hostility which has divided you for so long. It might even create a situation in which naval expansion becomes as unnecessary as it is economically wasteful."

The Grayson side of the table had stared at him in mounting, horrified disbelief; now they turned as one to look at Courvosier, and the admiral clenched his teeth. He'd warned Yanakov to watch his blood pressure, but he hadn't counted on quite how difficult it would be to watch his own.

"Admiral Courvosier," Prestwick asked very carefully, "does this constitute a rejection of our request for assistance in naval expansion?"

"No, Sir, it does not," Courvosier said, and ignored Houseman's flush. He'd warned the man against going off half-cocked, but Houseman had been too convinced of his own moral superiority to listen. Under the circumstances, his embarrassment weighed very little with Raoul Courvosier.

"Her Majesty's Government," he went on firmly, "is well aware of the Masadan threat to Grayson. In the event that Grayson allies itself with Manticore, the government intends to take all necessary and prudent steps to safeguard Grayson's territorial integrity. If, in the view of your own government and military, those steps include the expansion and modernization of your fleet, we will assist in every practical way."

"Mr. Chancellor," Houseman cut in, "while Admiral Courvosier is a direct representative of Her Majesty, the fact remains that he is primarily a military man, and military men think in terms of military solutions. I'm simply trying to point out that reasonable men, negotiating from reasonable positions, can sometimes—"

"Mr. Houseman." Courvosier's deep, normally pleasant voice was very, very cold, and the economist turned to glare resentfully at him.

"As you've just pointed out," Courvosier went on in that same cold voice, "I *am* Her Majesty's direct representative. I am also the chief of this diplomatic mission." He held the other's eyes until they dropped, then nodded and returned his own attention to Prestwick.

"Now, then," he said as if nothing had happened, "as I was saying, Mr. Chancellor, we will assist your naval expansion in any way we can. Of course, as you yourself have indicated, you have other needs, as well. The equipment and materials already being transferred from our freighters to your custody will make a start towards meeting some of them, but their long-term solution is going to be an extensive and difficult task. Balancing them against your military requirements will require some careful tradeoffs and allocations, and I'm sure Mr. Houseman will agree that the best way to meet all of them will be to upgrade your own industrial and technical base. And I think we can assume your major trading partner will be Manticore, not Masada, at least—" he allowed himself a wintry smile "—for the foreseeable future."

A ripple of laughter with an undeniable undertone of relief answered from the Grayson side of the table, and Houseman's face turned ugly for just a moment, then smoothed into professional non-expression.

"I believe that's probably a safe assumption," Prestwick agreed.

"Then we'll proceed on that basis," Courvosier said calmly. He glanced back at his economic adviser, and there was a hint of steel in his voice as he said, again, "Mr. Houseman?"

"Well, yes, of course," Houseman said. "I was merely—" He cut himself off and forced a smile. "In that case, Mr. Chancellor, I suppose we should first consider the question of government guarantees for loans to Grayson industrial consortiums. After that—"

The last of the strain dissipated among the Grayson delegates, and Yanakov leaned back with a sigh of relief. He met Courvosier's eyes across the table, and the two of them exchanged a brief smile.

Space was deep and dark and empty sixty-five light-minutes from Yeltsin's Star, but then, suddenly, two starships blinked into existence, radiating the blue glory of hyper transit from their Warshawski sails in a brief, dazzling flash no eye or sensor observed. They floated for a moment, sails reconfiguring into impeller wedges, and then they began to move, accelerating at scarcely half a dozen gravities in an arc which would intersect the outer edge of the asteroid belt, and no one saw them coming at all.

"Admiral Courvosier, I resent the way you humiliated me in front of the Grayson delegation!"

Raoul Courvosier leaned back behind his desk in the Manticoran Embassy, and the look he gave Reginald Houseman would have been recognized by whole generations of errant midshipmen.

"There was no need for you to undercut my position and credibility so blatantly! Any *diplomat* knows all possibilities must be explored, and the possibilities for reducing tensions in this region would be incalculable if Grayson would even consider the benefits of peaceful trade with Masada!"

"I may not be a diplomat," Courvosier said, "but I know a little something about chains of command. I specifically told you *not* to raise that point, and you gave me your word you wouldn't. In short, you lied, and any humiliation you may have suffered in consequence leaves me totally unmoved."

Houseman paled, then reddened with fury. He was unaccustomed to hearing such cold contempt from anyone, much less ignorant uniformed Neanderthals. He was a master of his field, with the credentials to prove it. How *dared* this . . . this jingoistic *myrmidon* speak to him this way!

"It was my duty to present the truth, whether *you* can see it or not!"

"It was your *duty* to conform to my directives or tell me honestly that you couldn't do so in good conscience, and the fact that you came to this system with your own preconceptions and haven't bothered to learn a thing since only makes you as stupid as you are dishonest."

Houseman gaped at him, too furious to speak, and the admiral continued in a flat, deadly voice.

"The reason these people are expanding their population after centuries of draconian population control, the *reason* they need those orbital farms, is that Masada is getting ready to wipe them out and they need the man-power to fight back. I was prepared to learn their fears were exaggerated, but after studying their intelligence reports and the public record, it's my opinion, Mr. Houseman, that they have in fact understated the case. Yes, they have a stronger industrial base, but the other side outnumbers them three-to-one, and they need most of that industry simply to survive their planetary en-vironment! If you'd bothered to examine their library data base, or even the *précis* Ambassador Langtry's staff have assembled, you'd know that. You haven't, and I have absolutely no intention of allowing your unin-formed opinions to color the official position of this mission."

"That's preposterous!" Houseman spluttered. "Masada doesn't begin to have the capacity to project that kind of military power to Yeltsin!"

"I rather thought the military was *my* area," Cour-vosier said icily.

"It doesn't take a genius to know that—just someone with an open mind! Look at their per capita income figures, damn it! They'd ruin themselves if they made the attempt!"

"Even assuming that statement to be true, that doesn't mean they *won't* make the attempt. The point you seem consistently unwilling or unable to grasp is that rationality isn't their driving motivation. They're *committed* to the defeat of Grayson and the forcible imposition of their own way of life in both systems because they see it as their religious duty."

"Hogwash!" Houseman snorted. "I don't care what mystic gobbledygook they spout! The fact is that their economy simply won't support the effort—certainly not to 'conquer' such a hostile-environment planet!"

"Then perhaps you'd better tell *them* that, not their intended victims. Their fleet is twenty percent stronger overall than Grayson's, and *much* stronger in terms of hyper-capable units. They have five cruisers and eight destroyers to Grayson's three cruisers and *four* destroyers. That's not a defensive power mix. The bulk of the Masadan Navy is designed for operations in someone else's star system, but the bulk of the *Grayson* fleet consists of sublight LACs for local defense. And LACs, Mr. Houseman, are even less capable in combat than their tonnage might suggest because their sidewalls are much weaker than those of starships. The local orbital fortifications are laughable, and Grayson doesn't know how to generate spherical sidewalls, so their forts don't have *any* passive anti-missile defenses. And, finally, the Masadan government—which nuked planetary targets in the last war—has repeatedly stated its willingness to *annihilate* the 'godless apostates' of Grayson if that's the only way to 'liberate' and 'purge' the planet!"

The admiral stood, glaring across his desk at the diplomat.

"All that is available from the public record, *Mr.* Houseman, and our own Embassy reports confirm it. They also confirm that those industrially backward Masadans have committed over a *third* of their gross system product to the military for the last twenty years! Grayson can't possibly do that. They've only managed to stay in shouting distance because their larger GSP means the smaller percentage they *can* divert to the military is about half as large in absolute terms. Under the circumstances, only an idiot would suggest they ought to give their enemies more economic muscle to beat them to death with!"

"That's your opinion," Houseman muttered. He was white-faced with mingled fury and shock, for he'd looked only at absolute tonnages in the casual glance he'd given the comparative naval strengths. The difference in capabilities hadn't even occurred to him.

"Yes, it *is* my opinion." Courvosier's voice was calmer, but there was no yield in it. "And because it is, it's also the opinion of Her Majesty's Government and its diplomatic mission to this system. If you disagree with it, you'll have every opportunity to tell the Prime Minister and Parliament so once we return home. In the meantime, however, you will refrain from gratuitously and stupidly insulting the intelligence of people who've lived their whole lives facing that threat, or I will have you removed from this delegation. Is that clear, Mr. Houseman?"

The economist glared at his superior for one more moment, then nodded curtly and slammed out of the office.

• CHAPTER TWELVE

The buzzing com terminal jerked Raoul Courvosier awake. He sat up in bed quickly, scrubbing sleep from his eyes, and hit the acceptance key, then straightened as he recognized Yanakov. The Grayson admiral was bare-chested under a bathrobe, and his sleep-puffy eyes were bright.

"Sorry to wake you, Raoul." His soft Grayson accent was clipped. "Tracking just picked up a hyper footprint thirty light-minutes from Yeltsin. A big one."

"Masada?" Courvosier asked sharply.

"We don't know yet, but they're coming in from oh-oh-three oh-niner-two. That's certainly right for a straight-line course from Endicott."

"What do you have on impeller signatures?"

"That's mighty far out for us." Yanakov sounded a bit embarrassed. "We're trying to refine our data, but—"

"Pass the locus to Commander Alvarez," Courvosier interrupted. "*Madrigal's* sensor suite is better than anything you've got. Maybe he can refine it for you."

"Thank you. I hoped you'd say that." Yanakov sounded so grateful Courvosier frowned in genuine surprise.

"You didn't let that asshole Houseman make you think I wouldn't?"

"Well, no, but we're not officially allied, so if you—"

"Just because we don't have a piece of paper doesn't mean you and I aren't aware of what both our heads of state want, and one of the advantages of being an admiral instead of a *diplomat*—" Courvosier made the word an obscenity "—is that we can cut through the bullshit when we have to. Now pass that info on to

Madrigal." He paused, about to cut the circuit. "And may I assume I'm invited to Command Central?"

"We'd be honored to have you," Yanakov said, quickly and sincerely.

"Thank you. Oh, and when you contact Alvarez, see where he is on that project I assigned him Monday." Courvosier smiled crookedly. "We've been monitoring your C^3 systems, and I think he can probably tie *Madrigal's* sensors directly into Command Central's net."

"That *is* good news!" Yanakov said enthusiastically. "I'll get right on it. I'll pick you up in my car in fifteen minutes."

Printers chattered madly as the admirals arrived at Command Central, and the two of them turned as one to the main display board. A dot of light crept across it with infinitesimal speed. That was a trick of scale—any display capable of showing a half light-hour radius had to compress things—but at least gravitic detectors were FTL so they could watch it in real time. For all the good it was likely to do them.

Madrigal had, indeed, gotten her CIC tied into the net. The board couldn't display individual impeller sources at such a long range, but the data codes beside the single blotch of light were far too detailed for Grayson instrumentation. That was Courvosier's first thought; his second was a stab of dismay, and he pursed his lips silently. There were ten ships out there, accelerating from the low velocity imposed by translation into normal space. Not even *Madrigal* could "see" them well enough to identify individual ships, but the impeller strengths allowed tentative IDs by class. And if Commander Alvarez's sensor crews were right, they were four light cruisers and six destroyers—more tonnage than the entire Grayson hyper-capable fleet.

A projected vector suddenly arced across the display, and Yanakov cursed beside him.

"What?" Courvosier asked quietly.

"They're headed straight for Orbit Four, one of our belt mining processing nodes. Damn!"

"What have you got to stop them?"

"Not enough," Yanakov said grimly. He glanced up. "Walt! How long till they hit Orbit Four?"

"Approximately sixty-eight minutes," Commodore Brentworth replied.

"Anything we can intercept with?"

"*Judah* could reach them just short of the processors." Brentworth's voice was flat. "Nothing else could—not even a LAC."

"That's what I thought." Yanakov's shoulders slumped, and Courvosier understood perfectly. Sending a single destroyer out to meet that much firepower would be worse than pointless. "Signal *Judah* to stand clear of them," the Grayson admiral sighed, "then get me a mike. Orbit Four's on its own." His lips twitched bitterly. "The least I can do is tell them myself."

The holo sphere sparkled with individual lights and shifting patterns of information as Matthew Simonds stood in *Thunder of God*'s CIC. Captain Yu stood beside him, face relaxed and calm, and Simonds repressed a flare of disappointment. He should be on *Abraham*'s bridge, not standing here watching one of his juniors lead Masada's most powerful attack ever on Yeltsin's Star!

But he couldn't be. And powerful as this attack was, it was but one aspect of the overall plan—a plan whose entirety not even Captain Yu knew.

Orbit Four's CO watched his com, and a drop of sweat trickled down his face. The transmission had taken almost half an hour to reach him, but he'd known what it was going to say for over twenty minutes.

"I'm sorry, Captain Hill, but you're on your own," High Admiral Yanakov's voice was level, his face like stone. "Aside from *Judah*, nothing we've got can intercept, and sending her in alone would be suicide."

Hill nodded in silent agreement. His own lack of bitterness surprised him, but there was no point condemning *Judah* to share his command's death. And at least he'd gotten the collector ships out; three were down for repairs, but the others were well away, packed with Orbit Four's dependents, and his gravitics had already picked up the squadron headed towards them from Grayson. Unless the Masadans broke off from Orbit Four to pursue the fugitives in the next five minutes or so, they could never intercept short of the relief force. At least his wives and children would survive.

"Do your best, Captain," Yanakov said quietly. "God bless."

"Put me on record," Hill told his white-faced com officer, and the lieutenant nodded choppily.

"Recording, Sir."

"Message received and understood, Admiral Yanakov," Hill said as calmly as he could. "We'll do what we can. For the record, I concur completely in your decision not to send *Judah* in." He hesitated a second, wondering if he should add some last, dramatic statement, then shrugged. "And God bless you, too, Bernie," he ended softly.

Captain Yu's expression had yielded to a slight frown. He leaned to one side, checking a readout, then straightened with a small shrug. His frown disappeared, yet there was a new intentness in his eyes. It was almost a look of disappointment, Simonds thought. Or of disapproval.

He started to ask what Yu's problem was, but the range was down to three and a half million kilometers, and he couldn't tear his attention from the sphere.

"They're late." Admiral Courvosier's statement was barely a whisper, yet Yanakov heard him and nodded curtly. The Masadan commander had missed his best chance to kill Orbit Four from beyond its own range . . . not that it was going to make any difference to Captain Hill's men in the end.

The Masadan ships' velocities mounted steadily. Their

courses were already curving up in the arc which would take them inside Orbit Four and back the way they'd come, and weapons crews crouched over their consoles as the range dropped. There was tension in their faces, but no real fear. They had the protection of their impeller wedges and sidewalls; the weapon stations guarding Orbit Four were naked to their fire, protected only by point defense.

"We've got a good target setup, Sir."

Admiral Jansen looked up aboard the light cruiser *Abraham*, flagship of the Masadan Navy, as his chief of staff spoke.

"Range?"

"Coming down on three million kilometers."

Jansen nodded. His missiles were slower than *Thunder of God*'s. Their drives would burn out in less than a minute, and their maximum acceleration was barely thirty thousand gravities, but his fleet's closing speed was over 27,000 KPS. His missiles would take seventy-eight seconds to reach their targets from that initial velocity; Orbit Four's missiles would take a minute and a half to reach *him*. Only a twelve-second difference—but unlike asteroids, his ships could dodge.

"Commence firing," he said harshly.

Captain Hill's face tightened as his gravitics picked up missile separations. At this range, even given their closing speed, drive burnout would send his missiles ballistic and deprive them of their homing ability over 800,000 kilometers short of target. That was why he'd held his own fire, hoping against hope that they'd keep coming until he opened up. Not that he'd expected them to, but it had been worth praying for. There was little point throwing away birds that couldn't maneuver when they reached the enemy—missiles that had gone ballistic were easy for impeller drive ships to evade or pick off—but they'd already come closer than he'd had any reasonable right to expect, and even a ballistic bird was better than none when he and his men had at most three salvos before the Masadan missiles arrived.

"Open fire!" he barked, and then, in a softer voice, "Stand by point defense."

The range was too great even for *Madrigal*'s systems to plot single missile drives, but the display flashed as the destroyer's sensors noted a sudden background cascade of impeller sources. Courvosier stood silently beside Yanakov, watching the Grayson admiral's gray, clenched face, and knew there was nothing at all he could say.

Sword Simonds shivered as he watched the missiles on *Thunder of God*'s displays. They slashed out from attacker and defender alike, tiny drops of ruby blood that were somehow beautiful and obscenely tranquil. There should have been fury and thunder. Should have been the sights and sounds and smells of battle. But there was only the hum of ventilation systems and the calm, quiet murmur of sensor technicians.

The tiny dots moved with agonizing slowness across the holo sphere's vast scale, and time held its breath. Another salvo followed thirty-five seconds later, and another, answered by the Graysons' replies. Then the first salvo's dots vanished as their drives burned out, and Admiral Jansen altered course, twisting away from the defensive fire which had gone inert and clumsy. Simonds pictured Jansen's missiles driving on through God's own emptiness, invisible on passive sensors at such a range, and there was an inevitability, almost a dreaminess, about it now.

Orbit Four's defenses had never been intended to stand off eighty percent of the Masadan Navy all by themselves. The fixed fortifications were sitting ducks for missile solutions; anything fired at them was almost bound to hit, unless it was stopped by point defense, and there simply wasn't enough point defense to stop the scores of missiles coming at them.

Radar locked onto the incoming warheads, and counter missiles raced to meet them. The chances of interception were far lower than they would have been for more modern defensive systems, but Captain Hill's men did well. They stopped almost a third of them, and lasers and last-ditch autocannon went to continuous fire against the survivors.

Admiral Jansen stared at his visual display, ignoring the salvos of Grayson missiles flashing towards him. The first one didn't matter, anyway; it would be ballistic and harmless long before it reached him. The second would still have a few moments on its drives, but only enough for straight-in attacks with no last minute penetration maneuvers. Only the third posed a real threat, and his smile was a shark's as huge fireballs glared, eye-hurting and savage even at ten light-seconds and despite the display's filters.

Sword Simonds leaned closer to the holo sphere as the flashing time display counted down to impact for the first Grayson salvo. None of Jansen's impeller signatures vanished, and the task force altered course again to evade the second salvo. His eyes darted back to the secondary plot monitoring Orbit Four's launch times, and his mouth curved up in a smile of triumph.

Something like a soft, silent moan—sensed, not heard—swept through the background printer clatter of Central Command as the data codes blinked. More missile projections traced their way across the glass . . . and every one of them was headed *away* from the attackers.

Courvosier's shoulders slumped. They'd deserved better than that, he thought. They'd deserved—

"They *got* one of the bastards!" someone screamed, and his eyes jerked back to the board.

The missile was an orphan from Captain Hill's third and final salvo. In fact, it should have been from his *second* salvo, but its launch crew had suffered a momentary loss of power. By the time the frantic techs got their weapon back on line, their bird launched almost five seconds after the third salvo, and all of them were dead by the time it entered attack range. The orphan neither knew nor cared about that. It drove forward, still under power while its sensors listened to the beacon of its chosen target. The Masadan defensive systems almost missed the single missile entirely, then assigned it a far lower threat value as it tagged along behind the others.

Admiral Jansen's ships writhed and twisted far more frantically, for unlike the first salvo, this one still had drive power. But Tracking had its birds pegged to a fare-thee-well, and counter-missiles charged to meet the most dangerous ones.

Defensive fire smashed some of the orphan's fellows. Others immolated themselves uselessly against impeller wedges they couldn't possibly penetrate. A handful struck squarely at the far weaker sidewalls protecting the open sides of those wedges, and one of them actually penetrated. Its target lurched, damage alarms screaming, but the Masadan destroyer's damage was slight, and only the orphan was left. Only the orphan with the low threat value.

The two counter-missiles targeted on it flashed past, clear misses without the better seeking heads of more modern navies, and its target's sensors, half-blinded by the artificial grav wave of its own belly stress band, lost lock. There was no last-minute laser fire, and the missile bobbed up, programmed for a frontal attack, and threw every erg of drive power it still had into crushing deceleration. There wasn't time to kill much velocity, even at 30,000 gees—but it was enough.

The unprotected, wide open throat of the light cruiser *Abraham*'s impeller wedge engulfed the warhead like a vast scoop. Primary and backup proximity fuses flashed as one, and a fifty-megaton explosion erupted one hundred meters from the Masadan flagship.

Sword Simonds' face went bone-white as the impeller signature vanished. Air hissed in his nostrils, and he peered at the holo sphere for one, frozen moment, unwilling to accept it, then turned to stare at Captain Yu.

The Havenite returned his gaze gravely, but there was no shock, no horror, in *his* eyes. There wasn't even any surprise.

"A pity," Yu said quietly. "They should have launched from farther out."

Simonds clenched his teeth against a mad impulse to scream at his "adviser." Twenty percent of the Masadan wall of battle had just been obliterated, and all he could say was *they should have launched from farther out?!* His eyes blazed, but Yu flipped his own eyes to the members of the Sword's staff. Most of them were still staring at the sphere, shocked by the totally unanticipated loss, and the Havenite officer pitched his voice high enough for them to hear as he continued.

"Still, Sir, it's the final objective that matters. There are always losses, however good a battle plan may be, but Grayson has lost far more heavily than we have, and the trap is set, isn't it, Sir?"

Simonds stared at him, still quivering with fury, but he felt his staff behind him and sensed the potential damage to their confidence. He knew what Yu was doing, and the infidel was right—curse him!

"Yes," he made himself say calmly and levelly for his staff's benefit, and the word was acid on his tongue. "Yes, Captain Yu, the trap is set . . . exactly as planned."

● CHAPTER THIRTEEN

Bernard Yanakov's uniform tunic hung over a chair, the topmost button of his shirt was open, and he frowned at his CRT, then looked up with a weary smile of welcome as the door opened to admit Raoul Courvosier and the background chatter of printers.

Civilian clothing or not, no one could mistake Courvosier for anything but a naval officer now, and Yanakov was devoutly thankful for his presence. Not only had he made his destroyer's sensors available to Grayson, but he'd also placed his own vast experience at Yanakov's disposal. Despite, Yanakov knew, protests from certain members of his delegation that he ought to load them all aboard *Madrigal* and get them safely out of the line of fire.

"You need sleep," the Manticoran said bluntly, and Yanakov nodded.

"I know," he sighed, "but—" He broke off and shrugged, and Courvosier nodded in understanding. Not approval, just understanding.

A fatigue-dulled mind was scarcely the best tool for his system's defense, but Yanakov couldn't sleep. Orbit Four had been joined by Orbit Five and Six, and neither of their commandants had gotten as lucky as Hill. Or, rather, the Masadans had gotten smarter. They were launching from six million kilometers or more, ranges so long the defensive missiles' drives burned out over five full minutes short of their targets. It gave the defenders longer tracking times and better point defense kill probabilities, yet sheer numbers more than made up for that by saturating the defenses. It might cost the Masadans a lot of missiles, but *Grayson* had already lost nine percent of its orbital resource processing capacity . . . not to mention twenty-six hundred uniformed defenders and sixteen thousand civilian workers.

"You know," the Manticoran admiral mused, looking out through the glass wall across the bustling battle staff, "there's something peculiar about this whole attack pattern." He turned to face Yanakov. "Why aren't they either pulling completely out of the system or continuing straight along the belt?"

"They *are* continuing along the belt," Yanakov said in some surprise. "They're picking off our nodes in a straight-line sequence, directly against the belt's orbit."

"I know, but why take so much time? Why dash in, hit a single target, then pull back out again, when they could blow their way right along the belt in a fraction of the time?"

"This way they can watch us coming, then choose a different target or even break off entirely, and we can't preposition ourselves to intercept—unless we spread ourselves so thin any force that *does* catch them will be cut to dog meat," Yanakov pointed out bitterly.

"No, that's not it." Courvosier rubbed his chin and frowned as he considered the board. The Masadan raiders tracked slowly across it, retiring from their third attack, and he shook his head. "Their sensors are no better than yours, right?"

"Probably not as good, actually."

"All right. Your orbital sensor arrays give you real-time gravitic detection out to thirty-four light-minutes—eight light-minutes beyond the belt on their normal retirement vector. More than that, the Masadans *know* they do."

"Well, yes." Yanakov scrubbed at burning eyes, then rose and walked across to stand beside his friend and watch the display. "Of course, there's a lot of transmission lag from the more distant arrays—especially those on the far side of Yeltsin—but they're working our side of the primary, so Command Central's got real-time data where it really matters. That's why they pull back out beyond our detection range after each raid, pick a new attack vector, and come charging back in. As you say, our shipboard sensors have very limited range compared to yours. Even if we happened to guess right and place a force where it could intercept them, its commander couldn't see them soon enough to generate an intercept, and we probably couldn't pass him light-speed orders from Command Central in time for him to do it, either."

"I could buy that," Courvosier agreed, "but you're missing my point. They keep pulling back out to the same damned place after each attack, and they have to know you can see them doing it."

"Um?" Yanakov frowned, and Courvosier nodded.

"Exactly. They keep heading back to the same spot before your sensors lose them. And as they work their way along the belt, they keep extending their flight distance *back* to that same place with each target they hit. That not only makes them more vulnerable to interception but also vastly extends the time they're spending on the entire operation, yet they keep poking along at no more than point-three cee while they do it. Now why would they be doing that?"

"Well . . ." Yanakov scratched his head. "They're throwing a lot of missiles in each attack. That has to run their magazines low—maybe they've got colliers out there with reloads and they have to return to them to rearm. And I suppose the low velocities could be so they don't have to kill too much vee if we do manage to hide something in front of them."

"Possibly, possibly," Courvosier murmured. "But their timing suggests they had somebody hidden out there, watching when *Fearless*, *Apollo*, and *Troubadour* left. They may think that was our entire escort force, and they may not have any idea those ships are coming back, but they have to know there's a high probability *some* Manticoran squadron's likely to drop by. That should be a factor in their planning. They ought to be going for a fast decision, hoping to finish you off before some RMN admiral intervenes on your behalf."

"One already has, in a sense," Yanakov said with a tired grin.

"You know what I mean."

"True—but I'm not too sure about your basic premise. There's no commerce between Yeltsin and Endicott. That means no information flow, so how could they know you were ever here in the first place?"

"The fact that we were sending a diplomatic mission—and a convoy—has been general knowledge for months," Courvosier argued, "and they must've known we'd send along an escort. Once we arrived, all they'd have needed to make a pretty fair projection of what we were up to is a single hidden picket. And look at the timing. Allow a day or so for their picket to sneak back out to Masada after *Fearless* left, then another day to mobilize, and they'd be back here just about the time they started shooting." He shook his head. "They know at least some of the escorts pulled out, and they're trying to get in before any other Manticoran force gets here to replace them."

"I don't think they have the technical capability to pull off that kind of operation, Raoul. Oh, certainly they could get a ship in or out. All they'd have to do is translate beyond our detection range and come in with a low-powered wedge, then hide in the asteroid belt. Even if we saw them, we'd probably put them down as routine mining traffic, and getting out would be just as easy. But even if they did that, they'd need sensors almost as good as yours to tell what's happening in the inner system." Yanakov shook his head. "No, the timing has to be a coincidence."

"Maybe." Courvosier shook himself. "At any rate, Captain Harrington *will* be back within another four days."

"I can't wait that long," Yanakov said, and Courvosier looked at him in surprise. "They've taken out close to ten percent of our processors; if I give them another four days, they'll destroy forty years of investment—not to mention killing several thousand more people—especially if, as you yourself have pointed out they should, they drop this in-and-out nonsense and start working their way straight around the belt. I've got to stop them sooner than that . . . assuming I can figure a way to intercept the bastards in strength."

"I see." Courvosier chewed the inside of his lip for a minute, then frowned intently. "You know, there just might be something you *can* do."

"Such as?"

"You're too tired to think straight, Bernie. If they keep heading back to the same spot every time, you don't have to let them see you coming."

"You're right." Yanakov sat back down abruptly, then began punching keys. "If we know where they're going, we could wait till they pull back from this last attack, then put everything we've got on a course to intercept their retirement vector for the *next* one!"

"Exactly." Courvosier grinned. "Get your people out there, accelerate like hell once the bad guys are out of their sensor range of you, then kill your drives and coast until they start back out after their next attack. What's your max fleet acceleration?"

"Five hundred gees, more or less, for the hyper-capable units," Yanakov said. "Three seventy-five for the LACs." He studied his calculations for a moment, then grimaced and started changing numbers.

"Do the LACs add enough firepower to justify holding your starships back?"

"No. That's what I'm reworking." Yanakov nodded as new numbers began to come together. "Okay, that's better. Now, given their operational pattern to date, I think we can assume a sensor window of—" He tapped a quick calculation. "Call it three and a half hours. Three to be on the safe side."

"Which means you could be up to—?"

"Approximately fifty-three thousand KPS. And even if they don't come back in at all, that would take us to the point where our sensors keep losing them in . . . roughly four hours from Grayson orbit," Yanakov said, still working at his terminal. "Given their attack patterns, we can kick our drives back in . . . call it three hours into their next run and *still* intercept even if they pull back out the instant they pick us up!" His hands stilled on the keys and his tired eyes were almost awed. "By the Grace of God the Tester, you're right. We can do it."

"I know," Courvosier replied, but he sounded less enthusiastic. Yanakov looked a question, and he shrugged. "Oh, it's neat, and I like the notion of using their predictability against them, but there's still something I can't quite put my finger on. It just doesn't make sense for them to give us an opening like this."

"Didn't someone say the general who makes the last mistake loses?"

"Wellington, I think. Or maybe it was Rommel." Courvosier frowned. "Tanakov?" He shrugged it away. "The point is, we want *them* to make the mistake."

"I don't see how it can hurt us," Yanakov argued. "Holding the Fleet in-system accomplishes absolutely nothing. At least this gives us a chance. And, as you say, Captain Harrington will be back in four days. If they have missile colliers out there, we may be able to knock them out and choke off their supplies, even if we miss an actual interception. And even if we only derail their operations for a few days, that'll still be long enough to prevent further damage before she gets back and kicks the bas—"

He broke off, a curious expression on his face, and Courvosier cocked an eyebrow.

"Sorry," Yanakov half-muttered. "I was simply assuming you'd commit her ships to help us."

"Why in the galaxy shouldn't you assume that?" Courvosier demanded.

"But you're not— I mean, *we're* not—" Yanakov paused and cleared his throat. "We don't have a treaty yet. If you lose ships or take damage on your own responsibility without one, your government may—"

"My government will do what Her Majesty tells it to do," Courvosier said flatly, "and Her Majesty told *me* to come back with a treaty with Grayson." Yanakov looked at him wordlessly, and he shrugged. "I can't very well do that if I let Masada wipe you out, can I?" He shook his head. "I'm not too worried about the Crown's reaction, or even Parliament's. The Queen's honor is at stake here—and even if it weren't, I wouldn't sleep too well nights if I turned my back on you people, Bernie."

"Thank you," Yanakov said very softly, and Courvosier shrugged again, uncomfortably this time.

"Forget it. It's really just a sneaky maneuver to bring your own conservatives around."

"Of course it is." Yanakov smiled, and Courvosier grinned back.

"Well, I can pretend, can't I?" He rubbed his chin again and fell silent for a moment. "In fact, with your permission, I'm going to take *Madrigal* out with your interception force."

"What?!" Surprise betrayed Yanakov into the undiplomatic exclamation, but Courvosier only shook his head in mock sorrow.

"I told you you need sleep. *Madrigal's* sensors are better than anything you—and, ergo, the Masadans— have. If we include her in your intercept force, her gravitics'll pick them up a minimum of two light-minutes before they have the reach to see you. That means you can keep your force under power longer, build a higher base vector, because you'll only have to shut down when they *do* come back, not when we think they *might* come back. And just between the two of us, I don't think any Masadan cruiser out there is going to enjoy meeting up with *her*, Bernie."

"But . . . but you're the head of a diplomatic mission! If anything happens to you—"

"Mr. Houseman will be only too happy to take over in that unhappy event." Courvosier grimaced. "Not the happiest of outcomes, I agree, but scarcely disastrous. And I told the FO when I took the job that it was only temporary. As a matter of fact—" he grinned slyly "—I believe I may have slipped up and packed a uniform or two along with all these civvies."

"But, Raoul—!"

"Are you saying you don't *want* me along?" Courvosier asked in hurt tones.

"Of course I do! But the possible repercussions—"

"—are far outweighed by the probable benefits. If a

Queen's ship fights alongside you against your traditional enemy, it can only be a plus for the ratification of any treaty, don't you think?"

"Of course it would," Yanakov said, but the words cracked around the edges, for he knew it wasn't diplomatic considerations which shaped the offer. "Of course," he went on after he got his voice back under control, "you're senior to any of my other officers. Hell, you're senior to *me!*"

"I'll certainly waive seniority," Courvosier said wryly. "After all, my entire 'fleet' consists of a single destroyer, for God's sake."

"No, no. Protocol must be observed," Yanakov said with a tired smile. "And since this is all a sneaky diplomatic ploy, not a spontaneous and generous offer to help people who have done their best to insult your senior subordinate and half your other officers, we might as well play it to the hilt." He held Courvosier's eyes warmly and extended his hand.

"I hereby offer you the position of second in command of the Grayson-Manticoran Combined Fleet, Admiral Courvosier. Will you accept?"

• CHAPTER FOURTEEN

An admiral's vac suit looked out of place on HMS *Madrigal*'s cramped bridge, for a destroyer had never been intended as a flagship. The assistant astrogator had been squeezed out of his position at Lieutenant Macomb's elbow to provide Courvosier with a chair and a maneuvering display, and if Commander Alvarez seemed totally unbothered, almost everyone else was clearly a little ill at ease in his august presence.

But Lieutenant Commander Mercedes Brigham wasn't. *Madrigal*'s exec had other things on her mind as she stood at the tactical officer's shoulder and peered at her displays, and those displays were why Courvosier wouldn't have been anywhere else, for they gave *Madrigal* infinitely better information than any other ship in the small fleet accelerating away from Grayson.

The admiral leaned back, resting one hand on his chair's waiting shock frame, and watched his own readouts. His cramped screen wasn't as detailed as the one Brigham and Lieutenant Yountz studied so intently, but it showed the Grayson ships deployed protectively about *Madrigal*. They'd lost a half-hour of their anticipated "free time" because a single Masadan destroyer had lagged behind her withdrawing consorts for some reason; aside from that everything was exactly on schedule, and two Grayson destroyers led *Madrigal* by a lightsecond and a half, covered by her sensors yet interposing themselves between her and any threat. Not that they were likely to meet one with her to watch their backs, but the Graysons were guarding her like a queen.

It was odd, Courvosier thought. Manticoran

destroyers had excellent sensor suites for their displacement, but they were hardly superdreadnoughts. Yet at this moment, *Madrigal* was the closest thing around. She was a pygmy beside Honor's *Fearless*, much less a battlecruiser or ship-of-the-wall, but she massed barely twelve thousand tons less than Yanakov's flagship, and her command and control facilities—like her firepower—were light-seconds beyond the best the Graysons could boast.

Given the way Grayson's original colonists had marooned themselves, it was little short of miraculous their descendants had managed to rediscover so much— and survive—on their own, but their tech base was patchy. They'd been fifteen hundred years behind the rest of the galaxy when they were finally rediscovered, yet the progeny of Austin Grayson's anti-tech followers had demonstrated a positive genius for adapting what they already knew to any new scrap of technology they got their hands on.

Neither Endicott nor Yeltsin had been able to attract significant outside help until the Haven-Manticore confrontation spilled over on them. Both were crushingly impoverished; no one in his right mind voluntarily immigrated to an environment like Grayson's; and Masada's theocratic totalitarians didn't even *want* outsiders. Under the circumstances, the Graysons had made up a phenomenal amount of ground in the two centuries since their rediscovery by the galaxy at large, but there were still holes, and some of them were gaping ones.

Grayson fusion plants were four times as massive as modern reactors of similar output (which was why they still used so many fission plants), and their military hardware was equally out of date—they still used *printed circuits*, with enormous mass penalties and catastrophic consequences for designed lifetimes— though there were a few unexpected surprises in their mixed technological bag. For example, the Grayson Navy had quite literally invented its own inertial compensator thirty T-years ago because it hadn't been able to get anyone else to explain how it was done. It was a clumsy, bulky thing, thanks to the components they had to use, but from what he'd seen of its stats, it might just be marginally more efficient than Manticore's.

For all that, their energy weapons were pitiful by modern standards, and their missiles were almost worse. Their point defense missiles used *reaction* drives, for God's sake! That had stunned Courvosier—until he discovered that their smallest impeller missile massed over a hundred and twenty tons. That was fifty percent more than a Manticoran ship-killer, much less a point defense missile, which explained why they had to accept shorter-ranged, less capable counter missiles. At least they were small enough to carry in worthwhile numbers, and it wasn't quite as bad as it might have been, if only because the missiles they had to stop were so limited. Grayson missiles were slow, short-legged, and myopic. Worse, they required direct hits, and their penaids might as well not exist. They weren't even in shouting range of *Madrigal's* systems, and the destroyer could take any three Grayson—or Masadan—light cruisers in a stand-up fight.

Which, he reflected grimly, might be just as well in the next several hours, for something still bothered him about the entire Masadan operational pattern. It was too predictable, too . . . stupid. Of course, closing to three million klicks before engaging Orbit Four hadn't exactly been a gem of genius, either, but the Graysons and Masadans had fought their last war with chem-fuel missiles and no inertial compensators at all. Their capabilities had leapt ahead by eight centuries or so in the last thirty-five years, so perhaps closing that way resulted from simple inexperience with their new weapons mix.

But Grayson wouldn't have done it, his doubts told him, for Yanakov had seen to it that his people knew exactly what their systems could do. Then again, Yanakov was a remarkable man in many ways, not simply as an officer, and Courvosier regretted the brevity of his lifespan, already nearing its end after less than sixty years, almost as much as he regretted *Fearless's* absence.

He snorted to himself. Perhaps he shouldn't apply Yanakov's standards to his opponents, but he'd never met any Masadans. Maybe that was his problem. Maybe he was giving them too much credit because, despite their crude hardware, the Graysons were so good. Their opposition might really be as bad as their ops patterns suggested.

He shrugged. He was going to discover the truth soon enough, and—

"Ma'am, I've got—"

"I see it, Mai-ling." Brigham touched the ensign at the assistant tactical officer's station lightly on the shoulder and looked at Alvarez.

"We've got them on gravitics, Skipper, bearing three-five-two by zero-zero-eight. Range nineteen-point-one light-minutes, speed three-zero-eight-eight-nine KPS, accelerating at four-point-nine-zero KPS squared." She leaned closer to the display, studying data codes, then nodded. "All there, Sir. And they're on course for Orbit Seven."

"Closure time?" Alvarez asked.

"They'll cross our track port to starboard and begin opening the range in two-three-point-two-two-niner minutes, Sir," Lieutenant Yountz replied. "At present acceleration, we'll reach the crossover point in niner-seven-point-six minutes."

"Thank you, Janice." Alvarez glanced at the ensign beside his tac officer. Mai-ling Jackson was a petite young lady who reminded Courvosier a great deal of Dr. Allison Harrington, and he'd already noted the way her seniors trusted her judgment, especially where Grayson systems capabilities were concerned. "How long until their sensors can pick us up, Mai-ling?"

"Assuming we both maintain our current accelerations, make it . . . two-zero-point-niner minutes, Sir."

"Thank you." Alvarez turned to Courvosier. "Admiral?"

"Admiral Yanakov will have the data from CIC," Courvosier said, "but double-check to be certain."

"Aye, aye, Sir," Alvarez replied, and Lieutenant Cummings became very busy at his com panel.

"Flag confirms copy of our data, Skipper," he said after a moment. "*Grayson* is feeding us a fleet course change."

"Understood. Do you have it, Astro?"

"Aye, aye, Sir—coming up on the computers now." Lieutenant Macomb studied his panel. "Course change to one-five-one two-four-seven true with impeller shutdown in one-niner minutes, Sir."

"Make it so," Alvarez replied, and Yountz punched buttons.

"That brings us across their projected track in one-one-two minutes," she reported. "Assuming their acceleration remains unchanged, the range will be four-point-one-one-six light-minutes at crossover, but if they maintain heading and acceleration, they'll reach the point of no return for their recovery vector in just over nine minutes from our shutdown, Sir."

Alvarez nodded, and Courvosier echoed his gesture with a mental nod of silent satisfaction. Yanakov might be cutting his drives a little sooner than he had to, but it was probably better to be conservative.

He made quick calculations on his own number pad, and his smile grew predatory as the solution blinked. If the task force coasted for just thirteen minutes, then went back to max accel on an intercept vector, the Masadans would have to accept action or cut and run for the hyper limit the instant they saw its impeller signatures. If they ran, Yanakov would never catch them, but if he was right about their having supply ships out here, that would be tantamount to abandoning them to his mercy. And *that* would spell the defeat of their current operations at least until Honor got back.

And, his smile grew even more predatory, it was unlikely the Masadan commander *would* break off. He might have lost a light cruiser, but he still had nine ships to Yanakov's seven, and Yanakov had left the *Glory* in Grayson orbit. She was his oldest, least capable cruiser, and she'd been completing a routine maintenance cycle when everything broke loose. She needed another twenty hours to get back on line, but her absence had left a hole in Yanakov's order of battle for *Madrigal* to fill. With any luck, the Masadans would accept battle with their outnumbered enemies without realizing Grayson's third "cruiser" was, in fact, a Manticoran destroyer, and wouldn't that just be too bad?

High Admiral Yanakov sat on his own bridge and yearned silently for the nest of repeaters which surrounded the captain's chair on a Manticoran warship. He had a clear view of all really critical readouts, but he didn't have anything like a Manticoran CO's ability to manipulate data.

Still, the situation was clear enough just now—thanks to *Madrigal's* keen eyes. He felt an odd, godlike sense of detachment, for he could see every move the Masadans made, but they couldn't even guess he was watching them. Their ships slid onward, driving ever deeper into the trap as his own vector angled towards theirs, and he smiled.

"Where are their LACs?" Sword of the Faithful Simonds fretted yet again as he stared into *Thunder of God's* holo sphere, and Captain Yu suppressed a desire to bite his head off.

Damn it, the man was supposed to be a naval officer! He ought to know no plan—especially one this complex—survived contact with the enemy. No one could cover all the variables, which was why Jericho had been planned with plenty of redundancy. Only a fool relied on a plan in which *everything* had to go right, and killing LACs was completely unnecessary.

For that matter, the entire trap was unnecessary. Left to his own devices, Yu would have preferred a direct, frontal assault, trusting *Thunder's* missile batteries to annihilate any defenders before they ever reached their own combat range of her. But for all their vocal faith in their own perfection as God's Chosen, what passed for Masada's General Staff held the Grayson military in almost superstitious dread. They seemed unaware of the true extent of the advantage *Thunder* gave them, but then, most of them had been very junior officers during Masada's last attempt to conquer Yeltsin's Star. That had been the sort of disaster even the most competent military people tended to remember with dread . . . and most of the senior officers who'd launched it and escaped death at Grayson hands had found it from the Church their failure had "betrayed." The consequences to fleet morale and training had been entirely predictable, and Yu had to concede that the present Grayson Navy was at least half again as efficient as his own allies.

The Masadans refused to admit that . . . but they'd also insisted the Grayson Navy must be wiped out, or at least crippled, before *Thunder*'s existence was revealed to the enemy. The possible intervention of a Manticoran warship had made them even more insistent, yet despite all *Thunder of God* could do for them, it was the Graysons and their primitive weapons that really worried them. Which was stupid, but telling them so wouldn't be the most diplomatic thing he could possibly do, now would it?

"They've clearly left them home, Sir," he said instead, as patiently as he could. "Given what they know, that was the best decision they could have made. LACs would have reduced their fleet acceleration by twenty-five percent, and the LACs themselves are much more fragile than proper starships."

"Yes, and they don't *need* them, do they?" Anxiety put a venomous edge in Simonds' question, and he pointed to a single light code. "So much for your assumption the Manticoran warship would sit this operation out, Captain!"

"Its intervention was always a possibility, Sir. As I said at the time." Yu smiled, carefully not saying that, contrary to what he'd told the Council of Elders, he'd assumed from the beginning that the Manticorans probably *would* pitch in. If he'd told them that, the Masadan Navy would have sat in its corner and shit its vac suits rather than commit to Jericho. "And, Sir," he added, "please note that sh—*he* is, indeed, only a destroyer. A nasty handful for your people, yes, but no match for *Thunder* and *Principality*."

"But they're not coming in on the vector we wanted," Simonds stewed.

One or two people turned to glance at the Sword, then whipped back around as they caught their captain's cold stare, yet Simonds hadn't even noticed. He was too busy glaring at Yu, as if challenging the captain to dispute his statement, but Yu said nothing. There really wasn't any point.

There'd never been any way to guarantee the exact course the enemy might follow once their own forces were spotted. In point of fact, Yu was quite pleased with how close his predictions *had* come. *Thunder of God* had enough tracking range to put the regular Masadan ships on the proper incursion vector even with light-speed communications, and the Grayson commander had selected very nearly the exact course change Yu had projected. Anyone but an idiot—or someone as badly rattled as Sword Simonds—would have allowed for how vast the field of maneuver was. Yu would have settled for getting one of his ships into attack range; as it was, both of them would have the reach, if only barely.

"They'll cross your range more than six hundred thousand kilometers out at almost point-five cee!" Simonds went on. "And look at that vector! There's no way we'll be able to fire down their wedges, and that makes *Thunder*'s energy weapons *useless*."

"Sir," Yu said even more patiently, "no one can count on having an enemy voluntarily cross his own T. And if we have to take on their sidewalls, that's the reason our missiles have laser heads."

"But—"

"They may not be on the exact vector we wanted, Sir, but our flight time will be under forty seconds at their closest approach. *Principality*'s will be somewhat longer, true, but they won't even know we're here until we launch, and there's no way they can localize us to shoot back."

Yu himself would have been happier if his targets had come straight at him, though he had no intention of telling Simonds that. Had they done so, he could have punched his missiles straight down the wide-open throats of their wedges. Even better, he could have used his shipboard lasers and grasers against those same unprotected targets.

As it was, *Thunder of God*'s energy weapons would never penetrate their targets' sidewalls at their closest range, and he'd have to launch at better than three million klicks if his missiles were going to catch them as they passed, while *Principality* was even more poorly placed. He'd had to spread the ships to cover the volume through which the Graysons might pass, which meant the destroyer's closest approach would be over a hundred million kilometers, and that *she* would have to launch at something like eight million. But even *Principality*'s actual flight time would be under a minute, and the two ships' salvos would arrive within twenty seconds of one another.

Of course, *Thunder* would have time for only one effective broadside, though *Principality* could probably get two off. Even in rapid fire, their best reload time was a tad over fifteen seconds, and the Graysons' crossing velocity was almost twice his missiles' highest speed from rest. That made it physically impossible for him to get off more than one shot per launcher before the Grayson fleet zipped across his engagement range at a velocity his birds could never overtake. But this was an almost classic ambush scenario, and Commander Theisman already had his ship spinning on her central axis. *Thunder* was too slow on the helm and too close, but Theisman could bring both broadsides to bear in *his* window of engagement. He'd fire the first one with its missiles' drives programmed for delayed activation, then fire the second as his other broadside rolled onto the target, which would bring them in together and let him get off almost as many birds as *Thunder*.

And, in a way, Yu was just as happy his energy weapons would be out of it. His jamming and other precautions should make it almost impossible for even the Manticorans to localize him if he used only missiles, but energy fire could be back-plotted far too precisely, and hiding his ships had required him to shut down his own drives, which deprived him of *any* sidewalls. Besides, *Principality* was one of the new city-class destroyers. She was short on energy weapons . . . but she packed a missile broadside most light cruisers might envy.

"I don't like how long the range is," Simonds muttered after a moment, more quietly but still stubborn. "They'll have too much time to spot our missiles after launch and take evasive action. They can roll and interpose their belly bands if they react quickly enough."

"It's a longer range than I'd really prefer myself, Sir," Yu said winningly, "but they're going to have to detect our birds, realize what they are, *and* react. That will take time, and even if they do manage to interpose their wedges, our birds will still have the power to maneuver to get at their sidewalls. And unlike your own weapons, these have a stand-off range. The Grayson defensive systems will have very little chance of stopping them far enough out, and if we take out only the Manticoran and both cruisers, there's no way the others can escape Admiral Franks."

"*If.*" Simonds fidgeted a moment, then turned away from the sphere, and Yu sighed in silent relief. For a moment, he'd been afraid the Masadan would actually scrub the entire operation because of one stupid destroyer.

"May I suggest we adjourn to the bridge, Sir?" he suggested. "It's getting close to starting time."

GNS *Austin Grayson*'s drive had been shut down for over twelve minutes while her enemies continued on course, and Admiral Yanakov checked his projections once more. The Masadan fleet was well past the point of no return; they couldn't possibly retire on whatever was so damned important to them without his intercepting them, which left ignominious flight or a resolute turn to engage as their only options.

He ran a hand down the arm of his command chair, wondering if the Masadan commander would cut and run or counterattack. He hoped for the latter, but at this point he would settle for the former.

He turned his head and nodded to Commander Harris.

"Signal from Flag, Sir," Lieutenant Cummings said suddenly. "Resume maximum acceleration at zero-eight-five by zero-zero-three in twenty seconds."

"Acknowledge," Alvarez said, and then, twenty seconds later, "Execute!"

Courvosier felt his nerves tighten as the shock frame dropped into place and locked about him. He hadn't seen combat in thirty T-years, and the adrenaline rush was almost a shock after so long.

The Masadan ships could see them now, but it was too late for them to do anything about it. The Grayson Navy—and HMS *Madrigal*—snarled around, bending their vector into one that arced across to cut their enemies off from escape.

"Right on schedule, Sir," Captain Yu said quietly as the ships of Admiral Franks' squadron altered course abruptly. They turned directly away from the Graysons in what was clearly an all-out bid to run, and the Grayson commander did exactly what any admiral worth his braid would do: he went in pursuit at his own maximum acceleration—on the exact vector Yu had projected.

He watched his display and felt an edge of sympathy. Based on what he knew, that man had done everything exactly right. But because he didn't know about *Thunder of God*, he was leading his entire navy into a death trap.

Admiral Courvosier checked the numbers once more

and frowned, for the current Masadan maneuvers baffled him. They were obviously trying to avoid action, but on their current course the Grayson task force would overtake well before they reached the .8 *C* speed limit imposed by their particle shielding. That meant they couldn't run away from Yanakov in normal space, yet they were already up to something like .46 *C*, much too high for a survivable Alpha translation, and if they kept this nonsense up much longer, they'd put themselves in a position where he would overrun them in short order if they tried to decelerate to a safe translation speed. Which meant, of course, that for all their frantic attempts to avoid action, they were painting themselves into a corner where they had no *choice* but to fight.

"Captain, I'm getting something a little witchy on my active systems," Ensign Jackson said.

"What do you mean 'witchy'?"

"I can't really say, Sir." The ensign made careful adjustments. "It's like snow or something along the asteroid belt ahead of us."

"Put it on my display," Alvarez decided.

Jackson did better than that and dropped the same data onto Courvosier's plot, and the admiral frowned. He wasn't familiar with the idiosyncrasies of the Yeltsin System, but the two clumps of cluttered radar returns certainly looked odd. They were fairly far apart and neither was all that big, yet the returns were so dense *Madrigal* couldn't see into them, and his frown deepened. Micrometeor clusters? It seemed unlikely. He saw no sign of energy signatures or anything else unnatural out there, and they were too far off the task force's vector to pose a threat with Masadan weaponry, but their illogic prodded at his brain, and he keyed his private link to Yanakov.

"Bernie?"

"Yes, Raoul?"

"Our active systems are picking up something str—"

"Missile trace!" Lieutenant Yountz snapped suddenly, and Courvosier's eyes jerked towards her. *Missiles?*

They were millions of kilometers outside the Masadan's effective missile envelope! Not even a panicked commander would waste ammo at this range!

"Multiple missile traces at zero-four-two zero-one-niner." Yountz's voice dropped into a tactical officer's flat, half-chant. "Acceleration eight-three-three KPS squared. Project intercept in three-one seconds—mark!"

Courvosier blanched. Eight hundred and thirty KPS^2 was 85,000 gees!

For just a moment, a sense of the impossible froze his mind, but then the missile origins registered. They were coming from those damned "clusters"!

"We've been suckered, Bernie!" he snapped into his com. "Roll your ships! Those are *modern* missiles!"

"Second missile launch detected," Yountz chanted. Brilliant lights flared in Alvarez's and Courvosier's plots. "Second launch interception in four-seven seconds—mark!"

Alvarez whipped his ship up on her side relative to the incoming fire, and Yanakov's order to the rest of his command came while Courvosier was still speaking. But his lead destroyers were two light-seconds from his flagship, and it took time. Time to pass the word. Time for stunned captains to wrench their attention from the Masadan warships clearly visible before them. Time to pass their own orders and for their helmsmen to obey.

Time too many Graysons no longer had.

The destroyers *Ararat* and *Judah* vanished in savage flashes. They were the flankers, closest to the incoming fire. It reached them thirteen seconds sooner than it did *Madrigal*, and they never had a chance. They'd barely begun to roll their wedges up to interdict when the incoming missiles detonated, and they carried laser heads—clusters of bomb-pumped X-ray lasers that didn't need the direct hits Grayson missiles required. They had a stand-off range of over twenty thousand kilometers, and every primitive point defense system aboard the destroyers had been trained in the wrong direction.

Just as *Madrigal's* were.

Stunned Manticoran brains raced to keep up with their computers as their weapons went into action without them. *Madrigal*'s people were only human, but her cybernetic reflexes—and a quite inordinate amount of pure luck—saved her from destruction in that first volley. Nine missiles tore down on her, but counter missiles went out at almost a thousand KPS^2 and point defense lasers tracked and slewed with calm technological haste. A dozen X-ray lasers lashed harmlessly at her impenetrable belly band, yet the two laser heads which might have pierced her sidewalls were picked off just short of detonation.

But simply surviving wasn't enough, and Courvosier cursed with silent ferocity. Their attackers *had* to be in those "clusters," and in order to hide, they'd had to shut down their own impellers and sidewalls. That meant they were not only immobile targets but buck naked to any return fire. Yet, small as the clusters might be on a solar system's scale, they were far too vast to cover with area fire. *Madrigal* needed a target, and she didn't have one.

"Point defense to task force coverage!" he snapped to Alvarez.

"Make it so, Tactical!" The commander listened to Yountz's acknowledgment and watched her punch the command into her console, then said, almost conversationally, "That's going to leave us mighty weak ourselves, Sir."

"Can't be helped." Courvosier never looked up from his display. "Whoever's shooting at us can't have time for more than one or two broadsides each at this velocity. If we can get the Graysons through them—"

"Understood, Sir," Alvarez said, then wheeled back to Yountz. "Can you get me any kind of target?" he demanded harshly.

"We can't even *find* them, Skipper!" The tac officer sounded more frustrated than afraid . . . but the fear would come, whether it showed or not, Courvosier thought. "They *must* be inside that crap, but my radar's bouncing right back in my face. That's got to be some kind of reflectors, and—" She broke off for a moment, and her voice went flat. "Now something's jamming hell out of me, too, Skip. There's no way I can localize."

Alvarez swore, but Courvosier made himself ignore the commander and his tactical officer and stared at his own display. The Grayson destroyer *David* streamed a tangled blood-trail of atmosphere, but she was still there, and she was up on her side, showing only the impenetrable belly of her impeller wedge to the second broadside already rushing down upon them.

Her sister *Saul* looked untouched on the far side of the formation, but both light cruisers had been hit. *Covington* held her course, trailing air but with little other sign of damage, while her crude point defense lasers continued firing after missiles which had already passed. She didn't have a prayer of hitting them, and it wouldn't have mattered if she had, yet the volume of her fire indicated she couldn't be too badly hurt.

Austin Grayson was another story. Debris and atmosphere trailed in her wake, and she wasn't under complete control. She'd completed her roll but was still rolling, as if she'd lost her helm, and her impeller wedge fluctuated as Courvosier watched.

"Bernie?" There was no reply. "*Bernie!*" Still nothing.

"Second salvo impact on *David* in seventeen seconds," Yountz snapped, but Courvosier hardly heard her.

"What's the status of the Flag, Tactical?" he demanded harshly.

"She's been hit several times, Sir." Ensign Jackson's voice quivered, but her answer came promptly. "I can't tell how badly, but she took at least one in her after impellers. Her accel's down to four-two-one gees and falling."

Courvosier nodded and his mind raced even as *Madrigal's* counter missiles went out once more. This time her human personnel knew what was happening as well as her computers did; that should have made her fire even more effective, but she was spread thinner, trying to protect her consorts as well as herself. There

were almost as many missiles in this salvo—with fewer
targets to spread themselves among—and whoever had
planned their targeting clearly knew what *Madrigal* was.
The missile pattern was obviously a classic double
broadside from something fairly powerful—probably a
light cruiser—and he'd allocated six of the birds in his
second launch to *Madrigal*. Whether it was an all-out
bid for a kill or only an effort to drive her anti-missile
systems back into self-defense was immaterial.

All of that flickered at the back of Courvosier's mind,
yet he couldn't tear his eyes from *Austin Grayson's*
silent light code. Then—

"Raoul?" Yanakov's voice was twisted and breathless,
and Courvosier bit his lip. There was no visual, but that
breathless quality told him his friend was hurt—hurt
badly—and there was nothing at all he could do for him.

"Yes, Bernie?"

Even as Courvosier replied, two missiles slashed in
on the damaged *David*. The destroyer's outclassed
defenses nailed one of them; the other popped up to
cross her starboard quarter at less than five hundred
kilometers. The sides of her impeller wedge were
protected by the focused grav fields of her sidewalls—
far more vulnerable than the wedge's "roof" and "floor,"
but powerful enough to blunt the heaviest energy
weapon at anything above pointblank range. But this
was pointblank for the laser head . . . and Grayson
sidewalls were weak by modern standards.

A half-dozen beams ripped at *David's* sidewall. It
bent and degraded them as it clawed at their photons,
and the radiation shielding inside the wedge blunted
them a bit more, but not enough.

Three of them got through, and the destroyer belched air. Her impeller wedge flashed—then died as the
ship broke almost squarely in half. Her forward section
vanished in an eye-tearing glare as her fusion plant's
mag bottle went, and her frantically accelerating sisters
left the madly spinning derelict of her after hull—and
any survivors who might still cling to life within it—
astern as they raced for salvation.

No less than four missiles attacked *Saul*, yet once again, *David's* sister ship emerged miraculously untouched. Her crude counter missiles were useless, but this time her gunners were ready. Primitive as their fire control was, they nailed two of her attackers; *Madrigal* got a third, and the single laser head they missed wasted itself harmlessly against her upper impeller band.

Covington was next as the missiles sleeted across what was left of the fleet. Three went after her, but *Madrigal* picked two of them off just short of detonation. The third got through, and the cruiser took yet another hit, but she shook it off and kept charging.

Grayson didn't.

Only a single missile had targeted her, but it came in on a wicked, twisting flight path, and *Madrigal's* own evasive maneuvers had taken her away from the cruiser. Her counter missiles went wide, none of her lasers had a shot, and *Grayson's* faltering drive made her easy meat for its terminal attack maneuver. At least four lasers—possibly more—slashed through her weakened sidewall. The Grayson flagship's impeller wedge went dead, and Courvosier heard the scream of damage alarms over his com link to her flag deck.

"It's up to you, Raoul." Yanakov's voice was weaker, and he coughed. "Get my people out of it if you can."

"I'll try," Courvosier promised softly as *Madrigal's* laser clusters opened up against the quartet of missiles still homing on her.

"Good man." Yanakov coughed again, the sound harsh through the voice and electronic chatter of *Madrigal's* point defense. "I'm glad I knew you," he said faintly. "Tell my wives I love th—"

The cruiser *Austin Grayson* blew up with the silent fury of deep-space death. A sliver of a second later, a single missile penetrated *Madrigal's* over-extended defenses.

Admiral of the Faithful Ernst Franks gloated as he remembered another battle—one in which Grayson had forced Subofficer Franks's crude destroyer to surrender with demeaning ease. Not this time. This time was different, and his teeth flashed in a feral smile.

The Grayson Navy had been savagely mauled. They were still too far away for him to make out details, but there were only three impeller signatures left, and he nodded as he watched them twist onto a new heading. They must have cleared *Thunder's* active missile envelope as she crouched amid the asteroids; now they were trying desperately to break away from his own ships. But unlike them, he'd known the ambush was coming and shaped his vector accordingly. He had just as much acceleration as they did, and his apparently suicidal course had placed him inside them. Not by much, but his nine ships would intercept them in scarcely two hours as they struggled to reach home.

No, he thought, in *less* than two hours, for the survivors must have taken impeller damage. Their acceleration was less than 4.6 KPS^2, under four hundred seventy gravities.

"Commodore, I have a signal from *Madrigal*."

Commodore Matthews looked up from the damage control reports. *Covington* was badly hurt—still a fighting force, but with a quarter of her weapons out of action. Worse, the forward third of her starboard sidewall was down, leaving a deadly chink in her armor, yet something about his com officer's tone cut through his own shock and near despair.

"Put it on the main screen," he said

The big com screen blinked to life, but not with the face he'd expected to see. He recognized Commander Alvarez, instead. The commander's helmet was sealed, and a gaping bulkhead hole behind him explained why. Matthews could actually see stars through it.

"Commodore Matthews?" Alvarez's voice was harsh and strained.

"Here," Matthews replied. "Where's Admiral Courvosier, Captain?"

"Dead, Sir." There was more than harshness in Alvarez's voice now. There was pain—and hate.

"Dead?" Matthews repeated almost numbly. *God the Tester, aid us now*, his mind whispered, and only then did he realize how desperately he had depended on the Manticoran to save what was left of Grayson's fleet.

"Yes, Sir. You're in command now." Matthews couldn't see Alvarez's face clearly through his suit visor, but the other man's mouth seemed to tighten before he spoke again. "Commodore, what shape are your impellers in?"

"Untouched." Matthews shrugged. "Our weapons have been badly hit, and my forward starboard sidewall isn't there anymore, but our drive's fine."

"And *Saul's* undamaged," Alvarez said flatly. Then he nodded. "We're slowing you down, aren't we, Sir?"

Matthews didn't want to answer that question. The Manticoran ship had taken at least two hits from the last broadside, and one must have gone home in her impellers. Her acceleration was dropping even further as Matthews watched, but they would all have been dead already if not for Courvosier's warning . . . and if the Manticoran ship hadn't exposed herself to save them. Besides, abandoning *Madrigal* would only delay the inevitable a dozen minutes or so.

"Aren't we?" Alvarez pressed, and Matthews clenched his jaw and made himself nod.

The commodore heard Alvarez inhale deeply, then the commander straightened in his chair. "That makes things much simpler, Commodore. You're going to have to leave us behind."

"No!" Matthews snapped in instant, instinctive response, but Alvarez shook his head.

"Yes, you are, Sir. That's not a suggestion. I have my orders from Admiral Yanakov and Admiral Courvosier, and we're all going to obey them."

"Orders? What orders?"

"Admiral Yanakov told Admiral Courvosier to get you home, Sir . . . and Admiral Courvosier lived long enough to confirm those orders to me."

Matthews stared at the hole behind the commander and knew that was a lie. There was no way anyone killed by that hit had lived even briefly, much less issued any orders. He started to say so, but Alvarez went on too quickly.

"*Madrigal* can't outrun them anyway, Sir. That means we're dead. But we've still got our weapons. You don't, but you've still got your drive. We're elected to play rearguard whatever happens. Don't waste that, Commodore."

"*Saul's* still undamaged—and we're not completely out of it!"

"Both of you together wouldn't make a damn bit of difference to what happens to us," Alvarez said harshly, "but if we hit them head-on—" Matthews saw his bared teeth even through his visor. "Commodore, these assholes have never seen what a Manticoran destroyer can do."

"But—"

"Please, Commodore." There was an edge of pleading in the harsh voice. "It's what the Admiral would have wanted. Don't take it away from us."

Matthews' fists clenched so hard they hurt, but he couldn't tear his eyes from the com, and Alvarez was right. It wasn't much of a chance for *Saul* and *Covington* . . . but refusing it wouldn't save *Madrigal*.

"All right," he whispered.

"Thank you, Sir," Alvarez said. Then he cleared his throat. "Admiral Yanakov passed one more message before he died, Sir. He . . . asked Admiral Courvosier to tell his wives he loved them. Will you pass that on for us?"

"Yes." Tears glittered under the word, but Matthews made himself get it out, and Alvarez squared his shoulders.

"I'm not sure what hit us, Sir, but assuming they both fired double broadsides, I'd guess one was a light cruiser. The other was bigger—maybe a heavy cruiser. They're both modern ships. We couldn't get a read on them, but they have to be Havenite. I wish we could tell you more, but—"

He broke off with a shrug, and Matthews nodded again.

"I'll inform Command Central, Captain Alvarez—and I'll see to it Manticore knows, as well."

"Good." Alvarez inhaled deeply, then laid his hands on the arms of his chair. "Then I guess that's about it," he said. "Good luck, Commodore."

"May God receive you as His own, Captain. Grayson will never forget."

"Then we'll try to make it worth remembering, Sir." Alvarez actually managed a smile and sketched a salute. "These bastards are about to find out how a Queen's ship kicks ass."

The signal died. GNS *Covington* went back to full power, racing desperately for safety while her single remaining destroyer covered her wounded flank, and there was silence on her bridge.

Astern of her, HMS *Madrigal* turned alone to face the foe.

• CHAPTER FIFTEEN

Fearless decelerated towards Yeltsin's hyper limit once more, and this time Honor Harrington awaited translation in a very different mood.

Alistair had been right, she thought, smiling at her display. *Troubadour* led *Fearless* by half a light-second, and even her light code seemed insufferably pleased with itself. Part of that was any tin-can's cheeky disdain for the heavier ships trailing in her wake, but there was more to it, this time. Indeed, the entire squadron had a new air of determination.

Much of it stemmed from the simple joy of stretching their legs. Once they'd handed off the freighters who'd lumbered them for so long, Honor's ships had made the run back from Casca well up into the eta band, and the sense of release had been even greater because they hadn't realized quite how heavy-footed they'd really felt on the outward leg.

But that explained only a part of her people's mood. The rest stemmed from the conferences she'd had with Alistair and Alice Truman—the conferences whose purpose she'd made certain were known to all of her ships' companies.

She'd been livid when Venizelos brought Ensign Wolcott into her cabin. Wolcott's experience had crystallized her determination in a way all the insults to *her* hadn't managed, and she'd launched a full-scale investigation aboard all three ships to see what else someone hadn't reported to her.

The response had been sobering. Few of her other female personnel had experienced anything quite so blatant, yet once she started asking questions dozens came forward, and she suspected—not without a sense of shame—that they'd been silent before for the same reasons as Wolcott. She hadn't had the heart to pin the ensign down, but her red-faced circumlocutions as she described what the Grayson had said about Honor had told their own tale. Honor *hoped* the ensign hadn't hesitated to speak up for fear her captain would blame the bearer of the news for its content, but whether Wolcott had been afraid of her or not, it was clear her own failure to fight back was at least partly to blame for the general silence. What she'd put up with had inhibited Wolcott (and others) from coming forward, either because they felt she'd proven she could endure worse than they had experienced (and expected them to do the same), or because they figured that if she wouldn't stand up for herself, she wouldn't for them.

Honor knew her own sense of failure was what had made her fury burn so bright, but she'd done an excellent—and deliberate—job of redirecting her anger since. However much of it was her fault, *none* of it would have happened if Graysons weren't bigoted, chauvinistic, xenophobic cretins. Intellectually, she knew there had to be at least a few Grayson officers who hadn't allowed their cultural biases free rein; emotionally, she no longer cared. Her people had put up with enough. *She*'d put up with enough. It was time to sort Grayson out, and she felt the fierce support of her crews behind her.

Nimitz made a soft sound of agreement from the back of her chair and she reached up to rub his head. He caught her thumb and worried it gently in needle-sharp fangs, and she smiled again, then leaned back and crossed her legs as DuMorne prepared to initiate translation.

"Now *that's* peculiar," Lieutenant Carstairs murmured. "I'm picking up three impeller signatures ahead of us, Captain, range about two-point-five light-seconds. Our vectors are convergent, and they look like LACs, but they don't match anything in my Grayson data profile."

"Oh?" Commander McKeon looked up. "Put it on my—" He broke off as Carstairs anticipated his command and transferred his data to the command chair's tactical repeater. McKeon didn't particularly like his tac officer, but despite a certain cold superciliousness, Carstairs was damned good.

"Thank you," he said, then frowned. Carstairs's ID had to be correct. The impeller drives were too small and weak to be anything except LACs, but what were they doing clear out here beyond the asteroid belt? And why weren't they saying anything? It would be another sixteen minutes before any transmission from Grayson could reach *Troubadour*, but the LACs were right next door, and their courses were converging sharply.

"Max?"

"Sir?"

"Any idea what these people are doing way out here?"

"No, Sir," Lieutenant Stromboli said promptly, "but I can tell you one weird thing. I've been running back my astro plot, and their drives weren't even on it until about forty seconds ago."

"Only forty seconds?" McKeon's frown deepened. LACs were very small radar targets, so it wasn't surprising *Troubadour* hadn't spotted them if their drives had been down. But the squadron's impeller signatures had to stick out like sore thumbs, even on Grayson sensors. If the LACs had wanted to rendezvous with them, why wait nine minutes to light off their own drives?

"Yes, Sir. See how low their base velocity is? They were sitting more or less at rest relative to the belt, then they got underway." A green line appeared on McKeon's plot. "See that jog right there?" A cursor blinked beside a sharp hairpin bend, and McKeon nodded. "They started out away from us under maximum accel, then changed their minds and altered course through more than a hundred seventy degrees *towards* us."

"Do you confirm that, Tactical?"

"Yes, Sir." Carstairs sounded a bit peeved with himself

for letting the astrogator get in with the information first. "Lighting off their impellers was what attracted my attention to them in the first place, Captain."

"Um." McKeon rubbed the tip of his nose, unconsciously emulating one of Honor's favorite thinking mannerisms. *Troubadour* was up to barely twenty-six hundred KPS, still building velocity from translation. The closing rate was a little higher, given the LACs' turn to meet her, but what were they up to?

"How do they differ from your profile, Tactical?"

"Almost across the board, Captain. Their drive strength is too high, and their radar's pulse rate frequency is nine percent low. Of course, we haven't seen everything Grayson has, Sir, and I don't have anything at all on a LAC class of this mass, much less details on its sensor suite."

"Well, we may not have seen them before, but LACs are intrasystemic," McKeon thought aloud, "so these have to be from Grayson. I wonder why they never mentioned them to us, though?" He shrugged slightly. "Com, ask Captain Harrington if she wants us to investigate."

Commander Isaiah Danville sat very still on *Bancroft*'s deathly silent bridge. He could feel his crew's fear, but it was overlaid by resignation and acceptance, and in a way, their very hopelessness might make them even more effective. Men who knew they were about to die were less likely to be betrayed into mistakes by the desire to live.

Danville wondered why God had chosen to kill them all this way. A man of the Faith didn't question God's Will, but it would have been comforting to know why He'd placed his small squadron square in the invaders' path. Anywhere else, and they could have lain low, impellers shut down. As it was, they were bound to be seen. And since it was impossible for them to survive anyway. . . .

"Range?" he asked softly.

"Coming down to six hundred thousand kilometers,

Sir. They'll enter our missile envelope in thirty-two seconds."

"Stand by," Danville almost murmured. "Don't engage until I give the word. We want them as close as they'll come."

Honor wrinkled her forehead. She had the LACs on her own sensors, and she was as puzzled by their presence as Alistair.

"Reaction, Andy?"

"They're only LACs, Ma'am," Venizelos replied. "It's not like they were big nasties, but I've been running the military download Grayson gave us. They're not in it, and I'd feel better if they were."

"Me, too." Honor nibbled the inside of her lip. There might be any number of reasons Grayson had inadvertently omitted a single light warship class from its download, but she was darned if she could think of one for LACs to be swanning around this far out-system. "Hail them, Com."

"Aye, aye, Ma'am. Hailing now." Lieutenant Metzinger transmitted the hail, then sat back. Four seconds passed. Five. Then ten, and she shrugged.

"No response, Ma'am."

"They're hailing us, Captain." *Bancroft*'s communications officer sounded calmer than Danville knew he could possibly be. "Their hail confirms Tactical's ID. Shall I respond?"

"No." Danville's lips thinned. So it *was* the Manticore escort force and its bitch of a commander. There was a certain satisfaction in that. If God had decided it was time for his men to die, what better way could they to do so than striking at a woman who blasphemed against His Will by assuming a man's role?

"They may be suspicious if we don't reply, Sir." His exec's voice was pitched too low for anyone else to hear. "Maybe we should try to bluff them?"

"No," Danville replied just as quietly. "We didn't recover enough of their secure codes to avoid giving ourselves away. Better to leave them a puzzle they can't quite figure out than give them a clear clue."

The exec nodded, and Danville kept his eyes on the plot. The Manticorans had much more range than he did, and their defenses were far better . . . yet none of those defenses were active, and they were already inside the extreme limit of his powered missile envelope. The temptation to fire was great, but he thrust it aside once more, knowing he must wait for the shortest possible flight time. And they'd been out of the system too long to know what was happening, he told himself. No, they'd try to talk to him again, try to figure out why he wasn't responding, and every second they delayed brought them thirty-three hundred kilometers closer to his missiles.

"Get me Commander McKeon," Honor said with a frown, and Alistair McKeon appeared on her com screen.

"I don't know what's going on," she told him without preamble, "but you'd better take a look."

"Yes, Ma'am. It's probably just some kind of communications failure. They're still accelerating towards us, so they must want to make contact."

"It'd take something pretty drastic to affect communications aboard all three of them. Hail them again when you reach one light-second."

"Aye, aye, Ma'am."

"The destroyer is hailing us, Sir."

The com officer sounded harsh and strained this time, and Danville didn't blame him. *Troubadour* had cracked on a few more MPS^2 of acceleration directly towards *Bancroft*, and the range was down to a single light-second. That was far closer than he'd dared hope God would let them come. In fact, the destroyer was inside energy range now, still without a sign he suspected a thing. Even the cruisers were now inside the LACs' effective missile envelope.

"Stand by, Lieutenant Early." He spoke very formally,

though his own voice was less calm than he might have wished. "We'll go for the destroyer with our lasers. Lay your missiles on the cruisers."

His tactical officer passed orders over the squadron net, and Danville bit his lip. *Come a little closer*, he told the destroyer. *Just a little. Bring the flight time to your cruisers down just a little more . . .* damn *you.*

"This is ridiculous," McKeon muttered. The LACs were less than a light-second away and still not saying a word! Unless he wanted to assume Grayson had suffered some sort of fleet-wide communications failure, these turkeys had to be up to something. But what? If this was some sort of oddball exercise, he was less than amused by it.

"All right, Tactical," he said finally. "If they want to play games, let's play back. Get me a hull map off their lead unit."

"Aye, aye, Sir!" There was a grin in Carstairs's normally cold voice, and McKeon's lips twitched as he heard it. The radar pulse it would take to map a ship's hull at this range would practically melt the LACs' receivers, and most navies would understand the message he was about to send as well as Carstairs did—it was a galaxy-wide way of shouting "Hey, stupid!" at someone. Of course, these people had been isolated for so long they might not realize how rude *Troubadour* was being . . . but he could hope.

"What the—?!" Early gasped, and Danville winced as a threat receiver squealed in raucous warning.

"*Engage!*" he snapped.

HMS *Troubadour* had no warning at all. Lasers are light-speed weapons; by the time your sensors realize someone has fired them at you, they've already hit you.

Each of the Masadan LACs mounted a single laser, and if *Troubadour*'s sidewalls had been up, the crude, relatively low-powered weapons would have been harmless. But her sidewalls weren't up, and Commander

McKeon's face went whiter than bone as energy fire smashed into his ship's starboard bow. Plating shattered, damage and collision alarms shrieked, and *Troubadour* lurched as the kinetic energy bled into her hull.

"My God, they've *fired* on us!" Carstairs sounded more outraged than frightened, but McKeon had no time to worry about his tac officer's sensitivities.

"Hard skew port!" he snapped.

The helmsman was as startled as anyone else, but twenty years of trained reflex took charge. He snapped the ship up on her port side, simultaneously slewing her bow around to jerk the throat of her impeller wedge away from the enemy, even before he acknowledged the order. It was well he did, for the next salvo of lasers struck harmlessly against the belly of *Troubadour's* wedge just as her general quarters alarm began to scream.

An icicle of relief stabbed through McKeon as his wedge intercepted the incoming fire, but lurid damage and pressure loss signals flashed, and none of his people had been expecting a thing. None of them had been vac-suited, and that meant some of them were dead. He prayed there weren't too many of them, yet even that was almost an afterthought, for he'd already seen the missiles streaming past *Troubadour* towards the cruisers astern of her.

"Skipper! Those LACs have *fired* on *Troubadour!*" Lieutenant Cardones blurted. And then— "Missiles incoming! Impact in four-five seconds—mark!"

Honor's head whipped up in pure disbelief. *Fired?* That was insane!

"Point defense free! Sound general quarters!"

Ensign Wolcott stabbed the GQ button at Cardones's elbow. The tac officer was too busy; he'd anticipated his captain's orders, and his hands were already flying across his panel.

"Zulu-Two, Chief Killian!" Honor snapped.

"Aye, aye, Ma'am. Executing Zulu-Two."

Killian sounded almost detached, not with professional calm, but as if the real shock hadn't hit him yet,

yet his response was almost as quick as Cardones's. *Fearless* squirmed into evasive action—not that she had the base velocity to make it very effective—and Honor heard the pop of pierced upholstery as Nimitz's claws sank into the back of her chair.

A distant corner of her mind remembered a hesitant puppy of a junior-grade lieutenant, but there was no sign of that uncertain young officer today. Rafael Cardones had his priorities exactly right, and the green standby light of the point defense lasers blinked to crimson even before he brought the sidewalls up. There was no time for counter missiles—only the lasers had the response time, and even they had it only under computer command.

The sidewall generators began spinning up just as the lasers opened fire. An incoming missile vanished, then another and another as the computers worked their way methodically through their assigned threat values. More missiles ripped apart as *Apollo*'s point defense opened up on the ones speeding towards her, and Honor gripped the arms of her command chair while Nimitz's tail curled protectively about her throat.

She'd screwed up. She couldn't conceive of any reason for Grayson to be doing this, but she'd *let* them do it. Dear God, if they'd held their fire only another twenty seconds, not even Rafe Cardones' reactions could have saved her ship! Three wretched little LACs from a planet so primitive it didn't even have molycircs would have *annihilated* her entire squadron!

But they hadn't held their fire, and her thundering pulse slowed. The Grayson missiles' low acceleration not only lengthened their flight times but made them easier targets, and they didn't have laser heads. They needed direct hits, and they weren't going to get them. Not against Rafe Cardones.

She looked down again, and her lips drew back. Many of her people must still be rushing to their stations, most of her weapon crews must still be understrength, but her energy weapons flashed uniform crimson readiness.

"Mr. Cardones," she said harshly, "you are free to engage."

Commander Danville bit off a savage curse. He hadn't been present for Jericho, and he hadn't really believed the reports of how a single Manticoran ship had killed two light cruisers and a pair of destroyers before the rest of the Fleet took him down. Now he knew he should have. He'd gotten two clean hits on *Troubadour*, and a drop in impeller strength indicated he'd gotten a piece of the destroyer's drive, yet he'd whipped over faster than a Masadan ferret to hide his vulnerable flanks.

The one ship he should have been guaranteed to nail had escaped him, but even the speed of *Troubadour's* response paled beside that of the cruisers' point defense. *Bancroft* and his brothers massed barely nine thousand tons each. That was far too small to mount worthwhile internal magazines, so they carried their missiles in single-shot box launchers. It reduced the total number they could stow only slightly and let them throw extremely heavy broadsides for their size. Only once per launcher, perhaps, but LACs were eggshells armed with sledgehammers. LAC-versus-LAC engagements tended to end in orgies of mutual destruction; against regular warships, the best a LAC could realistically hope for was to get his missiles off before he was wiped from the universe.

But Danville's squadron had been given every possible edge. They'd sent thirty-nine missiles streaking towards *Fearless* and *Apollo* with the advantage of total surprise against defenses that weren't even active—surely *one* of them should have gotten through!

But it hadn't.

He watched the last missile of his first salvo die a thousand kilometers short of the light cruiser, and threat signals warbled afresh as targeting systems locked onto his tiny ships. *Bancroft* finished his frantic roll, bringing his unfired broadside to bear, and Lieutenant Early sent a fresh salvo charging towards their enemies, and it was useless. Useless.

God was going to let them all die for *nothing*.

Rafe Cardones' point defense was fully on line now. He didn't bother with ECM—the range was too short, and according to his data base, Grayson missiles were almost too stupid to fool, anyway. His counter missiles went out almost as the enemy launched, but he left them to Ensign Wolcott. He had other things on his mind.

His heavy launchers were still coming on line as their crews closed up, but his energy weapons were ready. Dancing fingers locked in the targeting schedule, and a single, big key at the center of his panel flashed, accepting the commands.

He drove it flat.

Nothing at all happened for one endless moment. Then Chief Killian's maneuvers swung *Fearless*'s starboard side towards the LACs. It was only for an instant . . . but an instant was all the waiting computers needed.

A deadly flicker sparkled down the cruiser's armored flank, heavy energy mounts firing like the breath of God, and the range was little more than a quarter-million kilometers. No Grayson-built sidewalls could resist that fury at such short range. They did their best, but the beams stabbed through them as if they were paper, and each of those LACs was the target of two lasers and a graser, each vastly more powerful than they themselves mounted.

Atmosphere spumed out in a shower of debris as HMS *Fearless* blew *Bancroft* and her consorts into very tiny pieces.

• CHAPTER SIXTEEN

"How bad is it, Alistair?"

"Bad enough, Ma'am." Alistair McKeon's face was grim. "We've lost Missile Two and Radar Three. That leaves point defense wide open on the starboard beam. The same hit carried through into the forward impellers—Alpha Four's gone, and so is Beta Eight. The second hit came in right on Frame Twenty and carried clear back through sickbay. It took out the master control runs to Laser Three and Missile Four and breached Magazine Two. The magazine's a total write-off; Laser Three and Missile Four are on line in local control, and we're repressurizing and rigging new runs to them now, but we lost thirty-one people, including Dr. McFee and two sick berth attendants, and we've got wounded."

His voice was harsh with pain, and Honor's eyes were dark as she nodded, but for all that, they both knew *Troubadour* had been incredibly lucky. The loss of one of her forward missile tubes and an entire magazine had hurt her offensive capability, and Radar Three's destruction left a dangerous chink in her anti-missile defenses. But her combat power was far less impaired than it might have been, and the casualties could have been much, much worse. She'd been lamed, and until the alpha node was replaced she couldn't generate a forward Warshawski sail, but she could still maneuver and fight.

"I came in too fat and stupid," McKeon went on bitterly. "If I'd only had my sidewalls up, maybe—"

"Not your fault," Honor interrupted. "We didn't have any reason to expect Grayson to open fire on us, and even if we had, it was *my* responsibility to go to a higher readiness state."

McKeon's lips tightened, but he said no more, and Honor was glad. Whatever was happening, one thing they didn't need was for both of them to blame themselves for it.

"I'll have Fritz Montoya over there in five minutes," Honor went on when she was certain he'd dropped it. "We'll transfer your wounded to our sickbay once he's sure they're stabilized."

"Thank you, Ma'am." There was less self-blame in McKeon's voice, but no less anger.

"But why in God's name did they fire?" Alice Truman asked from her quadrant of the split screen, green eyes baffled as she voiced the question for them all. "It's crazy!"

"Agreed." Honor leaned back, her own eyes hard, but Alice was right. Even if negotiations had broken down completely, the Graysons must be insane to fire on her. They were already worried over the Masadans—surely they must realize what the Fleet would do to them for this!

"It seems crazy to me, too," she went on after a moment, her voice grim, "but as of right now, this squadron is on a war footing. I intend to enter attack range of Grayson and demand an explanation and the stand-down of their fleet. I also intend to demand to speak to our people planet-side. If any of my demands is refused, or if our delegation has been harmed in any way, we will engage and destroy the Grayson Navy. Is that understood?"

Her subordinates nodded.

"Commander Truman, your ship will take point. Commander McKeon, I want you tucked in astern. Stay tight and tie into *Fearless*'s radar to cover the gap in your own coverage. Clear?"

"Yes, Ma'am," her captains replied in unison.

"Very well, then, people. Let's be about it."

"Captain? I have a transmission from Grayson," Lieutenant Metzinger said, and the tension on *Fearless*'s bridge redoubled. Barely five minutes had passed since the ambush, and unless the Graysons were stupid as well as crazy, they couldn't possibly expect to talk their way out of this with a message sent before their ships had even opened fire!

But Metzinger wasn't finished.

"It's from Ambassador Langtry," she added, and Honor's eyebrows rose.

"From Sir Anthony?"

"Yes, Ma'am."

"Put it on my screen."

Honor felt a surge of relief as Sir Anthony's face appeared before her, for the wall of his embassy office was clearly visible behind him, and Reginald Houseman stood beside the ambassador's chair. She'd been afraid the entire diplomatic staff was in Grayson custody; if they were still in the safety of their own embassy, the situation might not be totally out of control after all. But then the ambassador's grim, almost frightened expression registered. And where was Admiral Courvosier?

"Captain Harrington." The ambassador's voice was taut. "Grayson Command Central has just picked up a hyper footprint which I assume—hope—is your squadron. Be advised Masadan warships are patrolling the Yeltsin System." Honor stiffened. Could it be those LACs *hadn't* been Grayson ships? Only, if they weren't, then how had they gotten here, and why had they—?

But the prerecorded message was still playing, and the ambassador's next words shattered her train of thought like a hammer on crystal.

"Assume any ship encountered is hostile, Captain, and be advised there are at least two—I repeat, at least *two*—modern warships in the Masadan order of battle. Our best estimate is that they're a pair of cruisers, probably Haven-built." The ambassador swallowed, but he'd been a highly decorated Marine officer, and he carried through grimly. "No one realized the Masadans had them, and Admiral Yanakov and Admiral Courvosier took the Grayson fleet out to engage the enemy four days ago. I'm . . . afraid *Madrigal* and *Austin Grayson* were lost with all hands—including Admirals Courvosier and Yanakov."

Every drop of blood drained from Honor's face. No! The Admiral *couldn't* be dead—not the *Admiral!*

"We're in serious trouble down here, Captain," Langtry's recorded voice went on. "I don't know why they've held off this long, but nothing Grayson has left can possibly stop them. Please advise me of your intentions as soon as possible. Langtry clear."

The screen blanked, and she stared at it, frozen in her command chair. It was a lie. A cruel, vicious lie! The Admiral was alive. He was *alive*, damn it! He wouldn't die. He *couldn't* die—he wouldn't *do* that to her!

But Ambassador Langtry had no reason to lie.

She closed her eyes, feeling Nimitz at her shoulder, and remembered Courvosier as she'd left him. Remembered that impish face, the twinkle in those blue eyes. And behind those newer memories were others, twenty-seven *years* of memories, each cutting more deeply and cruelly than the last, as she realized at last—when it was too late—that she'd never told him she loved him.

And behind the loss, honing the agony, was her guilt. She'd run out on him. He'd wanted her to stay and let her go only because she insisted, and because *Fearless* hadn't been there—because *she* hadn't been there—he'd taken a single destroyer into battle and died.

It was her fault. He'd needed her, and she hadn't been there . . . and that had killed him. *She'd* killed him, as surely as if she'd sent a pulser dart through his brain with her own hand.

Silence enfolded *Fearless*'s bridge crew as all eyes turned to the woman in the captain's chair. Her face was stunned as even the total surprise of the LACs' attack had not left it, and the light had gone out of her treecat's eyes. He crouched on her chair back, tail tucked in tight, prick ears flat, and the soft, heartrending keen of his lament was the only sound as tears rolled silently down her cheeks.

"Orders, Captain?" Andreas Venizelos broke the

crew's silence at last, and more than one person flinched as his quiet voice intruded upon their captain's grief.

Honor's nostrils flared. The sound of her indrawn breath was harsh, and the heel of her hand scrubbed angrily, brutally, at her wet face as she squared her shoulders.

"Record for transmission, Lieutenant Metzinger," she said in a hammered-iron voice none of them had ever heard, and the communications officer swallowed.

"Recording, Ma'am," she said softly.

"Ambassador Langtry," Honor said in that same, deadly voice. "Your message is received and understood. Be advised that my squadron has already been engaged by and destroyed three LACs I now presume to have been Masadan. We've suffered casualties and damage, but my combat power is unimpaired."

She inhaled again, feeling her officers' and ratings' eyes on her.

"I will continue to Grayson at my best speed. Expect my arrival in Grayson orbit in—" she checked her astrogation readout "—approximately four hours twenty-eight minutes from now."

She stared into the pickup, and the corner of her mouth twitched. There was steel in her brown eyes, smoking from anger's forge and tempered by grief and guilt, and her voice was colder than space.

"Until I have complete information, it will be impossible to formulate detailed plans, but you may inform the Grayson government that I intend to defend this system in accordance with Admiral Courvosier's apparent intentions. Please have a complete background brief waiting for me. In particular, I require an immediate assessment of Grayson's remaining military capabilities and assignment of a liaison officer to my squadron. I will meet with you and the senior Grayson military officer in the Embassy within ten minutes of entering Grayson orbit. Harrington clear."

She sat back, her strong-boned face unyielding, and her own determination filled her bridge crew. They knew as well as she that the entire Grayson Navy, even if it had suffered no losses at all, would have been useless against the weight of metal she'd just committed them to face. The odds were very good that some of them, or some of their friends on the other ships of the squadron, were going to die, and none of them were eager for death. But other friends had already died, and they themselves had been attacked.

None of Honor's other officers had been Admiral Courvosier's protégée, but many had been his students, and he'd been one of the most respected officers in their service even to those who'd never known him personally. If they could get a piece of the people who'd killed him, they wanted it.

"On the chip, Captain," Lieutenant Metzinger said.

"Send it. Then set up another conference link with *Apollo* and *Troubadour*. Make certain Commander Truman and Commander McKeon have copies of Sir Anthony's transmission and tie their coms to my briefing room terminal."

"Aye, aye, Ma'am," Metzinger said, and Honor stood. She looked across the bridge at Andreas Venizelos as she started for the briefing room hatch.

"Mr. DuMorne, you have the watch. Andy, come with me." Her voice was still hard, her face frozen. Grief and guilt hammered at the back of her brain, but she refused to listen to them. There would be time enough to face those things after the killing.

"Aye, aye, Ma'am. I have the watch," Lieutenant Commander DuMorne said quietly to her back as the hatch opened before her.

She never heard him at all.

• CHAPTER SEVENTEEN

Commander Manning paused outside the briefing room and drew a deep breath.

Manning liked Captain Yu. In a service where too many senior officers came from Legislaturist families, Yu was that rarest of birds: a self-made man. It couldn't have been easy for him, but somehow the Captain had won his way to the very brink of flag rank without forgetting what he himself had been through on the way up. He treated his officers firmly but with respect, even warmth, and he never forgot those who served him well. Thomas Theisman commanded *Principality* because he'd served with Captain Yu before and Yu had wanted him for the slot, and Manning had been handpicked as *Thunder*'s exec for the same reasons. That sort of treatment earned the Captain a remarkable degree of personal loyalty and devotion, but he was only human. He had his bad days, and when a CO—*any* CO—was out of sorts, his subordinates trod warily.

And if the Captain had ever had reason to feel out of sorts, now was certainly the time, Manning thought as he pressed the admittance button.

"Yes?" The voice over the intercom was as courteous as ever, but it held a dangerous, flat undertone for ears which knew it well.

"Commander Manning, Sir."

The hatch opened. Manning stepped across the sill and braced to attention, and some instinct told him to do it Havenite style.

"You wanted to see me, Sir?"

"Yes. Sit down, George."

Yu pointed to a chair, and the commander relaxed just a tad at the use of his first name.

"What's the status of Tractor Five?"

"Engineering says another ten or twelve hours, Sir."
Yu's face tightened, and Manning tried to keep any
defensiveness out of his voice. "The components were
never intended for this sort of continual power level,
Captain. They have to strip it clear down to the flux
core to make replacements."

"God*damn* it." Yu ran a hand through his hair in a
harried gesture he never let a Masadan see, and then
his free hand suddenly slammed the table top.

Manning managed not to flinch. It wasn't like the
Captain to carry on, but these Masadans were enough
to try the patience of a saint. The cliché was less amusing than it might have been, but the fact that the
Captain was allowing himself to use the sort of language
he hadn't let himself use since arriving here was a fair
indication of how far he'd been pushed.

Yu smashed the table again, then sat back in his chair
with a groan.

"They're idiots, George. Fucking *idiots!* We could
wipe out everything Grayson has left in an hour—in
fifteen *minutes!*—and they won't let us do it!"

"Yes, Sir," Manning said softly, and Yu shoved himself
up to stalk back and forth across the briefing room like
a caged tiger.

"If anyone back home had told me there were people
like this anywhere in the galaxy, I'd have called him a
liar to his face," Yu growled. "We've got Grayson by the
balls, and all they can see is how bad *they* got hurt!
Goddamn it, people *get* hurt in wars! And just because
Madrigal chewed the hell out of their piss-ant navy,
they're shitting their drawers like they were up against
the Manticoran Home Fleet!"

This time Manning was tactfully silent. Anything he
said could only make it worse at this point.

No one, Captain Yu included, had been prepared for
just how good Manticoran anti-missile systems had
turned out to be. They'd known the RMN's electronic
warfare capability was better than theirs, and they'd
assumed a certain margin of superiority for their other

systems as well, but the speed and accuracy of *Madrigal's* point defense had shocked all of them. It had turned what should have been a complete kill into something far less, and if the destroyer's defenses hadn't been overextended by her efforts to protect her consorts, she probably would have gotten out completely undamaged.

It would have been different in a sustained engagement, when their own computers could have gotten a read on *Madrigal's* responses and they could have shifted their firing patterns and penaid settings until they found a way through them. But they'd only had one shot each, and the destroyer had knocked down entirely too many of their missiles.

That had smarted badly enough for the "immigrants" in *Thunder's* crew—it had been their hardware that showed up so poorly, after all—but it had more than smarted for the Masadans. Sword Simonds had been livid as *Madrigal* and the two surviving Graysons raced out of their missile envelope. Manning was still astonished the Captain had managed to hang onto his temper as the Sword ranted and railed at him, and despite his outward calm, Manning knew he'd been as close to murder as the exec had ever seen him when Simonds refused to order Franks to bypass *Madrigal* and pursue the Grayson survivors.

Simonds had practically danced with rage as he rejected Yu's suggestion. The extent to which *Madrigal* had degraded the ambush had not only infuriated but frightened him, and he'd known perfectly well that at least some of Franks' ships would have been exposed to her fire, however widely they dispersed, if the squadron spread out to over-fly her.

Well, of course they would have been, but the Sword's response to the threat had proven once and for all that he was no tactician. If his ships had dispersed, he might have had to write off one or two cruisers to *Madrigal's* missiles, but the others would have been outside the destroyer's effective engagement range. She simply wouldn't have had the reach to hit that many targets. But he'd insisted on backing Franks' decision to go in together for mutual support—and paid the price hesitant tactics almost always exacted. The Masadan ships had actually *decelerated* to meet *Madrigal* in an effort to bring their own weapons into effective range and keep them there!

It had been like a mob armed with clubs charging a man with a pulser. *Madrigal's* missiles had blown the cruisers *Samson* and *Noah* and the destroyer *Throne* right out of space as they closed, and then the Masadans entered her energy range and it only got worse. The cruiser *David* had survived, but she was little more than a hulk, and the destroyers *Cherubim* and *Seraphim* had been crippled before they ever got into *their* energy range.

Of course, the clubs had had their own turn after that. Crude as Masadan energy weapons were, there'd simply been too many of them for her, and they'd battered her to bits. But even after she'd been mortally wounded, *Madrigal* had set her teeth in the destroyers *Archangel* and *Angel*. She'd pounded them until she didn't have a single weapon left, and she'd taken *Archangel* with her. Of the entire squadron which had closed with her, only the cruiser *Solomon* and the destroyer *Dominion* remained combat effective . . . and, of course, Franks' decision to slow for the suicidal engagement meant the surviving Graysons had escaped.

It shouldn't have mattered. If nothing else, what *Madrigal* had done should have made Simonds even more confident. If a *destroyer* could wreak that kind of carnage, what did he think *Thunder* could do?!

"Do you know what that insufferable little prick said to me?" Yu whirled to face his exec, one finger pointed like a pistol, and his eyes blazed. "He told me—told *me*, damn him!—that if I hadn't *lied* to him about my ship's capabilities, he *might* be more inclined to listen to me now!" A snarl quivered in the Captain's throat. "What the *fuck* does he expect is going to happen when his frigging '*admirals*' have their heads so far up their asses they have to pipe in air through their navels?!"

Manning maintained his silence and concentrated on looking properly sympathetic, and Yu's lips worked as if he wanted to spit on the decksole. Then his shoulders slumped, and he sank back into his chair.

"God, I wish the Staff had found someone else to dump this on!" he sighed, but the fury had left his voice. Manning understood. The Captain had needed to work it out of his system, and for that he had to yell at one of his own.

"Well," Yu said finally, "if they insist on being stupid, I suppose there's nothing we can do but try to minimize the consequences. There are times I could just about kill Valentine, but if this weren't so completely unnecessary, I might almost admire the cleverness of it. I don't think anyone else ever even considered *towing* LACs through hyper space."

"Yes, Sir. On the other hand, they couldn't have done it with their own tractors or hyper generators. I guess by the time you've got the technical ability, you've figured out how to build good enough ships that you don't need to use it."

"Um." Yu inhaled deeply and closed his eyes for a moment. Stupid as he thought the whole idea was, he also knew that only his chief engineer's suggestion had kept the Masadans going at all.

They'd flatly refused to attack Grayson with their remaining combat strength in Yeltsin. As near as Yu could figure out, they were afraid Manticore might have slipped some sort of superweapon to the Graysons. That was the stupidest idea they'd had yet, but perhaps it shouldn't be so easy to blame them for it. They'd never seen a modern warship in action before, and what *Madrigal* had done to their antiquated fleet terrified them. Intellectually, they had to know *Thunder* and *Principality* were many times as powerful as *Madrigal* had been, but they'd never seen "their" two modern ships in action. Their capabilities weren't quite real to them . . . and Yu's credibility had been damaged by *Madrigal's* escape from the ambush, anyway.

For one whole day, Simonds had been adamant about

the need to suspend all operations and seek a negotiated settlement. Yu didn't think Masada had a hope in hell of pulling *that* off after their sneak attack and *Madrigal's* destruction, but the Sword had dug his heels in and insisted he simply didn't have the tonnage in Yeltsin to continue.

That was when Commander Valentine made his suggestion, and Yu didn't know whether to strangle his engineer or kiss him. It had wasted three days already, and Tractor Five's breakdown was going to stretch that still further, but it had gotten Simonds to agree, if only hesitantly, to press forward.

Valentine had pointed out that both *Thunder* and *Principality* had far more powerful hyper generators than any Masadan starship. In fact, their generators were powerful enough to extend their translation fields over six kilometers beyond their own hulls if he redlined them. That meant that if they translated from rest, they could take anything within six kilometers with them when they did. And *that* meant that if Masadan LACs clustered closely enough around them, they could boost the lighter vessels into hyper space.

Normally, that would have been little more than an interesting parlor trick, but Valentine had taken the entire idea one stage further. No LAC crew could survive the sort of acceleration ships routinely pulled in hyper for the simple reason that their inertial compensator would pack up the instant they tried it. But if they took the entire crew off and removed or secured all loose gear, Valentine suggested, there was no reason the ships *themselves* couldn't take the acceleration on the end of a tractor beam.

Yu had thought he was out of his mind, but the engineer had pulled up the numbers on his terminal and demonstrated the theoretical possibility. Simonds had jumped at it, and to Yu's considerable surprise, it had worked.

So far, they'd lost only two of the tiny ships. The LACs were just big enough it took three tractors to zone each of them, and one tractor had lost lock during acceleration. That LAC had simply snapped in half; the second had survived the journey only to have its crew find a ragged, three-meter hole torn half the length of their ship where a twelve-ton pressure tank had come adrift and crashed aft like an ungainly cannonball.

Of course, the towing ships had been crowded almost beyond endurance by packing in the crews who couldn't survive aboard their own ships and, as Manning had said, the strain on their tractors had been enormous. But it had worked—and Yu had found *Thunder* and *Principality* playing tugboat back and forth between Endicott and Yeltsin's Star.

It was a short hop, barely twelve hours either way for a modern warship, even towing LACs behind her, but there were only two vessels capable of pulling it off, and they could tow only three LACs at a time: two behind *Thunder* and one behind *Principality*. They simply didn't have enough tractors to move more than that. In three days, they'd transferred eighteen of Masada's twenty LACs to Yeltsin—well, sixteen, discounting the two they'd lost. This final trip by *Thunder* would move the last of them, and if he couldn't see that their firepower afforded any particular tactical advantage, it seemed to have bolstered the Masadans' confidence, so perhaps it hadn't been an entire waste.

"I need to talk to the Ambassador," he said suddenly, and Manning's eyebrows rose at the apparent *non sequitur*. "About getting out from under Simonds' thumb," Yu clarified. "I know we have to maintain the fiction that this is a purely Masadan operation, but if I can give them a good, hard push just *once*, we can tie this whole thing up in a couple of hours."

"Yes, Sir." Manning felt oddly moved by his captain's openness. It wasn't the sort of thing one normally encountered in the People's Navy.

"Maybe repairing Tractor Five will give me enough time ground-side," Yu mused. "It'll have to be face-to-face; I don't trust our com links."

Actually, Manning knew, the Captain didn't trust his

com *officer*, since that was one of the slots now filled by a Masadan.

"I understand, Sir."

"Good." Yu rubbed his face, then straightened. "Sorry I screamed at you, George. You were just handy."

"That's what execs are for, Sir," Manning grinned, not adding that few other captains would have apologized for using an exec for one of his designed functions.

"Yeah, maybe." Yu managed a smile. "And at least this will be the *last* tow trip."

"Yes, Sir. And Commander Theisman will keep an eye on things in Yeltsin till we get back."

"Better him than that asshole Franks," Yu growled.

Sword of the Faithful Matthew Simonds knocked on the door and walked through it into the palatially furnished room. His brother, Chief Elder Thomas Simonds of the Faithful of the Church of Humanity Unchained, looked up, and his wizened face was not encouraging. Senior Elder Huggins was seated beside Thomas, and he looked even less encouraging.

Deacon Ronald Sands sat opposite Huggins. Sands was one of the youngest men ever to attain the rank of deacon, and his face was much less thunderous than his seniors'. Part of that was probably because he was so junior to them, but Sword Simonds suspected most of it was because Masada's spy master was smarter than either of them and knew it.

Cloth rustled, and he turned his head to see his brother's junior wife. He couldn't recall her name, and she wore the traditional form-shrouding dress of a Masadan woman, but her face was unveiled, and the Sword suppressed a grin as he suddenly realized that at least a portion of Huggins' obvious anger was directed at that shocking breach of propriety. Thomas had always been vain about his virility, and it had pandered to his *amour propre* to take a wife barely eighteen T-years of age. He already had six others, and Matthew doubted he still had the endurance to mount any of them, but Thomas had taken to flaunting his new prize's beauty whenever his associates met in his home.

The practice drove Huggins berserk—which was one reason Thomas did it. Had the wench belonged to anyone else, the fire-and-brimstone elder would have sent her to the post for a public flogging prefaced by a few pointed words on the laxity of the man who allowed his wife to behave in such ungodly fashion. If the man in question had been unimportant enough, he might even have called for his stoning. As it was, he had to pretend he hadn't noticed.

The Sword advanced across the carpet, ignoring her presence, and sat in the chair at the foot of the long table. The appearance of a tribunal, with himself in the role of the accused, was not, he was certain, a coincidence.

"So you're here." Thomas' voice was creaky with age, for he was the eldest child of Tobias Simonds' first wife, while Matthew was the second son of their father's fourth wife.

"Of course I am." Matthew was well aware of the danger in which he stood, but if he showed any consciousness of his vulnerability his enemies would close in like a rathound pack pulling down a Masadan antelope.

"I'm gratified to see you can follow at least *some* orders," Huggins snapped. The rancorous elder considered himself the Sword's main competition for the Chief Elder's chair, and Matthew turned to him, ready to strike back, but Thomas' raised hand had already rebuked the elder. So. At least his brother wasn't yet ready to cut him totally adrift.

"Peace, Brother," the Chief Elder said to Huggins. "We are all about God's Work, here. Let there be no recriminations."

His wife moved silently about the table, refilling their glasses, then vanished as a jerk of his head banished her back to the women's quarters. Huggins seemed to relax just a bit as she disappeared, and he forced a smile.

"I stand rebuked, Chief Elder. Forgive me, Sword

Simonds. Our situation is enough to try even Saint Austin's Faith."

"Indeed it is, Elder Huggins," the Sword said, with just as much false graciousness as Huggins, "and I can't deny that, as commander of our military, the responsibility for straightening that situation out is mine."

"Perhaps so," his brother said impatiently, "but it was no more of your making than ours—except, perhaps, in that you supported that infidel's plans." The Chief Elder's jaw worked, and his head seemed to squat lower on his shoulders.

"In fairness to Sword Simonds," Sands put in in the diffident tone he always assumed before his superiors, "Yu's arguments were convincing. And according to my sources, they were generally sincere, as well. His motives were his own, of course, but he truly believed he had the capabilities he claimed."

Huggins snorted, but no one disputed Sands. The Masadan theocracy had gone to great lengths to deny its "ally" any participation in its own covert activities, and everyone in this room knew how extensive Sands's network was.

"Nonetheless, we're in serious trouble because we listened to him." The Chief Elder gave his brother a sharp glance. "Do you think he's right about his ability to destroy what's left of the Apostate fleet?"

"Of course he is," the Sword said. "He overestimated Jericho's initial effectiveness, but my own people in his tactical section assure me his fundamental assessments are correct. If a single destroyer could do so much damage to *our* fleet, *Thunder* and *Principality* together could make mincemeat of the Apostate."

Matthew was aware that Huggins no longer trusted Yu—or anyone who agreed with him, for that matter—a millimeter. Yet what he'd just said was self-evidently true . . . and he'd avoided mentioning what those same people of his in Yu's tactical section had had to say about his own decision to support Franks's tactics in Yeltsin. He hadn't been too happy to hear it himself, but if he punished them for it, they would almost certainly start telling him what he wanted to hear, not what they truly thought.

"Deacon Sands? Do you agree?"

"I'm not a military man, Chief Elder, but, yes. Our own sources had already indicated that Manticoran systems are better than those of Haven, but their margin of superiority is vastly less than *Thunder*'s superiority to anything the Apostate have."

"So we can let him proceed if we must?" the Chief Elder pressed.

"I don't see any option but to let him if Maccabeus fails," Sands said unflinchingly. "In that event, only a military solution can save us. And with all due respect, time is running out. Maccabeus wasn't able to tell us if the Manticoran escort was returning, but we must assume it will be back within days. One way or the other, we must control both planets by that time."

"But Maccabeus is our best hope." Huggins shot a venomous glance at the Sword. "Your operations were supposed to support him, Sword Simonds. They were supposed to be a *pretext*, not a serious attempt at conquest!"

"With all respect, Elder Huggins," Matthew began hotly, "that—"

"Peace, Brothers!" The Chief Elder rapped a bony knuckle on the table and glared at them both until they sank back into their chairs, then turned his basilisk gaze on Huggins. "We're all aware of what was supposed to happen, Brother. Unfortunately, we couldn't exactly tell the Havenites that, nor could we proceed without their support in case Maccabeus failed. God has not yet decided our efforts merit His Blessing, but neither has He condemned us to failure. There are two strings to our bow, and neither has snapped yet."

Huggins glowered for a moment, then bobbed his head stiffly. This time he didn't even pretend to apologize to the Sword.

"Very well." Thomas turned back to his brother. "How much longer can you stall direct military action without arousing Haven's suspicions?"

"No more than another thirty or forty hours. *Thunder's* tractor damage buys us a little time, but once all of our LACs are in Yeltsin, we'll either have to move or admit we have no intention of doing so."

"And your last contact with Maccabeus?"

"*Cherubim* lagged far enough behind on our fourth strike to speak with his courier. At that time, Maccabeus believed there was still too much popular support for the current regime, despite our attacks. We've been unable to contact him since, of course, but he indicated that he was prepared to move if public morale began to crack, and Jericho must have weakened it further."

"Do you concur, Deacon Sands?"

"I do. Of course, we can't know how *much* it's weakened. Our own losses and the fact that any of their ships escaped may have an offsetting effect. On the other hand, they now know that we have at least some modern vessels, and the Apostate media has no Synod of Censors. We can assume, I think, that at least some accounts of the battle—and the odds they face—have found their way into the planetary news net."

"Does Maccabeus know what strength we have?" Huggins demanded.

"No," Sands said. "He and Jericho were completely compartmentalized for operational security. Given his position under the current regime, however, he must know that what we have outclasses anything in the Apostate navy."

"That's true," Elder Simonds mused, then inhaled deeply. "Very well, Brothers, I think we have reached our moment of decision. Maccabeus remains our best hope. If he can secure control of Grayson by domestic means, we'll be in a far better position to stave off further Manticoran intervention. No doubt they'll demand steep reparations, and I am prepared even to bend my neck to publicly apologize for our 'accidental' attack on a ship we didn't realize wasn't Apostate-built, but the destruction of any local regime to support their aims in the region should cause them to cut their losses. And, given their traditional foreign policy, it's unlikely they'll have the will and courage to conquer us to gain the base they desire. Most importantly, if Maccabeus succeeds, we can gain gradual control of Grayson without further overt military action, which means we will no longer need Haven, either, so I think we must delay *Thunder*'s return to Yeltsin for at least one more day to give him time.

"Nonetheless, we must also face the possibility that he will fail—or, at any rate, require a further demonstration of the hopelessness of the Apostate military position to succeed."

He paused and looked at his brother.

"Bearing all of this in mind, Sword Simonds, I hereby direct you to begin military operations to reduce the Apostate navy, followed, if necessary, by demonstration nuclear strikes on their less important cities, to create the conditions for Maccabeus' success. You will begin those operations within twelve hours of your return to Yeltsin with the last of our LACs."

He looked around the table, his rheumy old eyes flat as a snake's.

"Is there any disagreement with my directions?"

• CHAPTER EIGHTEEN

The cold stench of panic hung in Honor's nostrils as she stepped out of her pinnace, and armed sentries were everywhere. She'd met the tight-faced Army captain who greeted her before, and she hadn't enjoyed it, but at this particular moment other worries had pushed his bigotry into the background.

That, she thought bitterly as he escorted her stiffly to a ground car, was one good thing about a first-class military disaster. Like the prospect of hanging, it concentrated one's thoughts wonderfully.

Nimitz shifted on her shoulder, ears flattened and one true-hand plucking nervously at her white beret as the tension about him assaulted his empathic sense, and she reached up to stroke him. She'd intended to leave him behind, but he'd made his reaction to that idea abundantly plain, and truth to tell, she was glad he had. Even now, no one understood exactly how a 'cat's empathic link to his human functioned, but Honor—like every human who'd ever been adopted—was convinced it helped her retain her own stability.

And she needed all the help she could get with that just now.

The ground car whisked her to the Embassy through deserted streets. The few people in evidence hurried along, necks turning again and again as they peered furtively up at the sky. The car's sealed air system was clean and fresh smelling, but once again she could smell panic.

She understood it, for Langtry's staff had done better than she'd asked. They'd sent her the requested background brief an hour out of Grayson orbit, and its grim content told her exactly what Grayson faced. For six centuries, these people's mortal enemies had promised to destroy them; now they had the ability to do so, and Grayson's only hope was a squadron of foreign warships which *might* stand between it and Masada. A squadron commanded by a *woman*.

Oh, yes. She understood their fear, and understanding woke a sympathy deep within her despite the way they'd treated her.

The car arrived at the Embassy, and she swallowed fresh anguish as she saw Sir Anthony Langtry waiting alone. There should have been another figure beside the tall, broad ambassador. A small figure, with Puck's face and a special smile for her.

She climbed the steps past the Marine guard, noting his body armor and loaded pulser, and the Ambassador came halfway down them to meet her.

"Sir Anthony." She shook his hand, letting no sign of her pain color her voice or expression.

"Captain. Thank God you're here." Langtry had been a Marine colonel. He understood their grim position, and she thought she saw just a hint of a Marine's traditional deference to the captain of a Queen's ship in his deep-set eyes as he ushered her into the Embassy's filtered air. He was a tall man, but much of his bulk was in his torso, and he had to half-trot to match her long-legged stride as they moved down the central hall.

"Has the senior Grayson officer arrived?"

"Ah, no. No, he hasn't." She looked sharply at him, and he started to say something else, then shut his mouth, pressed an admittance key, and waved her through the opening door into a conference room. Two other people were waiting for her. One was a commander in the blue-on-blue of Grayson's Navy, the other was the Honorable Reginald Houseman.

"Captain Harrington, this is Commander Brentworth," Langtry said by way of introduction. "Mr. Houseman you know, of course."

Honor nodded to Houseman and extended her hand to the commander. She might as well test his reaction now, she thought, and felt a slight surprise as he took it without hesitation. There was discomfort in his eyes, but for a change it didn't seem to be directed at her. Or not *directly* at her, anyway.

"Commander Brentworth will be your liaison to the Grayson Navy," Langtry went on, and there was an odd note in his voice.

"Welcome aboard, Commander." Brentworth nodded, but his discomfort seemed to sharpen. "I'd hoped your senior officer would already be here," Honor went on, "since I don't believe we can accomplish much until I've had a chance to speak with him and coordinate our planning."

Brentworth started to speak, but Langtry cut him off with a curiously compassionate gesture.

"I'm afraid Admiral Garret isn't coming, Captain," the ambassador answered for Brentworth, and his voice was flat. "He feels his time is better spent monitoring the situation from Command Central. He's charged Commander Brentworth with your instructions under his current deployment plan."

Honor stared at him, then looked at Brentworth. The Grayson was beet-red, and now she recognized the discomfort in his eyes. It was shame.

"I'm afraid that's not acceptable, Sir Anthony." She was surprised by the steel in her own voice. "Admiral Garret may be a fine officer, but he can't possibly have a full understanding of my ships' capabilities. As such, he can't know how to wring the fullest advantage from them." She looked at Brentworth. "With all due respect, Commander, my assessment of the situation is that your navy simply doesn't begin to have the capacity to defeat this threat."

"Captain, I—" Brentworth began, then stopped, his face redder than ever, and Honor took pity on him.

"I understand your position, Commander Brentworth," she said more quietly. "Please don't consider anything I've just said a criticism of you."

The Grayson officer's humiliation actually grew at her understanding tone, but there was gratitude in his expression, as well.

"Very well, Sir Anthony." Honor returned her attention to Langtry. "We're just going to have to change Admiral Garrett's mind. I must have full access and cooperation to defend this planet, and—"

"Just a moment, Captain!" Houseman's interrupting voice was strained, almost strident, unlike the polished enunciation whose edge of smug superiority Honor remembered so well, and he leaned forward over the conference table.

"I don't think you understand the situation, Captain Harrington. Your primary responsibility is to the Kingdom of Manticore, not this planet, and as Her Majesty's representative, it's my duty to point out that the protection of her subjects must take precedence over any other consideration."

"I fully intend to protect Her Majesty's subjects, Mr. Houseman." Honor knew her personal dislike was coloring her voice, but she couldn't help it. "The best way to do that, however, is to protect the entire *planet*, not just the part of it Manticorans happen to be standing on!"

"Don't you take that tone with *me*, Captain! With Admiral Courvosier's death, *I* am the senior member of the delegation to Grayson. I'll thank you to bear that in mind and attend to my instructions!"

"I see." Honor's eyes were hard. "And what might those 'instructions' be, Mr. Houseman?"

"Why, to evacuate, of course!" Houseman looked at her as if she were one of his slower students at Mannheim University. "I want you to begin immediate planning for an orderly and expeditious evacuation of all Manticoran subjects aboard your ships and the freighters still in orbit."

"And the rest of the Grayson population, Mr. Houseman?" Honor asked softly. "Am I to evacuate all of *them* as well?"

"Of course not!" Houseman's jowls reddened. "And I won't remind you again about your impertinence, Captain Harrington! The Grayson population isn't your responsibility—our subjects *are!*"

"So my instructions are to abandon them." Honor's voice was flat, without any inflection at all.

"I'm very sorry for the situation they face." Houseman's eyes fell from her hard gaze, but he plowed on stubbornly. "I'm very sorry," he repeated, "but this situation is not of our making. Under the circumstances, our first concern must be the safety and protection of our own people."

"Including yourself."

Houseman's head jerked back up at the bottomless, icy contempt in that soft soprano voice. He recoiled for just a second, then slammed a fist on the conference table and yanked himself erect.

"I've warned you for the last time, Captain! You watch your tongue when you speak to me, or I'll have you *broken!* My concern is solely for my responsibilities—responsibilities *I* recognize, even if you don't—as custodian of Her Majesty's interests in Yeltsin!"

"I was under the impression we had an ambassador to look after Her Majesty's interests," Honor shot back, and Langtry stepped closer to her.

"So we do, Captain." His voice was cold, and he looked much less like an ambassador and much more like a colonel as he glared at Houseman. "Mr. Houseman may represent Her Majesty's Government for purposes of Admiral Courvosier's mission here, but *I* represent Her Majesty's continuing interests."

"Do you feel I should use my squadron to evacuate Manticoran subjects from the line of fire, Sir?" Honor asked, never taking her eyes from Houseman's, and the economist's face contorted with rage as Langtry answered.

"I do not, Captain. Obviously it would be wise to evacuate as many dependents and noncombatants as possible aboard the freighters still available, but in my opinion your squadron will be best employed protecting Grayson. If you wish, I'll put that in writing."

"*Damn* you!" Houseman shouted. "Don't you split legal hairs with *me*, Langtry! If I have to, I'll have *you* removed from Foreign Office service at the same time I have *her* court-martialed!"

"You're welcome to try." Langtry snorted contemptuously.

Houseman swelled with fury, and the corner of Honor's mouth twitched as her own rage raced to meet his. After all his cultured contempt for the military, all his smug assumption of his own superior place in the scheme of things, all he could think of now was to order that same despised military to save his precious skin! The polished, sophisticated surface had cracked, and behind it was an ugly, personal cowardice Honor was supremely ill-equipped to understand, much less sympathize with.

He gathered himself to lash back at Langtry, and she felt the Grayson officer standing mutely to one side. It shamed her to know what he was seeing and hearing, and under all her shame and anger was the raw, bleeding loss of the Admiral's death and her own responsibility for it. This man—this *worm*—was not going to throw away everything the Admiral had worked and, yes, *died* for!

She leaned across the table towards him, meeting his eyes from less than a meter away, and her voice cut across the beginning of his next outburst like a scalpel.

"Shut your cowardly mouth, Mr. Houseman." The cold words were precisely, almost calmly, enunciated, and he recoiled from them. His face went scarlet, then white and contorted with outrage, but she continued with that same, icy precision that made each word a flaying knife. "You disgust me. Sir Anthony is entirely correct, and you know it—you just won't *admit* it because you don't have the guts to face it."

"I'll have your commission!" Houseman gobbled. "I have friends in high places, and I'll—"

Honor slapped him.

She shouldn't have. She knew even as she swung that she'd stepped beyond the line, but she put all the strength of her Sphinx-bred muscles into that backhand blow, and Nimitz's snarl was dark with shared fury. The explosive *crack!* was like a breaking tree limb, and Houseman catapulted back from the table as blood burst from his nostrils and pulped lips.

A red haze clouded Honor's vision, and she heard Langtry saying something urgent, but she didn't care. She grabbed the end of the heavy conference table and hurled it out of her way as she advanced on Houseman, and the bloody-mouthed diplomat's hands scrabbled frantically at the floor as he propelled himself away from her on the seat of his trousers.

She didn't know what she would have done next if he'd shown a scrap of physical courage. She never would know, for as she loomed above him she heard him actually *sobbing* in his terror, and the sound stopped her dead.

Her raw fury slunk back into the caves of her mind, still flexing its claws and snarling, but no longer in control, and her voice was cold and distant . . . and cruel.

"Your entire purpose here was to conclude an alliance with Yeltsin's Star," she heard herself say. "To show these people an alliance with Manticore could *help* them. That was a commitment from our Kingdom, and Admiral Courvosier understood that. He knew the Queen's *honor* is at stake here, Mr. Houseman. The honor of the entire Kingdom of Manticore. If we cut and run, if we abandon Grayson when we *know* Haven is helping the Masadans and that it was our quarrel with Haven that brought us both here, it will be a blot on Her Majesty's honor *nothing* can ever erase. If you can't see it any other way, consider the impact on every other alliance we ever try to conclude! If you think you can get your 'friends in high places' to cashier me for doing my duty, you go right ahead and try. In the meantime, those of us who aren't cowards will just have to muddle through as best we can without you!"

She trembled, but her rage had turned cold. She stared down at the weeping diplomat, and he shrank from her eyes. They were hard with purpose, but all he saw was the killer behind them, and terror choked him.

She glared at him a moment longer, then turned to

Langtry. The ambassador was a bit pale, but there was approval in his expression and his shoulders straightened.

"Now, then, Sir Anthony," she said more calmly, "Commander Truman is already working on plans to evacuate your staff's dependents. In addition, we'll need the names and locations of all other Manticoran subjects on Grayson. I believe we can fit everyone into the freighters, but they were never designed as transports. Facilities are going to be cramped and primitive, and Commander Truman needs the total number of evacuees as soon as possible."

"My staff already has those lists, Captain," Langtry said, not even glancing at the sobbing man on the floor behind her. "I'll get them to Commander Truman as soon as we're finished here."

"Thank you." Honor drew a deep breath and turned to Brentworth.

"I apologize for what just happened here, Commander," she said quietly. "Please believe Ambassador Langtry represents my Queen's true policy towards Grayson."

"Of course, Captain." The commander's eyes gleamed as he looked back at her, and she realized he was no longer seeing a woman. He was seeing a Queen's officer, perhaps the first Grayson ever to look beyond her sex to the uniform she wore.

"All right." Honor glanced at the upended table and shrugged, then turned one of the chairs to face the two men. She sat and crossed her legs, feeling the residual tremors of her anger in her limbs and the quiver of Nimitz's body against her neck.

"In that case, Commander, I think it's time we turned our minds to how best to secure the cooperation we need from your military."

"Yes, Sir—Ma'am." Brentworth corrected himself quickly, but there was no more hesitation in him. He actually grinned a little at his slip. But then his grin faded. "With all due respect, Captain Harrington, that's not going to be easy. Admiral Garret is . . . well, he's extremely conservative, and I think—" He gathered himself. "I think the situation is so bad he's not thinking very clearly, Captain."

"Forgive me, Commander," Langtry said, "but what you mean is that Admiral Garret is an old woman—if you'll pardon the expression, Captain Harrington—who's hovering on the edge of outright panic."

Brentworth flushed, but the ambassador shook his head.

"I'm sorry for my bluntness, Commander, and I'm probably doing the Admiral something of a disservice, but we need brutal candor now, with no misunderstandings. I'm perfectly well aware that no one could fill High Admiral Yanakov's shoes, and God knows Garret has every reason to be scared to death. I don't mean to imply that it's for his own safety, either. He never expected to have this job dumped on him, and he knows this is a threat he can't defeat. That's enough to keep anyone from 'thinking very clearly.' But the fact remains that he isn't going to voluntarily relinquish his command to a foreign officer who's not only a mere captain but also happens to be a woman, doesn't it?"

"I didn't say anything about assuming command!" Honor protested.

"Then you're being naive, Captain," Langtry said. "If this planet is going to be defended, your people are going to do the lion's share of the fighting—give Garret credit for understanding that much. And as you yourself said, no Grayson officer knows how to use your capabilities to fullest advantage. Their plans are going to have to conform to *yours*, not the other way around, and that makes you the de facto SO. Garret knows that, but he can't admit it. Not only would it be an abandonment of his own responsibilities in his eyes, but you're a woman." The ambassador glanced at Commander Brentworth but continued without flinching. "To Admiral Garret that means, automatically, that you're unfit for command. He can't entrust the defense of his homeworld to someone he *knows* can't handle the job."

Honor bit her lip, but she couldn't refute Langtry's assessment. The old warhorse behind the ambassadorial facade knew too well how fear could shape human reactions, and few physical fears cut as deep or killed as many people as the moral fear of failing. Of *admitting* failure. That was the fear which made a commander out of her depth cling to her authority, unable to surrender it even when she knew she couldn't discharge it, and Langtry was also right about the way Garret's prejudices would dovetail with his fear.

"Commander Brentworth." Her voice was soft, and the Grayson officer's eyes darted to her face. "I realize we're putting you in an invidious position," she went on quietly, "but I have to ask you—and I need the most honest answer you can give me—if Ambassador Langtry's assessment of Admiral Garret is correct."

"Yes, Ma'am," Brentworth said promptly, though manifestly against his will. He paused and cleared his throat. "Captain Harrington, there isn't a man in Grayson uniform who's more devoted to the safety of this planet, but . . . but he isn't the man for this job."

"Unfortunately, he's the man who's *got* it," Langtry said, "and he isn't going to cooperate with you, Captain."

"Then I'm afraid we have no choice but to go over his head." Honor squared her shoulders. "Who do we talk to, Sir Anthony?"

"Well. . . ." Langtry rubbed his lip. "There's Councilman Long, the Navy Minister, but he doesn't have any military service background of his own. I doubt he'd overrule an experienced flag officer on something this critical."

"I'm almost certain he wouldn't, Sir Anthony," Brentworth put in. The Grayson officer took a chair of his own with an apologetic little smile, but the gesture was a statement, ranging him firmly on the foreigners' side against his own military commander in chief. "As you say, he doesn't have any Fleet background. Except in administrative matters, he always deferred to Admiral Yanakov's judgment. I don't see him changing that policy now, and if you'll forgive me, Captain, he's a bit on the conservative side, too."

"Commander," Honor surprised herself with a genuine laugh, "I've got a notion we're never going to get anything done if you keep apologizing for everyone who's going to have trouble with the fact that I'm a woman." She waved a hand as he started to speak. "It's not your fault, and it's not really theirs, either—and even if it were, assigning fault is one thing we *definitely* don't have time for. But my skin's thick enough to take what it has to, so just plow right ahead and let the chips fall where they may."

"Yes, Ma'am." Brentworth smiled at her, relaxing even further, then furrowed his brow in thought.

"What about Admiral Stephens, Sir Anthony?" He glanced at Honor. "He's—or, rather, he was until last year—Chief of the Naval Staff."

"No good," Langtry decided. "As you say, he's retired. Even if he weren't, he and Long hate each other's guts. A personal thing." He made a shooing gesture with one hand. "Doesn't have anything to do with naval policy, but it'd get in the way, and we don't have time for that."

"Then I don't know who's left." Brentworth sighed. "Not short of the Protector, anyway."

"The Protector?" Honor cocked an eyebrow at Langtry. "That's a thought. Why don't we ask Protector Benjamin to intervene?"

"That would be completely without precedent." Langtry shook his head. "The Protector *never* intervenes between ministers and their subordinates."

"Doesn't he have the authority to?" Honor asked in surprise.

"Well, yes, technically, under the written constitution. But the *un*written constitution says otherwise. The Protector's Council has the right to advise and consent on ministerial appointments. Over the last century or so, that's turned into de facto control of the ministries. In fact, the Chancellor, as First Councilman, really runs the government these days."

"Wait a minute, Sir Anthony," Brentworth said. "I agree with what you just said, but the Constitution doesn't exactly cover this situation, either, and the

Navy's more traditional—" he smiled at Honor "—than the civilians. Remember, our oaths are sworn to the *Protector*, not the Council or Chamber. I think if he asserted his written powers, the Fleet would listen."

"Even if it's to put a woman in command of it?" Langtry asked skeptically.

"Well. . . ." It was Brentworth's turn to hesitate, but Honor sat up crisply and put both feet on the floor.

"All right, gentlemen, we're not going to get this ship off the field if we don't decide who to talk to, and I don't think we have much option. From what you're both saying, it has to be the Protector if we're going to cut through all the layers of insulation."

"I could put it to him," Langtry mused aloud, "but first I'll have to get Chancellor Prestwick's okay. That'll mean going through the Council, and I know some of them will stonewall, despite the situation. It's going to take time, Captain. A day or two, at least."

"We don't *have* a day or two."

"But—" Langtry began, and Honor shook her head.

"No, Sir Anthony, I'm sorry, but if we go that route, I'll end up defending this planet all by myself. Assuming the Masadans intend to continue operations now that my squadron's returned, I can't believe they'll delay that long. And, frankly, if they've moved all their LACs to this system to support their remaining hyper-capable units *and* two Peep cruisers, I'll need all the help I can get to keep them off my back while I deal with the big ones."

"But what *else* can we do?"

"We can take advantage of the fact that I'm a bluff, plain-spoken spacedog without the least notion of diplomatic niceties. Instead of putting a written proposal or diplomatic note through channels, request a direct meeting between Protector Benjamin and myself."

"My God, they'd never do it!" Langtry gasped. "A personal meeting between the Protector and a *woman?* A foreign *naval officer* who's a woman?! No, that's out of the question!"

"Then make it part of the question, Sir Anthony,"

Honor said grimly, and she was no longer seeking his guidance. She was giving an order, and he knew it. He stared at her, mind working in an effort to find a way to obey her, and she suddenly smiled.

"Commander Brentworth, you're about to not hear something. Can you do that? Or should I ask you to leave the room for real?"

"My hearing is pretty erratic, Ma'am," Brentworth said, and his grin was almost conspiratorial. Clearly nothing short of force could have gotten him out of that conference room.

"All right then. Ambassador, you're going to tell the Grayson government that unless I'm allowed a direct, personal meeting with Protector Benjamin, I will have no alternative but to assume that Grayson doesn't feel it requires my services, in which case I will have no option but to evacuate all Manticoran subjects and withdraw from Yeltsin within the next twelve hours."

Brentworth gawked at her, his enjoyment of a moment before turned suddenly to horror, and she winked at him.

"Don't panic, Commander. I won't really pull out. But if we put it to them in those terms, they won't have any choice but to at least listen, now will they?"

"Uh, no, Ma'am, I don't guess they will," Brentworth said shakenly, and Langtry nodded in reluctant approval.

"They've already got a military crisis. I suppose we might as well give them a constitutional one to go with it. The Foreign Minister will be horrified when he hears we've been issuing ultimata to friendly heads of state, but I think Her Majesty will forgive us."

"How soon can you deliver the message?"

"As soon as I get to my office com terminal, but if you don't mind, I'd like to spend at least a few minutes working on a properly grim delivery. Something formal and stiff with the proper overtones of laboring under the demands of a military hard case who doesn't understand she's violating every diplomatic precedent." Despite the tension, Langtry chuckled. "If I handle this right, I may even get away with holding a gun to a friendly government's head without chucking my career out the airlock!"

"You can make me as big an ogre as you like as long as saving your career doesn't slow us down too much," Honor said with another smile. She stood. "As a matter of fact, why don't you work on your delivery while we walk to your office?"

Langtry nodded again, grinning even though his eyes were just a bit dazed from her ruthless dispatch. He walked out of the conference room with Honor on his heels, and an even more dazed-looking Commander Brentworth trailed in their wake.

None of them even looked back at the diplomat still sobbing quietly in the shadow of the overturned table.

• CHAPTER NINETEEN

"How *dare* they?!" Jared Mayhew glared around the council room as if hunting a Manticoran to attack with his bare hands. "Who do they think they *are?!*"

"With all due respect, Councilman Mayhew, they think they're the only people who can keep those fanatics on Masada from conquering this star system," Chancellor Prestwick replied far more calmly.

"God wouldn't *want* us to save ourselves at the cost of such . . . such *sacrilege!*"

"Calmly, Jared. Calmly." Protector Benjamin touched his cousin's shoulder. "Remember that they don't see this as a sacrilegious demand."

"Perhaps not, but they have to know it's insulting, degrading, and arrogant," Howard Clinkscales, Grayson's Minister of Security growled. He and Jared Mayhew were the most conservative Council members, and his mouth worked bitterly. "It spits on all our institutions and beliefs, Benjamin!"

"Hear, hear!" Councilman Phillips murmured, and Councilman Adams, the Minister of Agriculture, looked like he wanted to say something even stronger. Barely a third of the faces present showed disagreement, and Prestwick looked around the long table despairingly.

He and Mayhew had been genial opponents for the five years since Benjamin became Protector, sparring with elegant good manners over the authority the last six protectors had lost to Prestwick's predecessors. Yet Prestwick remained deeply and personally committed to the Mayhew dynasty, and they'd worked closely to secure the Manticoran alliance. Now it was crashing down in ruins, and there was anguish in his eyes as he cleared his throat.

"At the moment, our concerns—" he began, but the Protector's raised finger stopped him.

"I know it looks that way to you, Howard," Protector Benjamin said, focusing on Clinkscales' face as if to exclude everyone else, "but we have to consider three questions. Do they truly realize how insulting this demand is? Will they really pull their warships out of this system if we reject it? And can we hold Grayson and *preserve* those institutions and beliefs if they do?"

"Of course they realize how insulting it is!" Jared Mayhew snapped. "No one could have put so many insults into one package by *accident!*"

The Protector leaned back in his chair and regarded his cousin with a mix of weariness, patience, disagreement, and exasperated affection. Unlike his own father, his Uncle Oliver had steadfastly refused to have any of *his* sons contaminated by off-world education, and Jared Mayhew was bright, talented, and the quintessential product of a conservative Grayson upbringing. He was also next in line for the Protectorship after Benjamin's brother and ten years older than Benjamin himself.

"I'm not at all sure 'insult' is the proper word, Jared. And even if it were, surely we've given them just as many 'insults' as they've given us."

Jared stared at him in astonishment, and Benjamin sighed mentally. His cousin was a gifted industrial manager, but he was so confident of the rectitude of his own beliefs that the notion anyone else might find his attitudes or behavior insulting was irrelevant. If they didn't like the way he treated them, then they should stay away from his planet. If they insisted on contaminating his world by their presence, he would treat them precisely as God wanted him to, and if they felt insulted, that was their problem.

"If you'll forgive me, Protector," a resonant voice said, "I rather think that whether they realize they're insulting us or not is somewhat less important than the last two questions you raised." The Reverend Julius Hanks, spiritual head of the Church of Humanity Unchained, seldom spoke up in Council meetings, but now he gave Prestwick a very hard look indeed. "Do you think they truly would withdraw and leave us to Masada's mercy, Chancellor?"

"I don't know, Reverend," Prestwick said frankly. "Were Admiral Courvosier still alive, I'd say no. As it is . . . " He shrugged. "This Harrington woman is now in complete control of their military presence, and that means her policies are driving their diplomatic position. I doubt Ambassador Langtry would support any decision to withdraw, but I don't know if he could stop her from doing it. And—" he hesitated a moment, glancing at Clinkscales and Jared Mayhew "—I have to say the experiences on Grayson of Captain Harrington and the other women in her crews may well incline her to do exactly that."

"Of course she feels inclined to!" Clinkscales snorted. "What d'you expect when you put women in uniform? Damn it, they don't have the self-control and stability for it! She got her *feelings* hurt when she was here before, did she? Well, at least that explains why she's cracking the whip over us this way now! It's for *revenge*, damn it!"

Prestwick clamped his lips on a hasty retort, and the Protector hid another sigh. Actually, this one was more of a groan. His was the third Mayhew generation Clinkscales had served, and not just as Minister of Security. He was the personal commander of the Protectorate Security Detachment, the bodyguards who protected Benjamin and his entire family every hour of their lives.

He was also a living fossil. The old man was an unofficial uncle—a curmudgeonly, irascible, often exasperating uncle—but an uncle—and Benjamin knew he treated his own wives with great tenderness. Yet fond as Benjamin was of the old man, he also knew Clinkscales treated them so because they were *his* wives. He knew them as people, separated from the general concept "wife" or "woman," but he would never dream of treating them as equals. The notion of a woman—*any* woman—asserting equality with a man— *any* man—was more than merely foreign to him. It was totally incomprehensible, and as the personification of that notion, Captain Honor Harrington was a fundamental threat to his entire way of life.

"All right, Howard," Benjamin said after a moment, "assume you're right—that she's just likely to pull her ships out of here for revenge because she's a woman. Distasteful as all of us may find the notion of submitting to her ultimatum, doesn't her very instability make it even more imperative for *us* to maintain an open mind as we consider it?"

Clinkscales glared at him. For all his conservatism, the old man was no fool, and his Protector's attempt to turn his own argument against him was the sort of thing the overly clever young sprout had been doing for years, ever since his return from that fancy university. His face reddened, but he clamped his jaws and refused to be drawn to the obvious conclusion.

"All right, then," Councilman Tompkins said. "If there's a real possibility this woman will abandon us, do we stand any chance at all of holding off the Faithful without her?"

"Of course we do!" Jared Mayhew snapped. "My workers are drawing weapons, and my shipyards are converting every freighter we have into missile carriers! We don't need *foreigners* to defend ourselves against scum like Masadans—just God and ourselves!"

No one else said a word, and even Clinkscales looked away in discomfort. Jared's fiery hatred of—and contempt for—Masada had always been very public, but no amount of rhetoric could hide Grayson's nakedness. Yet even though they all knew Jared's strident assertions were nonsense, no one had the will—or the courage— to say so, and Benjamin Mayhew surveyed the council room with a sense of despair.

Phillips and Adams had opposed the Manticore treaty from the outset, as had Jared and Clinkscales, though

Phillips had seemed to be coming around under Courvosier's influence once Harrington disappeared from the equation. Most of the rest of the Council had been in cautious agreement with Prestwick, Tompkins, and the others who believed the alliance was critical to Grayson's survival. But that had been when an attack by Masada had merely seemed likely. Now it had become a fact, and the destruction of their own navy had filled too many councilmen with terror. Knowing the despised, backward Masadans had somehow acquired state-of-the-art military technology only made their panic complete, and panicked men thought with their emotions, not their intellects.

Despite the desperation of their situation, if Prestwick polled the Council at this moment, a majority would undoubtedly vote to reject Captain Harrington's demand. The Protector felt his heart sink as that certainty filled him, but then an unexpected voice spoke up in support of sanity.

"Forgive me, Brother Jared," Reverend Hanks said gently. "You know my own view of the proposed alliance. The Church has learned from Masada's example not to meddle willfully in political decisions, yet I, as many in the Faith, have entertained serious doubts of the wisdom of such a close relationship with a power whose fundamental values differ so radically from our own. But that was when we had near parity with Masada's military."

Jared met the Reverend's eyes with an expression of betrayal, but Hanks continued quietly.

"I have no doubt you and your workmen would fight valiantly, that all of you would willingly die for your people and your Faith, but you *would* die. And so would our wives and children. Masada has always proclaimed its willingness to destroy all life on Grayson if that should prove the only way to cleanse this planet of our 'apostasy.' I fear we have no choice but to assume they mean what they say, and if that be true, Brother Jared, it leaves us only three options: secure the support of this foreign woman's ships in any way we must, surrender all we love and hold dear to Masada, or die."

Silence trembled in the council room as Grayson's spiritual leader put the decision into stark relief. Many of the councilmen seemed more shocked by Hanks's statement than they'd looked when they learned of the Fleet's destruction, and Benjamin Mayhew's pulse throbbed as he felt a moment of balance shivering about him.

The Council had chipped away at the protectorship's authority for a century, hemming successive protectors about with more and more restrictions. Benjamin himself was little more than a figurehead, but a figurehead who'd always known the Protector retained far more authority in the eyes of Graysons' citizens than the Council knew, and now the men in this room faced a decision they wanted desperately to avoid. They were frozen, their supremacy over the protectorship singing with the crystalline brittleness of ice, and he suddenly realized history and Captain Honor Harrington had given him a hammer.

He drew a deep breath and brought that hammer down.

"Gentlemen." He stood, assuming a dominant stance none of them had ever seen before. "This decision is too grave, and time is too short, for us to debate it endlessly. I *will* meet with Captain Harrington."

Breaths hissed all around the table, but he continued in that same, firm voice.

"Under the circumstances, I would be criminally remiss as Protector of Grayson not to act. I will meet Captain Harrington and, unless her demands are totally unreasonable, I will accept them in Grayson's name."

Howard Clinkscales and his cousin stared at him in horror, and he turned his head to meet Jared's eyes.

"I realize many of you will disagree with my decision, and it wasn't an easy one to make. Bowing to ultimatums never *is* easy. Nonetheless, my decision is final. I believe, however, that we can arrange to have differing viewpoints represented by placing this meeting in a familial setting. I will invite Captain Harrington to join myself and my family for supper, and I will extend that same invitation to you, Jared."

"*No!*" Jared Mayhew surged to his feet, glaring at his cousin. "I will *never* break bread with a woman who spits on everything I believe!"

Benjamin looked at his cousin and hoped his pain didn't show. They'd always been close, despite their philosophical differences. The thought that those differences might force a breach between them at last twisted his heart, but he *had* to meet with the Manticoran captain. The survival of his planet required it, and he could feel the political structure of Grayson realigning itself about him. If he hesitated, neither his home world nor his chance to forge a new, progressive power base would survive.

"I'm sorry you feel that way, Jared," he said quietly. "We'll miss you."

Jared stared at him, his face twisted, then wheeled and stormed out of the Council Room. A ripple of agitation washed over the councilmen at his flagrant breach of protocol, but Benjamin made himself ignore it.

"Very well, gentlemen. I believe that concludes our debate."

He turned on his heel and walked through the door to the private quarters of the palace. The frozen Council watched him go, and as the door closed behind him, they knew it had closed on their own control of the government, as well.

There was no image on the com in the small shop's back room. That was a security measure, yet it also meant the man who'd answered it could never be certain the blank screen wasn't a trap, and he drew a deep breath.

"Hello?"

"The Abomination of the Desolation will not be suffered twice," a familiar voice said.

"Nor shall we fear defeat, for this world is God's," the man replied, and his shoulders relaxed. "How may I serve, Maccabeus?"

"The time has come to reclaim the Temple, Brother. The Protector will meet privately with the blasphemer who commands the Manticoran squadron."

"With a *woman?!*" the shopkeeper gasped.

"Indeed. But this time sacrilege will serve God's Work. Word of his decision will be announced within the hour. Before that happens, you must mobilize your team. Is all in readiness?"

"Yes, Maccabeus!" The shopkeeper's horror had turned into something else, and his eyes gleamed.

"Very well. I'll com back within forty-five minutes with final instructions and the challenges and counter-signs you'll need. After that, God's Work will be in your hands, Brother."

"I understand," the shopkeeper whispered. "My team and I won't fail you, Maccabeus. This world is God's."

"This world is God's," the faceless voice responded. Then there was a click, and only the hum of the carrier.

• CHAPTER TWENTY

She was certainly a *big* woman.

That was Benjamin Mayhew's first thought as Captain Harrington was ushered into the sitting room, but he changed it almost instantly. She wasn't so much "big" as "tall." She towered over her Security escort, but though she was broad-shouldered for a woman, with the solid, well-muscled look of a heavy-worlder, she moved like a dancer, and there wasn't a gram of excess weight on her.

He watched Captain Fox, the head of his personal Security detachment, bristle like a terrier confronted by the tall elegance of a borzoi and felt an almost uncontrollable desire to laugh. Fox had been Mayhew's personal guardsman since boyhood, and laughing would have been an unforgivable insult to his utterly loyal henchman, but Harrington was twenty centimeters taller than he, and Fox was only too obviously irked by that.

He was also irked by the six-legged, cream-and-gray creature riding her shoulder. One didn't normally bring pets to formal state occasions, but then, the Protector had decreed that this *wasn't* a state occasion. Officially, it was simply a dinner invitation to a foreign officer. The fact that this horrible woman had issued an ultimatum to the entire planet to extort that "invitation" was beside the point—officially—but it certainly didn't give her a right to bring her horrid alien creature and God alone knew what off-world parasites or diseases into the Protector's presence!

Unfortunately for Fox, Captain Harrington was all done deferring to Grayson's tender sensibilities. She hadn't even discussed bringing the beast along; she'd simply appeared with it on her shoulder. Mayhew had used the palace surveillance system to observe her arrival, and he hadn't quite been able to suppress a grin as she ignored Fox's pointed hints that its presence might be unwelcome. When he'd tried to persist, she'd given him the sort of look nannies reserved for rambunctious boy children not yet out of the nursery.

Fox had surrendered, but the chemistry between him and Harrington should add a certain something to the evening's atmosphere.

Mayhew rose from his armchair as Fox escorted her across the room to him. Unlike his Security team's commander, he'd spent six years at Harvard University's Bogota campus on Old Earth. That gave him a degree of experience with off-world women virtually no other Grayson could match, yet even he was struck by Captain Harrington's assurance. Her height didn't hurt any, but neither that, nor her startling, unconventional attractiveness, nor even the gliding grace with which she moved, explained it.

She paused, tall and erect in her black-and-gold uniform with the snarling, scarlet-and-gold Manticore shoulder patch, and removed her white beret. Mayhew recognized the gesture of respect, but his Security men exchanged grimaces behind her as she bared her short, curly mop of close-cropped hair. Grayson women were spared the veils of their Masadan sisters, but none of them would have dared wear trousers in public, and tradition still forbade uncovered female heads in the presence of men. Besides, no Grayson woman would ever cut her hair so short.

But Captain Harrington wasn't a Grayson woman. One look into those dark, cool almond eyes made that perfectly clear, and Mayhew extended his hand as he would have extended it to a man.

"Good evening, Captain Harrington." He allowed himself an ironic smile. "It was so kind of you to come."

"Thank you, Protector Mayhew." Her grip was firm, though he had the impression its strength was carefully restrained, and her soprano voice was surprisingly soft

and sweet. It was also admirably grave, but he thought
he saw a hint of a twinkle in her dark eyes. "It was very
generous of you to invite me," she added, and he felt
his lips twitch.

"Yes. Well, it seemed appropriate, under the
circumstances."

Her inclined head conceded him the match, and he
gestured graciously for her to accompany him. She fell
in at his side, her stride slow and unhurried to match
his shorter legs, and he looked up at her.

"I thought I'd introduce you to my family before we
dine, Captain," he went on. "My younger brother
Michael is particularly interested in meeting you. He
holds a bachelor's degree from Anderman University on
New Berlin, but he hopes to pursue graduate work on
Manticore if our negotiations prosper."

"I certainly hope he'll be able to, Protector."
Harrington's tone acknowledged the implication that
Michael, like Mayhew himself, had been exposed to
independent-minded women. Of course, the Protector
thought with an inner smile, that wasn't the only reason
Michael wanted to meet her.

They passed down the hall to the dining room, and
two of Fox's men peeled off to station themselves on
either side of its door. The other four accompanied
their captain and the Protector through it and moved to
the corners of the large room. They were used to looking unobtrusive, and Harrington showed no particular
awareness of their watchful presence. Fox gave her one
last baleful look, then assumed his own position beside
the Protector's chair as Mayhew's family joined him.

"Allow me to present my wives, Captain Harrington,"
he said. "This is my first wife, Katherine."

Katherine Mayhew was a small woman, even by
Grayson standards; next to Harrington she was tiny. But
she combined the graciousness of a traditional Grayson
wife with a first-class mind, and her deplorably non-
traditional husband had actively abetted her voracious
pursuit of a course of private study which would have
qualified her for half a dozen degrees at any off-world

university. Now she looked up at their visitor and offered her hand without hesitation.

"Madam Mayhew," Harrington responded, shaking it gravely.

"And this is Elaine," Mayhew went on, presenting his second wife.

Elaine Mayhew was obviously pregnant, and she shook the Captain's hand more warily than Katherine, but she relaxed as Harrington smiled at her.

"Madam Mayhew," she repeated.

"Our daughters are already in bed, I'm afraid," Mayhew went on, "but permit me to introduce my brother and heir, Michael, Steadholder Mayhew."

"Captain Harrington." Michael Mayhew was taller than his brother, though still considerably shorter than their guest. He was also twelve years younger and Navy mad, and he grinned boyishly. "I certainly hope you'll be kind enough to let me tour your ship before you return to Manticore, Captain."

"I'm sure something can be arranged, Lord Mayhew," she responded, with only the faintest hint of a smile, and Mayhew shook his head as servants began to materialize out of the woodwork.

"I see you've already made at least one convert, Captain," he said lightly, smiling at his brother, and Michael blushed.

"I'm sorry if I sounded pushy, Captain," he began, "but—"

"Don't apologize, Lord Mayhew," Harrington said as she took her seat. A servant placed a tall, backless stool beside her at a gesture from the Protector, then retreated with more haste than dignity as she coaxed her treecat down onto it. "I'd be honored to show you around her personally, if circumstances permit. I'm quite proud of her."

"I'll bet you are!" Michael said enviously. "I've read everything I could get my hands on about her class, but Cousin Bernie says—"

He broke off, happiness suddenly quenched, and Harrington smiled sadly at him.

"I regret that I never got to know High Admiral Yanakov very well, Lord Mayhew, but Ambassador Langtry tells me he and Admiral Courvosier had become very close. I believe Admiral Courvosier had the greatest respect for him, and I hope we'll have the chance to welcome you on board so you can judge *Fearless's* capabilities for yourself."

The Protector sat back to let the servants pour wine and nodded to himself. Harrington's voice held none of the stridency or challenge he'd been half afraid of when he first learned of her "ultimatum." He'd suspected—or hoped, perhaps—that the Council's fear she might truly abandon them had been exaggerated; now he was certain of it.

The servants finished placing the appetizers before each diner, and Mayhew bent his head to offer thanks . . . and not for the meal, alone.

The last of Honor's inner tension faded as the supper progressed. Her host's family appeared completely relaxed, despite the guards in the corners and the sour-faced Security captain hovering at the Protector's shoulder. She knew Queen Elizabeth was guarded with equal attentiveness, though Manticore's tech base made it possible for her protectors to be much less evident. It wasn't a way of life Honor would have cared for, but she supposed it was the sort of thing any ruler had to grow used to, however beloved she—or he—was.

Yet aside from the guards, these people seemed amazingly unthreatened by her presence. The Protector was younger than she'd expected—at least ten years younger than she, she suspected, allowing for the absence of prolong on Grayson—but his disarming conversation hid neither his self-assurance nor his authority. His brother, on the other hand, was something Honor understood perfectly. She'd met scores of youngsters like him at Saganami Island.

But it was the Protector's wives who truly surprised her. She'd known Benjamin and Michael Mayhew had attended off-world schools, but it didn't take her long to realize Katherine Mayhew was far better educated than she herself, in nontechnical fields, at any rate. Elaine was younger and tended to defer to her tiny fellow wife—she was clearly the more traditional of the two—yet she was just as articulate. That was heartening after Honor's own experiences, and though she had no idea how typical the Protector's household might be, she began to suspect how Admiral Courvosier had become so close to Admiral Yanakov despite the high admiral's stiffness with her.

Clearly her host had decided business—and any potential unpleasantness—could wait until after supper. Conversation flowed amiably as they worked their way through the sumptuous meal, but it was restricted largely to discussion of the differences between Grayson and Manticore, and Lord Mayhew and Elaine Mayhew were fascinated when she requested a plate for Nimitz. The Security captain looked ready to burst, but Lord Mayhew and his sister-in-law took turns slipping Nimitz tidbits . . . which he accepted as his just due. He was on his best behavior, though. Even when Elaine discovered his fondness for celery, he managed to devour the crunchy sticks neatly despite his carnivore's teeth, and his obvious comfort with these people was the most reassuring element yet. Honor had brought him along partly to make a point, but even more because of his empathic sense, for she'd learned to rely on him as a barometer of others' emotions long ago.

The meal ended at last. The servants withdrew, leaving the Protector's family alone with their guest and their guards, and Mayhew leaned back in his chair and regarded her thoughtfully.

"Why do I suspect, Captain Harrington, that the, um, persuasion you used to 'request' this meeting was a bit . . . overstated, shall we say?"

"Overstated, Sir?" Honor asked innocently. "Well, perhaps it was. On the other hand, I thought I might need an argument to catch your attention."

Captain Fox wore the wooden expression of a man

accustomed to hearing sensitive discussions which were none of his business, but his mouth twitched.

"You found one, I assure you," Mayhew said dryly. "Now that you have it, however, what, precisely, can I do for you?"

"It's very simple, Sir," Honor said, grasping the nettle firmly. "In order to employ my squadron effectively in defense of your planet, I need the cooperation of your high command. However able and determined, your commanders simply aren't sufficiently familiar with my ships' capabilities to make best use of them without the closest coordination."

"I see." Mayhew regarded her for a moment, then cocked an eyebrow. "Should I assume from your statement that you've been denied that cooperation?"

"Yes, Sir, you should," she said flatly. "Admiral Garret has assigned me a fine liaison officer in Commander Brentworth, but I have only the most incomplete knowledge of your surviving naval strength, and he's issued orders for the deployment of my vessels which make very poor use of them."

"Issued *orders?*" There was an ominous note in Mayhew's voice, and Honor didn't think it was assumed.

"Yes, Sir. In fairness to him, I believe he assumed I meant to place my ships under his command when I informed your government through Ambassador Langtry of my intention to assist in Grayson's defense."

"And did you mean to?"

"I suppose I did, to the extent of tying them into an integrated defense plan. The plan he evolved, however, is far from ideal in my opinion, and he declines to discuss it with me."

"After all Admiral Courvosier and *Madrigal* already did for us?!" Lord Mayhew burst out. He glared at his brother. "I told you Garret didn't know his ass from his elbow, Ben! He knows how badly we need Captain Harrington's ships if we're going to stand a chance, but he's not to admit it if it means he has to take orders from a *woman*. Cousin Bernie always said—"

"Yes, Mike, I know," Mayhew interrupted, and looked

squarely at Honor. "I take it, then, Captain Harrington, that the real reason for this meeting was to ask me to order Admiral Garret to cooperate with you?"

"Yes, Sir, more or less," she said.

"You mean 'more' more than 'less,' I suspect." The Protector propped his right elbow comfortably on the arm of his chair. "If I direct him to cooperate, I expect he'll accept the order—officially, at least—but he's not going to forget that you went over his head to get it, Captain."

"Protector Benjamin," Honor said evenly, "what you do within your own navy is no business of mine. My sole concern is to protect this planet in accordance with what I believe to be my Queen's desires. To accomplish that, I need the cooperation I've requested. If Admiral Garret can give it to me, I'm entirely prepared to work with him."

"But *he's* not prepared to work with *you*. My impetuous, big-mouthed brother's right about that, I'm afraid—which means I'll have to relieve him."

Honor hid an inner quiver of relief, but all she said quietly was, "You know the Admiral better than I, Sir."

"Yes, I do, and it's a pity he's so set in his ways." The Protector rubbed his cheek, then nodded. "Very well, Captain. Admiral Garret will cease to be a problem." He looked at his brother. "You're the one who's so informed on naval affairs, Mike. Who's the next most senior officer we've got left?"

"With command experience, or on the staff?"

"Command experience."

"Commodore Matthews, unless you want to bring someone out of retirement," Lord Mayhew said without hesitation, "and he's a good one, Ben." The younger Mayhew smiled almost shyly at Honor. "You won't have any problems working with *him*, Ma'am."

"Commodore Matthews it is, then," the Protector said, and despite herself, Honor sighed with relief. Mayhew heard it and smiled at her.

"I gather you're not really accustomed to high-stakes diplomacy, Captain Harrington?"

"No, Sir, I certainly am not," she replied with feeling.

"Well, you did rather well, then," he told her. "In fact, you may have done even better than you realize, considering the domestic situation." Captain Fox made a small sound, and the Protector grinned up at him. "Contain yourself, Fox," he teased. "There are no spies from the Council here."

Fox abandoned his wooden expression to give his Protector a very old-fashioned look, then glowered at Honor and resumed his parade-ground stance beside Mayhew's chair.

"Tell me, Captain," Mayhew said lightly, "are you a student of Old Earth history, by any chance?"

"I beg your pardon, Sir?" Honor blinked at the question, then shrugged. "I'd hardly claim to be an authority on the subject, Sir."

"Neither was I, before my father sent me to Harvard, but you remind me rather strongly of Commodore Perry at this particular moment. Are you familiar with his career?"

"Perry?" Honor thought for a moment. "The . . . American commander at the Battle of Lake Champlain?"

"Lake Erie, I believe," Mayhew corrected, "but that was Oliver Perry. I was referring to his brother Matthew."

"Oh. Then I'm afraid the answer is no, Sir."

"A pity. He was a bit on the pompous side, I'm sorry to say, but he also dragged the Empire of Japan kicking and screaming out of its isolation in the Fourth Century Ante Diaspora. In fact, it was Japan that got me interested in Perry, though the parallel between Grayson and the Japanese only goes so far, of course. They wanted to be left alone, whereas we've been trying for two centuries to *get* someone—anyone!—to 'drag' us into the present, but I'm beginning to suspect you're going to have as big an impact on us as Perry had on them." He smiled faintly. "I trust we'll avoid some of their worst mistakes—and they made some big ones—but the social and domestic consequences of your visit may prove even greater than the military and technological ones."

"I see." Honor regarded him cautiously. "I trust you don't believe those consequences will be unhappy ones, Sir?"

"On the contrary," Mayhew said as the dining room door opened and two uniformed Security men stepped into the anteroom-like entry alcove. He glanced up casually as the newcomers walked towards Captain Fox and a second pair followed them into the dining room. "I expect they'll be highly beneficial, though it may take some of us a while to—"

Fox frowned as the new arrivals approached him, then relaxed as one of them extended a dispatch case. He reached out to take it . . . and Nimitz suddenly catapulted from his stool with a snarl like tearing canvas.

Honor's head whipped around as the treecat landed on the back of the Security man closest to her. The guard howled as the treecat's true-feet sank centimeter-long claws bone-deep into his shoulders, and his howl became a shriek of raw, terrified agony as Nimitz's uppermost limbs reached around his head and scimitar-clawed fingers buried themselves to the knuckles in his eyes.

Blood and fluids erupted down the shrieking guard's cheeks, and his hands rose frantically to clutch at his assailant. But his sounds died in a horrible, whistling gurgle as the clawed hand-paws of the treecat's middle limbs ripped his throat open to the spine.

The dead man crumpled like a felled tree, but the 'cat was already somersaulting away from him. His rippling snarl rose even higher as he slammed into a second newcomer, all six sets of claws ripping and tearing, and Fox and his men stared at him in horror. They'd been surprised by the length of his sixty-centimeter body when he uncoiled from Honor's shoulder, but he was narrow and supple as a ferret, and they hadn't realized he massed over nine kilos of bone and hard muscle. It wasn't really their fault—Honor had grown so accustomed to his weight over the years that it scarcely even inconvenienced her, and they hadn't made sufficient allowance for how easily her own Sphinx-bred muscles let her carry him.

Yet whatever their reasoning, they'd dismissed him as a simple pet, without guessing how powerful and well-armed he actually was. Nor had they even suspected his intelligence, and the totally unexpected carnage stunned them. But they were trained bodyguards, responsible for their head of state's safety, and their hands jerked to their weapons as the beast ran amok.

Captain Fox grabbed the Protector without ceremony, yanking him out of his chair by brute force and throwing him behind him as he went for his own sidearm. Lord Mayhew recoiled as the dead man's blood splashed the tablecloth and spouted over him, but he, too, reacted with admirable speed. He grabbed both his sisters-in-law, shoved them under the table, and fell across them to protect them with his own body.

Honor saw it all only peripherally. She'd always known Nimitz could feel *her* emotions, but she'd never knowingly felt his.

This time she did—and as she also felt the emotions of the fresh "Security detachment" *through* him, she exploded out of her chair. The heel of her hand slammed into the face of the newcomer closest to the Protector, and cartilage crunched horribly as she drove his nose up into his brain—just as his companion dropped the dispatch case, raised his other hand, and fired at pointblank range into Captain Fox's chest.

The handgun made a whining noise and a sound like an axe sinking into a log, and the Security captain flew backward, his pistol less than half-drawn. His corpse knocked Mayhew to the carpet, and a corner of Honor's mind cringed as she recognized the sound of an off-world sonic disrupter.

She reached out and caught the killer by the nape of the neck with one hand and reached past him to clamp her other over his gun before he could get a clear shot at Mayhew. She missed the gun but captured his wrist, and he dropped the weapon with a howl of anguish as her fingers squeezed and the hand on his neck yanked him off the floor. His eyes started to roll towards her in disbelief as he hurtled through the air, and then she slammed him back over the table. Dishes flew, crystal shattered, and his eyes bulged, shock become agony as the point of her elbow smashed down. It hit his solar plexus like a hammer, driven by all of her weight and strength, and she whipped away from him, leaving him to die as his lungs and heart forgot to function.

Nimitz's second victim was down, screaming on the floor as he clutched at the remnants of his face, but there were more whining disrupter shots in the hall—mixed with the single, explosive crack of a regular firearm. A horde of fresh "Security" men charged through the door, all armed with disrupters, and Honor snatched a heavy metal tray from the table. It flew across the room, as accurate as Nimitz's frisbee but far more deadly, and the leading intruder's forehead erupted in blood. He went down, tripping the man behind him, tangling them all up briefly, and then the chaos became total as the Protector's bodyguards suddenly realized who the enemy truly was.

Gunfire thundered across the dining room, bullets crisscrossing with the solid-sound fists of disrupter bolts. Bodies went down on both sides, and aside from the disrupters, there was no way Honor could tell who was friend and who was foe.

But Nimitz was unhampered by any confusion. The high-pitched snarl of his battle cry wailed in her ears as he hurled himself into the face of another assassin like a furry, six-limbed buzz saw. His victim went down shrieking, and the man beside him swung his weapon towards the treecat, but Honor flew across the carpet towards him. Her right leg snapped straight, her boot crunched into his shoulder, breaking it instantly, and a hammer blow crushed his larynx as she came down on top of him.

All the Mayhews' guards were down now, but so

were many of the assassins, and Honor and Nimitz were in among the others. She knew there were too many of them, yet she and Nimitz were all that was left, and they had to keep them bottled up in the entry alcove, away from the Protector and his family, as long as they could.

The killers had known she'd be here, but she was "only" a woman. They were totally unprepared for her size and strength—and training—or the mad whirl of violence that wasn't a bit like it was on HD. Real martial arts aren't like that. The first accurate strike to get through unblocked almost always ends in either death or disablement, and when Honor Harrington hit a man, that man went down.

More feet pounded down the hallway and fresh gunfire crackled and whined as Palace Security reacted to the violence, but the remaining assassins were between Honor and the reinforcements. She tucked and rolled, taking the legs out from under two more men, then vaulted to her feet and drove a back-kick squarely into an unguarded face. A disrupter bolt whizzed past her, and iron-hard knuckles crashed into the firer's throat. Nimitz howled behind her as he took down another victim, and she smashed a man's knee into a splintered, backward bow with a side-kick. He fired wildly as he went down, killing one of his own companions, and her boot pulped his gun hand as she turned on yet another. She snaked an arm around his neck, pivoted around her own center of balance, and bent explosively, and the crack of snapping vertebrae was like another gunshot as he flew away from her.

Shouts and screams and more shots echoed from the hallway, and the assassins turned on Honor with panicky fury while their rearmost ranks wheeled to confront the reinforcements. Someone thrust a disrupter frantically in her direction, but she took out his gun arm with one chopping hand, cupped the other behind his head, and jerked his face down to meet her driving kneecap. Bone crunched and splintered, blood soaked the knee of her trousers, and she twisted towards a fresh enemy as the real Security people broke through the doorway at last.

A sledgehammer smashed into her face. She heard Nimitz's shriek of fury and anguish as it hurled her aside, twisting her in midair like a doll, but all she could feel was the pain the pain the *pain,* and then she crashed down on the side of her face and bounced limply onto her back.

The pain was gone. Only numbness and its memory remained, but her left eye was blind, and her right stared up helplessly as the man who'd shot her raised his disrupter with a snarl. She watched the weapon rise in dreadful slow motion, lining up for the pointblank final shot—and then her killer's chest exploded.

He fell across her, drenching her in steaming blood, and she turned her head weakly, hovering on the edge of the blackness. The last thing she saw was Benjamin Mayhew and Captain Fox's autopistol smoking in his hand.

• CHAPTER TWENTY-ONE

"Captain? Can you hear me, Ma'am?"

The voice trickled through her head, and she opened her eyes. Or, rather, *an* eye. She forced it to focus and blinked dizzily at the face above her.

A familiar, triangular jaw pressed into her right shoulder, and she turned her head to look into Nimitz's anxious green eyes. The 'cat lay beside her, not curled up on her in his preferred position, and he was purring so hard the bed vibrated. Her hand felt unnaturally heavy, but she raised it to his ears, and the anxious power of his purr eased slightly. She stroked him again, then looked back up at a soft sound. Andreas Venizelos stood beside Surgeon Commander Montoya, and her dapper exec looked almost as worried as Nimitz had.

"How am I?" she tried to ask, but the words came out slurred and indistinct, for only the right side of her lips had moved.

"You could be a lot better, Ma'am." Montoya's eyes sparked with anger. "Those bastards damned near killed you, Skipper."

"How bad is it?" She took her time, laboring to shape each individual sound, but it didn't seem to help a great deal.

"Not as bad as it might have been. You were lucky, Ma'am. You only caught the fringe of his shot, but if he'd been a few centimeters to the right, or a little higher—" The doctor paused and cleared his throat. "Your left cheek took the brunt of it, Skipper. The muscle damage isn't as bad as I was afraid, but the soft tissue damage is severe. It also broke the zygomatic arch—the cheekbone just below your eye—and you broke your nose when you went down. More seriously, there's near total nerve mortality from your eye to your chin and reaching around to a point about a centimeter in front of your ear. It missed your ear structure and aural nerves, luckily, and you should still have at least partial control of your jaw muscles on that side."

Montoya's was a doctor's face; it told his patients precisely what he told it to, but Venizelos' was easier to read, and his definition of "lucky" clearly didn't match Montoya's. Honor swallowed, and her left hand rose. She felt her skin against her fingers, but it was like touching someone else, for her face felt nothing at all, not even numbness or a sense of pressure.

"In the long-run, I think you'll be okay, Ma'am," Montoya said quickly. "It's going to take some extensive nerve grafting, but the damage is localized enough the repairs themselves should be fairly routine. It's going to take time, and I wouldn't care to try it, but someone like your father could handle it no sweat. In the meantime, I can take care of the broken bones and tissue damage with quick heal."

"An' m' eye?"

"Not good, Skipper," the surgeon said unflinchingly. "There are an awful lot of blood vessels in the eye. Most of them ruptured, and with muscle control gone, your eye couldn't close when you hit the carpet. Your cornea is badly lacerated, and you put some debris—broken glass and china—through it and into the eyeball itself." She stared at him through her good eye, and he looked back levelly.

"I don't think it can be repaired, Ma'am. Not enough to let you do much more than distinguish between light and dark, anyway. It's going to take a transplant, regeneration, or a prosthesis."

"I don' regen'." She clenched her fists, hating the slurred sound of her voice. "M' mom check' m' profile years 'go."

"Well, there's still transplants, Skipper," Montoya said, and she made herself nod. Most of the human race could take advantage of the relatively new regeneration techniques; Honor was one of the thirty percent who could not.

"How's th' rest 'f m' face look?" she asked.

"Awful," Montoya told her frankly. "The right side's fine, but the left one's a mess, and you're still getting some blood loss. I've drained the major edemas, and the coagulants should stop that in a little while, but frankly, Skipper, you're lucky you *can't* feel anything."

She nodded again, knowing he was right, then shoved herself into a sitting position. Montoya and Venizelos glanced at one another, and the surgeon looked as if he might protest for a moment. Then he shrugged and stood back to let her look into the mirror on the bulkhead behind him.

What she saw shocked her, despite his warning. Her pale complexion and the startlingly white dressing over her wounded eye made the livid blue, black, and scarlet damage even more appalling. She looked as if she'd been beaten with a club—which, in a sense, was exactly what *had* happened—but what filled her with dismay was the utter, dead immobility of the entire left side of her face. Her broken nose ached with a dull, low-key throb, and her right cheek felt tight with a sympathetic reaction; to the left, the pain just stopped. It didn't taper off—it just *stopped*, and the corner of her mouth hung slightly open. She tried to close it, tried to clench her cheek muscles, and nothing happened at all.

She looked into the mirror, making herself accept it, telling herself Montoya was right—that it could be fixed, whatever it looked like—but all of her self-assurances were a frail shield against her revulsion at what she saw.

"'V look' be'er," she said, and watched in numb horror as the untouched right side of her mouth and face moved normally. She drew a deep breath and tried again, very slowly. "*I*'ve look*ed* bet*t*er," she got out, and if it still sounded strange and hesitant, at least it sounded more like *her*.

"Yes, Ma'am, you have," Montoya agreed.

"Well." She wrenched her eye from the mirror and looked up at Venizelos. "Might as well get up, I guess."

The words came out almost clearly. Perhaps if she remembered the need to concentrate on speaking slowly and deliberately it wouldn't be too bad.

"I'm not sure that's a good i—" Montoya began.

"Skipper, I can handle things un—" Venizelos started simultaneously, but they both broke off as she swung her legs over the side of the bed. She put her feet on the deck, and Montoya reached out as if to stop her.

"Captain, you may not be able to *feel* it, but you've taken one hell of a beating! Commander Venizelos has things under control here, and Commander Truman's doing just fine with the squadron. They can manage a while longer."

"The doc's right, Ma'am," Venizelos weighed in. "We've got everything covered." His voice sharpened as Honor ignored them both and heaved herself to her feet. "Oh, for God's sake, Skipper! Go back to bed!"

"No." She gripped the bed for balance as the deck curtsied under her. "As you say, Doctor, I *can't* feel it," she said carefully. "I might as well take advantage of that. Where's my uniform?"

"You don't need one, because you're getting right back into bed!"

"I had one when I came in." Her eye lit on a locker. She started towards it, and if her course wavered just a bit, she ignored that.

"It's not in there," Montoya said quickly. She paused. "Your steward took it away. He said he'd *try* to get the blood out of it," he added pointedly.

"Then get me another one."

"Captain—" he began in even stronger tones, and she swung to face him. The right corner of her mouth quirked in an ironic smile that only made the hideous deadness of the left side of her face more grotesque, but there was something almost like a twinkle in her remaining eye.

"Fritz, you can get me a uniform or watch me walk

out of here in this ridiculous gown," she told him. "Now which is it going to be?"

Andreas Venizelos rose as Commander Truman stepped through the hatch. Honor didn't. She'd carried Nimitz here in her arms instead of on her shoulder because she still felt too unsteady to offer him his usual perch, and she had no intention of displaying her knees' irritating weakness any more than she could help.

She looked up at her second in command and braced herself for Truman's reaction. She'd already seen MacGuiness's shocked anger when he brought her the demanded uniform and saw her face, and Venizelos wasn't making any effort to hide his opinion that she was pushing herself too hard, so she wasn't too surprised when Truman rocked back on her heels.

"My God, Honor! What are you doing out of sickbay?!" Truman's green eyes clung to her wounded face for just a moment, then moved deliberately away, focusing on her single uncovered eye. "I've got most of the fires under control, and I'd have been perfectly happy coming down there to see you."

"I know." Honor waved to a chair and watched her subordinate sit. "But I'm not dead yet," she went on, hating the slowness of her own speech, "and I'm not going to lie around."

Truman glared at Venizelos, and the Exec shrugged.

"Fritz and I *tried*, Commander. It didn't seem to do much good."

"No, it didn't." Honor agreed. "So don't try anymore. Just tell me what's going on."

"Are you sure you're up to this? You— I'm sorry, Honor, but you have to know you look like hell, and you don't sound too good, either."

"I know. Mostly it's just my lips, though," she half-lied. She touched the left side of her mouth and wished she could feel it. "You talk. I'll listen. Start with the Protector. Is he alive?"

"Well, if you're sure." Truman sounded doubtful, but Honor nodded firmly and the commander shrugged.

"All right—and, yes, he and his family are all unhurt. It's been—" she checked her chrono "—about twenty minutes since my last update, and only about five hours since the assassination attempt, so I can't give you any hard and firm details. As far as I can make out, though, you wound up square in the middle of a coup attempt."

"Clinkscales?" she asked, but Truman shook her head.

"No, that was my first thought, too, when we thought it was Security people, but they weren't real Security men, after all. They were members of something called 'The Brotherhood of Maccabeus,' some kind of fundamentalist underground no one even suspected existed." Truman paused and frowned. "I'm not too sure I'm entirely ready to accept that they didn't know *anything* about it."

"I believe it, Ma'am." Venizelos turned to Honor. "I've been monitoring the planetary news nets a bit more closely than Commander Truman's had time for, Skipper. Aside from some pretty graphic video," he looked at her a bit oddly, "it's all conjecture with a hefty dose of hysteria, but one thing seems pretty clear. Nobody down there ever heard of the 'Maccabeans,' and no one's sure what they were trying to accomplish, either."

Honor nodded. She wasn't surprised the Graysons were in an uproar. Indeed, it would have amazed her if they hadn't been. But if Protector Benjamin was unhurt there was still a government, and at the moment, that was all she really had time to concern herself with.

"The evacuation?" she asked Truman.

"Underway," the commander assured her. "The freighters pulled out an hour ago, and I sent *Troubadour* along as far as the hyper limit to be on the safe side. Her sensors should give them plenty of warning to evade any bogeys they meet before translating."

"Good." Honor rubbed the right side of her face. The muscles on that side ached from having to do almost the whole job of moving her jaw by themselves, and the thought of trying to chew appalled her.

"Any movement out of the Masadans?" she asked after a moment.

"None. We know they know we're here, and I'd have expected them to try something by now, but there's not a sign of them."

"Command Central?"

"Not a peep out of them, Ma'am," Venizelos said. "Your Commander Brentworth is still aboard, but even he can't get much out of them right now."

"I wouldn't be too surprised by that, Honor," Truman cautioned. "If these crazies really did blind-side Grayson Security, they have to be worrying about moles in the military, at least until they get some kind of fix on how extensive the plot really was. In fact, I wouldn't be surprised if some idiot's already come up with the theory that what happened to their navy was part of some Machiavellian 'betrayal by the high command' to set up the assassination."

"So we're all there is for now," Honor said even more slowly than her damaged mouth required. "What's the status on *Troubadour*'s alpha node?"

"The Grayson yard people confirm Alistair's original estimate," Truman replied. "It's completely gone, and they can't repair it. Their Warshawski technology's even cruder than I thought, and their components simply won't mate with ours, but their standard impellers are a lot closer to our levels, and Lieutenant Anthony got with their chief shipwright before I sent *Troubadour* off with the freighters. By the time she gets back, the Graysons should have run up jury-rigged beta nodes to replace the damaged beta *and* alpha nodes. She still won't have Warshawski capability, but she'll be back up to five-twenty gees for max acceleration."

"Time to change over?"

"Anthony estimates twenty hours; the Graysons say fifteen. In this case, the Graysons are probably closer to right. I think Anthony's less than impressed by their technical support and underestimates its capabilities."

Honor nodded, then snatched her hand away before it could begin massaging her face again.

"All right. If we can stand her down long enough, then—"

Her terminal beeped, and she pressed the answer key. "Yes?"

"Captain, I've got a personal signal for you from Grayson," Lieutenant Metzinger's voice said. "From Protector Benjamin."

Honor looked at her subordinates, then straightened in her chair.

"Switch him through," she said.

Her terminal screen blinked instantly to life, and a drawn and weary Benjamin Mayhew looked out of it. His eyes widened, then darkened with distress as he saw her face and covered eye.

"Captain Harrington, I—" His voice was husky, and he had to stop and cough, then blinked hard and cleared his throat noisily.

"Thank you," he said finally. "You saved my family's lives, and my own. I am eternally in your debt."

The live side of Honor's face heated, and she shook her head.

"Sir, you saved *my* life in the end. And I was only protecting myself, as well."

"Of course." Mayhew managed a tired smile. "That's why you and your treecat—" His eyes cut suddenly to her unoccupied shoulder. "He *is* all right, isn't he? I understood—"

"He's fine, Sir." She kicked herself for speaking too quickly in her haste to reassure him, for the words had come out so slurred they were almost incomprehensible. Rather than embarrass herself by repeating them, she scooped Nimitz up and exhibited him to the com pickup, and Mayhew relaxed bit.

"Thank God for that! Elaine was almost as worried over him as we've all been over you, Captain."

"We're tough, Sir," she said slowly and distinctly. "We'll be all right."

He looked doubtfully at her crippled face and tried to hide his dismay. He knew Manticoran medical science was better than anything available on Grayson, but he'd seen the bloody wreckage of her eye as the RMN medics—and grim-faced Royal Manticoran Marines in full battle dress—whisked her away. The rest of the damage looked even worse now, and her slurred speech and paralyzed muscles were only too evident . . . and hideous. The swollen, frozen deadness of a face which had been so mobile and expressive was a desecration, and despite any off-world sophistication, he was a Grayson. Nothing could completely eradicate the belief that women were supposed to be protected, and the fact that she'd suffered her injuries protecting *him* only made it worse.

"Really, Sir. We'll be fine," she said, and he decided he had no choice but to take her at her word.

"I'm glad to hear it. In the meantime, however," his voice turned suddenly harsher, "I thought you might like to hear who was behind the coup."

"You know?" Honor leaned forward and felt Venizelos and Truman stiffen with matching interest.

"Yes." Mayhew looked almost physically ill. "We've got his confession on tape. It was my cousin Jared."

"Your *cousin?*" Honor gasped before she could stop herself, and he nodded miserably.

"Apparently all his anti-Masadan rhetoric's been nothing more than a cover, Captain. He's been working for them for over eight years. In fact, Councilman Clinks- cales now thinks he was the second 'Maccabeus,' not the first. He thinks my Uncle Oliver passed the position on to him when he died."

"My God," Honor whispered.

"We're just starting to put it all together," Mayhew went on in that same wretched tone, "but Security got several assassins alive, mainly thanks to your treecat. Aside from the first one he attacked, he seems to have settled for blinding his opponents. I'm afraid only one of the ones *you* hit survived."

Honor said nothing. She merely sat watching his expression and feeling his pain. She was an only child, but the Harrington clan was an extensive one. She didn't need anyone to tell her how terribly it must hurt to know his own cousin had plotted his family's murder.

"At any rate," the Protector continued after a moment, "Howard and his people took them into custody, patched them up, and interrogated them. Howard won't tell me exactly how. I think he's afraid I wouldn't approve of his methods, but whatever he did to them, some of them talked fairly quickly, and he's been able to put together at least a rough chronology.

"Apparently Masada's been building a fifth column out of our own reactionaries ever since the last war. We never even guessed—something else Howard blames himself for—but that was because, religious fanatics or not, these 'Maccabeans' apparently realized their ideals were too divorced from the mainstream for them to achieve anything by open resistance or guerrilla warfare. So instead of coming into the open and alienating the population as a whole—not to mention warning Security of their existence—they've been waiting until they thought they had a chance to decapitate the state in one blow."

"And replace you with your cousin," Honor said flatly.

"Precisely." Mayhew's voice was equally flat. "None of the assassins had ever actually met him, but the support they'd been given—genuine uniforms and IDs, the exact guard schedule, detailed maps, Palace Security's challenges and countersigns—all pointed to someone inside the palace itself. And they *could* tell Howard's people how to locate the 'Maccabean' communications net, which led him to a couple of plotters who *did* know who 'Maccabeus' was."

Mayhew looked away for a moment.

"Howard was devastated. He and Jared have been close Council allies for years, and he felt personally betrayed. But instead of arresting him immediately, Howard confronted him in person, and Jared was stupid enough—or desperate enough—to *admit* he was Maccabeus. Apparently he hoped Howard shared enough of his beliefs to join him. I imagine he thought the two of them together could still kill me and put Jared in my place . . . instead, Howard recorded the entire conversation, then called in his people to arrest him."

"Protector Benjamin," Honor said softly, "you have my sincere sympathy. To know your cousin—"

"If Jared could betray my planet to Masada, if he could plot to kill my family and *succeed* in killing men who protected me from birth," Mayhew said harshly, "he is no cousin of mine! The law of Grayson sets only one penalty for what he's done, Captain Harrington. When the time comes, he'll pay it."

Honor bent her head silently, and the Protector's nostrils flared. Then he shook himself.

"At any rate, he's clammed up since his arrest. Whatever else he may be, he seems to hold his beliefs honestly. But he made the mistake of keeping records. They've told Howard a lot, and he believes he can break the entire organization with them.

"It seems Jared's position as Minister of Industry was the key to the entire plot. His father, my uncle, held the same position before him, and they'd placed entire crews of Maccabeans on some of the mining and construction ships. The Masadans have been slipping in and out of Yeltsin for some time—Mike tells me it probably wasn't difficult if they translated into n-space beyond detection range, then came in under minimal power— and Jared's Maccabean crews have been rendezvousing with them as his couriers to Masada.

"Howard isn't positive, but he now believes this war was launched not as a genuine bid to conquer us militarily but to create panic. According to one of Jared's people, the plan was for him to have Michael and myself killed at what he judged was the proper psychological moment. That would have made him Protector, and if there'd been enough fear and confusion, he could have made himself dictator, as well, on the pretext of dealing with the crisis—at which point he would have 'negotiated an end to the hostilities.' Ending the war without Masada's actually attacking the planet itself was supposed to cement his hold on power, after which he'd have appointed like-minded cronies to positions of power in order to 'reform' us into voluntarily accepting the Masadan line and, eventually, amalgamating with Endicott."

"I can't believe he'd have succeeded," Honor murmured.

"I don't think so either, but *he* did, and he'd managed to convince Masada. And if it could have been pulled off, it would have been perfect from the Faithful's viewpoint. They'd have gotten their hands on us and our industry without all the damage a fight to the finish would inflict, and Jared would have terminated our negotiations with you as his very first step. With your Kingdom out of the way, Masada—which, Howard tells me, is definitely working with Haven—would've had the only outside ally. If his 'reform' approach failed, they still could have used that edge to pick us off any time."

"But do the Peeps know what's going on, Sir?" Commander Truman leaned diffidently into the com pickup's field, and the Protector raised his eyebrows at her. "Commander Alice Truman, Sir," she identified herself, and he gestured for her to continue.

"It just seems unlikely to me that Haven would willingly attack a Queen's ship and risk war with Manticore as part of any such long-term, iffy operation, Sir. Even assuming we didn't wind up at war with *them*—and I'm not at all sure they *would* assume that—there'd be too many opportunities for something to go wrong on Grayson that might get us invited back in."

"I'm afraid we don't know the answer to that yet, Commander," Mayhew said after a moment's thought. "I'll ask Howard to look into it. On the face of it, however, I can't see that it matters much. The Faithful are committed now, and they've lost their 'Maccabeus.' I don't see that they've got any choice but to follow through on the military option."

"Agreed." Honor realized she was rubbing the left side of her face again and lowered her hand. "Of course, if they did know the truth, and if they expected Maccabeus to make his try, that may explain why they've held off this long. They're waiting to see if he succeeded."

"If they knew his timetable, then they also know he's failed," Mayhew said, and Honor's eyebrows rose. At least both of *them* still worked, she thought, but her mordant humor vanished as Mayhew went on. "If his plan had succeeded, Captain, your next in command—Commander Truman, is it?" Honor nodded, and he shrugged. "Well, then, Commander Truman would already have pulled your vessels out of here."

Alice Truman bristled at his assumption that anything could have induced her to abandon Grayson to Masada.

"And why might that have been, Sir?" she asked stiffly.

"Because the entire idea was to place responsibility for my death on Captain Harrington," he said quietly, and all three Manticorans stared at him in disbelief.

"That was why they were armed with disrupters, Captain. Those aren't Grayson—or, for that matter, Masadan—weapons. The plan was to claim your demand for a meeting was only a pretext to get close to me, at which point you were supposed to have produced your off-world weapon, murdered my guards and family as part of a *Manticoran* plot to seize Grayson, and then been shot down by other Security people when you tried to escape."

"He 'as ou' 'f his mind!" The right side of Honor's face tightened as the clarity of her speech vanished, but Mayhew seemed not to notice, and she went on doggedly. "No one would have believed that!" she said more distinctly.

"I don't know about that, Captain," Mayhew admitted with manifest reluctance. "I admit it would have sounded insane, but remember what a pressure cooker Grayson is right now. With me dead and your body as 'evidence,' he probably could have produced enough panic and confusion to at least get himself into office and summarily break off the negotiations. If he managed that and informed Commander Truman your ships were no longer welcome in Yeltsin space, what could she do but leave? Especially when he could construe any decision to remain as further 'proof' of a Manticoran plot to seize Yeltsin's Star?"

"He's got a point, Honor," Truman muttered, tugging at a lock of golden hair. "Damn. I hate to admit it, but he does have a point."

"So if they knew his timetable, and if they're monitoring the inner system for outbound impeller signatures, they know he failed," Honor said.

"Unless we get dead lucky and they're dumb enough to think the freighters are all of us," Truman agreed.

"Which they're very unlikely to do," Mayhew pointed out from the com screen. "They know precisely how many of your vessels are present. Jared saw to that . . . just as he told them exactly what classes of warship you have."

"Oh, *shit!*" Venizelos muttered audibly, and a bleak smile flitted across the Protector's lips.

"Then we can expect them to react militarily shortly." Honor realized she was rubbing her numb face again, but this time she let herself go on doing so. "Protector Benjamin, that makes it imperative that we waste no more time. I *must* be able to confer with your navy immediately."

"I agree, and you won't have any further problems in that regard."

"Then Admiral Garret's been relieved?" she asked hopefully.

"Not precisely." Her good eye narrowed, but Mayhew smiled almost naturally at her. "I've managed to save face a little for him, Captain—which is important, given the state of nerves down here right now. Instead of relieving him, I've appointed him to command Grayson's fixed orbital defenses. Commodore Matthews has been promoted to admiral, and he'll command our *mobile* units. I've made it very clear to him that that means he's to adapt his movements and resources to yours, and he has no problem with that."

"That might work," Honor said while her mind raced,

"but Command Central's still our central com node, Sir. If Garret decides to sulk—"

"He won't, Captain. He won't dare to do anything that *anyone* down here might perceive as an insult to you." Honor's eyebrows rose once more at the total assurance in his voice, and it was his turn to look surprised.

"Haven't you been monitoring our news nets, Captain?"

"Sir, I just got out of sickbay forty minutes ago." Honor frowned, wondering what news nets had to do with anything, then remembered Venizelos' odd expression when *he'd* mentioned them. She gave him a sharp look, and he shrugged with something suspiciously like a grin.

"I see." Mayhew's voice drew her eye back to the com screen. "In that case, you wouldn't know. Just a second." He killed his audio for a moment while he turned his head to speak to someone else, then looked back at her.

"What you're about to see has been playing practically nonstop over the video nets ever since the assassination attempt, courtesy of the palace surveillance system, Captain. I'd estimate it's already been seen more often and by more eyes than any other news report in our history."

His face disappeared before she could ask what he was talking about. The screen was completely blank for a second—then something else appeared.

It left a lot to be desired from an artistic viewpoint, a corner of her brain thought, but the imagery was remarkably clear for something as crude as video tape. It was the dinner party, and she saw herself leaning towards the Protector and listening attentively to him just as Nimitz erupted from his stool and attacked the first assassin.

She stared at the screen, appalled by the carnage, as her own image lunged up from its chair and killed the second assassin. Captain Fox went down, and she watched herself take out his killer, then whirl towards the others charging towards her. The thrown platter dropped their leader, and then people fell in all directions as gunfire ripped back and forth across the room.

She felt a stab of terror there'd been no time to feel then as she watched men crumple and die and wondered how she and Nimitz could possibly have been missed in that crossfire, and then she saw her own desperate charge as the last of the Protector's guards died.

The tape went to slow motion after that, but it still didn't last long. Indeed, it had seemed much longer at the time. Bodies seemed to fly away from her, she saw flashes of a raging Nimitz taking others down, and that same corner of her mind wondered how her Academy instructors would have rated her form.

It seemed impossible that she'd survived, and as she watched Nimitz claw down a man who'd been about to shoot her in the back she knew she wouldn't have without her diminutive ally. She reached out to him, still staring at the screen, and he purred reassuringly as he pressed his head against her palm.

Dead and crippled assassins littered the floor around her as the Security response team broke through at last, and she felt her entire body tense as the man who'd shot her did it all over again. Her image went down on the screen, and sweat beaded her forehead as the disrupter swung towards her once more, and then he was down and dead and the screen went blank.

Mayhew's face reappeared, and he smiled soberly at her.

"That's what all of Grayson's been seeing for the last several hours, Captain Harrington—a tape of you saving the lives of my family," he said softly, and the living side of her face flamed.

"Sir, I—" she began hesitantly, but his raised hand silenced her.

"Don't say it, Captain. I won't embarrass you by saying it again, but I don't have to, either. That tape should rather conclusively discredit any claim that *you* were behind the assassination attempt, I think. And after seeing it, no one on this planet—including Admiral Garret—will ever dare to question your fitness as an officer again, now will they?"

• CHAPTER TWENTY-TWO

It was the first time she'd been to Command Central. Its size impressed her, but the noisiness of the status room was startling, and the shrill ringing of priority com signals, the rumble of voices, and the clatter of printers did more than startle Nimitz. He rose high on her shoulder, ears half-flattened, and his high-pitched bleek of protest cut through the background noise like a knife.

Heads turned all over the huge room, and Honor felt the ugliness of her wounded face like a brand. Commander Brentworth bristled at her side and stepped forward, glaring back at all comers, regardless of rank, but she stopped him with a tiny gesture. There was curiosity in all those stares, and shock, even repugnance, in some of them as they saw her face, but not intentional rudeness, and most of them flushed and looked away almost as quickly as they'd turned towards her.

Commodore Brentworth had been waiting for her small party. Now he materialized out of the crowd and offered his hand with only the slightest hesitation.

"I'm Commodore Walter Brentworth, Captain," he said, and if there'd been any hesitation when he held out his hand, there was none in his use of her rank. "Welcome to Command Central."

"Thank you, Commodore," she said as clearly as she could. She'd practiced hard to master her stiff lips, but his eyes flickered at the slurring she couldn't quite overcome. She knew they wanted to cling to the crippled side of her face, but he kept them resolutely under control.

"These are my captains," she went on. "Commander Truman of the *Apollo*, and Commander McKeon of the

253

Troubadour. I believe—" the mobile corner of her mouth quirked slightly "—that you know Commander Brentworth."

"Yes, I believe I do." The commodore smiled at her, then nodded to his son and shook hands with Truman and McKeon. Then he turned back to Honor. "Captain," he began, "please allow me to apologize for any—"

"No apologies are necessary, Commodore," she interrupted him, but the commodore clearly shared his son's stubborn integrity. He seemed about to disagree, and she went on in the short sentences her impaired speech enforced. "We come from very different backgrounds. There was bound to be some friction. What's important is seeing to it that there isn't any more."

He looked up at her, letting his gaze rest frankly on her swollen, paralyzed face at last, then nodded slowly.

"You're right, Captain," he said, then smiled. "Mark said you had your head on straight, and I've always had considerable faith in his judgment."

"Good, because I do, too," Honor said firmly, and the commander blushed. His father chuckled and waved for the Manticorans to follow him.

"Let me escort you to Admiral Garret, Captain." There was a hint of amusement in his voice. "I believe he's been awaiting you with some anticipation."

Admiral Leon Garret was a craggy-faced man whose hooded eyes watched Honor with a sort of hypnotized fascination as she stepped into the conference room. It was a fascination which extended itself to Nimitz, as well, and she wondered which of them he found more *outré*—the six-limbed "animal" who'd proved so unexpectedly deadly, or the woman who wore a captain's uniform?

He rose at her approach, but he didn't extend his hand. Had his inner confusion been less evident, she might have construed that as an insult. As it was, and despite the gravity of the situation, his expression almost betrayed her. A totally inappropriate giggle fluttered at the base of her throat, and she suppressed it only with difficulty as Commodore Brentworth introduced her small group to Garret and his officers.

The man at the admiral's right hand had already attracted her attention. He wore a commodore's uniform but an admiral's collar insignia, and she wasn't surprised when he was introduced as Admiral Wesley Matthews. She sized him up carefully, not rudely but without making any effort to hide her one-eyed evaluation, and he squared his shoulders and looked back frankly.

She liked what she saw. Matthews was short, even for a Grayson, stocky and solid, with an intelligent, mobile face, and there were no sex-based reservations in his hazel eyes. She remembered what Lord Mayhew had said and decided he'd been right. She wouldn't have any problems working with this man.

"Thank you for coming, uh, Captain Harrington." Garret flushed as he stumbled over her rank, then pointed at the empty chairs on her side of the conference table and went on more naturally. "Please, be seated."

"Thank you, Admiral." She sat, followed by her subordinates. She felt Nimitz's expressive tail twitch against her back, but he was aware of the need to mind his manners. She lifted him down to sit beside the blotter before her and noted the way the Grayson officers watched him move. Clearly they'd been impressed by the video of his bloody handiwork, and one or two of them looked a bit uneasy. Well, it was hard to blame them; few *Manticorans* realized how lethal a 'cat could be when he or his human was threatened.

"Yes, well." Garret cleared his throat. "As you know, Captain," he got her title out without hesitation this time, "Com—Admiral Matthews has been placed in command of our mobile units. It's my understanding that you believe it would be more advantageous to employ them with your vessels in a forward defense rather than from an orbital position."

He hid the chagrin he must be feeling (given that the orbital idea had been his) quite well, Honor thought with unexpected sympathy.

"Yes, Sir, I do." Her sympathy helped her keep any hint of satisfaction out of her voice. "Our current estimate is that one heavy and one light Havenite cruiser are supporting Masada. If that's true, my squadron should be able to take them on without the assistance of your orbital defenses. At the same time, Masada used nuclear weapons against planetary targets thirty-five years ago and has repeatedly stated its willingness to do so again. Now that 'Maccabeus' has failed, we must assume they'll do just that. Under the circumstances, I believe we must keep them as far from Grayson as possible."

"But if you deploy yourself on the wrong bearing," one of Garret's staff officers said quietly, "they may slip past and get the attack in anyway. And with your ships out of position, our own defensive systems are unlikely to stop warheads with modern penetration aids, Captain."

"I'm sure the Captain's thought of that, Commander Calgary," Garret said uncomfortably. It was clear Protector Benjamin had had a long talk with him, but Honor simply nodded, for Commander Calgary's point was well taken.

"You're correct, Commander. But there are offsetting considerations." She spoke firmly, minimizing the slurring of her words. "They know where Grayson is. If their goal is simply to bombard, they can launch from extreme range at near-light velocity. Once their missile drives go dead, even our sensors will have trouble localizing them for point defense. My ships could intercept most of them, but we're talking about nukes. We have to catch them *all*, and our best chance for that is while they're still in boost phase."

Calgary nodded his understanding, and she went on.

"Admittedly, moving away from Grayson will open the threat window. We have, however, certain technical advantages we believe are unknown to Haven."

A stir went through the Graysons, and she felt Truman's residual unhappiness beside her. What she proposed to describe to the Graysons was still on the

Official Secrets List, and Truman had opposed its revelation. On the other hand, even Alice had to admit they didn't have any choice but to use it, and that meant telling their allies about it.

"Advantages, Captain?" Garret asked.

"Yes, Sir. Commander McKeon is our expert on the system, so I'll let him explain. Commander?"

"Yes, Ma'am." Alistair McKeon faced the Grayson officers. "What Captain Harrington refers to, gentlemen, is a newly developed reconnaissance drone. RDs have always played a role in our defensive doctrine, but like every surveillance system, light-speed data transmission has always limited the range/response time envelope. In essence, the RD can tell us someone's coming, but if we're too far out of position, we can't respond in time."

He paused, and several heads nodded.

"Our R&D people have been working on a new approach, however, and for the first time, we now have a limited FTL transmission capability."

"An *FTL* capability?" Calgary blurted, and he was far from alone in his astonishment, for the human race had sought a way to send messages faster than light for almost two thousand years.

"Yes, Sir. Its range is too limited for anything other than tactical purposes—our best transmission radius is only about four light-hours at this time—but that's quite enough to give us a marked advantage."

"Excuse me, Commander McKeon," Admiral Matthews said, "but how does it *work?* If, that is," he looked at Honor, "you can tell us without compromising your own security."

"We'd rather not go into details, Admiral," Honor replied. "Less because of security, than because it's too technical for a quick explanation."

"And," Matthews grinned wryly, "because it's probably too technical for our people to duplicate even if we *understood* the explanation."

Honor was appalled by his remark, but then a rumble of chuckles came from the other side of the table. She'd been afraid of stepping on sensitive toes by flaunting her ships' technical superiority, but it seemed Matthews understood his people better than she did. And perhaps it was his way of telling her not to worry.

"I imagine that's true, Sir," she said, smiling with the right side of her mouth, "at least until we bring you up to speed on molycircs and super-dense fusion bottles. Of course," her smile grew, "once the treaty is signed, I expect your navy is going to get *much* nastier all around."

The Grayson chuckles were even louder this time, tinged with more than an edge of relief. She hoped they didn't expect a God weapon to come out of her technological bag of tricks, but anything that bolstered their morale at this moment was well worth while, and she nodded for Alistair to continue.

"Basically, Admiral," he said, "it's a reversion to old-fashioned Morse code. Our new-generation RDs carry an extra gravity generator which they use to create extremely powerful directional pulses. Since gravitic sensors are FTL, we have effective real-time receipt across their maximum range."

"That's brilliant," a captain with Office of Shipbuilding insignia murmured. Then he frowned. "And difficult, I'd imagine."

"It certainly is," McKeon said feelingly. "The power requirement is enormous—our people had to develop an entire new generation of fusion plants to pull it off—and that's only the first problem. Designing a pulse grav generator and packing it into the drone body came next. As you can probably imagine, it uses up a lot more mass than a drive unit, and it was a monster to engineer. And there are certain fundamental limitations on the system. Most importantly, it takes time for the generator to produce each pulse without burning itself out, which places an insurmountable limit on the data transmission speed. At present, we can only manage a pulse repetition rate of about nine-point-five seconds. Obviously, it's going to take us a while to transmit any complex messages at that rate."

"That's true," Honor put in, "but what we propose to

do is program the onboard computers to respond to the most likely threat parameters with simple three or four-pulse codes. They'll identify the threat's basic nature and approach in less than a minute. The drones can follow up with more detailed messages once we've started responding."

"I see." Matthews nodded quickly. "And with that kind of advance warning, we can position ourselves to cut them off short of optimum launch range against the planet."

"Yes, Sir." Honor nodded to him, then looked at Admiral Garret. "More than that, Admiral, we'll have time to build an intercept vector that lets us stay with them instead of finding ourselves with a base velocity so low as to give us only a limited engagement time before they break past us."

"I understand, Captain." Garret plucked at his lip, then nodded. "I understand," he repeated, and she was relieved at the absence of acrimony in his tone. "If I'd realized you had this capability, I would have approached the entire problem differ—" He stopped himself and smiled crookedly. "Of course, if I'd bothered to ask you, I might have known about it sooner, mightn't I?"

Honor saw amazement on more than one Grayson face, as if they couldn't quite believe what they'd just heard him say, and she wondered how to respond, but then he shrugged and smiled more naturally.

"Well, Captain, they say there's no fool like an old fool. Do Manticorans use that expression?"

"Not to senior officers, Sir," Honor said demurely, and Garret startled her by bursting into laughter. His guffaws reminded her of a neighing horse, but no one could have doubted their genuineness. He couldn't get a word out through them, though he pointed a finger at her and tried hard, and she felt herself grinning lopsidedly at him.

"Point taken, Captain," he gasped at last, and there were smiles on other faces on his side of the table. "Point taken, indeed." He settled himself in his chair and nodded. "Do you have any other ideas, Captain Harrington?"

"Well, Sir, as you know, we've evacuated our own noncombatants aboard our freighters." Garret nodded, and Honor shrugged. "Commander Truman's report included an urgent request for reinforcements. I'm certain that request will be granted, but those are slow ships, Sir. I'd have preferred to send one of my warships, but I can't spare *Apollo* if we may be facing two modern cruisers, and *Troubadour*'s node damage would restrict her to impeller drive. More, she couldn't get much above the gamma band without reliable Warshawski sails. If one of *your* hyper-capable ships could be sent—?"

She paused, for Garret and Matthews were both shaking their heads. Matthews glanced at Garret, and his superior nodded for him to explain.

"We can do it, Captain, but our hyper technology is much cruder than yours. Our ships are restricted to the middle gamma bands, and our Warshawski sails won't let us pull anywhere near as much accel from a given grav wave. I doubt we could cut more than a day or so off your freighters' time. Under the circumstances, I think we'll be better employed keeping what's left of the Masadan Navy off your back while you deal with the Havenites."

Honor glanced at Truman and McKeon. Truman gave her a small nod, and McKeon simply shrugged. None of them had realized Grayson hyper capability was that limited, but Matthews was right. The small time saving would be much less useful than the support of another warship here, especially since it was unlikely the Masadans would delay their attack more than another few hours.

"I think you're right, Admiral Matthews," she agreed. "In that case, I'm afraid all we can do is get our mobile units ready for action and deploy the RDs. Unless—"

Someone knocked on the conference room door, then opened it to admit the chatter of printers, and Honor's eyebrows rose. The newcomer was a burly, white-haired man in the uniform of a Security general, not a naval officer.

"Councilman Clinkscales!" Garret exclaimed. He and his staff stood quickly, and the Manticorans followed them. "What can I do for, you, Sir?"

"Sorry to interrupt you, gentlemen . . . ladies." Clinkscales paused, his fierce old eyes examining Honor and Alice Truman with frank but wary curiosity. He advanced and held out his hand rather abruptly. "Captain Harrington." She took his hand, and he squeezed hard, as if he were determined to reject the least suggestion that he was concerned about feminine frailty.

"Councilman Clinkscales," she murmured, squeezing back with equal strength, and his mouth twitched into a wintry smile.

"I wanted to thank you," he said abruptly. "Grayson owes you a tremendous debt—and so do I." He was clearly uncomfortable saying that, but his determination to get it out was obvious.

"I just happened to be there, Sir. And it was actually Nimitz who saved the day. If he hadn't reacted so quickly—" She shrugged.

"True." Clinkscales gave a quick bark of laughter. "Wonder if he'd be willing to join Palace Security?"

"I'm afraid not, Sir." The undamaged side of Honor's mouth smiled, and she realized that he, alone of everyone she'd met since the attack, seemed unembarrassed by the condition of her face. Apparently once he decided someone was a real officer, he expected them to bear their battle scars the same way *he* would have, and she discovered that she actually liked this old dinosaur.

"Pity," he said, then looked at Garret. "As I say, I'm sorry to interrupt, but my people've got one of the Maccabean resource ship pilots, and he's singing like a bird."

"He is?" Garret's eyes sharpened, and Honor felt a matching interest.

"He is," Clinkscales said grimly. "He doesn't know

shi—" He stopped and looked at Honor and Truman, and Honor forced herself not to smile again.

"He doesn't know anything about the Havenite ships' actual classes," the councilman corrected himself, "but he *does* know that Masada's put in an advanced base in this system."

"In *Yeltsin?*" Garret sounded shocked, and Clinkscales shrugged.

"That's what he says. He's never seen it, and according to his friends who have, it wasn't easy to build. But he does know where it is, *and* he says their 'biggest ship,' whatever it is, may be in Endicott right now."

"It may?" Honor leaned towards him. "Did he say why?"

"Something about towing their LACs over here," Clinkscales said, and Honor's eye widened in surprise. She'd never heard of anyone trying that! Which didn't mean it was impossible. And it certainly explained how they'd gotten them here. But if they had modern ships, why were they wasting time bringing over something as crude as Masadan LACs in the first place?

"How positive is he that she's gone?" she asked, shaking off the irrelevant questions. "And does he know when she's due back?"

"He knows she was due to leave," Clinkscales said. "He doesn't know if she's still gone, but it occurred to me that her absence might explain why they haven't already attacked, and if it does, their continued lack of activity could be an indication that she hasn't gotten back yet."

"It could be, Sir," she murmured. She glanced at Truman and McKeon. "On the other hand, we've been in-system for almost twenty-six hours. Even if she left just before we arrived, she should have had time to get back by now. Unless. . . ." She rubbed the numb side of her face, then looked back at Truman. "Any idea what their transit time might be towing LACs, Alice?"

"I don't think there's any way to know without actually trying it ourselves. No one else ever did it, as far as I know. In fact, I don't think *they* could have, if

Yeltsin and Endicott were any further apart. As for how fast they can make the passage, they'd probably have to take it pretty easy, but as for *how* easy—" Truman shrugged.

"A lot would depend on what they're using as a tug, Skipper," McKeon offered. "The mass ratio would be fairly critical, I'd think. And they'd have to use something with enough tractor capacity to completely zone a LAC, too."

Honor nodded, still rubbing her dead cheek, then shrugged. "Either way, just knowing where to find them should be a major plus. Assuming the information is reliable."

She looked at Clinkscales, and the hard gleam in the Security commander's eye was almost frightening.

"Oh, it's reliable, Captain," he assured her in a chilling tone. "They've put in a base on Blackbird—that's one of Uriel's moons," he added for Honor's benefit, and she nodded. That made sense. Uriel—Yeltsin VI—was a gas giant larger than Sol's Jupiter, with an orbital radius of almost fifty-one light-minutes, which put it well beyond sensor range of anything Grayson had.

"What sort of basing facilities do they have?" Admiral Matthews asked sharply, and Clinkscales shrugged.

"That I don't know, Admiral, and neither does he. Not in any detail." The councilman produced an old-fashioned audio tape. "I brought along everything he could tell us in case your people could make a better estimate from it. All he could tell us for sure is that 'Maccabeus'—" the old man refused to use Jared Mayhew's name "—diverted some of our own construction ships with Maccabean crews to help them build it. His wasn't among them, unfortunately, but he heard one of the other captains commenting on the fact that they've put in modern sensors. They may have a few Havenite heavy weapons, as well, though he's not sure about that."

"Damn," someone muttered from the Grayson side of the table, and the right side of Honor's face tightened.

"I don't think they could have turned Blackbird into

any kind of real fortress," Matthews said quickly. "Not unless they can generate a sidewall bubble around a moon eight thousand kilometers in diameter." He looked questioningly at Honor, and she shook her head.

"No, Sir. Not even Manticore can work miracles yet," she said dryly.

"Then whatever they've got was probably designed to stop *us*. They certainly haven't put up any orbital platforms. They took a risk just setting up a moon-side base, because we conduct periodic exercises in the area. Maccabeus—" like Clinkscales, Matthews refused to use Mayhew's name "—had access to our schedules, so he could have warned them when to lie low, but they couldn't have counted on hiding orbital installations from us."

Honor nodded again, following his logic.

"And fixed defenses would be far more vulnerable than my ships." She spoke more rapidly, and her words slurred badly, but no one seemed to notice.

"Exactly. And if there's a chance most of their Havenite firepower is elsewhere—" Matthews suggested.

Honor looked at him for a moment and realized she was rubbing her face much harder. She made herself stop before she further damaged the insensitive skin, then nodded decisively.

"Absolutely, Admiral. How soon can your units be ready to move out?"

• CHAPTER TWENTY-THREE

"Skipper?"

Thomas Theisman jerked awake, and his executive officer stepped back quickly as he sat up and swung his legs over the edge of the couch.

"What?" he asked thickly, rubbing at sleep-crusted eyes. "Is it the Captain?"

"No, Sir," Lieutenant Hillyard said unhappily, "but we're picking up an awful lot of impeller signatures headed this way."

"This way? Towards *Uriel?*"

"Slap bang towards Blackbird, Skipper." Hillyard met his eyes with an anxious grimace.

"Oh, *fuck*." Theisman shoved himself erect and wished he'd never left the People's Republic. "What kind of signatures? Harrington's?"

"No, Sir."

"I'm in no mood for bad jokes, Al!"

"I'm not kidding, Skipper. We don't see her anywhere."

"Damn it, there's no way the Graysons would come after us alone! Harrington *has* to be out there!"

"If she is, we haven't seen her yet, Sir."

"Goddamn it." Theisman massaged his face, trying to knead some life back into his brain. Captain Yu was forty hours overdue, the reports coming up from moonside were enough to turn a man's stomach, and now *this* shit.

"All right." He straightened with a spine-cracking pop and picked up his cap. "Let's get to the bridge and see what's going on, Al."

"Yes, Sir." The exec followed him from the cabin. "We only picked them up about five minutes ago," he went on. "We've been getting some funny readings from in-system, some kind of discrete gravity pulses." Theisman looked at him, and Hillyard shrugged. "Can't make anything out of them, Skipper. They're scattered all over the place, and they don't seem to be *doing* anything, but trying to run them down had our sensors looking the wrong way. They may have been decelerating for as much as thirty minutes before we picked them up."

"Um." Theisman rubbed his chin, and Hillyard looked at his profile.

"Skipper," he said hesitantly, "tell me if I'm out of line, but have you heard anything about what's happening ground-side?"

"You *are* out of line!" The lieutenant recoiled, and Theisman grimaced. "Sorry, Al. And, yes, I've heard, but—" He slammed a fist explosively into the bulkhead beside him, then jerked to a stop and swung to face his exec.

"There's not a goddamned thing I can do, Al. If it was up to me, I'd shoot every one of the sons-of-bitches—but don't you breathe a word of that, even to *our* people!" He held Hillyard's eyes fiercely until the exec nodded choppily, then rubbed his face again.

"Jesus, I hate this *stinking* job! The Captain never figured on this, Al. I know how he'd feel about it, and I made my own position as clear to Franks as I can, but I can't queer the deal for the Captain when I don't know how *he'd* handle it. Besides," he smiled crookedly, "we don't have any Marines."

"Yes, Sir." Hillyard looked down at the deck, and his mouth worked. "It just makes me feel so . . . dirty."

"You and me both, Al. You and me both." Theisman sighed. He started back down the passage, and Hillyard had to half-trot to keep up with him. "When I get home—*if* I get home—" Theisman muttered savagely, "I'm gonna find whatever Staff puke thought this one up. I don't care who the bastard is, he's dog shit when I find him. I didn't sign up for this kind of garbage, and rank won't help the son-of-a-bitch in a dark alley!" He broke off and looked sidelong at Hillyard. "You didn't hear that, Lieutenant," he said crisply.

"Of course not, Sir." Hillyard took another few steps and looked back up at his commander. "Want a little help in that alley, Skipper?"

She missed Nimitz. The back of her command chair seemed empty and incomplete without him, but Nimitz was tucked away in his life-support module. He hadn't been any happier at being parted than she was, yet he'd been there before, and he'd settled down without demur when she sealed him in. Now she put the lonely feeling out of her mind and studied her plot.

A solid wedge of LACs led her ship, its corners anchored by Grayson's three surviving starships, while *Troubadour* and *Apollo* were tucked in tight on *Fearless's* port and starboard quarters. It was scarcely an orthodox formation, especially since it put the best sensor suites behind the less capable Grayson units, but if it worked the way it was supposed to . . .

She heard a soft sound and looked up to see Commander Brentworth playing with his helmet beside her chair. His bulky vac gear marked him as a stranger among her bridge crew's skin suits, and, unlike everyone else, he had nothing to do but stand there and worry.

He felt her eye and looked down, and she smiled her lopsided smile.

"Feeling out of place, Mark?" she asked quietly, and he gave her a sheepish nod. "Don't worry about it. We're glad you're aboard."

"Thanks, Ma'am. I just feel sort of useless with nothing to do, I guess." He nodded at her plot. "In fact, the whole Fleet probably feels that way right now."

"Well, we certainly can't have that, Commander!" a cheerful voice said, and Honor's good eye twinkled, as Venizelos appeared on the other side of her chair. "Tell you what," the exec went on, "leave us the Peeps, and we'll let you have all the Masadans. How's that?"

"It sounds fair to me, Commander." Brentworth grinned.

"Good enough." Venizelos looked down at his captain. "Steve makes it another hour and fifty-eight minutes, Skipper. Think they know we're here?"

"They're down to two-six-oh-five-four KPS, Sir," Theisman's plotting officer reported as *Principality's* captain stepped onto his bridge. "Range niner-two-point-two million klicks. They should come to rest right on top of us in another one-one-eight minutes."

Theisman crossed to the main tactical display and glowered at it. A tight-packed triangle of impeller signatures came towards him across it, decelerating at the maximum three hundred seventy-five gravities of a Grayson LAC. Three brighter, more powerful signatures glowed at its corners, but they weren't Harrington. *Principality* had good mass readings on them, and they had to be what was left of the Graysons.

"Anybody in position to see around that wall?"

"No, Sir. Aside from *Virtue*, everybody's right here."

"Um." Theisman rubbed an eyebrow and cursed himself for not convincing Franks to send one of the Masadan destroyers to Endicott as soon as Harrington returned. The admiral had refused on the grounds that *Thunder of God* was already two hours overdue and so must be back momentarily, and the most Theisman had been able to get him to do was send *Virtue* out to *Thunder's* planned translation point to warn the Captain the instant he did return.

He thrust that thought aside and concentrated on the plot. It certainly looked as if Grayson had launched this little expedition without Harrington, but that would have required an awful lot of guts—not to say stupidity—if they knew what they were getting into.

But did they? Obviously they knew *something*, or they wouldn't be here at all. Theisman didn't know how they'd tumbled to the Masadan presence on Blackbird, yet it seemed unlikely Harrington had recovered any usable data from Danville's LACs. No other Masadan ships had been in range to assist Danville (luckily for them), but the destroyer *Power* had been close enough for long-range grav readings, and Harrington hadn't even slowed down. That suggested there hadn't been any wreckage large enough to search, which was precisely what Theisman would have expected.

But if *Harrington* hadn't learned about Blackbird, then something must've slipped on the Grayson end. The original base predated Haven's involvement, and the Masadans had always been mighty cagey about how they'd put it in. Yet they almost had to have recruited local assistance to build it, so whoever their assistant had been might have spilled the beans.

And if that were the case, the Graysons still might not realize who was waiting for them here. Or, he amended sourly, who *ought* to be waiting for them if the Captain weren't so long overdue. Damn, damn, *damn!* He could feel the wheels coming off, and there was no way to find out what the Captain would want him to do about it!

He drew a deep breath. Assume a worst-case scenario. The Graysons had discovered Blackbird, learned about *Principality* and *Thunder of God*, and told Harrington all about it. What would he do if he were she?

Well, he damned straight wouldn't come after them— not if he knew about *Thunder!* What he'd probably do was send his destroyer for help, hold his cruisers in the inner system to cover Grayson, and hope like hell the cavalry arrived in time.

On the other hand, Harrington was good. The People's Navy had studied her carefully since Basilisk, and *she* might just figure she could take *Thunder* if the Graysons kept the Masadans off her ass while she did it. Theisman couldn't imagine how she'd do it, but he wasn't prepared to say categorically that she couldn't. Only, in that case, where *was* she?

He looked at the Grayson formation again. If she was

out there at all, she was behind that triangle, following it closely enough for its massed impellers to screen her from any gravity sensors in front of it.

The only thing was, her record said she was sneaky enough to send in the Graysons like this to make him think just that while she was someplace else entirely . . . like waiting for any Haven-built ships to abandon their Masadan allies and make a run for it.

His eyes switched to a direct vision display filled with Uriel's bloated sphere. The planet was so enormous it created a hyper limit of almost five light-minutes—half as deep as an M9's. That meant *Principality* would have to accelerate at max for ninety-seven minutes before she could translate the hell out of here, and Harrington might have her cruisers smoking in on a ballistic course to pick off anyone who tried to run. With her drives down, he'd never see her coming till she hit radar range, but she'd see *him* the instant he lit off his impellers. That would give her time to adjust her own vector. Probably not by enough for a classic broadside duel, but certainly by enough for two cruisers to reduce a destroyer to glowing gas.

Assuming, of course, that she didn't know about *Thunder*—and that she expected him to run.

He swore to himself again and rechecked the Grayson ETA. A hundred seven minutes. If he was going to run, he'd better start doing it soon . . . and if he had his druthers, running was exactly what he'd do. Thomas Theisman was no coward, but he knew what was going to happen if Harrington hit this force with *Thunder* absent—and, in the longer run, if she'd sent for help, it was going to arrive long before anything got here from Haven. Besides, the idea had been to pull this thing off *without* a war with Manticore! Everyone knew that was coming, but this wasn't the time or place for it to begin.

Then again, wars often started somewhere other than when and where "the plan" called for. He squared his shoulders and turned from the display.

"Get me a link to Admiral Franks, Al."

* * *

"Don't be ridiculous, Commander!" Admiral Ernst Franks snorted.

"Admiral, I'm telling you Harrington and her ships are right behind those people."

"Even if you're correct—and I'm not at all certain you are—our weapons on Blackbird will more than even the odds. We'll annihilate her allies, then close in and finish *her* off, as well."

"Admiral," Theisman clung to his temper with both hands, "they wouldn't be here if they didn't have some idea what they were heading into. That means—"

"That means nothing, Commander." Franks's eyes narrowed. He'd heard rumors about this infidel's opinion of his battle with *Madrigal*. "Your own people supplied our missiles. You know their effective powered range—and that nothing the Apostate have could possibly stop them."

"Sir, you won't be *engaging* Grayson defenses," Theisman said almost desperately, "and if you think *Madrigal's* point defense was bad, you don't even want to *think* about what a *Star Knight*-class cruiser's will do to us!"

"I don't believe she's back there!" Franks snapped. "Unlike you, I know precisely what data could have fallen into Apostate hands, and I'm not running from ghosts! This is a probe to examine little more than wild tales someone heard from someone who heard it from someone else, and they wouldn't dare pull the infidel bitch's ships off Grayson to chase down *rumors* when they can't know *Thunder* won't pounce on the planet in her absence."

"And if you're wrong, Sir?" Theisman asked in a tight voice.

"I'm not. But even if I were, she'd be coming to us on our own terms. We'll shoot the Apostate out of our way, then overwhelm her with close-range fire, just as we did *Madrigal*."

Theisman locked his teeth on a curse. If Harrington was out there, this was suicide. Franks had gotten his ass kicked up between his ears by a frigging destroyer—what did he think two *cruisers* were going to do to him?!

But there was no point arguing. Franks had heard too much criticism of his previous tactics, insisted too doggedly that only the superior range of *Madrigal's* missiles and the way they'd reduced his force before he ever engaged had caused his heavy losses. This time *he* had the range advantage from Blackbird Base, and he was determined to prove he'd been right the first time.

"What are your orders, then, Sir?" Theisman demanded in a curt voice.

"The task force will form up behind Blackbird as planned. Our base launchers will engage when the Apostate enter their range. Should any of the Apostate—or your Manticorans—survive that, we will be able to engage them with equivalent base velocities at close range."

"I see." That was probably the stupidest battle plan Theisman had ever heard, given the quality of the two forces, but short of running on his own, there was nothing he could do about it. And, from Franks's expression, he suspected the Masadans had their energy weapons dialed in on *Principality*. If they thought she was pulling out, they'd blow her out of space themselves.

"Very well, Sir." He cut the circuit without further ado and cursed for two minutes straight.

"Coming down on forty minutes, Ma'am," Stephen DuMorne reported. "Range is approximately ten-point-six million kilometers."

"Com, ask Admiral Matthews to open the wall. Let's take a look," Honor said. If the Peeps had given the Masadans what she was afraid they had, she and Matthews would be finding out about it in approximately one hundred and forty seconds.

"I frigging well *knew* it!" Commander Theisman spat. His own sensors were blind from back here, but the base's systems were now feeding *Principality's* displays . . . for what it was worth. The tight wall of LACs had just spread, revealing the far stronger—and larger—impeller signatures behind it. It was Harrington . . . and she was just as good as ONI said she was, damn it! Even as he watched, her ships were sliding forward through the Grayson wall, spreading out into a classic anti-missile pattern and deploying decoys while the Graysons vanished behind them.

Admiral Matthews watched his display and waited. *Covington* was still short five missile tubes, but her energy weapons and sidewall generators had been repaired in record time. For all that, he knew just how helpless she would have been before the attack Captain Harrington was deliberately inviting. He'd been horrified when she first told him about the endurance their larger, more robust drives gave Haven's ground-based missiles, but she'd seemed confident.

Now it was time to see if that confidence had been justified. If those missiles had the endurance she estimated, they would accelerate to an incredible 117,000 KPS and reach eight million-plus kilometers before burnout. Given their ships' closing velocity, that equated to an effective powered engagement range of well over nine million kilometers, and that meant the base should be launching right . . . about . . . *now.*

"Missile launch!" Rafael Cardones snapped. "Birds closing at eight-three-three KPS squared. Impact in one-three-five seconds—mark!"

"Implement point defense Plan Able."

"Aye, aye, Ma'am. Initiating Plan Able."

Commander Theisman managed to stop swearing and raised his eyes from his plot to glare at Lieutenant Trotter as the first Manticoran counter missiles scorched out. It wasn't Trotter's fault he was one of the very few Masadan officers aboard *Principality*. In fact, Trotter was a pretty decent sort, and he seemed to have become even more so by a sort of process of spiritual contamination during his time aboard Theisman's ship. Unfortunately, he was Masadan and he was handy.

Trotter felt his captain's eyes, and his face reddened with a curious blend of humiliation, apology, and answering resentment. He opened his mouth, then closed it, and Theisman made himself stop glaring. He gave the Masadan an apologetic half-shrug, then looked back at his plot.

There were thirty missiles in the salvo, more than Honor had expected, and they were big, nasty, and dangerous. Each of them massed a hundred and sixty tons, more than twice as much as her own missiles, and they put all that extra mass into tougher drives, better seekers, and penaids no shipboard Havenite missile could match.

But she'd suspected what was coming, and Rafe Cardones and Lieutenant Commander Amberson, *Apollo*'s tac officer, had the squadron in a classic three-tiered defense plan. *Fearless*'s counter missiles were responsible for long-range interceptions, with *Apollo*'s and *Troubadour*'s taking the leakers. Any that got through both missile layers would be engaged by the massed laser clusters of all three ships under *Fearless*'s control.

Now Honor punched a plotting overlay into her tactical display, tracking the vectors of the incoming fire back to Blackbird to pinpoint their launchers.

"Engage the launchers, Captain?" Cardones asked tensely as his counter missiles began to launch.

"Not yet, Mr. Cardones."

If she could get it, Honor wanted that base intact, for she still had no positive identification of what she faced in the way of modern warships. She might find that out the hard way very shortly; if she didn't, somewhere in that base were the records—or the people—who could tell her.

A second missile salvo launched. It contained exactly the same number of birds, and she nodded as she checked the time. Thirty-four seconds. ONI estimated three-round ready magazines and a firing cycle of thirty to forty seconds for the newest Peep ground-based systems, so the launch times suggested thirty tubes were all there were. Now the question was how many missiles each tube really had.

She looked back to the first salvo. Their ECM was better than ONI had predicted. Fifteen of its birds had broken through Cardones' outer intercept zone, but his computers were already updating their original solutions and feeding them to *Apollo* and *Troubadour*. The attacking missiles' powerful drives gave them an incredible velocity—they were already moving fifty percent faster than anything of *Fearless*'s could have managed from rest—but simple speed was no magic wand, and the range gave lots of time to plot intercepts.

Her plot beeped as a third salvo launched, and she bit the inside of her lip—too hard on the dead left side; she tasted blood before she could ease the pressure. That made ninety missiles, and that was already more than she'd believed Haven would have handed over to fanatics like the Masadans. If there was a fourth launch, she was going to have to forget about taking that base intact and blow it away.

Four missiles from the first salvo broke through the middle intercept zone, and lights blinked on *Fearless*'s tactical panels. Her computers were working overtime, already plotting solutions for her own missiles on the third salvo even as they targeted *Apollo*'s and *Troubadour*'s missiles on the second and brought all three ships' lasers to bear on the remnants of the *first*, and Honor felt a fierce stab of pride in her squadron as the last missile of the first flight blew apart thirty-thousand kilometers ahead of *Fearless*.

Admiral Wesley Matthews' heart had gone into his throat when he saw the sheer density and acceleration of the hostile launches and remembered what far smaller and slower missiles had done to the Grayson Navy. But this was no ambush, and Harrington's ships had been built by sorcerers, not technicians! There was a smooth, clean efficiency to them, a lethal, beautiful precision that cut down the attacking missiles in threes and fours and fives.

His bridge crew forgot professionalism, cheering and whistling like spectators at some sporting event, and Matthews wanted to join them, but he didn't. It wasn't professionalism that stopped him. It wasn't even dignity or an awareness of the example he ought to be setting. It was the thought that somewhere beyond those incoming missiles was at least one other ship which could *match* what Harrington's were doing.

"There go the last of them, Skipper," Hillyard said bitterly, and Theisman grunted. Just like Franks to throw good money after bad, he thought savagely. Good as Harrington's point defense had proven itself, her systems had to be working at full stretch. If Franks had been willing to hold his follow-up salvos till the range closed and she had less response time . . . But, no! He was trying to swamp her with sheer volume, when anyone but an idiot would have realized *timing* was more critical than numbers.

He checked his plot. Harrington was still thirty-five minutes out. There was time for a little judicious adjustment of his position . . . assuming Franks didn't think he was trying to run and burn him down.

It wouldn't make much difference in the end, but the professional in him rebelled against going down without achieving *anything*. His fingers flew as he punched a trial vector across his display, and he nodded to himself.

"Astrogation, download from my panel!"

"Aye, Sir. Downloading now."

"Prepare to execute on my command," Theisman said, then turned to Lieutenant Trotter. "Com, inform the Flag that I will be adjusting my position to maximize the effectiveness of my fire in—" he glanced at his chrono "—fourteen-point-six minutes from now."

"Aye, Sir," Trotter said, and this time Theisman

smiled at him, for there was no more question in his com officer's voice than there had been in his astrogator's.

Blackbird's second salvo fared even worse than its first, and Honor relaxed slightly when there was no fourth launch. Either they'd shot their wad or they were being sneaky, and the rapidity of those first three salvos made her doubt it was the latter. She looked up at Venizelos.

"I don't think we'll have to nuke the base after all, Andy," she said as the last wave of missiles came in.

"That's good. I'm still hoping we—"

A crimson light glared, and Honor's head whipped around as an alarm squealed.

"Point Defense Three's rejecting the master solution!" Cardones' hands flew across his console. "Negative response override."

Honor's fists clenched as three missiles charged through a hole that shouldn't have been there.

"Baker Two!" Cardones snapped, still fighting the malfunction lights.

"Aye, aye, Sir!" Ensign Wolcott's contralto voice was tight, but her hands moved as rapidly as his. "Baker Two engaged!"

One of the missiles disappeared as *Apollo* responded to Wolcott's commands and blew it away, but two more kept coming. *Fearless*'s computers had counted them as already destroyed before Point Defense Three put itself out of the circuit; now they were scrambling frantically to reprioritize their firing sequences, and Honor braced herself uselessly. It was going to be tight. If they didn't stop them at least twenty-five thousand kilometers out—

Another missile died at twenty-seven thousand kilometers. The port decoy sucked the other off course, but it detonated six hundredths of a second later, fine off the port beam, and HMS *Fearless* bucked in agony.

Her port sidewall caught a dozen lasers, bending most of them clear of her hull, but two struck deep through the radiation shielding inside her wedge. The composite ceramic and alloys of her heavily armored battle steel hull resisted stubbornly, absorbing and deflecting energy that would have blown a Grayson-built ship's titanium hull apart, but nothing could stop them entirely, and damage alarms screamed.

"Direct hits on Laser Two and Missile Four!" Honor slammed a fist into her chair arm. "Magazine Three open to space. Point Defense Two's out of the loop, Skipper! Damage Control is on it, but we've got heavy casualties in Laser Two."

"Understood." Honor's voice was harsh, yet even as she grated the response, she knew they'd been lucky. *Very* lucky. Which wouldn't make the families of the people who'd just died feel any better than it made *her* feel.

"Point Defense Three is back on line, Captain," Ensign Wolcott reported in a small voice, and Honor nodded curtly.

"Put me through to Admiral Matthews, Com," she said, and the Grayson appeared on her command chair com.

"How bad is it, Captain?" he asked tautly.

"It could have been a lot worse, Sir. We're working on it."

Matthews started to say something else, then stopped at the expression on the mobile side of her face. He nodded instead.

"We'll clear Blackbird in—" Honor glanced at her plot "—twenty-seven minutes. May I suggest we shift to our attack formation?"

"You may, Captain." Matthews' voice was grim, but his eyes glittered.

Theisman grunted in relief as *Principality* began to move and none of her "friends" killed her. His ship was the wrong one for an action this close, for her heavy missile armament left little room for energy weapons, and at this range that was going to be fatal. But Harrington had made a mistake at last; she was holding her entire force together as she swept around Blackbird after the enemy she knew had to be hiding behind it— just as he'd expected.

She couldn't know exactly what she was up against, so she wasn't taking any chances on getting her units caught in isolation by something big and modern. It was the smart move, since anyone who hoped to take her would have to hold *his* forces together or run the same risk of defeat in detail. But there was no way in hell Franks was going to beat her; that meant *Principality* wasn't going to survive anyway, and the options were different for a kamikaze.

The Havenite destroyer accelerated, streaking around Blackbird in the same direction as her enemies.

"Engage at will!" Honor snapped as enemy impeller sources suddenly speckled the plot. There was no time for careful, preplanned maneuvers. It was a shoot-out at minimum range, and she who shot first would live.

The numbers were very nearly even, and the Grayson LACs were bigger and more powerful than their opponents while nothing in Masada's order of battle even approached Honor's ships. But Blackbird Base's sensors were feeding them targeting data before their enemies even saw them, and they got off their first shots before even *Fearless* could localize them.

The cruiser shuddered as a shipboard laser blasted through her starboard sidewall at pointblank range and a direct hit wiped away Laser Nine. A Grayson LAC blew up just astern of her, and *Apollo* took two hits in rapid succession, but fire was ripping back at the Masadans, as well. Two of their LACs found themselves squarely in *Covington's* path, and Matthews' flagship tore them apart in return for a single hit of her own. The destroyer *Dominion* locked her batteries on *Saul* and reduced the Grayson ship to a wreck, but *Troubadour* was on *Saul's* flank, and her fire shredded the Masadan ship like tissue paper. *Dominion* vanished in a ball of flame, and a pair of Grayson LACs went after her sister ship *Power* in a savage, twisting knife-range dogfight.

Ernst Franks cursed hideously as enemy ships tore through his formation. *Solomon's* lasers killed a Grayson

LAC, then another, but the action was too close and
furious for her computers to keep track of. She fired
again, at a target that was already dead, just as *Power*
blew apart, and then some sixth sense jerked his eyes to
the visual display as HMS *Fearless* flashed across his
flagship's bow.

The cruiser's massed beams ripped straight down the
open throat of *Solomon*'s impeller wedge, and the last
cruiser in the Masadan Navy vanished in an eye-tearing
flash as her fusion bottles let go.

Honor stared into her display, her single eye aching
with concentration. The Masadan ships were dying even
more rapidly than she'd hoped, but where were the
Havenites? Had they come all this way just to *miss*
them?

She winced as another Grayson LAC blew up, but
there were only a handful of Masadan LACs left, with
no starships to support them, and Matthews' units were
picking them off with methodical precision.

"Come to two-seven-zero, Helm!"

"Aye, aye, Ma'am. Coming to two-seven-zero."

HMS *Fearless* curved out from Blackbird, clearing
her sensors to look for the enemy Honor knew had to
be somewhere.

"Stand by," Commander Theisman whispered as his
ship flashed around the craggy moon with ever gathering speed. The base's sensors still fed his plot, and his
teeth drew back. "Stand . . . by. . . . *Now!*"

"Skipper! Astern of us—!"

Lieutenant Commander Amberson's shout wrenched
Commander Alice Truman's eyes back to her display,
and her face whitened in horror.

"Hard a-port!" she barked, and *Apollo* swerved wildly
in response.

It was too late. The destroyer behind her had timed
it perfectly, and her first broadside exploded just behind
the open rear of *Apollo*'s impeller wedge. X-ray lasers

opened the light cruiser's port side like huge talons, and damage alarms screamed like damned souls.

"Bring her around!" Truman shouted. "Bring her around, Helm!"

A second broadside was already roaring in, and a corner of her mind wondered why the Peep was using missiles at beam ranges, but she didn't have time to think about that. Her cruiser clawed around, interposing her sidewall, and two of the incoming missiles ran physically into it and perished before their proximity fuses could trigger. Four more detonated just short of it, stabbing through the sidewall into already shattered plating, and a seventh streaked all the way past her and detonated on her starboard side. Smoke and screams and thunder filled *Apollo*'s bridge, and Truman's face was bloodless as her starboard sidewall went down and the Havenite closed in for the kill.

Theisman snarled in triumph, yet under his snarl was the bitter knowledge that his triumph would be brief. He could finish the cruiser with another salvo, but he'd already crippled her. The Captain would finish her off; *his* job was to damage as many Manticorans as he could before *Thunder* came back.

"Take the destroyer!" he barked.

"Aye, Sir!"

Principality slewed to starboard, presenting her reloaded port broadside to *Troubadour*, but the Manticoran destroyer saw her coming, and her skipper knew his business. Theisman's entire body tensed as the Manticoran fired a laser broadside three times as heavy as his own into him, then snapped up to present the belly of his wedge before the missiles could reach him. *Principality* heaved in agony, and the plot flickered. Two of his birds popped up, fighting for a look-down shot through *Troubadour*'s upper sidewall, but her point defense picked them off, and Theisman swore as the Manticoran rolled back down with viperish speed to bring her lasers to bear once more.

But *Principality* was rolling, too, and her starboard

broadside fired before *Troubadour* had completed her maneuver. His ship bucked again as energy blasted deep into her hull, but this time one of his laser heads got through. There was no way to tell how much damage it had done—there wasn't enough time to tell what *his* damage was!—but he knew he'd hurt her.

"Come to oh-niner-three three-five-niner!"

Principality dived towards the moon, twisting to present the top of her own wedge to *Troubadour* while her surviving missile crews fought to reload. The single laser in her port broadside picked off a Grayson LAC that never even saw her, and then she shuddered as a Grayson light cruiser put a laser into her forward impellers. Her acceleration dropped and her wedge faltered, but the ready lights glowed on the four surviving tubes of her port broadside, and Theisman sent her rolling madly back to bring them to bear on the Grayson.

He never made it. *Fearless* came screaming back on a reciprocal of her original course, and a hurricane of energy fire ripped through *Principality*'s sidewall as if it hadn't existed.

"Sidewall down!" Hillyard shouted. "We've lost everything in the port broadside!" The Exec cursed. "Emergency reactor shutdown, Skip!"

Principality went to emergency power, and Theisman's face relaxed. His ship was done, but she'd accomplished more than Franks's entire task force, and there was no point throwing away those of her people who still survived.

"Strike the wedge," he said quietly.

Hillyard looked at him in shock for just one instant, then stabbed his panel, and *Principality*'s impeller wedge died.

Theisman watched his display, wondering almost calmly if he'd been in time. Striking the wedge was the universal signal of surrender, yet if someone had already committed to fire—or wasn't in the mood to accept surrenders. . .

But no one fired. *Troubadour* rolled up onto his port

side, streaming air from her own wounds, and Theisman sighed in relief when *Principality* trembled as a tractor locked onto her and he realized he and his remaining people would live after all.

"Sir," Lieutenant Trotter said softly, "*Fearless* is hailing us."

• CHAPTER TWENTY-FOUR

Honor leaned back as the hatch sighed open and a very ordinary-looking brown-haired man in the scarlet and gold of a Masadan commander walked through it, escorted by Major Ramirez.

Ramirez was six centimeters shorter than Honor, but San Martin, the single habitable planet of Trevor's Star, was one of the heaviest-gravity worlds man had settled. Its sea-level air pressure was high enough to produce near-toxic concentrations of carbon-dioxide and nitrogen, and the major reflected the gravity to which he had been born. He was built like a skimmer turbine with an attitude problem, and he hated the People's Republic of Haven with a passion no native-born Manticoran could match. At the moment, his complete non-expression showed exactly how he felt, and she sensed the battle between emotion and life-long discipline which held those feelings at bay.

Yet it was the major's prisoner who interested her. He looked far more composed than he could possibly be, and she felt an unwilling respect for him as he gazed levelly back at her. He'd done an outstanding job—better, she suspected, than *she* could have done under the circumstances—yet she sensed an odd sort of strain under his self-possessed surface and wondered if it had anything to do with his request for this interview with her.

The commander tucked his cap under his arm and braced to attention.

"Commander Thomas Theisman, Navy of the Faithful, Ma'am," he said crisply—in an accent that had never come from Masada.

"Of course you are, Commander." Honor's irony was impaired by her persistently slurred speech, and she

saw his eyes widen as he took in her dead, ravaged face
and bandaged left eye. But though she waited expectantly, he refused to rise to the bait of her response,
and she shrugged.

"What was it you wished to see me about,
Commander?"

"Ma'am, I—"

Theisman glanced at Ramirez, then back at her, his
appeal for privacy as eloquent as it was silent. The
major stiffened, but Honor regarded the Havenite
thoughtfully as he closed his mouth tight and stared
back at her.

"That will be all for the moment, Major," she said at
last, and Ramirez bristled for an instant, then clicked to
attention and withdrew in a speaking silence. "And now,
Commander?" she invited. "Was there something you
wanted to tell me about why the People's Republic
attacked Her Majesty's Navy?"

"Captain Harrington, I'm a registered Masadan
citizen," Theisman replied. "My vessel is—was—the
Masadan Naval Ship *Principality*."

"Your ship was the destroyer *Breslau*, built by the
Gunther Yard for the People's Republic of Haven,"
Honor said flatly. His eyes widened a fraction, and the
mobile corner of her mouth smiled thinly. "My boarding
parties found her builder's plaque, as well as her splen-
didly official Masadan registry, Commander Theisman."
Her smile vanished. "Shall we stop playing games now?"

He was silent for a moment, then replied in a voice
as flat as hers.

"My ship was purchased by the Masadan Navy, Captain Harrington. My personnel are all legally Masadan
citizens." He met her eye almost defiantly, and she
nodded. This man knew his duty as well as she knew
hers, and he was under orders to maintain his cover
story, patently false or not.

"Very well, Commander," she sighed. "But if you
intend to stick to that, may I ask why you wanted to see
me?"

"Yes, Ma'am," Theisman replied, yet for the first time

he appeared clearly uncomfortable. "I—" He clenched his jaw, then went on steadily. "Captain, I don't know what you intend to do about the base on Blackbird, but I thought you should know. There are Manticoran personnel down there."

"*What?!*" Honor half-stood before she could stop herself. "If this is some kind of—" she began ominously, but he interrupted her.

"No, Ma'am. Captain Y—" He cleared his throat. "One of my superiors," he went on carefully, "insisted that the survivors from HMS *Madrigal* be picked up. They were. Thereafter, they were delivered to Blackbird to be held by . . . the appropriate local authorities."

Honor sank back into her chair, and his painstaking choice of words sounded a warning deep in her brain. She had no doubt Masada would have happily abandoned any of *Madrigal's* survivors to their fate—indeed, she'd assumed that was what had happened and tried not to think of the deaths they must have died. Now she knew some of them had lived, instead, but something about the way Theisman had said "appropriate local authorities" chilled her instant surge of joy. He was distancing himself from those authorities, at least as much as his cover story allowed. Why?

She started to ask him, but the plea in his eyes was even stronger than before, and she changed her question.

"Why are you telling me this, Commander?"

"Because—" Theisman started sharply, then stopped and looked away. "Because they deserve better than getting nuked by their own people, Captain."

"I see." Honor studied his profile and knew there was more—much more—to it than that. He'd started to reply too angrily, and his anger frightened her when she added it to the distaste with which he'd first referred to "local authorities."

"And if we simply leave the base for the moment, Commander, do you feel they would be endangered?" she asked softly.

"I—" Theisman bit his lip. "I must respectfully

decline to answer that question, Captain Harrington," he said very formally, and she nodded.

"I see," she repeated. His face reddened as her tone accepted that he *had* answered it, but he met her gaze stubbornly. This man had integrity as well as ability, she thought, and hoped there weren't many more like him in Haven's service. Or did she?

"Very well, Commander Theisman, I understand." She touched a stud and looked past Theisman as the hatch behind him opened to readmit Ramirez.

"Major, please return Commander Theisman to his quarters." Honor held the major's gaze. "You are to hold yourself personally responsible for seeing to it that he and his personnel are treated with the courtesy of their rank." Ramirez's eyes flashed, but he nodded, and she looked back at Theisman. "Thank you for your information, Commander."

"Yes, Ma'am." Theisman came back to attention.

"When you've returned the Commander to his quarters, Major, return straight here. Bring your company commanders with you."

Captain Harrington and her officers started to rise as Admiral Matthews walked through the hatch, but he waved them back, embarrassed by their deference after all they'd done. He nodded to Commander Brentworth and noticed that Harrington's Marine officers were also present.

"Thank you for coming, Admiral," Harrington said. "I know how busy you must have been."

"Not with anything my chief of staff and flag captain can't handle," Matthews said, waving away her thanks. "How bad are your own damages, Captain?"

"They could have been worse, but they're bad enough, Sir." Her slurred soprano was grim. "*Apollo*'s impellers are undamaged, but she has almost two hundred dead and wounded, her port broadside is down to a single laser, and her starboard sidewall is beyond repair out of local resources."

Matthews winced. He had far more casualties, and

his entire navy had been reduced to two cruisers—one of which, *Glory*, was badly damaged—and eleven LACs, but it was the Manticoran vessels which truly mattered. Everyone in this room knew that.

"*Fearless* got off more lightly," Harrington went on after a moment. "We've lost our long-range gravitics, but our casualties were low, all things considered, and our main armament, radar, and fire control are essentially intact. *Troubadour* has another twenty dead, and she's down two tubes and her Number Five Laser. She's also lost most of her long-range communications, but her sensor suite is undamaged. I'm afraid *Apollo* is out of it, but between them, *Fearless* and *Troubadour* are still combat effective."

"Good. I'm very sorry about Commander Truman's ship—and her people—but I'm relieved to hear the rest of it, Captain. And grateful for all you and your people have done for us. Will you tell them that for me?"

"I will, Sir. Thank you, and I know your own losses were heavy. Please tell your people how much we admire the job they did on the Masadans."

"I will." Matthews allowed himself a weary chuckle. "And now that we've got that out of the way, why don't you tell me what's on your mind?"

The Manticoran officer gave him one of her strange, half-frozen smiles, and he tried to hide how shocking the expressiveness of the living side of her face made the other side's damage—just as he tried to hide his own instinctive thought that her injuries underscored exactly why women had no business in combat. He knew that perception was parochial of him, but it was a part of his cultural baggage, and two days was far too brief a period to divest himself of it.

"I've been discussing the problem of the base with my own officers," she replied. "May I assume the situation remains unchanged?"

"You may," Matthews said grimly. The two of them had agreed he was the only choice to demand Blackbird's surrender, lest seeing a woman on the other end of the com link push the fanatics below into suicidal defiance—not that they seemed inclined towards reason, anyway. "They continue to refuse to surrender. I think they hope they can stall us long enough for their other Havenite ship to return and rescue them."

"Or at least long enough to leave Grayson uncovered against her," Honor agreed. She looked at Venizelos, then back at Matthews. "None of our prisoners are able—or willing—to tell us exactly what their other ship is, Admiral. On the other hand, many of them seem to have a rather disturbing confidence that, whatever she is, she's a match for *all* of us."

"I know." Matthews' mouth pursed in distaste for his next suggestion, but it had to be made. "Under the circumstances, I'm afraid we have little choice. I know we need information, but we have neither the time nor, speaking for Grayson, the means for a ground attack. If they won't surrender, our only options are to let the base wither until we can come back with a proper ground force, or else take it out from orbit and hope some of the prisoners we've already got prove more communicative with time."

"I'm afraid we have a problem there," Honor said carefully. "In fact, that's why I asked you to come aboard, Sir. According to one of our prisoners, there are survivors from *Madrigal* down there."

"Are you serious?!" Matthews jerked upright in his chair, then waved a hand quickly. "No, of course you are." He bit his lip. "That *does* change things, Captain Harrington. Of course we can't just bombard the base now!"

"Thank you, Sir," Honor said quietly. "I appreciate that."

"Captain, *Madrigal* saved my ship at the cost of her own life, and only the damage she did the Masadans prevented them from conquering or bombarding my planet before your own return. If any of her people are still alive down there, Grayson will do everything in its power to get them out alive." He paused and frowned. "And given the Masadans' intransigence, we'd better get them out as quickly as we can, too."

Honor nodded. Commander Brentworth had told her the admiral would react in just that way, but it was a vast relief to hear it.

"The problem, Sir, is that they have a lot more men down there than we have up here."

"I'm sure of that," Matthews agreed, plucking at his lower lip. "Unlike yours, none of our ships carry Marine complements, but we do have some smallarms aboard."

"Yes, Sir. We, however, as you've just pointed out, *do* have Marines, and I've been discussing the best way to employ them with Major Ramirez. With your permission, I'll ask him to share our conclusions with you."

"Of course." Matthews turned to the Manticoran major, and Ramirez cleared his throat.

"Basically, Admiral, I have three companies aboard *Fearless*." Ramirez's accent differed from most of the Manticorans Matthews had heard, with liquid consonants that were oddly musical in such a massive man. "*Apollo* has another company embarked, although they suffered about twenty casualties in the engagement. That gives me the better part of a battalion, including just over a company's worth of battle armor. Our best current estimates suggest the Masadan base is much larger than we'd originally thought, with a complement of about seven thousand men. How many of those have the training and equipment to be considered combat effective is an unknown, but the total numbers give them a considerable edge over our own five hundred troopers.

"I doubt any pure Masadan ground force could stand up to our battle armor, but the Peeps may have given them modern weapons, and three-quarters of my people would be in skin suits. In this kind of environment—" He shrugged, and Matthews nodded.

"We also lack any detailed plans of the base itself," Ramirez went on. "The best we've been able to get from prisoner interrogation is some idea of how the immediate entry areas are laid out and where the blast doors are located. But the Captain tells me tying ourselves down in methodical operations isn't an acceptable option—that we can't allow ourselves to be drawn away from Grayson for any length of time—and we also have reason to believe our people down there are in danger if we leave them in Masadan hands. That rules out probing the defenses to develop tactical information.

"Bearing all that in mind, the best plan I can come up with is one the tactics instructors back home would bust me to civilian for suggesting. Visual and radar mapping of the base have identified three main entry points, including the hangars for their small craft. I intend to pick one of those entries—the hangar area—and use brute force to blast my way inside, then punch right through anything in front of us and just keep going until we find our people, the central control room, or the power plant. Finding the prisoners would be the best-case option and allow us to pull straight back out. Failing that, the garrison will have no choice but to surrender once we control their life-support systems—or put ourselves in a position to shut them down by blowing their reactors. I hope."

"I see." Matthews looked from Ramirez to Harrington and back again. "How can we assist you, Major?"

"I realize your people aren't trained Marines, Admiral, and your vac suits are a lot more fragile than Marine skin suits." Matthews' mouth quirked at Ramirez's diplomatic tone. "Because of that, using them to reinforce my Marines would represent an unwarrantable risk to your personnel, but you do have quite a large number of men, and I'd like to use them for a diversion."

"A diversion?"

"Yes, Sir. What I'd like to do is use your pinnaces and shuttles to mount a big, noisy mock attack on both of the other main entry points. Our own pinnaces are designed for ground assaults, among other things, and two of them will lay in supporting fire to make your 'attacks' as convincing as possible and persuade the defenders to concentrate their combat forces against you. *Our* attack will go in fifteen minutes after you begin landing operations to give them time to deploy

against you. By the time they start redeploying against
us, we ought to be inside the base, where the close
confines will make our battle armor even more effective
and allow me to deploy my skin suits behind them."

"I see." Matthews sucked his teeth for a moment,
then grinned. "Some of my men are going to be irked,
Major. We did fairly well against the Faithful in several
boarding actions in the last war, and the notion that
they're more or less holding your coats is going to upset
them. But I think we can do it—and you're right about
the difference in our combat capabilities."

He nodded again, but then he frowned.

"At the same time, Captain Harrington, this *is* going
to be time-critical. Not only do we have to worry about
the other Havenite's return, but any of your people
being held down there aren't going to have vac suits. If
the fighting depressurizes their area, they'll be killed.
And if it occurs to the Masadans to use them against
you as hostages—" His expression was grim.

"Agreed, Sir," Honor said quietly, "but your freighters
have deployed our recon drones, and *Troubadour* and
Apollo still have the gravitic sensors to read their transmissions. Should the other Peep return, we should have
enough warning to get under way and intercept him with
Fearless and *Troubadour*, particularly since he's most likely to be headed for Blackbird, anyway. As for the threat to
Madrigal's survivors," the living side of her face hardened,
"I'm very much afraid it's lower than the danger to them
if we don't go in. Our information on their treatment is
limited but disquieting. Under the circumstances, any
reasonable risk to get them out quickly has to be considered acceptable. And, despite Major Ramirez's
deprecation of his battle plan, I have great faith in him
and in his people." She met Matthews' eyes squarely.
"Given the information we have, I believe this is the very
best we can do. I'd like your permission to try it."

"*My* permission?" Matthews smiled almost sadly. "Of
course you have my permission—and my prayers for
your success."

• CHAPTER TWENTY-FIVE

Captain of the Faithful Williams paced back and forth across the command room and gnawed his lower lip. He'd been picked for this post in no small part for his piety—now that very piety fanned his fury at the disaster wreaked by a *woman*. And violently though he tried to deny it, there was fear in his fury. Fear for himself and for God's Work. The Apostate admiral whoring for the Manticoran bitch had stopped demanding his surrender; that could only mean they were prepared to try something more direct.

But what? Williams didn't know, and ignorance shuddered in his blood like another layer of anger. That *bitch!* If she hadn't come back—back to a star system neither she nor her whore of a queen had any business in—Masada would have completed God's Work. But she *had* come back, she and her accursed ships, and smashed the entire remaining navy except *Virtue* and *Thunder* in two short days. She'd set herself against God's Work and Will, just as women always had, and Williams cursed her with silent ferocity as he paced.

It wasn't supposed to happen like this. As Blackbird Base's CO, he'd known about Maccabeus, known all the military maneuvers were but window dressing for the real operation, and he'd wondered, deep inside, if perhaps the Elders weren't being just a bit too clever. Yet they'd spent decades creating the Maccabeans, and the Apostates' security had never suspected a thing. Surely that had been a sign God approved! And then the heathen Havenites had offered the final, crucial ingredient, the means to create the crisis Maccabeus needed. What better proof of the workings of God's Will could there be than the opportunity to use infidels against the Apostate?

Yet Williams had doubted, and in the nightmares which had haunted him since Jericho—and especially since the bitch's return—a fresh doubt had tormented him. Had *his* lack of Faith turned God's Heart from them? Had it been *he* who allowed Satan's bitch and her ships to thwart the Work?

Such thoughts could not be allowed, yet neither could he stop them. Even prayer and penance had failed him, but his sleepless nights had revealed another truth. Satan's servants must be punished, and so he had punished them, hoping to turn God's Wrath from the Faithful by proving his own Faith anew.

And he'd failed. God still turned His Heart against His Faithful. Why else had *Thunder of God* not returned to destroy the bitch? Why else had Blackbird's missiles failed to destroy even a single LAC? There could be no other answer, and as he paced and worried and fury knotted his belly, he prayed desperately for God to turn once more to His People and save them.

"Covington reports ready, Major."

"Thank you." Tomas Ramirez acknowledged the report and looked up. Sergeant Major Babcock stood beside him in the crowded pinnace troop bay, her gray eyes cool and very still in the open visor of her battle armor, and a pulser tri-barrel thrust up behind her right pauldron. "Are *we* ready, Gunny?"

"Aye, Sir. All weapons checked, and Cap'n Hibson's company and the HQ section are armored up. We had to downcheck one set of armor, but *Apollo* had a prepped spare. The Captain says she's ready to drop."

"Good, Gunny," Ramirez murmured, and silently thanked God that Susan Hibson's last assignment had been with one of the heavy assault battalions. She'd spent it practicing exactly the sort of thing her people faced today, which was why he'd made her *Fearless's* designated assault commander the day she came aboard.

"Give me a direct feed to *Covington*."

"Aye, Sir," the com tech replied, and a tone beeped as Ramirez's armor com dropped into the circuit.

"*Covington*, this is Ramrod. Do you copy?"

"*Covington* copies, Ramrod. Go ahead."

"Begin your drops, *Covington*. I say again, begin your drops."

"*Covington* copies," the voice in his earphones said. "Beginning drops now. May God go with you, Ramrod."

"Thank you, *Covington*. Ramrod clear." The major punched a chin switch to plug into the Manticoran net. "Ramrod to Decoy Flight. Commence your runs."

"Aye, Ramrod. Decoy Flight copies. Beginning our runs."

"Captain Williams!"

Williams whirled at the shout. His plotting officer pointed urgently at the master display, and the captain swallowed in sudden fear. Dozens of small craft were plummeting from the orbiting warships, and leading the way were two pinnaces with impossible energy signatures.

They gathered speed even as he stared at them, slicing down into Blackbird's wispy hydrogen atmosphere, and crimson projections showed their targets.

"They're going for the vehicle entrances!" Williams snapped. "Alert the ready teams and get Colonel Harris's men moving!"

The Manticoran flight crews were tense faced, nerves clenched against the ground fire they all expected. But there was none, and the pilots pulled out of their steep approaches, kicking the counter-grav to a hundred twenty percent and riding their thrusters to convert momentum into howling dives straight for their targets.

"Coming up on IP. Arm, arm, arm," the master weapons officer aboard *Fearless* chanted into his com. Amber standby lights blinked to red aboard each pinnace, and the gunners' hands curled about the triggers on their joysticks.

"*Launch* your birds! *Launch* your birds!" the weapons officer sang out, and two waiting fingers squeezed.

Quad-mounted fifty-centimeter rockets ripple-fired like brief-lived, flame-tailed meteors. Twelve of them blasted ahead of each pinnace—twenty-four one thousand-kilo warheads with a yield man once could have gotten only from atomic weapons—and the pinnaces charged onward down their wakes.

Captain Williams went white as a rumbling fist of thunder smashed through Blackbird Base. The entire facility shuddered, lighting flickered, and eyes jerked anxiously up as overhead rock groaned. Dust sifted down over the command room equipment, and the first bellow of destruction was followed by another. And another. And *another!*

The final rockets smashed home, and the pinnaces' bow-mounted pulsers opened fire. Thirty thousand thirty-millimeter shells per second ripped into the smoke and dust billowing in Blackbird's thin atmosphere, and then they flashed directly over their targeting points and the plasma bombs dropped.

Most of the men guarding those portals were already dead; the rest died instantly as the heart of a sun consumed them.

"God the Merciful, be with us now!" Williams whispered in horror. He'd lost all of his pickups in the immediate lock areas, but remote cameras showed the smoke and dust—and the thick plumes of atmosphere howling up through it—and his eyes whipped to the base schematic. They'd blown their way over a hundred *meters* into the base! Emergency blast doors slammed, and the captain licked his lips in terror as troop shuttles grounded two kilometers from the breaches and began disgorging hundreds of suited figures.

"Tell Harris to *hurry!*" he shouted hoarsely.

*   *   *

"Well," Ramirez murmured, "*that* was impressive, wasn't it, Gunny?"

"As the Major says," Sergeant Major Babcock's smile was predatory. "Think they took the hint, Skipper?"

"Oh, I'd say it was probable," Ramirez said judiciously. "At least we knocked on the door hard enough to get their attention." He glanced at the chrono and keyed his mike. "Ferret Leader, this is Ramrod. Stand by for run-in in one-zero minutes."

Decoy Flight screamed upward, then pushed over and came in again. The remaining Masadan surface arrays saw them coming, but even as Colonel Harris screamed a warning to his troops, the anti-radiation missiles blasted off the racks. Six seconds later, they put out Blackbird Base's eyes, and then the pinnaces rolled back onto their original attack headings and bored straight in.

The Masadan defenders went flat, rolling off into side passages wherever possible, and then the entire base leapt and convulsed again. This time each pinnace fired only a single missile, but those missiles' onboard radar took them straight into the airlocks their predecessors had blown open and down the passages inside them at eight thousand MPS. They carried no explosives, but their super-dense "warheads" struck the first sets of internal blast doors with the force of twenty-three and a half tons of old-style TNT apiece, and another two hundred odd Masadans died as the doors disintegrated in white-hot gas and murderous shrapnel.

More troop shuttles landed, and Colonel Harris cursed his survivors to their feet and sent them stumbling through the rock dust and the howl of escaping atmosphere to find firing positions even as the core base's main blast doors slammed shut behind them.

"Ramrod, the Ferret is rolling. I say again, the Ferret is rolling."

"Roger, Ferret. Ramrod copies." Ramirez looked up at his own pilot. "Follow them in, Max."

* * *

Captain Williams tried not to twitch in impatience while his damaged sensors strove to sort out what was happening. Most of Harris's men seemed to have survived, and he heard snatches of chatter as their officers harried them into some sort of defensive positions amid the rubble, but his surface arrays were gone. He couldn't tell where the attackers were, how soon they would hit Harris, or what they were armed with.

Nor could he see the fresh flight of small craft streaking towards the hangars on the far side of Blackbird Base.

"Launch your birds!"

Fresh rockets streaked downward, but these were much lighter than the ones which had ripped the vehicle entrances apart. Their warheads massed barely three hundred kilos each, and hangar doors blew open and surface domes peeled back like broken bone. A hundred and twenty battle-armored men and women fell from pinnace belly hatches like lethal snow, riding their counter-grav down into the gaping holes, and four hundred more Royal Manticoran Marines debarked from cutters and shuttles to follow in their wake.

Fresh alarms screamed, and Captain Williams' head twisted around as new swatches of crimson blazed on the base schematic.

Speed was everything, and the handful of suited Masadan service techs who got in the point teams' way died before anyone found out whether they were trying to fight or surrender. Then the Marines came up against the closed blast doors, and engineers slapped shaped charges against the massive panels even as other engineers sealed in the portable plastic airlocks behind them.

Battle armor wasn't built to let someone tap an impatient toe, so Captain Hibson was reduced to snapping her chewing gum as her people worked. Not that she could fault their speed and precision. It was just that it took time, however good they were.

"Sealed!" Lieutenant Hughes' voice crackled in her earphone.

"Do it," she grunted back.

"Fire in the hole!" Hughes called, and armored shapes turned away from the locks just in case.

There was an instant of taut silence, and then Blackbird's rock transmitted the smothered *ka-CHUNK!* to them. One lock failed as back-blast leaked around the face of a charge and split a plastic wall, but the engineers were on it before more than a few cubic meters of air escaped, and even as they worked, a dozen more locks were passing Marines into the base six at a time.

Colonel Harris looked around wildly. Smoke and dust settled about his knees with dreamy slowness in Blackbird's low gravity and tenuous atmosphere, but there was no sign of the ground attack. There should have been. The attackers should be following up their initial breaching strike as closely as they dared, not letting his men get set to receive them. So where *were* they?

"The hangars!" a voice shouted in his earphones. "They're coming in through the hangars, too!"

Too? Harris looked around once more, then punched the side of his helmet. They weren't coming against *his* positions at all! It had all been a feint—and all his men were on the wrong side of the base's sealed blast doors!

Captain Hibson's people went down the passage with the speed only battle armor allowed. There wasn't room to use thrusters, and their exoskeletal "muscles" were real energy hogs, but in this gravity they let them advance in gliding, thirty-meter jumps, and terror went before them like pestilence.

Here and there a firearm barked and metal slugs whined off a Marine's armor, but Hibson's troopers carried tri-barrels and plasma rifles, and they moved with the smooth precision she'd drilled into them for months.

She watched a squad team move down the passage before her. They came to an intersection, and a plasma gunner turned each way. White light flashed off their armor as they hosed the perpendicular corridors, and the next squad leapfrogged past them while their demolition numbers slapped beehives onto the seared tunnel roofs. They pulled back, the charges thundered, the intersecting passages collapsed for over ten meters, and the squad was moving again.

The entire operation had taken sixteen seconds by her chrono.

Harris started his men cycling through the personnel locks in the core blast doors, but each lock would admit only three men at a time, and the only sitrep he could get from Captain Williams was a half-hysterical babble about demons and devils.

"Ramrod, this is Ferret One," Captain Hibson's voice said in Ramirez's earphone. "Ferret One has penetrated two kilometers. I've got corridor markings indicating the route to the control room and to the power section. Which should I follow?"

"Ferret One, Ramrod," Ramirez replied without hesitation. "Go for the control room. I repeat, go for the control room."

"Ramrod, Ferret One copies. Go for the control room."

Colonel Harris' central reserve was small, with none of the Havenite weapons issued to his primary maneuver units, but it was stationed deep inside Blackbird Base to move to any threatened sector. The Colonel had a very clear idea what would happen to those men if he committed them against the juggernaut rolling towards them, yet he had no choice, and they went racing down the tunnels to meet the intruders.

Some of them came up against sealed passages

choked with fallen rubble and stalled. Others were less fortunate; they found the enemy.

The Marines' belt-fed tri-barrels pumped out a hundred four-millimeter explosive darts per second, with a muzzle velocity of two thousand MPS. That kind of firepower could chew through armored bulkheads like a hyper-velocity band saw; what it did to unarmored vac suits was indescribable.

"Ramrod, Ferret One. We have contact with organized resistance—such as it is. No problems so far."

"Ferret One, Ramrod copies. Keep it moving, Captain."

"Aye, Sir. Ferret One copies."

Colonel Harris shoved through a blast door airlock and ran down the passage at the head of everyone he'd gotten back inside. Captain Williams' voice had gone beyond mere hysteria in his headphones. The base CO was babbling prayers and promises to punish Satan's whores, and the Colonel's mouth twisted in distaste. He'd never liked Williams, and what he and others like him had been doing for the last two days sickened Harris. But it was his job to defend the base or die trying, and he exhorted his men to ever greater efforts even while the premonition of failure settled in his bones.

"Ramrod, Ferret One. My point is one passage from the control room. Repeat, my point is one passage from the control room."

"Ferret One, Ramrod. Good work, Captain. Send them in—but remind them we want the place intact."

"Aye, Sir. We'll take it in one piece if we can. Ferret One clear."

Captain Williams heard the thunder coming closer and slammed his hand down on the button that closed the control room hatch. He stared at it with wide eyes, then whirled and cursed his technicians as they began to scramble for the still open hatch on the far side of the chamber. They ignored him, and he snatched out his sidearm.

"Get back to your posts!" he screamed.

A terrified lieutenant turned to run, and Williams shot him in the back. The man went down, and his shriek of agony galvanized the others. They darted through the hatch, and Williams howled curses after them, firing until his magazine was empty. Then he turned back to the control room, and his eyes were mad as he calmly replaced the empty magazine and switched the selector to full auto. The sobbing lieutenant dragged himself towards the hatch, his blood a thick, crimson smear on the floor, and Williams stepped over beside him.

He emptied the entire magazine into the dying man.

Private Montgomery slapped her beehive on the sealed panel, stepped back, and hit the button. The hatch blew apart, and Sergeant Henry went through it in a swooping leap.

A single Masadan officer's pistol spat fire at less than ten meters' range, and steel-jacketed slugs whined uselessly from the Sergeant's armor. He felt them bouncing away and started to bring up his pulser, then remembered his orders to take the place intact. He grimaced and waded through the fire, and an armor-augmented fist clubbed the Masadan to the floor.

A corridor blast door slammed shut with no warning at all, crushing the man in front of Colonel Harris in an explosion of gore, and the Colonel slithered to a halt in shock. Someone screamed over his suit com, and the Colonel whirled to see another man shrieking and twisting as the door at the far end of the corridor segment ground his leg to paste. But then, through the screams, he heard something even more terrifying.

"Attention. Attention, all Masadan personnel!" His face went white, for the voice in his earphones spoke with an accent he'd never heard before . . . and it was female.

"This is Captain Susan Hibson of the Royal Manticoran Marine Corps," the cold, flat voice said. "We are
now in possession of your central control room. *We* now
control your blast doors, sensors, and life support. Lay
down your arms immediately or face the consequences."

"Oh, God," someone whimpered, and Harris swallowed hard.

"W-what do we do, Sir?" His exec was trapped on
the far side of the blast door behind the Colonel. Harris
could almost feel the man's struggle to suppress his own
terror, and he sighed.

"There's only one thing we *can* do," he said heavily.
"Lay down your weapons, boys. It's over."

• CHAPTER TWENTY-SIX

The cutter grounded amid the ruins of Blackbird Base's hangars, and a tall, slim figure in a navy captain's skin suit walked down the ramp while a squad of battle-armored Marines at its foot snapped to attention.

"Sergeant Talon, Second Squad, Third Platoon, Able Company, Ma'am," the squad sergeant announced.

"Sergeant." Honor returned the salute, then looked over her shoulder at her pilot.

None of *Fearless*'s small craft had yet returned, so she'd grabbed *Troubadour*'s number two cutter. Commander McKeon, still dealing with his own ship's damages, would much preferred to have told her she couldn't have it. Unfortunately, she was senior to him, and since he couldn't keep her upstairs where it was safe, he'd assigned Lieutenant Tremaine as her pilot. Now the Lieutenant trotted down the ramp in her wake, and Honor's lip twitched as she saw the heavy plasma carbine slung over his shoulder.

Pockets of Masadans still held out inside the base, and the chance of walking into trouble couldn't be totally ruled out—that was why Ramirez had assigned a full squad to babysit her and why she herself wore a sidearm—but Tremaine's weapon of choice seemed a bit extreme.

"I really don't need any more babysitters, Scotty."

"No, Ma'am. Of course not," Tremaine agreed, double-checking the charge indicator on his carbine.

"At least leave that cannon behind!" He looked up at her with a pained expression. "You're not a Marine, Lieutenant. You could hurt someone with that thing."

"That's the idea, Ma'am. Don't worry. I know what I'm doing with it," he assured her, and she sighed.

"Scotty—" she began again, but he gave her a sudden grin.

"Ma'am, the Skipper will skin me alive if anything happens to you." He looked over Honor's shoulder at Sergeant Talon, and his grin grew broader as the Marine glowered at him. "No offense, Sarge, but Commander McKeon can be a mite unreasonable at times." Sergeant Talon glared at his carbine, sniffed audibly over her com, and then looked pointedly at Honor.

"Are you ready, Ma'am?"

"I am, Sergeant," Honor replied, abandoning the attempt to dissuade her over-zealous bodyguard.

Talon nodded and waved her first section out to take point while Corporal Liggit's section brought up the rear. Talon herself accompanied Captain Harrington, completely ignoring the Lieutenant trudging along beside his long-legged superior, and Corporal Liggit chuckled to himself behind her.

"What's so funny, Corp?" a private asked over the section circuit.

"He is," Liggit replied, gesturing at Tremaine and chuckling even harder as he did a hop-skip-hop to catch back up with the Captain.

"Why? What about him?"

"Oh, nothing much . . . except for the fact that I used to be a small arms instructor at Saganami Island, and I happen to know he's qualified High Expert with the plasma carbine." The private looked at Liggit in disbelief for a moment, and then she began to laugh.

"I still think it would have been wiser to delay your landing." Major Ramirez greeted Honor in the mess hall which had become a POW cage. "There's still shooting going on in here, Ma'am, and these idiots are certifiable. I've had three people killed by grenade attacks from 'surrendered' Masadans."

"I know, Major." Honor held her helmet in the crook of her arm and noted the unlimbered tri-barrels of

Sergeant Talon's squad. Even Lieutenant Tremaine had abandoned his cheerful pose, and his forefinger rested lightly beside his carbine's firing stud. She looked back at Ramirez, and the living corner of her mouth twitched a brief, half-apologetic smile.

"Unfortunately, we don't know how much time we've got," she went on quietly. "I need information, and I need it quickly. And—" her slurred voice turned grim "—I want *Madrigal*'s people found. I am *not* going to leave them behind if we're forced to pull out suddenly!"

"Yes, Ma'am." Ramirez inhaled and indicated a Masadan officer in a captain's uniform. "Captain Williams, Ma'am. The base CO."

Honor studied the Masadan curiously. The right side of his face was almost as badly bruised and swollen as the left side of her own; the other side was tight and sullen, and it tightened further as he glared back at her.

"Captain Williams," she said courteously, "I regret—"

He spat in her face.

The glob of spittle hit the dead skin of her left cheek. She couldn't feel it, and for just one moment she couldn't quite believe it had happened, but Major Ramirez's left arm shot out. Armored fingers twisted in the neck of the Masadan's one-piece uniform, and exoskeletal muscles whined as he snatched Williams off his feet. He slammed him back against the wall like a puppet, and his right fist started forward.

"*Major!*" Honor's voice cracked like a whip, and Ramirez diverted the blow in the nick of time. His gauntlet smashed into the stone wall beside Williams' head like a mace, so hard flying stone chips cut the Masadan's cheek, and the red-faced, strangling captain flinched aside with a gasp of terror.

"Sorry, Ma'am." The major was white with fury as he muttered his apology—to Honor, not Williams—and dropped the Masadan. He rubbed his left hand on his equipment harness as if to scrub away contamination, and Sergeant Talon handed Honor a napkin from a dispenser on one of the mess tables. She wiped her numb face carefully, her eyes still on the major, and wondered if Williams truly understood how close to death he'd just come.

"I understand your feelings, Major," she said quietly, "but these people are our prisoners."

"Yes, Ma'am. I understand." Ramirez drew a deep breath and turned his back on Williams while the captain wheezed for breath. "They're scum, and one of them killed a medic trying to patch him up, but they're our prisoners. I'll remember that, Ma'am."

"See that you do," Honor said, but she laid her hand on his armored shoulder as she spoke, and he managed a brief smile.

"Yes, Ma'am," he replied more naturally, then gestured at a large chart spread out on one of the tables. "Let me show you where we are, Ma'am."

Honor followed him to the table, and he ran a finger across the captured ground plan.

"We now control the three upper levels," he said, "and I've got one of Captain Hibson's squads down onto Level Five to secure the power plant, but the Masadans still holding out on Four and parts of Five had too much time to get set before we penetrated that deep. It looks like the most fanatical members of the garrison headed that way when we took over the control room, and some of them knew how to override the blast doors locally, so we couldn't keep them from flowing together into some fairly tough knots."

Honor studied the plan and nodded in understanding.

"The specialists Admiral Matthews loaned us are interrogating the computers," Ramirez went on, "and, in some respects, I'd as soon leave them down there while we got what we came for and pulled out. Unfortunately," his voice turned harsh, "we've begun picking up indications *Madrigal*'s survivors are being held somewhere in this area—" his finger tapped "—on Level Four."

"'Indications'?" Honor asked sharply. "Not confirmation?"

"No, Ma'am. That's what worries me. None of these people—" he waved at the Masadans crowded against the messhall walls "—will say a word about them, but they look awfully uneasy when we ask. We haven't really had time for systematic interrogation, and, as you say, they're our prisoners, so there are limits to the way we can ask, but after Commander Theisman's hints, I don't like it, Ma'am. I don't like it at all."

"Neither do I," Honor murmured, staring at the map with her good eye. "Do we know—"

She broke off as a Marine lieutenant marched up with a fresh Masadan prisoner. He came to attention and saluted his superiors; the Masadan didn't, but he looked less sullen than many of his fellows.

"Captain, Major," the Lieutenant said, "this is Colonel Harris, the commander of the ground defense force."

"I see." Ramirez examined the Masadan. "Colonel, I'm Major Ramirez, Royal Manticoran Marines. This is Captain Harrington of Her Majesty's Navy."

Harris's gaze snapped to Honor as she was named, and his eyes narrowed. She saw a flash of repugnance in them, yet she wasn't certain whether it was because of who and what she was—the woman whose forces had defeated the Faithful—or because of the ruined side of her face. He looked at her for a moment, then bobbed a stiff, wordless nod.

"Allow me to commend you for instructing your people to surrender," Ramirez continued, and Honor was content to let his less threatening, male voice handle the conversation. "It undoubtedly saved their lives."

Harris gave another nod, still without speaking.

"However, Colonel," Ramirez went on, "we seem to have a problem here." He tapped the plan of the base. "Some of your men are still resisting in these sectors. They don't have the firepower to stop us, and an awful lot of them are going to get killed if we have to go in after them. I would appreciate it if you would instruct them to lay down their weapons while they still can."

"I can't do that." Harris spoke for the first time, his voice quiet but firm, despite an edge of bitterness. "Anyone who was going to surrender already has, Major. My talking to them won't change their minds."

"Then I'm afraid we're going to have to call out the

really heavy weapons," Ramirez said, watching the Colonel's face closely. Harris's eyes seemed to go very still, and then he inhaled deeply.

"I wouldn't do that, Major." He put his finger on the map, five centimeters from Ramirez's. "There are Manticoran prisoners in this area."

"Harris, you fucking traitor!"

Honor's head snapped around, and her single eye flashed with rage as Captain Williams writhed and twisted in the hands of a Manticoran Marine. He was actually frothing at the mouth, screaming imprecations at the Colonel, and this time she chose not to intervene when he was slammed back against the wall. His torrent of abuse died in a hoarse, anguished cough as the impact knocked the breath from him, and she looked back at Harris.

"Please continue, Colonel," she said quietly. He flinched at the sound of her voice, but he tapped the plan again.

"This is where they are, Major," he said as if Honor hadn't spoken. "And if I were you, I'd get in there quickly," he added. "Very quickly."

"Captain, will you *please* get further back?!" Sergeant Talon grated. Smoke hazed the corridor, and grenade explosions and a savage crackle of small-arms fire thundered up ahead.

"No, I won't, Sergeant," Honor didn't—quite—snap. She knew perfectly well she had no business in a ground battle. That wasn't her area of expertise. But her pistol was in her hand as Captain Hibson's leading elements smashed ahead down the passageway.

"If anything happens to you, the Major'll have my ass!" Talon growled, then added, as an afterthought, "Begging the Captain's pardon."

"Nothing's going to happen to me," Honor said, and Scotty Tremaine rolled his eyes heavenward behind her.

"Ma'am, I—" The fire ahead rose to a crescendo, then died, and Talon listened to her command net. "That's it. They're clear to Corridor Seven-Seventeen."

She gave Honor another glare. "This time, stay *behind* me, Captain!"

"Yes, Sergeant," Honor said meekly, and Talon snorted again.

They waded forward through the smoke and debris, past bodies and bits of bodies and blood-splashed corridor walls. A few Marines were down, for if none of the Masadan infantry weapons were remotely equal to theirs, these defenders had had a little more time to prepare, and the most fanatic among them had charged from concealment with suicide charges of blasting compound. Few had reached their targets, and most of those they'd hit were only lightly injured, thanks to their armor, but such rabid fanaticism was frightening.

Honor was just stepping over a tangled heap of dead Masadans when an armored Marine lieutenant swooped up the passage and slammed to a halt.

"Captain Harrington, Major Ramirez's respects, and could you please come straight ahead. We've . . . found the prisoners, Ma'am."

His voice was flat and harsh, and Honor's stomach clenched. She started to ask a question, then stopped herself at the look in his eyes. Instead, she simply nodded and started forward at a half-run.

This time Sergeant Talon raised no demur; she just sent her lead section leaping ahead to clear the way. When Honor stumbled over a corpse, the Sergeant caught her without a word, then swung her up in armored arms and went bounding ahead at a pace she could never have matched on her own feet. Corporal Liggit did the same for Tremaine, and the corridor walls blurred with the speed of their passage.

They emerged into a wider area, clogged by Marines who seemed struck by a strange stillness, and Talon set her down. She squirmed forward between the bulky, towering suits of battle armor, hearing Scotty wiggling through them behind her, then came to an abrupt halt as Ramirez loomed suddenly before her.

The major's eyes were hard, his nostrils flared, and he radiated pure, murderous fury. A barred door stood open behind him, and a pair of medics knelt in a pool of blood as they worked frantically over a man in the filthy uniform of a Manticoran petty officer. A Masadan officer's corpse sprawled against the wall opposite the cell, and he hadn't been killed by pulser fire. His head had been twisted off like a bottle cap, and the right arm of the battle-armored Marine private beside his body was bloody to the elbow.

"We've found six dead so far, Ma'am," Ramirez grated without preamble. "Apparently this bastard—" he jerked a savage gesture at the headless Masadan "—just started walking down the corridor shooting prisoners when our point broke into the cell block. I—"

He broke off as the senior medic rose from beside the petty officer. He met the Major's gaze and shook his head slightly, and Ramirez swallowed a savage curse.

Honor's single eye burned as she stared at the body, and the memory of how she'd kept Ramirez from smashing Williams was gall on her tongue while the Major got himself back under a semblance of control.

"I'm afraid this isn't all of it, Ma'am," he said in a harsh, clipped voice. "If you'll come with me?" She nodded and started forward, but he waved Tremaine back as he began to follow. "Not you, Lieutenant."

Tremaine looked a question at Honor, but something in Ramirez's voice warned her, and she shook her head quickly. His expression turned mutinous for just a moment, then smoothed, and he stepped back beside Sergeant Talon.

Ramirez led Honor another forty meters, to a bend in the passage, then stopped and swallowed.

"Captain, I'd better stay here."

She started to ask him a question, but his face stopped her. Instead, she nodded once and stepped around the corner.

The dozen Marines in evidence looked odd. For a moment, she couldn't understand why, then she realized: they'd all removed their helmets, and every one of them was a woman. The realization struck a terrible icicle through her, and she quickened her pace, then slid to a halt in the open door of a cell.

"Honey, you've got to let us have her," someone was saying softly, gently. "Please. We've got to take care of her."

It was Captain Hibson, and her strong, confident voice was fogged with tears as she bent over the naked, battered young woman on the filthy bunk. The prisoner's face was almost unrecognizable under its cuts and bruises, but Honor knew her. Just as she knew the equally naked, even more terribly battered woman in her arms.

The young woman clung to her companion desperately, trying to shield her with her own body, and Honor stepped forward numbly. She knelt beside the bunk, and the young woman—the girl—on it stared at her with broken, animal eyes and whimpered in terror.

"Ensign Jackson," Honor said, and a spark of something like humanity flickered far back in those brutalized eyes. "Do you know who I am, Ensign?"

Mai-ling Jackson stared at her an endless moment longer, then jerked her head in a spastic, uncoordinated nod.

"We're here to help you, Ensign." Honor would never know how she kept her voice soft and even, but she did. She touched the stiff, matted hair gently, and the naked ensign flinched as if from a blow. "We're here to help you," Honor repeated while tears slid down her face, "but you have to let us have Commander Brigham. The medics will help her, but you have to let her go."

Ensign Jackson whimpered, clinging even more tightly to the limp body in her arms, and Honor stroked her hair again.

"Please, Mai-ling. Let us help her."

The ensign looked down at Mercedes Brigham's blood-caked face, and her whimpers collapsed into a terrible sob. For a moment, Honor thought she would refuse, that they'd have to take Brigham from her by force, but then her desperate grip loosened. Hibson stepped in quickly, lifting the barely breathing Commander in armored arms, and Mai-ling Jackson screamed like a soul in hell as Honor gathered her in a protective embrace.

It took ten minutes and all the medics could do to break Ensign Jackson's hysteria, and even then Honor knew it was only a calm in the storm. There was too much hell in those broken, almond eyes for anything more, but at last she lay still on the stretcher, torn by great, heaving shudders under the blanket. She clung to her CO's hand like a child, eyes begging her to make it all a nightmare, not real, and Honor knelt beside her.

"Can you tell us what happened?" she asked gently, and the ensign jerked as if she'd been struck. But this time she licked her scab-crusted lips and gave a tiny, frightened nod.

"Yes, Ma'am," she whispered, but then her mouth worked soundlessly and fresh tears spangled her eyes.

"Take your time," Honor murmured in that same, gentle voice, and Jackson seemed to draw a sort of fragile strength from its encouragement.

"T-they picked us up," she whispered in a tiny thread of a voice. "The Captain, and Exec, and I w-were the only o-officers alive, Ma'am. I-I think there were twenty or . . . or thirty others. I'm not sure."

She swallowed again, and one of the medics pressed a cup of water into Honor's free hand. She held it to the ensign's lips, and Jackson sipped shallowly. Then she lay back on the stretcher, eyes closed. When she spoke again, her voice was flat, mechanical, without any human feeling.

"They brought us back here. For a while—a couple of days, maybe—it wasn't too bad, but they put all the officers in the same cell. They said—" her brief, frozen calm began to crack once more "—they said since we'd let women in uniform, the Captain could keep his w-whores with him."

The living side of Honor's face was as mask-like as the dead side, but she squeezed the ensign's hand.

"Then . . . then they just went crazy," Jackson whispered. "They came and took . . . me and the Commander. W-we thought it was just for interrogation, but then they threw us into . . . into this big room, and there were all these *men*, and they . . . they—"

Her voice broke, and Honor stroked her face as she sobbed.

"They said it was because we were women," she gasped. "They . . . they *laughed* at us, and they *hurt* us, and they said . . . they said it w-was G-G-God's will to . . . to punish Satan's w-w-whores!"

She opened her eyes and dragged herself up, staring into Honor's face while her hand tightened like a claw.

"We fought them, Ma'am. We *did!* B-but we were handcuffed, and t-there were so *many* of them! *Please*, Ma'am—we tried! We *tried!*"

"I know, Mai-ling. I know you did," Honor said through her own tears, hugging the brutalized young body, and the ensign relaxed convulsively. Her head rested on Honor's shoulder, and her voice was broken and dead.

"W-when they were . . . done, they . . . threw us back. The Captain—Captain Alvarez—did what he could, b-but he hadn't known, Captain. He hadn't known what they were going to *do*."

"I know," Honor whispered again, and the ensign's teeth clenched.

"T-then they came back, a-and I couldn't fight any more, Ma'am. I-I just *couldn't*. I tried, but—" She dragged in a ragged breath. "Commander Brigham could. I-I think she hurt some of them really bad b-before they got her down, and then they beat her and beat her and *beat* her!" The broken voice climbed, and a medic stepped in with a hypo as she trembled violently in Honor's arms.

"The Captain tried to stop them, Ma'am. H-he tried, and . . . and they knocked him down with their rifle butts, and then they . . . they—" She twisted in agony, and Honor covered her mouth with her hand, stilling her voice while the hypo took effect. She'd already seen the huge, dried bloodstain on the cell floor and the ragged streaks where someone's heels had been dragged through it to the door.

"And then they raped us again," the ensign said at last, her eyes hazy. "Again and again, and . . . and they said how *nice* it was of their CO to . . . to give them their own whores."

Her thready voice faded to silence, and Honor eased her back down and bent to kiss the filthy, bruised forehead, then tucked the ensign's limp hand under the blanket and rose.

"Take care of her," she told the senior Marine medic, and the woman nodded, her own face wet with tears.

Honor nodded back, then turned towards the door of the cell. As she stepped through it, she drew her sidearm and checked the magazine.

Major Ramirez looked up as Captain Harrington came up the corridor.

"Captain, what shall I—?"

She brushed by him as if he hadn't spoken. There was no expression at all on her face, but the right side of her mouth twitched violently, and her gun was in her hand.

"Captain? Captain Harrington!"

He reached out to grasp her arm, and she looked at him at last.

"Get out of my way, Major." Each word was precisely, perfectly formed despite her crippled mouth. "Clean up this section. Find every one of our people. Get them out of here."

"But—"

"You have your orders, Major," she said in that same, chilled-steel tone, and twitched out of his grasp. She started up the corridor once more, and he stared after her helplessly.

She didn't look up when she reached the Marines in

the passageway. She just strode straight ahead, and they scattered like frightened children. Sergeant Talon's squad started to fall in around her, but she waved them back with a savage chop of her hand and kept walking.

Lieutenant Tremaine stared after her, biting his lip. He'd heard about the discoveries the Marines had made. He hadn't believed it at first—hadn't *wanted* to believe it—but then the medics had carried Commander Brigham's stretcher past him. He'd believed it then, and the Marines' fury had been dwarfed by his own, for he knew Mercedes Brigham well. Very well, indeed.

The Captain said she wanted to be alone. She'd *ordered* everyone to leave her alone. But Scotty Tremaine had seen her face.

She turned a bend in the corridor, and his own face tightened with decision. He laid aside his plasma carbine and went hurrying after her.

Honor climbed the rubble-strewn stairs, ignoring the labored breathing of whoever was trying to catch up with her. It didn't matter. Nothing mattered. She vaulted up the stairs, using her long legs and the light gravity, brushing past an occasional Marine, stepping through an occasional puddle of Masadan blood, and her single eye glowed like molten steel.

She walked down the final corridor, gaze fixed on the open mess hall door, and a voice was calling her from behind. It was distant and unreal, immaterial, and she ignored it as she stepped into the crowded room.

A Marine officer saluted, then flinched back from her in shock, and she went past him as if he didn't exist. Her eye swept the lines of prisoners, searching for the face she sought, and found it.

Captain Williams looked up as if he felt her hatred, and his face paled. She walked towards him, shoving people out of her way, and the voice calling her name was even louder as its owner pushed and shoved through the crowd behind her.

Williams tried to twist away, but her left hand tangled

in his hair, and he cried out in agony as she slammed his head back against the wall. His mouth worked, gobbling words she didn't bother to hear, and her right hand pressed the muzzle against his forehead and began to squeeze.

Someone else's hands locked on her forearm, shoving frantically, and the sharp, spiteful explosion of a pulser dart pocked the mess hall roof as her pistol whined. She wrenched at the hands on her arm, trying to throw whoever it was off, but they clung desperately, and someone was shouting in her ear.

More voices shouted, more hands joined the ones on her arm, dragging her back from Williams while the man sagged to his knees, retching and weeping in terror, and she fought madly against them all. But she couldn't wrench free, and she went to her own knees as someone snatched the pistol from her grip and someone else gripped her head and forced it around.

"Skipper! Skipper, you *can't!*" Scotty Tremaine half-sobbed, holding her face between his hands while tears ran down his cheeks. "*Please*, Skipper! You can't *do* this—not without a trial!"

She stared at him, her detached mind wondering what a trial had to do with anything, and he shook her gently.

"Please, Skipper. If you shoot a prisoner without a trial the Navy—" He drew a deep breath. "You *can't*, Ma'am, however much he deserves it."

"No, she can't," a voice like frozen helium said, and a trace of sanity came back into Honor's expression as she saw Admiral Matthews. "I came as soon as I heard, Captain," he spoke slowly and distinctly, as if he sensed the need to break through to her, "but your lieutenant's right. *You* can't kill him." She stared deep into his eyes, and something inside her eased as she saw the agony and shame—and fury—in his soul.

"But?" she didn't recognize her own voice, and Matthews' mouth twisted in contemptuous hate as he glared down at the sobbing Masadan captain.

"But I *can*. Not without a trial. He'll have one, I

assure you, and so will all the animals he turned loose on your people. They'll be scrupulously, completely fair—and as soon as they're over, this sick, sadistic piece of garbage and all the others responsible will be hanged like the scum they are." He met her eye levelly, and his icy voice was soft.

"I swear that to you, Captain, on the honor of the Grayson Navy."

• CHAPTER TWENTY-SEVEN

Honor Harrington sat staring out the view port, her soul cold as the space beyond the armorplast, and Admiral Matthews, Alice Truman, and Alistair McKeon sat silently behind her.

Nineteen. Nineteen of *Madrigal*'s people were alive, and that figure had been enough to crack Commander Theisman's reserve at last. There was no record of *any* survivors in the Blackbird data base. Apparently Williams had erased it, but it was Theisman who'd picked up *Madrigal*'s survivors, and there had been fifty-three of them. Twenty-six had been women. Of that number, only Ensign Jackson and Mercedes Brigham were still alive, and Fritz Montoya's face had been terrible as he described Brigham's internal injuries and broken bones.

Honor had made certain Theisman was present to hear Montoya's report, and the Commander had gone absolutely white as he turned to her in horror.

"Captain Harrington, I swear I didn't know how bad it really was." He'd swallowed harshly. "Please, you have to believe me. I-I knew it was bad, but there wasn't anything I could *do*, and . . . and I didn't know *how* bad."

His agony had been genuine—as had his shame. *Madrigal*'s bosun had confirmed that it was Theisman's missiles which had killed the Admiral. Honor had wanted to hate him for that, wanted to hate him so badly she could taste it, and his anguish had taken even that away from her.

"I believe you, Commander," she'd said wearily, then inhaled deeply. "Are you prepared to testify before a Grayson court on the matters of which you do have personal knowledge? No one will ask you why you 'immigrated' to Masada. I have Admiral Matthews' promise on that. But very few of the real Masadans are going to voluntarily testify against Williams and his animals."

"Yes, Ma'am." Theisman's voice had been cold. "Yes, Ma'am, I'll testify. And—I'm sorry, Captain. More sorry than I'll ever be able to tell you."

Now she sat gazing at the stars, and her heart was ice within her, for if Blackbird's data base hadn't mentioned the prisoners, it had held other information. She knew, at last, what she truly faced, and it wasn't a heavy cruiser. Not a heavy cruiser at all.

"Well," she said at last, "at least we know."

"Yes, Ma'am," Alice Truman said quietly. She paused for a moment, and then she asked the question in all their minds. "What do we do now, Ma'am?"

The right side of Honor's mouth quirked without humor, for deep inside she was afraid she knew the answer. She had one damaged heavy cruiser, one damaged destroyer, and one completely crippled light cruiser, and she faced an eight-hundred-and-fifty-thousand-ton battlecruiser. What was left of Grayson's Navy didn't even count. She might as well shoot their crews herself as commit them against a *Sultan*-class battlecruiser . . . and her own ship was no match for one, either. A *Sultan* carried almost twice her armament, five times her ammunition, and sidewalls far heavier than her own. Despite *Fearless's* superior electronics, there would be very few survivors if she and *Troubadour* went toe-to-toe against *Thunder of God*.

"We do the best we can, Alice," she said softly. She straightened her shoulders and turned from the view port, and her voice was crisper. "It's always possible they'll decide not to push it. They've lost virtually all their Masadan units. That leaves Haven without any sort of cover. This *'Thunder of God's'* skipper will be as well aware of that as we are, and he can't know how soon we expect reinforcements."

"But we know, Ma'am." McKeon's voice was quiet. "The freighters won't even make Manticore for another nine days. Add four days for the Fleet to respond, and—" He shrugged.

"I know." Honor looked at Truman. "*Apollo's* nodes and Warshawski sails are in good shape, Alice. You can cut five days off that response time."

"Yes, Ma'am." Truman's face was desperately unhappy, but there was absolutely nothing she could do to help here.

"Alistair, you and I will have to get our heads together on the way back to Grayson. We're going to have to fight smart, if it comes to it."

"Yes, Ma'am," McKeon said as quietly as Truman, and Honor looked at Admiral Matthews as he cleared his throat.

"Captain, none of us suspected just how heavy the odds against you really are, but your people have already done—and suffered—far more for us than we had any right to expect. I hope that whoever *Thunder of God's* captain may be, he'll have the sense, the sanity, to realize the game is lost and pull her out. If he doesn't, however, surely Grayson can survive whatever the Faithful may do until your relief force gets here."

He fell silent, and Honor knew what he was trying to say—and why he couldn't quite say it in so many words. He knew how unlikely her ships were to survive against a *Sultan*, and the man in him wanted to give her a way out, to find a reason for her to back off and survive. But the admiral in him knew how desperate the Masadans would become when they heard what had happened to Blackbird, their navy, and *Principality*. Desperate people did irrational things . . . and Masada had stated its willingness to nuke Grayson when it *wasn't* desperate.

Poor as her own chances against a *Sultan* might be, *Fearless* and *Troubadour* were all Grayson had, and if she pulled them out . . .

"Perhaps, Admiral," she said quietly, "but if they're insane enough to continue at all at this point, there's no way to predict what they may do. And even if there were, it's my job to protect the planet."

"But you're not Graysons, Captain." Matthews' voice was as quiet as her own, and she shrugged.

"No, we're not. But we've been through a lot with you people, and we owe Masada." She heard a soft growl of agreement in McKeon's throat. "Admiral Courvosier would have expected me to stand by you just as he did, Sir," she went on past a fresh stab of sorrow and guilt. "More importantly, it's what my Queen would expect of me—and what I would expect of myself." She shook her head. "We're not going anywhere, Admiral Matthews. If Masada still wants Grayson, they'll have to come through us to get it."

"Yes, Sir. I'm afraid it *is* confirmed." Captain Yu sat in the Honorable Jacob Lacy's office, and Haven's ambassador to Masada looked just as grim as he did. Unlike most of his diplomatic colleagues, Lacy was a retired naval officer, a fact for which Yu was profoundly grateful.

"Shit," the ambassador muttered now. "*Principality*, too?"

"All of them, Mr. Ambassador," Yu said harshly. "Tom Theisman squealed a download to *Virtue* just before Harrington began her final run, and Blackbird Base confirmed the complete destruction of the Masadan fleet before it went off the air. For all practical purposes, *Thunder* is all that's left, Sir."

Rage clogged his voice and smoldered like lava in the back of his throat as he admitted it. If only Tractor Five hadn't gone down. If only it hadn't turned out even the flux coil was shot. Twelve hours of repairs had turned into twenty, then twenty-five, and then that fat-headed, stupid, incompetent *fucker* Simonds had cost them another full day and a half with his fits and starts! If it hadn't been so insane, Yu would have sworn the idiot was *trying* to delay their return to Yeltsin's Star!

And the result had been catastrophe.

"What are Masada's chances now, Captain?" Lacy asked after a moment.

"They'd have better luck putting out Yeltsin's Star by

pissing on it, Sir. Oh, I could take Harrington. I'd get hurt—*Star Knights* are nasty customers—but I could take her out. Only it wouldn't do any damned good. She must have sent for help. All her warships were present at Blackbird, but if she sent her freighters away first, she could still have a relief force out here in ten or twelve days. And there *will* be a relief force—one that'll come in ready to kick ass and take names, Sir. We've destroyed at least one Manticoran ship; from Blackbird's final report, we killed some more Manticorans there, and Harrington undoubtedly has proof *Principality* was Haven-built. Whatever the Staff and Cabinet may think, the RMN won't take that lying down."

"And if Masada were in possession of Grayson when they arrived?" It was clear from Lacy's tone that he already knew the answer, and Yu snorted.

"It wouldn't matter a good goddamn, Mr. Ambassador. Besides, I doubt Grayson will surrender if they know help is coming, and that idiot Simonds is just likely to order demonstration nuclear strikes." He clenched his jaw. "If he does, Sir, I'll refuse to carry them out."

"Of course you will!" Yu relaxed just a bit at the ambassador's response. "There's no possible moral justification for slaughtering civilians, and the diplomatic repercussions would be catastrophic."

"Then what do you want me to do, Sir?" the Captain asked quietly.

"I don't know." Lacy scrubbed his hands over his face and frowned up at the ceiling for a long, silent moment, then sighed.

"This operation is shot to hell, Captain, and it's not your fault." Yu nodded and hoped—without much conviction—that the Staff would endorse Lacy's opinion.

"Grayson will fall all over itself to sign the treaty now. Not only has all this underlined the Masadan threat, but we've literally thrown them into Manticore's arms. Gratitude, as well as self-interest, is going to push them together, and I don't see any way to avert that. If the Masadans had pushed operations more vigorously, or allowed us to station a squadron or two in Endicott to back you up, that might not be the case, but now—"

The ambassador pinched the bridge of his nose, then went on slowly.

"In a lot of ways, I'd like to simply wash our hands of the entire situation, but once Grayson signs up with Manticore, we'll need a presence in Endicott worse than ever. And much as I'm rapidly coming to despise the 'Faithful,' *they*'ll need *us* worse than ever with Manticore and Grayson both itching to chop them up. The trick is going to be keeping them alive long enough to realize that."

"Agreed, Sir. But how do we go about doing that?"

"We stall. It's all we *can* do. I'll send my courier boat off to request a 'visit' by a battle squadron or two, but it's going to take at least a T-month for anything to come of that. Somehow, we're going to have to keep Masada from doing anything stupid—anything else stupid, that is—while we simultaneously fend off any Manticoran counterattack against Endicott."

"If you'll forgive my saying so, Mr. Ambassador, that would be a neat trick if you could do it."

"I don't know that I can," Lacy admitted, "but it's the best we can hope for now." He swung his chair slowly back and forth, then nodded. "If you can keep the Masadans from launching any more adventures against Yeltsin, then your ship will still be intact and in Endicott when the Manticorans turn up, right?" Yu nodded, and the ambassador leaned over his desk. "Then I need you to be completely honest with me, Captain. I know how close you are to Commander Theisman, but I have to ask this. Assuming he and his people survived, will they have stuck to their cover story?"

"Yes, Sir." Yu's response was definite. "No one'll believe it, but they'll follow orders, and they all have official Masadan documentation."

"All right. Then what we'll do is this. You'll stall Sword Simonds while I work on his brother and the Council of Elders. If we can prevent any further offensive against Grayson and keep *Thunder* intact, I'll try to run a bluff if Manticore moves to punish Masada. When they turn up, *Thunder* will revert to being PNS *Saladin*, an official Republican unit defending the territory of a Republican ally."

"My God, Sir—Manticore will never buy it!"

"Probably not," Lacy agreed grimly, "but if I can get them to hesitate, even briefly, over committing an open act of war against us, I'll have a toe in the door. And if I talk fast enough, and if Masada agrees to make massive enough reparations, we may just be able to prevent outright invasion of Endicott until *our* reinforcements get here."

"Mr. Ambassador, Masada doesn't have anything to pay reparations *with*. They've bankrupted themselves with their military budgets."

"I know. We'll have to bankroll them—which will be one more hook in our favor, if it works."

Yu shook his head. "I realize you don't have much to work with, Sir, but this sounds awfully thin. And I guarantee the Masadans won't go for it—not willingly, anyway. I'm beginning to think they're even crazier than we thought, and one thing I do know is that Simonds—both the Simondses—are determined to avoid becoming a Republican client state."

"Even when the only other option is their destruction?"

"I wouldn't bet against it, and that's assuming they're ready to admit their only other option *is* destruction. You know what a fruitcake religion they've got."

"Yes, I do." Lacy sighed. "That's why we're not going to tell them what we're doing until it's too late for them to screw it up. We're going to have to keep them in the dark about what we're really up to and hope they realize later that we were right."

"Jesus," Yu murmured, sagging back in his chair. "You don't want much, do you, Mr. Ambassador?"

"Captain," Lacy smiled wryly, "no one knows better than I do what a sack of snakes I'm handing you. Unfortunately, it's the only sack I've got. Do you think you can bring it off?"

"No, Sir, I don't," Yu said frankly. "But I don't see any choice but to try, either."

* * *

" . . . but to try, either," Captain Yu's voice said, and the click as Deacon Sands switched off the tape recorder echoed in the council chamber. He looked at Chief Elder Simonds, but the Chief Elder's fiery eyes were locked upon his brother's expressionless face.

"So much for your precious *allies*, Matthew. And your own men don't seem to have done much better!"

Sword Simonds bit his lip. The Council's terrified hostility was palpable; anything he said would be futile, and he closed his mouth, feeling sweat on his forehead, then looked up in astonishment as someone else spoke.

"With all respect, Chief Elder, I don't think this can all be laid on Sword Simonds' shoulders," Elder Huggins said flatly. "*We* instructed him to delay operations."

The Chief Elder gaped at Huggins, for his hatred for and jealousy of Matthew Simonds were legendary, but Huggins went on in a precise voice.

"Our instru ons to the Sword were the best we knew to give, it we made insufficient allowance for the forces of Satan, Brothers." He looked around the council table. "Our ships in Yeltsin were destroyed by this *woman*, this handmaiden of Satan, Harrington." His calm, almost detached tone gave his hatred an even more terrible power. "It is she who has profaned all we hold most holy. She has set herself against God's Work, and the Sword can scarcely be blamed because we exposed him to the Devil's venom."

A quiet rustle ran around the table, and Huggins smiled thinly.

"Then again, there are our 'allies.' They, too, are infidel. Have we not known from the beginning that their ends and ours differed? Was it not our fear of being engulfed by them which led us to prefer Maccabeus to outright invasion?" He shrugged. "We were wrong there, too. Maccabeus has failed us, if, indeed, he was ever truly ours. Either he made his attempt and failed, or else he will never make it at all, and after their joint battles, the Apostate and the harlot who rules Manticore will become closer than brothers. It is inevitable—if we allow the Devil to triumph."

He paused, and Thomas Simonds moistened his lips in the dead silence.

"May we assume from that last remark, Brother Huggins, that you have a proposal?" Huggins nodded, and the Chief Elder's eyes narrowed. "May we hear it?"

"The Havenite infidels clearly don't realize we've been able to listen to their plans to betray us," Huggins said conversationally. Sword Simonds shifted in his chair, swallowing any temptation to differ with Huggins' interpretation of Haven's purpose, and the Elder went on in the same everyday tone. "They think to play men who have set their hands to God's Work for fools, Brothers. They care nothing for the Work; their sole concern is to ensnare us in an 'alliance' against their enemies. Anything they say to us from this time forward will be shaped by that concern, and as such, they will be as words from Satan's own mouth. Is this not true?"

He looked around once more, and heads nodded. The assembled Elders' faces were those of men who have seen disaster staring back at them from their own mirrors. The catastrophe which had overwhelmed their plans, the trap into which they had thrust themselves and their planet, terrified them, and the only certitude in a universe which had turned to shifting sand was their Faith.

"Very well. If we cannot trust them, then we must make our own plans and bring them to fruition in God's Name even while we dissemble against the dissemblers. They believe our cause is hopeless, but we, Brothers, *we* know God is with us. It is His Work to which we are called, and we must not allow ourselves to falter and fail once more. There must be no Third Fall."

"Amen," someone murmured, and Sword Simonds felt a stir deep within him. He was a military man, whatever Captain Yu thought. Most of the decisions which infuriated the Havenite had sprung not from stupidity but from an agenda Haven knew nothing about, and he was only too well aware of the disastrous military position. Yet he was also a man of the Faith. He *believed*, despite all ambition, despite any veneer of sophistication, and as he listened to Huggins' quiet words, he heard his own Faith calling to him.

"Satan is cunning," Huggins went on. "Twice before he has sundered Man from God, each time using woman as his tool. Now he seeks to do so yet again, using the Harlot of Manticore and her handmaiden Harrington, and if we view our situation only through the eyes of the flesh, it is, indeed, hopeless. But there are other eyes, Brothers. How often must we succumb to the Devil's wiles before we recognize God's Truth? We must put our trust in Him and follow Him even as Meshach, Shadrach, and Abednigo followed into the furnace and Daniel followed into the lion's den. I say to you our position is *not* hopeless. I say it can *never* be hopeless so long as God is our Captain."

"No doubt that's true, Brother Huggins," even the Chief Elder's voice was touched with respect. "Yet we—all of us—are but mortal. What recourse have we with our navy gone if the Havenites deprive us even of *Thunder of God*? How can we stand off the entire power of Manticore if it comes against us?"

"We must only do our part, Chief Elder," Huggins said with absolute certainty. "The means to complete the Apostate's downfall before the Harlot's navy can intervene are in our hands. We must only grasp God's Sword and thrust It home to prove our constancy as His Faithful, and He will confound the Harlot—yes, and the infidels of Haven, as well."

"What do you mean, Brother Huggins?" Sword Simonds asked softly.

"Have we not known from the beginning that Manticore is weak and decadent? If our forces are in possession of Grayson, and if none of the Harlot's ships survive to dispute our version of how that came to pass, then what can she do? She will recoil from the Light of God, and His Hand will uphold us as He has promised It will always uphold the Faithful. And can you not see that He has given us the means to that end?"

Huggins' eyes burned with messianic fire, and his hand shot out to stab a long, bony finger at Deacon Sands's tape recorder.

"We know the infidels' plans, Brothers! We know they intend to divert and desert us, to enmesh us in their net—*but they don't know that we know!*" He turned his blazing eyes on the Sword. "Sword Simonds! If you held undisputed command of *Thunder of God*, how long would it take you to secure Yeltsin's Star against the Manticoran ships there?"

"A day," Simonds said. "Perhaps less, perhaps a little more. But—"

"But you don't hold undisputed command of it. The infidels have seen to that—but if we pretend to be duped by their lies, if we lull them by seeming to accept their delays, we can change that." He stabbed the Sword with another fiery stare. "How much of *Thunder of God*'s crew is of the Faith?"

"A little more than two-thirds, Brother Huggins, but many of the key officers are still infidels. Without them, our men would be unable to get full efficiency out of the ship."

"But they're infidels," Huggins said very, very softly. "Strangers to the Faith who fear death, even in God's Name, because they believe it is an end, not a beginning. If they were forced into combat, where they must fight or die, would they not choose to fight?"

"Yes," the Sword almost whispered, and Huggins smiled.

"And, Chief Elder, if the infidels of Haven were saddled with responsibility for an invasion of Yeltsin before the eyes of the galaxy, would they not be forced to at least pretend to have supported us knowingly? Endicott is but one, poor star system—would their credit survive if the galaxy learned that such as we had duped them into serving our ends, not their own?"

"The temptation to avoid embarrassment at any cost would certainly be great," the elder Simonds said slowly.

"And, Brothers," Huggins' eyes swept the table once more, "if the Harlot believed Haven stood behind us, with its fleet poised to grind her kingdom into dust, would she dare confront that threat? Or would she show her true weakness before the Light of God and abandon the Apostate to their fate?"

A low, harsh growl answered him, and he smiled.

"And so God shows us our way," he said simply. "We will let Haven 'delay' us, but we will use the delay to slip more of our own aboard *Thunder of God*, until we become strong enough to overpower the infidels in her crew. We will seize their ship and make her the *true* Thunder of God by giving the infidels the choice of certain death or the possibility of life if the Apostate and their allies are defeated. We will smash the ships of Satan's handm len and retake Grayson from the Apostate, and the harlot of Manticore will believe Haven stands behind us. And, Brothers, Haven *will* stand behind us. The infidels will have no stomach for admitting we made fools of them—and, best of all, we will have achieved their greatest desire by depriving Manticore of an ally in Yeltsin! The People's Republic is corrupt and ambitious. If we attain their end despite their own cowardice, they will embrace our triumph as their own!"

There was a stunned silence, and then someone began to clap. It was only one pair of hands at first, but a second joined them, then a third. A fourth. Within seconds the applause echoed from the ceiling, and Sword Simonds found himself clapping as hard as any.

He stood, still clapping, and not even the knowledge that Huggins had displaced him forever as his brother's successor could smother the hope flaming in his heart. He had entered this room knowing Masada was doomed; now he knew he'd been wrong. He had allowed his Faith to falter, forgotten that they were *God's Faithful*, not solely dependent on their own mortal powers. The great test of his people's Faith had come upon them, and only Huggins had recognized it for what it was—the chance to redeem themselves from the Second Fall at last!

He met the Elder's eyes and bowed, acknowledging

the passing of power, and if a corner of his mind knew Huggins' entire plan was a reckless gamble, a last death-or-glory challenge which must end in victory or doom them to utter destruction, he ignored it. Desperation had overwhelmed reason, for he had no other option. The thought that their actions—that *his* actions—had failed God and doomed the Faith was unacceptable.

It was as simple as that.

• CHAPTER TWENTY-EIGHT

"You're going home, Ensign," Honor said quietly.

She squeezed the shoulder of the young woman in the sickbay bunk while Nimitz crooned on her own shoulder, and Mai-ling Jackson managed a tiny, fragile smile. It wasn't much of a smile, but Honor forced her crippled mouth to smile back into the drug-clouded eyes even as she prayed the therapists could somehow put the ensign back together. Then she stepped back and looked at the life-support equipment enshrouding the bunk beside her. Mercedes Brigham was still unconscious, but Fritz Montoya did good work, and her breathing looked stronger. Honor made herself believe that.

She turned away and almost collided with Surgeon Lieutenant Wendy Gwynn. *Apollo*'s sickbay was small and cramped compared to *Fearless*'s, and the squadron's wounded spilled out of it to fill the wardroom, the officers' mess, and every other unoccupied—and pressure-tight—compartment of the savagely mauled light cruiser. Gwynn was going to have her hands full on the voyage to Manticore, Honor knew, but at least the wounded would be out of it. At least she could get *them* home alive.

"Take care of them, Doctor," she said, knowing even as she spoke that it was unnecessary.

"We will, Ma'am. I promise."

"Thank you," Honor said softly, and stepped into the passage before Gwynn could see the tears in her eye.

She drew a deep breath and straightened her aching spine, and Nimitz scolded gently. She hadn't slept since waking up in sickbay herself, and he didn't like her exhausted, depressed emotions. Honor didn't much care for them herself, but other people were just as tired as she was. Besides, the nightmares were waiting. She felt them whispering in the depths of her mind, and wondered whether it truly was duty alone which had kept her on her feet so long. Nimitz scolded again, harder, and she caressed his soft fur in mute apology, then headed for the lift to the bridge.

Lieutenant Commander Prevost had one plasticast-sheathed arm in a sling and moved with a painful limp, but her quiet voice was crisp as she spoke to the helmsman. *Apollo*'s executive officer was far from the only walking wounded member of the cruiser's crew. Over half Truman's people were dead or wounded; of her senior officers, only Prevost and Lieutenant Commander Hackmore, *Apollo*'s chief engineer, were still on their feet at all.

"Ready to pull out, Alice?"

"Yes, Ma'am. I wish—" Truman cut herself off with a little shrug and looked at the shattered ruin of *Apollo*'s tactical and astrogation stations and the patches on the bridge's after bulkhead. That hadn't been a direct hit, Honor knew—just a secondary explosion that had killed Lieutenant Commander Amberson, Lieutenant Androunaskis, and the astrogator's entire plotting party.

She held out her hand.

"I know. I wish you could stay, too. But you can't. I wish I could give you more medical staff, God knows Lieutenant Gwynn could use them, but—"

It was Honor's turn to shrug, and Truman nodded as she gripped the proffered hand firmly. If *Fearless* and *Troubadour* were called upon to fight *Thunder of God*, they would need every doctor and SBA they had.

"Good luck, Skipper," she said quietly.

"And to you, Alice." Honor gave her hand one last squeeze, stepped back, and adjusted her white beret. "You have my report. Just—" She paused, then shook her head. "Just tell them we tried, Alice."

"I will."

"I know," Honor repeated, and gave her a nod and a small half-wave, then turned away without another word.

Ten minutes later, she stood on her own bridge, watching the direct vision display as *Apollo* broke Blackbird orbit. The light cruiser's damage was hideously apparent in her mangled flanks, but she drove ahead at five hundred and two gravities, and Honor made herself look away. She'd done all she could to summon help, yet she knew, deep at the core of her, that if help were truly needed, it would arrive too late.

She felt her tired muscles listing under Nimitz's weight and made herself straighten as she switched the optical pickups to the surface of Blackbird. A time display clicked downward with metronome precision, and the visual dimmed suddenly as it hit zero. A huge, silent boil of white-hot light erupted from the frigid surface, swelling and expanding in the blink of an eye, and she heard her bridge crew's barely audible growl as it wiped away every trace of the Masadan base. Honor watched for a moment longer, then reached up to rub Nimitz's ears and spoke without looking away from the dying explosion.

"All right, Steve. Take us out of here."

The moon fell away from her, and she turned from the display at last as *Troubadour* formed up on her ship. They were together again—her entire remaining squadron, she thought, and tried to shake the bitterness of the reflection. She was tired. That was all.

"How's our com link to *Troubadour*, Joyce?" she asked.

"It's solid, Ma'am, as long as we don't get too far away from her."

"Good." Honor glanced at her com officer, wondering if her question made her sound a prey to anxiety. And then she wondered if perhaps she sounded that way because she *was*. Metzinger was a good officer. She'd tell her if there were any problems. But with her own gravitic sensors down, *Fearless* could no longer receive FTL transmissions from the recon drones mounting guard against *Thunder of God*'s return. Her ship was as one-eyed as she was, and without *Troubadour*'s gravitics to do her seeing for her . . .

She checked the chrono again and made a decision. Nightmares or no, she couldn't do her job with fatigue poisons clogging her brain, and she folded her hands behind her and walked across the bridge towards the lift.

Andreas Venizelos had the watch, but he rose from the command chair and followed her to the lift door. She felt him behind her and looked over her shoulder at him.

"You okay, Skipper?" he asked in a soft voice. "You look pretty shot, Ma'am." His eyes clung to her face, and she felt his concern for her.

"For someone who's lost half her very first squadron, I'm fine," she replied, equally softly, and the right side of her mouth quirked.

"I guess that's one way to look at it, Ma'am, but we kicked some ass along the way. If we have to, I figure we can kick a little more."

Honor surprised herself with a weary chuckle and punched him lightly on the shoulder.

"Of course we can, Andy." He smiled, and she punched him again, then drew a deep, tired breath. "I'm going to go catch some sleep. Call me if anything breaks."

"Yes, Ma'am."

She stepped into the lift. The door closed behind her.

Alice Truman watched her own display as *Fearless* and *Troubadour* headed towards Grayson and bit her lip at the thought of what they might face in the next few days. She hated herself for leaving them, but Commander Theisman had done too good a job on *Apollo*, and that was all there was to it.

She touched a com stud.

"Engineering, Commander Hackmore," an exhausted voice said.

"Charlie, this is the Captain. You people ready for translation?"

"Yes, Ma'am. About the only parts of this ship I *can* vouch for are her propulsive systems, Skip."

"Good." Truman never took her eyes from the

departing dots of Honor's other ships. "I'm glad to hear that, Charlie, because I want you to take the hyper generator safety interlocks off line."

There was a moment of silence, then Hackmore cleared his throat.

"Are you sure about that, Captain?"

"Never surer."

"Skipper, I know I said propulsion's in good shape, but we took a *lot* of hits. I can't guarantee there's not damage I haven't found yet."

"I know, Charlie."

"But if you take us that high and we lose it, or pick up a harmonic—"

"I know, Charlie," Truman said even more firmly. "And I also know we've got all the squadron's wounded with us. But if you kill the interlocks, we can cut twenty-five, thirty hours—maybe even a little more—off our time."

"Figure all that out on your own, did you?"

"I used to be a pretty fair astrogator, and I can still crunch numbers when I have to. So open up your little toolbox and go to work."

"Yes, Ma'am. If that's what you want." Hackmore paused a moment, then asked quietly, "Does Captain Harrington know about this, Ma'am?"

"I guess I sort of forgot to mention it to her."

"I see." Truman could feel the tired smile behind the words. "It just, um, slipped your mind, I suppose."

"Something like that. Can you do it?"

"Hell, yes, I can do it. Aren't I the most magnificent engineer in the Fleet?" Hackmore laughed again, more naturally.

"Good. I knew you'd like the idea. Let me know when you're ready."

"Yes, Ma'am. And I just want to say, Captain, that knowing you figured I'd go along with this makes me feel all warm and tingly inside. It must mean you must think I'm almost as crazy as you are."

"Flatterer. Go play with your spanners."

Truman cut the circuit and leaned back, rubbing her

hands up and down the arms of her chair while she wondered what Honor would have said if she'd told her. There was only one thing she *could* have said, by The Book, because Truman was about to break every safety reg there was. But Honor had enough on her plate just now. If *Apollo* couldn't be here to help take that big bastard on, the least she could do was bring back reinforcements as quickly as possible, and there was no point giving Honor something else to worry about.

The Commander closed her eyes, trying to forget the exhausted pain she'd seen in Honor's one good eye. The pain had been there from the moment she learned of Admiral Courvosier's death, but it cut deeper now, weighed down by every death her squadron had paid and might still be called upon to pay. Just as her exhaustion, anguish was the price a captain paid for the privilege of command. Civilians—and too many junior officers—saw only the courtesies and deference, the godlike power bestowed upon the captain of a Queen's ship. They never saw the other side of the coin, the responsibility to keep going because your people needed you to and the agony of knowing misjudgment or carelessness could kill far more than just yourself. Or the infinitely worse agony of sentencing your own people to die because you had no choice. Because it was their duty to risk their lives, and it was yours to take them into death's teeth with you . . . or send them on ahead.

Commander Truman could imagine no higher calling than to command a Queen's ship, yet there were times she hated the faceless masses she was sworn to protect because of what protecting them cost people like her crew. People like Honor Harrington. It wasn't patriotism or nobility or dedication that kept men and women on their feet when they wanted to die. Those things might have sent them into uniform, might even keep them there in the times between, when they knew what could happen but it hadn't happened yet. But what kept them on their feet when there was no sane reason for hope were the bonds between them, loyalty to one another, the knowledge others depended on them even as they depended on those others. And sometimes, all too rarely, it came down to a single person it was simply unthinkable to fail. Someone they knew would never quit on *them*, never leave *them* in the lurch. Alice Truman had always known there were people like that, but she'd never actually met one. Now she had, and she felt like a traitor for having no choice but to leave when Honor needed her.

She opened her eyes again. If the Lords of Admiralty chose to go by The Book, she would face a Board, certainly, possibly even a full Court, for recklessly hazarding her command. And even if she didn't, there were going to be captains who felt the risk was unjustifiable, for if she lost *Apollo*, no one in Manticore would even know that Honor needed help.

But hours might make the difference in Yeltsin, and that meant she would never be able to live with herself if she *didn't* take the chance.

Her intercom beeped, and she pressed the stud.

"Bridge, Captain."

"Safety interlocks disengaged, Skipper," Hackmore's voice said. "This beat-up bitch is ready to roll."

"Thank you, Charlie," Commander Alice Truman said firmly. She checked the maneuvering display. "Stand by to translate in eight minutes."

• CHAPTER TWENTY-NINE

Alfredo Yu knew he ought to be studying Engineering's report on *Thunder of God*'s overhauled tractors, but he frowned sightlessly at the data, unable to concentrate on it. Something about the Masadan reaction was out of kilter. It was *wrong*, and the fact that he couldn't put his finger on just what that wrongness was only made him even more uneasy.

He pushed back from the terminal to pace fretfully and tried to tell himself he was being silly. Of course something was "wrong" with Masada! He'd failed. Through no fault of his own, perhaps, but he'd failed, and the repercussions of that failure, and its consequences for them, had to be echoing through every Masadan mind and heart.

And yet . . .

He came to a stop, eyes unfocused but intent as he tried to chase down that "yet." Was it the Council of Elders' silence? The halfhearted way Sword Simonds had protested his excuses for keeping *Thunder* in Endicott? Or simply the sense of doom looming over them all?

He bared his teeth in a humorless smile at his own contrariness. He'd expected hysteria and a welter of conflicting orders from the Council, and the fact that he hadn't gotten those things should have been a vast relief. This stunned, silent lack of reaction was far better suited to his and Ambassador Lacy's purposes—was that why it worried him? Because it was too convenient?

And why should Simonds' pliancy puzzle him? The Sword must be astounded he was still alive. Surely he had to be wondering when his strange immunity would vanish, and a man who felt Death breathing quietly

339

down his neck, never knowing when it might strike,
wasn't very likely to be his old, prickly, meddlesome
self, now was he?

As for senses of doom, what else could he expect?
Despite the front he maintained for his inner circle of
Havenite officers, he himself had no hope at all that
Manticore would back off because a single Havenite
battlecruiser—especially the one who'd started the
shooting in the first place—got in the way. And if *he*
didn't believe it, how could he expect his crew to?
There was an air of caged lightning aboard *Thunder of
God*, and men did their duty without chatter and tried
to believe they would somehow be among the survivors
when it was finished.

All of those explanations for his unease were true.
Unfortunately, none of them got at the root of whatever
was worrying him.

He turned automatically, almost against his will, to
the bulkhead calendar display. Three days since
Blackbird's destruction. He didn't know exactly when
Harrington's freighters had pulled out, but if they hadn't
gone sooner, they *must* have gone as soon as she discovered *Thunder's* true weight of metal, and that gave
him a rough time window. He might have as many as
ten days or as few as eight before the Manticoran relief
arrived, and every slow-ticking second of anticipation
stretched his nerves tighter.

At least the Faithful seemed to realize they'd lost.
The Elders' relatively speedy acceptance of his argument that further attacks would be in vain had been a
welcome surprise, and if Simonds' decision to reinforce
the fortifications scattered about the Endicott System
was pointless, it also beat hell out of a do-or-die assault
on Grayson.

They were doing exactly what he and Ambassador
Lacy wanted them to, so why couldn't he feel any
satisfaction?

It was the futility, he decided. The sense that events
were in motion, proceeding down a foreordained path
no one could alter. His awareness that it simply didn't

matter anymore—that the end would be the same, whatever he did, or coaxed *them* into doing—made inactivity poisonously seductive.

Perhaps that was why he hadn't objected to the Sword's latest orders. *Thunder of God* had never been intended as a transport, but she was faster even sublight than anything Masada had, and if the thought of cluttering his ship with still more Masadans was unappealing, at least as long as she played passenger liner she wasn't being ordered back to Yeltsin. And it would at least give him the illusion of doing *something*.

He snorted. Perhaps he and Simonds were more alike than he cared to admit, for it seemed that was an illusion whose preservation they both craved.

He glanced at the calendar again. The first shuttles would be arriving in another nine hours, and he twitched his shoulders straight and headed for the cabin hatch. He and Manning were going to have a hell of a time figuring out where to put them, and that was good. It would give him something constructive to worry about for a while.

Admiral of the Green Hamish Alexander, Thirteenth Earl of White Haven, waited by the access tube as the pinnace docked in HMS *Reliant*'s boat bay. His flagship was already driving towards the hyper limit under maximum military power, and if his rugged face was calm, the skin around his ice-blue eyes was tight.

He folded his hands behind him and knew the full shock hadn't yet hit. Prolong made for long friendships and associations, and he'd known Raoul Courvosier all his life. He was twelve T-years younger than Raoul had been and he'd climbed the rank ladder faster, in no small part because of his birth, but there'd always been a closeness—personal, not just professional—between them. Lieutenant Courvosier had taught him astrogation on his midshipman's cruise, and he'd followed in Captain Courvosier's footsteps as senior tactical instructor at Saganami Island, and argued and planned strategy and deployment policies with Admiral Courvosier for years. Now, just like that, he was gone.

It was like waking up one morning to find he'd lost an arm or a leg in his sleep, but Hamish Alexander was familiar with pain. And terrible as this pain was, it was not what filled him with such fear. Beyond personal grief, beyond even his awareness of the outstanding leadership resource the navy had lost with Raoul, was the knowledge that four hundred other navy personnel had died with him, and that a thousand more were all too probably waiting for death in Yeltsin even now—if, indeed, they hadn't already died. *That* was what made Hamish Alexander afraid.

The tube pressure equalized, and a shortish, sturdy commander, her braided blond hair tucked under the white beret of a starship's commander, stepped out of it. Bosun's pipes shrilled, the side party came to attention, and she saluted crisply.

"Welcome aboard, Commander Truman," he said, returning her salute.

"Thank you, Sir." Truman's face was drawn and etched with weariness. It couldn't have been an easy voyage for her, Alexander thought, yet there was a fresh, peculiarly poignant sorrow he understood too well in her exhausted green eyes.

"I'm very sorry to have pulled you out of *Apollo*, Commander," he said quietly as they moved towards *Reliant's* lift, "but I needed to get under way immediately—and I need to know everything someone who was there can tell me. Under the circumstances—" He shrugged slightly, and she nodded.

"I understand, Sir. I hated leaving her, but she needs a dockyard, not me, and Commander Prevost can handle anything that comes up."

"I'm glad you understand." The door closed behind them, and Alexander examined his visitor as the lift started for the bridge. His ships had pulled out of Manticore orbit within fifteen minutes of receiving *Apollo's* squealed transmission, and he'd seen the cruiser's damage as she rendezvoused with *Reliant* to send Truman across.

He still had only the sketchiest knowledge of events in Yeltsin, but one look at that mangled hull had told him it was bad. It was a miracle *Apollo* had remained hyper capable, and he'd wondered then what Truman would look like when she came aboard. Now he knew.

"I noticed," he chose his words with care, "that you made excellent time from Yeltsin's Star, Commander."

"Yes, Sir." Truman's voice was uninflected, and Alexander smiled.

"That wasn't a trap, Commander. On the other hand, I know perfectly well you didn't cut thirty hours off the old passage record without playing games with your hyper generator."

Alice Truman looked at him for several silent seconds. Lord Alexander—no, he was the Earl of White Haven, since his father's death—was known for a certain willingness to ignore The Book when it got in his way, and there was an almost conspiratorial gleam under the worry in his eyes.

"Well, yes, My Lord," she admitted.

"How high did you take her, Commander?"

"Too high. We bounced off the iota wall a day out of Yeltsin."

Despite himself, Alexander flinched. Dear God, she must have taken out *all* the interlocks. No ship had ever crossed into the iota bands and survived—no one even knew if a ship *could* survive there.

"I see." He cleared his throat. "You were extremely lucky, Commander Truman. I trust you realize that?"

"Yes, Sir. I certainly do."

"You must also be extremely good," he went on in exactly the same tone, "considering that you held her together somehow."

"As you say, My Lord, I was lucky. I also have an extremely good engineer, who may even speak to me again someday."

Alexander's face blossomed with a sudden, almost boyish grin, and Truman grinned back at him. But it was a fragile, fleeting expression that died quickly, and she twitched her shoulders.

"I realize I violated every safety procedure, Sir, but knowing what Captain Harrington faced in Yeltsin, I felt the risk was justified."

"I agree completely—and I've so advised First Space Lord Webster."

"Thank you, Sir," Truman said quietly, and he nodded.

"As a matter of fact, Commander, we're going to be finding out just how good *my* engineers are. I'm afraid I can't justify taking two full squadrons of battlecruisers quite as high as you went, but I think we can shave a few hours off our return passage, and time is clearly the one thing we don't have."

It was Truman's turn to nod, but the worry was back in her eyes, because time wasn't something "we" didn't have; it was something Grayson and Captain Harrington might already have run out of.

The lift slid to a halt and the door opened onto the flag bridge's hustle and bustle. Alexander's task force was still shaking itself into order—three of his battlecruisers had been transferred abruptly to him to replace ships unready for instant departure—but Captain Hunter, his chief of staff, noted his presence. Hunter said something to the admiral's ops officer and crossed quickly to the lift, holding out his hand to Truman.

"Alice. I heard *Apollo*'s damage was wicked, but it's good to see you again. I only wish it were under other circumstances."

"Thank you, Sir. I do, too."

"Come into the briefing room, Byron," Alexander said. "I think both of us need to go over Commander Truman's story with her in some detail."

"Of course, Sir."

Alexander led the way into the briefing room and waved his juniors into chairs.

"I'm afraid I haven't met Captain Harrington, Commander," he said. "I know her record, but I don't know *her* or her present situation, so I want you to begin from the beginning and tell us everything that happened from the moment you first entered Yeltsin space."

"Yes, Sir." Truman drew a deep breath and straightened in her chair. "We arrived on schedule, My Lord, and—"

Alexander let her voice roll over him, listening as much to how she spoke as to what she said. His mind worked clearly and coldly, isolating bits of data, noting questions to be raised, filing other answers away, and under his concentration was that icy, personal core of fear.

For despite all the risks Truman had taken, the odds were very high that Honor Harrington and all of her people were already dead, and if they were, Hamish Alexander was about to begin the war Manticore had feared for almost forty years.

"Skipper?"

Honor looked up from her paperwork as Venizelos stuck his head in through the open hatch.

"Yes, Andy?"

"I thought you'd like to know we've got Laser Four back up—sort of. There's still a glitch in the fire control runs somewhere, and the crew's going to have to update the on-mount computers manually, but the bay's vacuum-tight again and all the test circuits are green."

"Well done, Andy!" Honor smiled with the right side of her mouth. "Now if you and James could just get the gravitics back up . . . ?"

She let her voice trail off on a teasing note, and he grimaced.

"Skipper, the difficult we do immediately; the impossible takes a shipyard."

"That's what I was afraid of." Honor waved at a chair, and the exec eyed her covertly as he parked himself in it.

She looked better, now that quick-heal was fading the horrible contusion which had disfigured her face. The left side was still frozen and dead, but Venizelos was getting used to that. And though her left eye's vision was as impaired as Montoya had feared, the neat black eye patch with which she'd replaced its bulky dressing gave her a sort of raffish toughness.

Yet it wasn't her appearance that mattered, he thought. She'd been madder than hell when she woke from her first sleep in fifty-three hours to discover Montoya and MacGuiness had slipped a mickey into her cocoa. For a while, Venizelos had thought not even the doctor's sworn oath that he could have had her back on her feet in less than thirty minutes had *Thunder of God* turned up would keep her from brigging both of them. But it had also put her to sleep for over fifteen hours, and deep inside she must have realized how desperately she'd needed that rest.

Venizelos hadn't known what Montoya intended, but if he had known, he would have drugged her cocoa himself. She'd been tearing apart before his eyes, and he'd been terrified—both for her and for all the people who needed her so badly. It had been dreadful enough when she learned of Admiral Courvosier's death; after what happened to *Madrigal's* people, it had become terrible to watch. He couldn't blame her for her hatred, and he'd understood her guilt, even if he didn't share her cruel self-conviction that she'd failed the Admiral, but he'd also known they needed her back. If it hit the fan, they needed Honor Harrington on *Fearless's* bridge, working her magic for them all once more, not an exhausted automaton who'd worn herself into a stupor.

"Well—" she leaned back, and her voice pulled the exec out of his thoughts "—I suppose we're as ready as we're going to get before she turns up."

"You really think she's coming, Skipper? It's been over four days. Wouldn't they've been here by now if they were going to come?"

"You'd think so, yes."

"But you don't, do you?" Venizelos asked, and his eyes narrowed as she shook her head. "Why not, Skipper?"

"I couldn't give you a logical reason." She folded her arms beneath her breasts, her single eye dark and deep. "Anything they do in Yeltsin at this point will only make their own situation worse. If they destroy us or nuke Grayson, the Fleet will turn them into a memory. Even if the Masadans don't know that, the Peeps do. And if they *were* going to do anything, they should already have done it without giving us time to make repairs and get set, much less giving a relief from Manticore time to get here. And yet. . ."

Her slurred voice trailed off, and Venizelos shivered deep inside. The quiet stretched out until he cleared his throat.

"And yet, Ma'am?" he asked quietly.

"She's out there," Honor said. "She's out there, and she's coming." Her eye focused on his face, and the right side of her mouth quirked at his expression. "Don't worry, Andy—I'm not turning mystic in my old age! But think about it. If they were going to be rational, they should have pulled out the instant the squadron got back. They didn't. Certainly they should have run instead of standing to fight when we came after them at Blackbird! And then—" her voice turned dark and grim "—there's the way they treated *Madrigal*'s people."

She fell silent for a moment, brooding down at the table once more, then shook herself.

"The point is, these aren't rational people. They don't even live in the same galaxy as the rest of us. I can't build a nice, neat enemy intentions analysis, but from what we've seen of them so far, I think—no, I *know*—they won't change now."

"Not even if the Peeps pull *Thunder of God* out on them?"

"Now that," Honor admitted, "is the one thing that might stop them. But the question is whether or not the PRH *can* pull her out, and after what happened at Blackbird, I'm not too optimistic on that point." She shook her head again. "No, I think she's coming. And if she is, we should be seeing her soon. Very soon."

• CHAPTER THIRTY

Cramming them in had been even harder than Yu had expected. Every spare compartment was packed to the deckhead with Masadan soldiers and their personal weapons. A man couldn't turn around without stepping on one of them, and Yu would be vastly relieved when he off-loaded the first consignment.

Their numbers put a strain on *Thunder*'s environmental plant, as well, which was what had prompted the current meeting. Yu, Commander Valentine, and Lieutenant Commander DeGeorge, *Thunder*'s purser, sat in the captain's day cabin, going over the figures, and DeGeorge was an unhappy man.

"The worst thing, Skipper, is that most of them don't even have vac suits. If we suffer an enviro failure, it's going to be ugly. *Very* ugly."

"Stupid bastards," Valentine grunted. Yu gave him a reproving glance, but he couldn't get much voltage into it, and the engineer shrugged. "All they had to do was put them into vac suits for the trip, Skipper. Their equipment sucks, and the poor pricks would've been miserable, but at least they'd have it with them!" He scowled. "And another thing. We're taking all these ground pukes out to their asteroid bases, right?" Yu nodded, and Valentine shrugged again. "Well, don't tell me they've got this many spare suits in stores out there!"

Yu frowned at that, for the engineer was right. They were hauling all these men out to hostile environment bases, and there wasn't a single vac suit among them. That was unusually stupid even for Masadans, and he wondered why that fact hadn't occurred to him sooner.

"Well, anyway," DeGeorge said, "I'm keeping a close

348

eye on the enviro monitors, and we're okay so far. I just hope we stay there!"

George Manning sat at the center of the bridge and concentrated on duplicating the confidence the Captain projected. Not that he felt particularly confident, but he'd had plenty of time to adjust to his own inner sense of doom, and it wasn't as if he had a lot of options.

He checked the time. They were running over a half-hour behind schedule for their first delivery, and he turned his head.

"Com, contact Base Three and update our ETA."

"Aye, Sir," Lieutenant Hart, his Masadan com officer replied, and something about the man's response nudged at Manning. There was an odd note in his voice, one that went deeper than the background anxiety all of them were feeling, and the exec gave him a sharper glance.

Hart seemed unaware of his scrutiny. He leaned to his left to bring up his com laser software, and Manning's eyes suddenly went very still. There was an angular shape under the Masadan's tunic, and there shouldn't have been—especially not one the shape of an automatic pistol.

The exec made himself look away. He might be wrong about what that shape was, but he didn't think so. Of course, even if he wasn't, there could be another explanation for its presence. Hart might be overcompensating for his own anxieties, or it might be a simple case of aberration, a single man about to snap under the strain. That would have been terrifying enough in the close confines of the bridge, but Manning would have infinitely preferred it to what he knew had to be the truth.

He pressed a stud on his intercom panel.

"Captain speaking," a voice said, and Manning made himself sound very, very natural.

"Commander Manning, Sir. I just thought you'd like to know I'm having Base Three updated on the arrival of their bounty of troops."

* * *

Alfredo Yu's face froze at the word "bounty." His eyes snapped up to his companions' faces, and he saw exactly the same shock looking back at him. He couldn't think for a moment, only feel the pit of his stomach falling away into infinite distance, but then his brain began to work again.

"Understood, Mr. Manning. Commander Valentine and I have just been discussing the environmental requirements. Do you think you could drop by my cabin to go over them with us?"

"I'm afraid I can't get away just now, Sir." Manning's voice was steady, and Yu's jaw clenched in pain.

"Very well, George," he said. "Thank you for informing me."

"You're welcome, Sir," Manning said quietly, and the circuit clicked.

"Jesus, Skipper!" Valentine began in an urgent voice, "we can't leave George up there by him—"

"Shut up, Jim." The very lack of emotion in Yu's voice only made it more terrible, and Valentine closed his mouth with a click. The captain shut his eyes in thought, and his subordinates sat in tight-faced silence.

Yu felt their fear and cursed his own complacency. He'd been so damned *pleased* when all Simonds wanted to do was reinforce his asteroid garrisons! Why in *hell* hadn't he thought about what putting that many more armed Masadans aboard *Thunder* could mean?!

Panic threatened, but he fought it back. At least George had been more alert than *he* had, yet his contingency plans had never contemplated having this many armed hostiles aboard. Barely a third of *Thunder's* regular crew were still Havenite; with all the Masadan soldiers packed aboard, they were outnumbered by over five-to-one.

He stood and crossed quickly to the hatch, opened it, and drew a deep breath of relief as he saw the Marine sentry in the corridor. The corporal looked up as the hatch slid open, then stiffened as Yu beckoned to him.

He stepped closer, and the captain pitched his voice very low.

"Get to Major Bryan, Marlin. Tell him it's Condition Bounty."

Yu hated to send the corporal in person, but he had no choice. He'd managed to hang onto his original Marine officers and most of his noncoms, and every one of them had been briefed on Bounty, but almost half *Thunder*'s enlisted Marines were Masadans, and they had the same personal com units as Yu's loyalists. If they were in on this (and they had to be) and one of them heard Marlin passing coded messages . . .

Corporal Marlin's face went white, but then he nodded, braced to attention, and marched briskly down the passage. Yu watched him go, hoping they had enough time for him to reach Bryan, and then withdrew into his cabin.

He thumbed a wall locker security plate, and the door swung open as the scanner recognized his print. The racked sidearms were in police-style shoulder holsters, not standard military ones, and he tossed one of them to each of his officers, then unsealed his tunic. He jerked on the shoulder rig and looked at Valentine as the engineer shrugged out of his own tunic.

"We're in deep shit here, Jim. I don't see any way we can hold the ship after I let the fuckers fill us right up." The engineer's nod was jerky but not panicked, and Yu went on grimly. "That means we have to cripple her."

"Aye, Sir." Valentine slid his tunic back on over his own shoulder harness and started shoveling magazines into his pockets.

"Who's got the Engineering watch?"

"Workman," Valentine replied in disgust, and Yu's face tightened.

"All right. You're going to have to get in there somehow and throw the fusion plants into emergency shutdown. Can you do it?"

"I can try, Sir. Most of his watch is Masadan, but Joe Mount shares it to keep them from fucking up."

"I hate to ask it of you, Jim—" Yu began, but Valentine cut him off.

"You don't have a lot of choice, Skipper. I'll give it my best shot."

"Thank you." Yu looked into his eyes for a moment, then turned to DeGeorge.

"Sam, you and I will try for the bridge. Major Bryan will know what to do when Marlin gets to him, and—

The cabin hatch opened behind him, and Yu froze for an instant, then turned his head sharply. A Masadan colonel stood in the opening, four armed men behind him, and his hand held a drawn autopistol.

"Don't you bother to knock on a superior officer's door, Colonel?" Yu snapped over his shoulder, sliding his own hand into his still open tunic.

"Captain Yu," the Colonel said as if he hadn't spoken, "it is my duty to inform you that this ship is now und—"

Yu turned, and his pulser whined. Its darts were nonexplosive, but it was also set on full auto, and the Colonel's back erupted in a hideous crimson spray. He went down without even a scream, and the same hurricane of destruction swept through his troops. The bulkhead opposite the hatch vanished under a glistening coat of blood, someone in the passage shouted in horror, and Yu charged for the hatch.

Six Masadans stood in the passage, gaping at the carnage. Five of them grabbed frantically at their rifle slings as the captain appeared before them, pulser in hand; the sixth thought more quickly. He turned and ran even as Yu squeezed the trigger again, and his quickness saved his life. His companions soaked up Yu's fire just long enough for him to make it around a bend in the passage, and the captain swore savagely.

He jerked back into the cabin, lunging for the com panel beside his desk terminal, and slammed his thumb down on the all-hands button.

"Bounty Four-One!" his voice blared from every speaker in the ship. "I say again, Bounty Four-One!"

* * *

Major Joseph Bryan drew his sidearm, turned, and opened fire without a word. The eight Masadan soldiers in the armory with him were still staring at the intercom in puzzlement when they died, and only then did Bryan allow himself to curse. He'd wondered why the Masadan lieutenant had wanted to tour the armory; now he knew, but thirty years of professional soldiering as one of the People's Republic's conquistadors made him double-check. He bent over the Lieutenant's pulser-mangled body and ripped the blood-soaked tunic open, and his face hardened with bleak satisfaction as he found the pistol inside it.

The armory hatch slid open, and he whirled in a half-crouch, but it was Corporal Marlin.

"What the fuck are *you* doing here?!" Bryan snarled. "You're supposed to be watching the Captain's back!"

"He sent me to find you before he came up over the intercom, Sir." Marlin looked down at the bodies and blood, and his eyes were bitter. "I guess he had less time than he thought he did."

Bryan only grunted. He was already yanking unpowered body armor over his uniform, and the corporal shook himself and followed his example. Both of them would vastly have preferred powered armor, or at least combat skin suits, but there was no time.

The Major sealed his clamshell breast-and-back plate and snatched a short, heavy-barreled flechette gun from one of the racks. He'd just slapped in a magazine when he heard the ear-splitting crack of a Masadan firearm. He whirled towards the hatch once more, then lowered his muzzle as pulsers whined in reply and Captain Young appeared in the opening.

"I've got nine men, Sir," the captain said without preamble.

"Good." Bryan's mind raced as he slid ammo bandoleers over his shoulders. Bounty Four-One meant Captain Yu didn't believe his people could hold the ship, and given the numbers of Masadan grunts on board, Bryan had no choice but to agree. His own mission under Four-One was clear and simple, but he'd expected to have more men available before he set off to accomplish it.

He latched the bandoleers and grunted approval as Young beckoned five men inside and all six of them began armoring up. The captain's four other men crouched outside the hatch, armed now with the flechette guns Marlin had tossed them, covering their companions while they grabbed their gear, and Bryan reached his decision.

"I'm taking Marlin and four of your people, Captain. Hang on here for thirty minutes or until I tell you different, but don't ride it down in flames. If you're forced out, inform me before you leave—and make damned sure nothing falls into Masadan hands."

"Yes, Sir." Young said. "Hadley, Marks, Banner, Jancowitz—you're with the Major." The detailed men nodded, not even slowing as they continued to festoon themselves with weapons. Bryan waited until they'd loaded themselves liberally with ammunition, then waved them out.

" . . . again, Bounty Four-One!"

Lieutenant Mount jerked in shock as the words crackled from the speaker. For just one moment, he stared at it in disbelief, feeling the confusion of the Masadans about him, then reached for his control panel.

Lieutenant Commander Workman had never heard of "Bounty Four-One," but he knew what Sword Simonds intended to happen, and the sudden, apparently meaningless message could mean only one thing. His pistol bullet shattered the Lieutenant's head before Mount reached the emergency shutdown switch.

Commander Manning didn't even twitch as Captain Yu's voice rolled from the com. He'd known it was coming, and he'd already accepted that he was trapped on the bridge. As soon as the Captain confirmed a Four-One condition, his right hand touched the underside of the command chair's arm rest. A small panel that didn't show on any engineering schematic slid open, and his index finger hooked up inside it even as Lieutenant Hart produced his pistol.

"Get out of the command chair, Commander Manning!" the Masadan snapped. "And keep your hands where I can see them!"

The Havenite helmsman lunged for the com officer's gun, but a pistol cracked twice somewhere behind Manning, and the petty officer slammed to the deck. His Masadan assistant stepped across his dying contortions to take over the controls, and Manning's face tightened in hatred. He snarled at Hart, but the com officer only jerked his gun hand.

"Out of the chair *now!*" he barked, and Manning shoved himself up with a contemptuous glare. The hidden panel slid shut once more as he stood, and the Masadan met his glare with a sneer of his own. "That's better, and now—"

"Lieutenant Hart!" It was the Masadan who'd taken over Maneuvering. "She won't answer the helm, Sir!"

Hart turned towards him, and Manning tensed to spring. But then he made himself relax, for there was at least one other armed man behind him.

The com officer leaned over the helmsman's shoulder and punched controls. Nothing happened, and he straightened to snarl at Manning.

"What did you do?" he demanded.

"Me? Nothing at all. Maybe PO Sherman did something before you murdered him," Manning grated.

"Don't lie to me, you fucking heretic!" Hart hissed. "I don't—"

An alarm shrilled, then another, and another, and his head twisted around in disbelief as Tactical, Astrogation, and Communications all went down at once. Warning lights and crimson malfunction codes glared on every panel, and Manning smiled thinly.

"You seem to have a problem, Lieutenant," he said. "Maybe you peo—"

He never heard the crack of Hart's pistol.

*   *   *

Captain Yu took a chance on the lift. He didn't have time to play safe, and Valentine and DeGeorge covered the passageway with drawn pulsers while he fed in his personal ID override and punched their destination.

"In!" he barked, but someone shouted even as they obeyed, and bullets spanged off the closing lift door.

"*Shit!*"

Valentine spun away from the door, clutching his left thigh, and Yu swore as he saw the wet, red stain. DeGeorge shoved the engineer down and ripped his trouser leg wide, and Valentine groaned through clenched teeth as he probed the wound with rough haste.

"I think it missed the major arteries, Captain," he reported quickly, then looked down at Valentine. "It's going to hurt like a son-of-a-bitch, Jim, but you'll be okay if we can get you out of here alive."

"Thanks for the qualifier," Valentine gasped. De-George laughed—a hard, sharp sound—and more cloth ripped as he fashioned a crude bandage.

Yu listened with only half his attention, for his eyes were locked on the lift position display. It blinked and changed steadily, and he started to feel a bit of hope, then punched the wall as the display suddenly froze and the lift stopped moving. DeGeorge looked up at the sound of his blow and raised an eyebrow even as he knotted Valentine's bandage.

"Bastards cut the power," Yu snapped.

"Just to the lifts, though." Valentine's voice was hoarse, but he raised a bloody hand to point at the status panel. The red light which should have indicated emergency power was dark, and his face twisted with more than pain. "Reactors're still up," he panted. "Means Joe didn't make shutdown."

"I know." Yu hoped Mount was still alive, but he had time to spare the Lieutenant only a single, fleeting thought. He was already wrenching up the decksole to get at the emergency hatch.

Major Bryan paused just inside the closed service crawlway hatch to catch his breath and wished fervently that he had some way to see through it. But he didn't. He and his men just had to go in blind and hope, and that wasn't the way Bryan had survived to become a major.

"All right," he said quietly. "I'll go right. Marlin, you go left. Hadley and Marks are with me; Banner and Jancowitz are on Marlin. Understood?"

A soft chorus of grunts answered him, and he gripped his flechette gun and rammed his shoulder into the release lever.

The hatch slammed open, and Bryan went through it in a dive. He hit on his belly, brain already noting people and positions, and fired his first shot even before he stopped sliding.

His weapon burped, and its bundle of flechettes screamed down the boat bay gallery. A Masadan officer exploded across the armorplast bulkhead in blood and scraps of tissue, and his three rifle-armed men whirled towards the Major in terrified surprise.

The flechette gun burped again, and again, so quickly only one of the Masadans even had time to scream before the razor-edged disks ripped him apart, and the Havenite personnel they'd been holding at gunpoint hurled themselves to the deck. Another flechette gun coughed to Bryan's left, this time on full auto, and Masadan firearms crackled in reply. He heard the wailing keen of ricocheting bullets, but he was already walking his own fire into the Masadan reinforcements trying to force their way through the boat bay hatch.

His flechettes chewed them into screaming, writhing hamburger, and then Hadley tossed a boarding grenade from behind him. The fragmentation weapon went off like the hammer of God in the confines of the passage beyond, and suddenly no one else was trying to come through the hatch.

Bryan climbed to his feet. Marlin was down, bleeding heavily where a rifle slug had shattered his left arm, but it could have been far worse. He counted at least eighteen dead Masadans, and the bastards had found time to herd over twenty Havenites into the boat bay for safe keeping.

"You men find yourselves weapons," the Major snapped, gesturing at the blood- and tissue-daubed Masadan rifles and pistols cluttering the deck. Shaken personnel scrambled up to obey him, and he punched his com. "Young, Bryan. We're on our position. What's your status?"

"I've got thirty-two men, including Lieutenant Warden, Major." The cough of flechette guns and rattle of rifles came over the link with Young's voice. "We're taking heavy fire from One-Fifteen and One-Seventeen, and they've cut One-Sixteen at the lift, but I blew the Morgue before they got in."

Bryan's mouth tightened. The armory was cut off from the rest of the ship. That meant no more of his men were going to be able to join Young there, and the fact that Young had been forced to destroy "the Morgue," the powered armor storage and maintenance area off Passage One-One-Five, meant the people he did have were going to have to fight in their own skins.

"Load up with all the ammo and weapons you can carry, then pull out," he said harshly. "Meet us here—and don't forget your going away present."

"Yes, Sir. I'll remember."

Alfredo Yu glided headfirst down the inspection ladder, grasping an occasional rung to pull himself along while the counter-grav collar hooked to his belt supported him. DeGeorge's people had cached a dozen collars under each lift at Yu's orders before *Thunder* ever arrived in Endicott, and the captain blessed his foresight even as he cursed himself for letting Simonds sucker him this way.

He glanced back up the lift shaft. DeGeorge had rearguard, with Valentine sandwiched between them. The engineer was still game, but his white face was sweat-streaked and his trouser leg was dark burgundy, and he needed both hands to cling to the ladder.

Yu reached a cross-shaft and checked the markings, then pulled himself into it. The shafts were only dimly lit, and his eyes ached from staring into the gloom, but the last thing he needed was a hand lamp to give himself away if any of the—

Something rattled ahead of him. His hand flew up, stopping the others, and he swam silently forward, left hand poised to snatch a handhold while he cradled his pulser in his right. Something moved in the dimness, and his free hand locked on a rung to anchor him against the recoil as he raised his pulser. His finger squeezed—then relaxed as he realized the three men in front of him were unarmed.

He swam slowly closer, and one of them saw him and gasped a strangled warning. Heads snapped up, faces turned, and then he saw them twitch in relief.

"Captain! Are we glad to see *you*, Sir!" a petty officer called, and his low-pitched voice warned Yu to keep his own voice down as he swam right up to them.

"We were headed for the boat bay, Sir," the noncom continued, "when we almost ran right into an ambush. They've got the lift doors open at Three-Niner-One."

"Have they, now?" Yu murmured. DeGeorge arrived behind him, towing Valentine. "Any idea how many men they've got with them, Evans?"

"Maybe half a dozen, Sir, but they were all armed, and none of us—" The petty officer gestured to his two companions, and Yu nodded. "Jim, give Evans your pulser and collar." The wounded engineer handed his gun to the petty officer, then started digging magazines out of his pockets while Evans unbuckled his grav collar. Yu looked at DeGeorge.

"We're going to have to clear the bastards out of the way, Sam, and not just for us." DeGeorge nodded, and Yu thumped the bulkhead that formed the rear wall of the shaft. "You come up this bulkhead. I'll take the overhead, and Evans will be opposite me." He looked up to be sure the petty officer was listening as well, and Evans nodded.

"This has to be fast. Keep your eyes on me. When I nod, go like hell. With a little luck, we'll be into the opening before they know it. Got it?"

"Yes, Sir," Evans said softly, and DeGeorge nodded.

"Okay, let's do it," Yu said grimly.

Major Bryan looked around the boat bay as Young climbed out of the service passage. He was the last of the party from the armory, but another fifteen men had arrived via other unlikely avenues of approach. Most had been unarmed, though a few had turned up carrying weapons Masadan soldiers no longer required, but Young and his men had brought enough flechette guns for everyone. In fact, Bryan still had a small reserve of them heaped on the deck, and the demolition charge Young had left in the armory meant the Masadans wouldn't get their hands on matching weapons.

Unfortunately, that only gave him about seventy men. He was confident he could hold the bay—for now, at least—but his options were limited, and none of the naval officers had gotten through to him.

"Breathers distributed, Sir," Sergeant Towers reported, and Bryan grunted. One thing about the boat bay—its emergency and service lockers held an enormous number of breath masks. Their distribution meant the Masadans couldn't use the ventilators to asphyxiate or gas his men, and two engineering petty officers had disabled the emergency hatches, so they couldn't depressurize the gallery on them, either. The Major had men holding the access corridor all the way to the blast doors, which gave him control of the lift shaft, but with power to the lifts cut, that was a limited advantage.

"Orders, Sir?" Young asked quietly, and Bryan scowled. What he *wanted* to do was launch a counterattack, but he wouldn't get far with seventy men.

"For right now, we hold in position," he replied in a soft voice, "but have the pinnaces pre-flighted."

Pinnaces were faster than most small craft, and they were armed, though none of them carried external ordnance at the moment. But they were far slower than *Thunder of God*, and her weapons could swat them like flies. Young knew that as well as Bryan did, but he only nodded.

"Yes, Sir," he said.

The ladder rung felt slick under Yu's sweaty hand, and his pulse raced. This wasn't his kind of a fight, but it was the fight he had, and he looked back to check on De-George and Evans. Both of them were in position, watching him tensely, and he drew a deep breath—then nodded.

The three of them hurled themselves forward, and Yu rolled on his side in midair, holding his pulser in a two-handed grip as he flashed across the open lift doors. A Masadan soldier saw him and opened his mouth to shout a warning, but the captain squeezed his trigger, and two other pulsers whined as the three of them sent a tornado of darts down the passage.

There was no time to pick targets, but those darts were no less deadly for being unaimed. They clawed down the Masadans who'd lurked in ambush, and Yu stuck out a foot. His toes hooked under one of the ladder rungs before the recoil of his pulser could push him away from it, and his leg muscles dragged him in close against the wall. He got an elbow through the opening, holding himself motionless, and his pulser whined again as someone tried to come around a bend in the passage. A shrill scream told him he'd scored, and he held his position, breathing hard, as Evans and DeGeorge crawled up beside him.

"See if you can get their weapons, Evans. Commander DeGeorge and I will cover you."

"Aye, Sir."

The petty officer looked both ways along the cross corridor, then eased himself over the lip of the opening and started dragging Masadan autorifles towards him. The rest of their small party came panting up to take the rifles as he passed them down, and DeGeorge sent a stream of darts up the passage as another Masadan tried to interfere.

One of the bodies had a grenade pouch, and Evans

smiled wickedly as he sent a grenade bouncing around the bend. Screams and shouts announced its arrival, and then a thunderous explosion wiped them away.

"Good man!" Yu said, and Evans grinned at him as he slid back into the shaft with his grenade pouch.

"Two more of our people just turned up, Sir," someone said, and Yu nodded. Aside from the service passages from Marine Country, this was the only way into the boat bay; any of his people from up-ship who managed to elude capture were going to have to get past this opening.

"Sam, you and Evans pick three more men and hold this position," he said. "I've got to get on to the boat bay and see what our situation there is."

"Yes, Sir," DeGeorge said.

"Who's got a com?" Two of the men in the shaft waved their arms. "You, Granger, give yours to the purser." The rating handed it over, and DeGeorge strapped it onto his left wrist.

"We're not going to retake her unless Bryan's managed to get more men into the boat bay than I think he has, Sam. If I can, I'll send some Marines back to help out. If I can't, hold on here until I call you forward, then come ahead as fast as you can. Clear?"

"Clear, Sir."

"Good." Yu squeezed the purser's shoulder, then launched himself on down the shaft.

"Sir! Major Bryan! The Captain's here!"

Bryan looked up in profound relief as Captain Yu crawled out of the lift doors. The captain loped down the hall, followed by a small group of navy types, two of whom carried a half-conscious Commander Valentine.

Bryan snapped to attention and started to report, but Yu's raised hand stopped him. The captain's dark eyes flitted over the assembled men, and his mouth tightened.

"This is it?" he asked in a low voice, and Bryan nodded. Yu looked as if he wanted to spit, but then he straightened and crossed to a control panel. He punched a security code into it and grunted in satisfaction.

Bryan followed him across and looked over his shoulder. The data on the small screen meant nothing to him, and he wouldn't have known how to access it, anyway, but it seemed to please the Captain.

"Well, that's *one* thing that worked," he muttered.

"Sir?" Bryan asked, and Yu gave him a grim smile.

"Commander Manning took out their bridge computers. Until they figure out how, they can't maneuver—and the entire tactical system is locked."

Bryan's eyes glowed, and Yu nodded.

"Have you pre-flighted the pinnaces?"

"Yes, Sir."

"Good." Yu chewed his lower lip for a moment, and then his shoulders slumped. "Good," he repeated more softly, "but I'm afraid we're going to have to leave an awful lot of people behind, Major."

"Yes, Sir," Bryan said grimly, then cleared his throat. "Sir, what do you think these bastards figure they can do with her?"

"I'm afraid to guess, Major," Yu sighed. "Whatever it is, *we* can't stop them. All we can do at this point is try to get our people out of it."

"What do you mean, you can't get into the boat bay?!" Sword Simonds shouted, and the army brigadier just stopped himself from licking his lips.

"We've tried, Sir, but they got too many men in there—Colonel Nesbit estimates at least three or four hundred."

"Bullshit! That's *bullshit!* There aren't six hundred of them aboard, and we've accounted for almost two thirds of them! You tell Nesbit to get his ass in there! That idiot Hart blew Manning away, and if Yu gets away from me, too—"

The Sword's sentence faded off ominously, and the brigadier swallowed.

*   *   *

"How many?" Yu asked.

"I make it a hundred sixty, Sir," Bryan said heavily. Yu's face was stone, but his eyes showed his pain. That was less than twenty-seven percent of his Havenite crew, but there'd been no new arrivals in almost fifteen minutes, and the Masadans were bringing up flamethrowers as well as grenades and rifles. He raised his wrist com to his mouth.

"Sam?"

"Yes, Sir?"

"Get your ass in here. It's time to go."

"They've *what?!*"

"They've launched pinnaces, Sir," the hapless officer repeated. "And . . . and there was an explosion in the boat bay right after they did," he added.

Sword Simonds swore savagely and restrained himself—somehow—from physically attacking the man, then wheeled on Lieutenant Hart.

"What's the status of the computers?"

"W-we're still trying to figure out what's wrong, Sir." Hart met the Sword's eyes fearfully. "It looks like some sort of security lock-out, and—"

"Of course it is!" Simonds snarled.

"We can get around it eventually," the white-faced Hart promised. "It's only a matter of working through the command trees, unless . . ."

"Unless what?" Simonds demanded as the Lieutenant paused.

"Unless it's a hard-wired lock, Sir," Hart said in a tiny voice. "In that case, we'll have to trace the master circuits till we find it, and without Commander Valentine—"

"Don't make excuses!" Simonds screamed. "If you hadn't been so fast to shoot Manning down, we could have made him tell us what he did!"

"But, Sir, we don't know it was him! I mean—"

"*Idiot!*" The Sword backhanded the Lieutenant viciously, then whirled to the brigadier. "Put this man under arrest for treason against the Faith!"

*   *   *

Captain Yu sat in the copilot's flight couch, watching his beautiful ship fall away astern, and the bitter silence from the pinnace's passenger bay mirrored his own. Like him, the men back there felt enormous relief at their own survival, but it was tempered by shame. They'd left too many of their own behind, and knowing they'd had no choice made them feel no better at all.

A part of Alfredo Yu wished he hadn't made it out, for his shame cut far deeper than theirs. That was *his* ship back there, and the men aboard it were *his* men, and he'd failed them. He'd failed his government, too, but the People's Republic wasn't the sort of government that engendered personal loyalty, and not even the knowledge that the navy would take vengeance upon him for his failure mattered beside his abandonment of his men. Yet he'd had no choice but to save as many as he could, and he knew it.

He sighed and punched up a chart of the system. Somewhere out there was a hiding place where he and his men could conceal themselves until the battle squadrons Ambassador Lacy had summoned arrived. All he had to do was find it.

• CHAPTER THIRTY-ONE

Honor cut another morsel of steak and slid it into her mouth. Eating, she'd found, was a monumental pain when only one side of your face worked. The left side of her mouth was useless for chewing, and she had a humiliating tendency to discover food was dribbling down her dead cheek and chin only when it dripped onto her tunic. She'd made progress over the past few days, but not enough to be willing to eat with an audience.

But at least worrying about eating was fairly mundane, almost comforting, compared to other things. Five days had passed since *Apollo*'s departure. If the Masadans were going to try something more—and despite all she'd said to Venizelos about the insanity of their doing so, she remained convinced they were—she knew it would be soon. Yet, to her own surprise, she could think about it almost calmly. She'd reached a state of balance, of acceptance. She was committed. She'd done all she could to prepare herself and her people. All that remained was to meet whatever came, and once that was accepted, grief and guilt and hatred, like terror, had faded into a strange sort of serenity. She knew it wouldn't last. It was simply the way she adjusted to the waiting, but she was grateful for it.

She chewed very carefully, keeping her numb inner cheek out from between her teeth and glad her tongue had escaped damage, then swallowed and reached for her beer. She sipped with equal care, cocking her head to minimize the chances of a spill. She was just setting her stein back down when the musical tone of a com terminal floated through the dining cabin hatch.

"Bleek?" Nimitz said from his end of the table.

"Beats me," she told him, and waited. After a moment, MacGuiness poked his head through the hatch with the expression of severe disapproval he reserved for occasions when his captain's meals were interrupted.

"Excuse me, Ma'am, but Commander Venizelos is on the com." The steward sniffed. "I told him you're eating, but he says it's important."

Honor's good eye twinkled, and she used her napkin to hide the smile that twitched the right corner of her mouth. MacGuiness had guarded her rare moments of privacy, especially during meals, like an irritable mastiff ever since she'd been wounded, and he would never forgive her if she giggled.

"I'm sure it really is, Mac," she soothed, and the steward stepped back with another sniff to let her pass, then crossed to the table and placed the warming cover over her plate. Nimitz looked up at him and, when MacGuiness shrugged his ignorance, hopped down and pattered after his person.

Honor hit the acceptance key to clear the "WAIT" prompt, and a worried-looking Venizelos appeared on the screen.

"What is it, Andy?"

"RD Niner-Three just picked up a hyper footprint at extreme range, Ma'am, right on the fifty light-minute mark."

Honor felt the right side of her face turn as masklike as the left. A crack yawned in her serenity, but she schooled herself into calm. At that range, there was time.

"Details?"

"All we've got so far is the alert sequence. *Troubadour's* standing by to relay the rest of the transmission as it comes in, but—" He paused as someone said something Honor couldn't quite catch, then looked back at his captain. "Scratch that, Skipper. Commander McKeon says Niner-Two is coming in now, reporting a low-powered wedge moving across its range. Niner-Three has the same bogey and makes it right on the ecliptic. Looks like they're heading around the primary to sneak up on Grayson from behind."

Honor nodded while her mind raced. That kind of course meant it could only be the Masadans, but they knew Masada still had at least one other hyper-capable ship, so it wasn't necessarily the battlecruiser either. And with *Fearless*'s gravitics down, she couldn't read the drones' FTL pulses direct, which meant she couldn't send *Troubadour* out to check without losing her real-time link to her main tactical sensors.

"All right, Andy. Alert Admiral Matthews and bring our own wedge up. Have Rafe and Stephen start a plot. Until we get mass readings from one of the drones, that's all we can do."

"Aye, aye, Ma'am."

"I'll be right up, and—" Honor paused as she felt a presence behind her. She turned to look over her shoulder, and James MacGuiness folded his arms. She met his eyes for a moment, then turned back to Venizelos. "I'll be right up as soon as I finish lunch," she corrected herself meekly, and despite his tension, the exec grinned.

"Yes, Ma'am. I understand."

"Thank you." Honor cut the circuit, stood, and marched straight back to the table under her steward's stern gaze.

Ensign Wolcott felt her own apprehension reflected from the people about her as she updated the rough plot. Commander Venizelos circulated between the control stations, yet Wolcott was more conscious of the Captain's absence than of the Exec's presence. She suspected she wasn't alone in that, either, for she'd seen more than one other glance being cast at the empty chair at the center of the bridge.

She finished and sat back, and a quiet voice spoke in her left ear.

"Don't sweat it, Ensign. If the shit were about to hit the fan, the Skipper wouldn't have taken time to finish lunch."

She turned her head and blushed as she met Lieutenant Cardones' knowing eyes.

"Was it that obvious, Sir?"

"Well, yes." Cardones smiled—grinned, really—at her. "Of course, that could be because *I* wish she were up here, too. On the other hand, this—" he gestured at their plot "—tells me nothing much is going to happen for a while, and I'd a lot rather have the Old Lady rested when it *does* happen than have her waste energy holding my hand in the meantime."

"Yes, Sir." Wolcott looked back down at the plot. They had tentative mass readings from three drones now, and CIC called it ninety-plus percent that the bogey was the Peep battlecruiser. It wasn't a comforting thought.

She stared at the innocent, unthreatening lines of light and felt her pulse race. Her chestnut hair felt damp with sweat, and there was a hollow, singing void where her stomach should have been. She'd been terrified as *Fearless* charged into the missiles at Blackbird, but this was worse. Much worse. This time she *knew* what could happen, for she'd seen ships blown apart, seen the consequences of the cruelty visited upon her classmate Mai-ling Jackson, and lost two close friends aboard *Apollo*, and she was afraid to her very bones. An awareness of her own mortality filled her, and the enemy's slow, dragging approach gave her too much time to think about it.

"Sir," she said softly, without looking up, "you've seen more action than me, and you know the Captain better. Can we—" She bit her lip, then met his gaze almost imploringly. "How much chance do we really have, Sir?"

"Well. . ." Cardones drew the word out and tugged on an earlobe. "Let me just put it this way, Carol. The first time the Skipper took *me* into action, I knew she was going to get me killed. I didn't think she was, I *knew* it, and I just about pissed myself, let me tell you."

He grinned again, and despite her fear, Wolcott's lips sketched a tremulous smile of their own.

"As it turned out, I was wrong," Cardones went on, "and it's a funny thing. You sort of forget to be scared with the Old Lady sitting behind you. It's like you know they'll never get *her*, and that means they won't get *you*. Or maybe it's just that you're too embarrassed to be scared when *she* isn't. Or something." He shrugged almost sheepishly.

"Anyway, she nailed a seven-and-a-half-million-ton Q-ship with a light cruiser. I figure that means she can take a battlecruiser with a *heavy* cruiser. And if she were worried, I imagine she'd be sitting up here fretting with the rest of us instead of finishing lunch."

"Yes, Sir." Wolcott smiled more naturally and turned back to her panel as her beeping earbug warned of fresh data from *Troubadour*. She updated the plot again, and Rafael Cardones looked at Commander Venizelos over her lowered head. Their eyes met with a certain sad empathy for Ensign Wolcott. They understood her need for reassurance perfectly . . . and they also knew there was a universe of difference between engaging a Q-ship while it tried to run and a battlecruiser which had come to kill you.

Honor opened the life-support module, and Nimitz hopped into it with an air of resignation. At least this time it wasn't an emergency, and he took time to check the water and food dispenser and arrange his nest to his satisfaction. Then he curled down and looked up at her with an admonishing little sound.

"Yeah, and you be careful, too," she told him softly, caressing his ears. He closed his eyes to savor her touch, and then she stepped back and sealed the door.

"CIC confirms the drone mass readings, Ma'am," Venizelos reported as he met her at the lift. "She's coming round the backside of the primary."

"ETA?"

"She's still close to two billion klicks out, Ma'am, and she's holding her accel down to about fifty gees, probably to avoid detection. Her base velocity's up to five-niner-point-five thousand KPS. Assuming she holds current acceleration, she'll hit Grayson in about eight hours at a velocity of approximately seven-four thousand."

Honor nodded, then turned her head as someone else stepped out of the lift. Stores had found Commander Brentworth a Manticoran skin suit, and only the Grayson insignia stenciled on its shoulders picked him out from the rest of her crew as he gave her a tense smile.

"Still time to put you planet-side, Mark," she said, her voice low enough no one else could hear.

"This is my assigned duty post, Ma'am." His smile might be tense, but his voice was remarkably level. Honor's good eye warmed with approval, yet that didn't stop her from pressing the point.

"It may be your assigned post, but we're not going to be doing much liaising over the next few hours."

"Captain, if you want me off your ship, you can order me off. Otherwise, I'm staying. There ought to be at least one Grayson officer aboard if you're going up against those fanatics for us."

Honor started to speak again, then closed her mouth and gave a tiny headshake. She touched him lightly on the shoulder, then crossed to DuMorne's astrogation station to look down at his display.

Thunder of God—or *Saladin*, or whatever she wanted to call the battlecruiser—was holding her acceleration down, but that was probably just a general precaution. She was over a hundred light-minutes from Grayson on her present course, and she was still over forty light-minutes out from Yeltsin, which put her well beyond any range at which any Grayson sensor array could possibly pick up her impellers.

Of course, her captain knew he was up against modern warships, but he certainly didn't see *Fearless* or *Troubadour* on his own sensors, nor would the heavily stealthed drones be visible to him. So assuming he didn't know they'd been deployed (which he couldn't) *and* about their detection range and FTL transmission capability, he had to believe he was undetected so far.

She rubbed the tip of her nose. It wasn't the way she would have proceeded, given the disparity in weight of metal, but he'd clearly opted for a cautious approach. By the time he crossed the outer edge of the Grayson sensor envelope, he'd be on the far side of Yeltsin, and he'd almost certainly cut his drive before he did. That would extend his flight time but bring him around the primary on a ballistic course, and without the betraying grav signature of his impellers, it meant he'd be into missile range of Grayson and firing before active sensors saw him coming.

But she'd already seen him. The question was what she did with her information, and she bent over DuMorne's panel and laid in a rough line for a shorter, tighter course that originated at Grayson and curved around the primary inside *Saladin's* projected parabola.

"Punch this up and refine it for me, Steve. Assume we go to maximum acceleration on this course. Where would we come into his sensor range?"

DuMorne started crunching numbers, and she watched a hypothetical vector build around Yeltsin as he turned her rough course into a finished one.

"He'd pick us up right about here, Ma'am, one-three-five million klicks out from Yeltsin, in about one-niner-zero minutes. Our base velocity would be five-six-six-six-seven KPS. He'd be right here—about four-niner-five million klicks from Yeltsin and one-point-three billion klicks short of Grayson on his present track. Our vectors would merge two-point-three million klicks short of Grayson five-point-two-five hours after that. Of course, that assumes accelerations remain unchanged."

Honor nodded at the qualification. If anything in this universe was certain, it was that *Saladin's* acceleration *wouldn't* remain unchanged once she saw *Fearless* and *Troubadour*.

"And if we go around Yeltsin on a straight reciprocal of his course?"

"Just a second, Ma'am." DuMorne crunched more numbers, and a second possible vector appeared on his display. "Going at him that way, he'd pick us up approximately one-point-five billion klicks out of Grayson orbit in two-five-zero minutes. Closing velocity would be one-four-one-four-niner-seven KPS, and vectors would intercept four-eight minutes after detection."

"Thank you." Honor folded her hands and walked across to her command chair while she contemplated her options.

The one thing she absolutely couldn't do was sit here and let the enemy come at her. With that much time to build her velocity advantage, *Saladin* would have every edge there was for the opening missile engagement, and she could overfly Grayson—and Honor's ships—with relative impunity.

To prevent that, Honor could meet her head-on by simply reversing the battlecruiser's course. *Saladin* couldn't evade her if she did, but their closing velocity would be high, severely limiting engagement time. They would cross the powered missile envelope in little more than four minutes, and energy range in barely seven seconds. *Saladin* would have to accept action, but her captain could count on its being a very short one.

Alternatively, Honor could shape her own, tighter parabola inside *Saladin's*. The battlecruiser would still have the higher base velocity when she detected *Fearless* and *Troubadour*, but they'd be on convergent courses, and Honor's ships would be inside her. Her ships would have less distance to travel, and the battlecruiser would be unable to cut inside them even if she stopped stooging along and went to maximum power on her wedge.

The drawback was that it *would* be a converging engagement, a broadside duel in which the battlecruiser's heavier missile batteries, bigger magazines, and tougher sidewalls could be used to best advantage. The very length of the engagement would give her more time to pound *Fearless* and *Troubadour* apart . . . but it would also give *them* more time to hurt *her*.

In essence, her choices were to go for a short, sharp closing engagement and hope she got lucky and *Saladin* didn't, or else go for a battering match.

Of course, she did have one major advantage, and she smiled hungrily at the thought, for it was the same one *Saladin* had enjoyed when Masada killed the Admiral; she knew where the enemy was and what he was doing, and he *didn't* know what she was up to.

She played with her projected course briefly, varying DuMorne's numbers on her command chair maneuvering repeater, then sighed. If *Saladin* had come in a bit more slowly or on a course with a broader chord, she might have had enough time to accelerate onto a converging course, then go ballistic to sneak into range with her own drives down. But *Saladin* hadn't, and she didn't.

And when she came right down to it, she couldn't risk the head-on interception, either. If that ship was irrational enough to press an attack now, then she had to assume its captain truly was crazy enough to nuke Grayson. That meant she couldn't engage hoping for a lucky hit when her failure to get it would let *Saladin* past her. It had to be the convergent approach.

She leaned back, rubbing the numb side of her face for a moment, and considered the way *Saladin* had chosen to come in. That was a cautious captain out there. Indeed, she was surprised to see such timidity, especially given that any attack on Grayson had to be an act of desperation. If the People's Navy had amassed one thing over fifty T-years of conquest, it was experience, but this fellow showed no sign of it. He certainly wasn't a bit like Theisman—not that she intended to complain about that!

But the point was that if she presented a cautious captain with a situation in which his only options were a fight to the death short of the planet or to break off, especially if she did it in a way which proved she'd been watching him when he'd believed it was impossible, he might just flinch. And if she got him to break away to rethink, it would use up hours of time . . . and every hour he spent dithering would bring the relief from Manticore one hour closer.

Of course, it was also possible he might decide he'd given sneakiness his best shot and do what *she* would have done from the beginning—go straight for *Fearless* and dare her to do her worst before he blew her out of space.

She closed her good eye, the living side of her face calm and still, and made her decision.

"Com, get me Admiral Matthews."

"Aye, aye, Ma'am."

Matthews looked anxious on Honor's screen, for *Troubadour*'s gravitic sensors had been feeding the drone data to his own plot aboard *Covington*, as well, but he met her gaze levelly.

"Good afternoon, Sir." Honor formed her words with care, making herself sound cool and confident, as the rules of the game required.

"Captain," Matthews replied.

"I'm taking *Fearless* and *Troubadour* out to meet *Saladin* on a convergent course," Honor told him without further preamble. "The cautious way she's coming in may mean this is mainly a probe. If so, she may break off when she realizes we can intercept her."

She paused, and Matthews nodded, but she could see his mind working behind his eyes and knew he didn't believe it was only a probe, either.

"In the meantime," she went on after a moment, "there's always the chance Masada has more of its own hyper-capable ships left than we think, so *Covington*, *Glory*, and your LACs are going to have to watch the back door."

"Understood, Captain," Matthews said quietly, and Honor heard the unspoken addition. If *Saladin* did get past *Fearless* and *Troubadour*, they might at least take a big enough piece out of her for the Grayson ships to have a chance against her.

Might.

"We'll be on our way, then, Sir. Good luck."

"And to you, Captain Harrington. Go with God and our prayers."

Honor nodded and cut the circuit, then looked at DuMorne.

"Update your first course for the helm and get us under way, Steve," she said quietly.

• CHAPTER THIRTY-TWO

"Sir, we're picking up another of those gravity pulses."

"Where?" Sword of the Faithful Simonds leaned over his tactical officer's shoulder, and Lieutenant Ash pointed at a blur on his display.

"There, Sir." Ash made painstaking adjustments, then shrugged. "It was only a single pulse this time. I don't know . . . it *could* be a ghost, Sir. I've never actually operated the recon drones solo."

"Um." Simonds grunted acknowledgment and resumed his restless prowl. He knew he should be sitting in *Thunder of God*'s command chair, radiating confidence as his ship slunk deeper into the Yeltsin System, but he couldn't. Even knowing Yu would have been doing just that—and making it look effortless—only made him more angry and restless, and fatigue wasn't helping. He hadn't slept in thirty hours, and his body cried out for rest, but he banished the temptation sternly. Sleep was out of the question.

It had taken over twelve hours to run down the circuits and find the lock-out in the command chair's arm rest. The Sword was humiliatingly certain the infidel engineers could have done it much more quickly, but Mount and Hara were dead, Valentine, Timmons, and Lindemann had escaped the ship, and that *ass* Hart had shot down the one senior bridge officer they'd actually taken!

Yu had gotten clean away by the time they'd regained control of the ship's systems, yet there'd been no possibility of aborting the attack. Seizing *Thunder* had been a declaration of war on Haven; only God and success in Yeltsin could save the Faithful from the consequences of that.

Simonds paced more rapidly, unwilling to admit, even to himself, how much he'd counted on having Yu, or at

376

least Manning, available. Lieutenant Commander Workman was doing an adequate job in Engineering, but Ash was the best tactical officer available, and his obsession with gravity anomalies at a time like this proved how poor a substitute for Manning he was.

Just as he himself was a poor substitute for Yu, a tiny, frightened voice whispered deep at the Sword's weary core.

"RD One-Seven reports another drone launch, Captain."

"Projected course?"

"Like the others, Ma'am. They're sweeping a sixty-degree cone in front of *Saladin*. There's no sign of anything on their flanks."

"Thank you, Carol." Honor was already turning towards her com link and missed the ensign's smile of pleasure at the use of her first name.

"You're our resident expert," she told the face on her small screen. "How likely are they to pick up the grav pulses?"

"Almost certain to, now that they're inside our drone shell," McKeon replied promptly, "but I doubt they'll figure them out. Until Admiral Hemphill got involved, no one on *our* side thought it was possible, after all."

Honor smiled sourly, and McKeon grinned at her. Both of them had reason to remember Lady Sonja Hemphill with less than joy, but Honor had to admit that, this time, "Horrible Hemphill" had gotten something right.

"Besides," McKeon went on, "the pulses are directional, and the repetition rate is so slow it's unlikely they'll get more than a few pulses off any one RD before they're out of the transmission path. Without more than that, even the best analysis won't recognize what they're actually hearing."

"Um." Honor rubbed the tip of her nose. No doubt Alistair was right, but if *she'd* been picking up grav pulses that shouldn't be there, she'd be wracking her brain to figure out what they might be.

"Well, there's nothing we can do about it." Except hope no one over there was feeling clever. McKeon nodded as if he'd heard her mental qualifier, and she checked the time.

They were two and a half hours out of Grayson orbit; they should enter *Saladin*'s sensor range in another forty minutes.

"Sir! Sword Simonds!" Simonds whipped around at Lieutenant Ash's excited cry. "Two impeller sources, Sir! They just popped up out of nowhere!"

Simonds crossed the bridge in a few, quick strides and peered at Ash's display. The crimson dots of hostile gravity signatures burned steadily, just under twenty-four light-minutes off *Thunder*'s port quarter.

"Enemy's base velocity five-six-six-seven-two KPS, Sir." Ash's voice was flatter as he took refuge in the mechanics of his report.

"Our velocity?"

"Six-four-five-two-eight KPS, Sir, but they're inside us. They're making up on us because their radius is so much smaller."

Simonds clenched his jaw and scrubbed at his blood-shot eyes. How? How had the bitch *done* this?! That course couldn't be a coincidence. Harrington had known exactly where he was, exactly what he was doing, and there was no way she could have!

He lowered his hand from his eyes and glared at the display while he tried to think. How she'd done it didn't matter. He told himself that firmly, even while a super-stitious voice whispered that it did. What mattered was that she was inside him . . . and her vector was curving out towards him. The closure rate was twelve thousand KPS and growing; that meant she'd be into missile range in three hours, long before he would be able to fire on Grayson.

He had plenty of acceleration still in reserve, but not enough. All she had to do was tighten her course back down and she could turn inside him forever. He couldn't get close enough to attack the planet without entering her range, and *Thunder* was the last hope of the Faithful.

"Come eighty degrees to starboard and increase acceleration to four hundred eighty gravities!"

"Aye, aye, Sir," the helmsman replied. "Coming eight-oh degrees to starboard. Increasing acceleration to four-eight-oh gravities."

Ash looked at his commander in surprise, and the Sword swallowed an urge to snarl at him. Instead, he turned his back and slid his aching body into the command chair. Its displays deployed smoothly, and he peered at the tactical repeater, waiting to see Harrington's response.

"I don't believe it! The sorry son-of-a—" Andreas Venizelos caught himself. "I mean, he's breaking off, Ma'am."

"No, he isn't. Not yet, anyway." Honor steepled her fingers under her triangular chin. "This is an instinct reaction, Andy. We surprised him, and he doesn't want to get any closer than he has to while he thinks it over."

"She's accelerating directly away at four-point-seven-zero KPS squared, Ma'am," Cardones reported, and Honor nodded. She didn't expect it to last, but for now *Saladin* was headed in the right direction.

"Punch us up a pursuit course, Steve. I want his relative accel held to two-fifty gees or so."

"Aye, aye, Ma'am," DuMorne replied, and she leaned back and watched *Saladin*'s light bead track down its new vector projection.

Simonds caught himself dry-washing his hands in his lap and made himself stop. *Thunder* had held his new heading and acceleration for over seventy minutes while the Harlot's handmaiden followed along in his wake, but Harrington was making no bid to overtake. She was letting *Thunder* make up velocity on her, despite the fact that her smaller ships had higher maximum acceleration rates, and that was more than merely ominous.

The range had opened to over twenty-four and a half light-minutes, yet Harrington knew *exactly* where they were. *Thunder* was able to see *Fearless* only through the drones Ash had deployed astern, but there was no sign of Manticoran drones. Unless Harrington's sensors were even better than Yu had believed, she shouldn't be able to see them at all, yet she'd adjusted to every course alteration he made! The implied technical superiority was as frightening as it was maddening, but the critical point was that he couldn't lose her and come in undetected on a new vector . . . and she'd already pushed him clear beyond the asteroid belt, far outside Grayson's orbit.

No wonder she was content to let him run! He'd wasted precious time trying to evade someone who could see every move he made, and by the time he killed his present velocity and came back into missile range—assuming she *let* him—over six *hours* would have passed since he'd first detected her.

He growled under his breath and kneaded his cheeks. What Manticoran ships had already done to the Faithful made him nervous about crossing swords with her, especially since Yu and Manning had been careful to preserve their own importance by seeing to it that their Masadan junior officers lacked their expertise. Ash and his people were willing enough, but they simply couldn't get the most out of their systems, and he could already feel their jagged tension as they, too, realized the enemy was somehow watching them at this preposterous range.

But that didn't change the fact that *Thunder of God* out-massed both his opponents more than twice over. If he had to fight his way through them, he could. Yet he also had to be able to carry through against Grayson. . . .

"Compute a new course," he said harshly. "I want to close to the very edge of the powered missile envelope and hold the range constant."

"Course change!" Cardones sang out. "She's coming back towards us at max acceleration, Ma'am."

Honor nodded. She'd known this would come—indeed, she'd expected it far sooner, and puzzlement stirred again, for cruisers and battlecruisers were built to close and destroy, not for this timid sort of long-range groping.

But he was coming in now with a vengeance.

"Take us to meet her, Astro," she said quietly, "but let's see if we can't tempt him into a missile duel. Hold our closing accel down to—" She thought for a moment. "Make it six KPS squared."

"Aye, aye, Ma'am."

Honor nodded, then pressed a stud on her arm rest.

"Captain's quarters, Steward MacGuiness."

"Mac, could you chase me up some sandwiches and a pot of cocoa?"

"Of course, Ma'am."

"Thank you." She closed the circuit and looked at Venizelos. The Manticoran Navy tradition was that crews went into battle well-fed and as rested as possible, and her people had been at general quarters for almost five hours. "Stand us down to Condition Two, Andy, and tell the cooks I want a hot meal for all hands." She gave him one of her lopsided grins. "The way this jackass is maneuvering, there should be plenty of time for it!"

Across the bridge from her, Ensign Carolyn Wolcott smiled down at her console at the confidence in the Captain's voice.

The command chair felt bigger, somehow, than it had looked when Yu sat in it, and Simonds' tired eyes burned as he watched his plot. Harrington had chosen to let *Thunder* close, but she was maintaining her position between him and Yeltsin. And when he'd reversed acceleration to slow his rate of approach, she'd matched him, almost as if she were *hoping* for a missile duel.

That worried Simonds, for *Thunder* was a battle-cruiser. His missiles were bigger and heavier, with a significantly greater penaid and ECM payload. The

Faithful had already seen bitter proof that Manticore's technology was better than Haven's, but did she believe her margin of superiority was enough to even the odds? And, far more frightening, could she be correct?

He made himself sit back, feeling the ache of fatigue in his bones, and held his course. They should reach extreme missile range in twelve minutes.

"All right, Andy—take us back up to GQ," Honor said, and the howl of the alarm resummoned her people to their battle stations as she slid her hands into her suit gloves and settled her helmet in the rack on the side of her chair. She supposed she ought to put it on—though *Fearless's* well-armored bridge was deep at the ship's heart, that didn't make it invulnerable to explosive depressurization—but she'd always thought captains who helmeted up too soon made their crews nervous.

At least she'd managed a three-hour catnap in the briefing room, and the quiet voices about her sounded fresh and alert, as well.

"What do you think he'll do, Ma'am?"

The quiet question came from her blind side, and she turned her head.

"That's hard to say, Mark. What he *should* have done the minute he saw us was come straight for us. There's no way he's going to sneak past us—the way we intercepted him should have proven that. All he's done so far is waste about six hours by trying to shake us."

"I know, Ma'am. But he's coming in now."

"He is, but not like he really means it. Look how he's decelerating. He's going to come just about to rest relative to us at six and three-quarters million klicks. That's extreme range for low-powered missile drives, which isn't exactly the mark of an aggressive captain." She shook her head. "He's still testing the waters, and I don't understand it."

"Could he be afraid of your technology?"

Honor snorted, and the right side of her mouth made a wry smile.

"I wish! No, if Theisman was good, the man they picked to skipper *Saladin* ought to be better than this." She saw the puzzlement in Brentworth's eyes and waved a hand. "Oh, our EW and penaids are better than theirs, and so is our point defense, but that's a battlecruiser. Her sidewalls are half again as tough as *Fearless*'s, much less *Troubadour*'s, and her energy weapons are bigger and more powerful. We could hurt him in close, but not as badly as he could hurt us, and even in a missile duel, the sheer toughness of his passive defenses should make him confident. It's—" She paused, seeking a comparison. "What it comes down to is that in a missile duel our sword's sharper, but his armor's a lot thicker, and once he gets in close, it's our sword against his battleaxe. He ought to be charging to get *inside* our missile envelope, not sitting out there where we've got the best chance of giving as good as we get."

Brentworth nodded, and she shrugged.

"I don't suppose I should complain, but I wish I knew what his problem is."

"Missile range!" Ash said, and Simonds straightened in his chair.

"Engage as ordered," he replied flatly.

"Missile launch! Birds closing at four-one-seven KPS squared. Impact in one-seven-zero seconds—mark!"

"Fire Plan Able." Honor said calmly. "Helm, initiate Foxtrot-Two."

"Aye, aye, Ma'am. Fire Plan Able," Cardones replied, and Chief Killian's acknowledgment was right behind him.

Troubadour rolled, inverting herself relative to *Fearless* to bring her undamaged port broadside to bear, and both ships began a snake-like weave along their base course as their own missiles slashed away and the decoys and jammers deployed on *Fearless*'s flanks woke to electronic life.

"The enemy has returned fire." Lieutenant Ash's

voice was taut. "Flight time one-seven-niner seconds. Tracking reports sixteen incoming, Sir."

Simonds nodded acknowledgment. *Thunder* had an advantage of two tubes, as well as his heavier missiles. He hoped it would be enough.

"Enemy jamming primary tracking systems," Ash announced, listening to his missiles' telemetry links. "Seekers shifting to secondary track."

Rafael Cardones fired his second broadside thirty seconds after the first, and *Troubadour's* launchers followed suit, slaved to his better fire control. A third broadside followed, then a fourth, and he nodded to Wolcott as *Saladin* launched *her* fourth salvo.

"Counter missiles now," he told his assistant.

Sword Simonds watched his plot and swallowed bile as half his first salvo lost lock and wandered away. The others charged onward, already up to more than fifty thousand KPS and still accelerating, but the Manticorans belched counter missiles to meet them at more than nine hundred KPS^2.

Honor frowned as Ensign Wolcott picked off *Saladin's* first missiles. The battlecruiser was splitting her fire between *Troubadour* and *Fearless*, and that was the stupidest thing her captain had done yet. He ought to be *concentrating* his fire, not dispersing it! His opponents were lighter and far more fragile; by targeting both of them, he was robbing himself of his best chance to overwhelm them in detail.

Simonds cursed under his breath as the last missile of his first launch vanished far short of target. Lieutenant Ash was updating the second salvo's jammers, but the bitch had already killed six of them, as well . . . and *Thunder* had stopped only nine of *her* first broadside.

His hands tightened like claws on the command chair's arms as the surviving Manticoran missiles streaked in. Two more perished, then a third, but three got through, and *Thunder of God* shuddered as X-ray lasers clawed at his sidewall. Damage alarms wailed, and a red light flashed on the damage control schematic.

"One hit, port side aft," Workman announced. "Tractor Seven is gone. Compartments Eight-Niner-Two and Niner-Three open to space. No casualties."

"I think we got one— Yes! She's streaming air, Ma'am!"

"Good, Guns. Now do it again."

"Aye, aye, Ma'am!" Rafael Cardones' grin was fierce, and his sixth broadside belched from *Fearless*'s launchers. Ensign Wolcott's face was almost blank at his side, and her fingers flew across her console as her sensors noted changes in the incoming missiles' ECM and she adjusted to compensate.

Thunder of God's second salvo fared almost as badly as the first, and Simonds wrenched around to glare at his tactical section, then bit back his scathing rebuke. Ash and his assistants were crouched over their panels, but their systems were feeding them too much data to absorb, and their reactions were almost spastic, flurries of action as the computers pulled it together and suggested alternatives interspersed by bouts of white-faced impotence as they tried to anticipate those suggestions.

He needed Yu and Manning, and he didn't have them. Ash and his people simply didn't have the exper—

Thunder of God heaved as two more lasers ripped through his sidewall and gouged into his hull.

"Lord God, but he's fighting dumb," Venizelos murmured, and Honor nodded. *Saladin*'s responses were slow and heavy-handed, almost mechanical, and she felt a tingle of hope. If this kept up, they might actually be—

Ensign Wolcott missed an incoming missile. The heavy warhead detonated fifteen thousand kilometers off *Fearless*'s starboard bow, and half a dozen savage rods of energy slammed at her sidewall. Two broke through, and the cruiser leapt in agony as plating shattered.

"Two hits forward! Laser Three and Five destroyed. Radar Five is gone, Ma'am. Heavy casualties in Laser Three!"

The right side of Honor Harrington's mouth tightened, and her good eye narrowed.

"A hit, Sir! At least one, and—"

A thundering concussion ripped across Lieutenant Ash's voice. The command deck lurched, the lighting flickered, and damage alarms howled.

"Missile Two-One and Graser One gone! Heavy damage in the boat bay and Berthing Compartment Seven-five!"

Simonds blanched. That was six hits—*six!*—and they'd scored only one in return! Powerful as *Thunder* was, he couldn't take that kind of exchange rate for long, and—

The battlecruiser bucked yet again, more crimson lights glared, and the Sword made up his mind.

"Starboard ninety degrees—maximum acceleration!"

"She's breaking off, Ma'am!" Cardones crowed, and Honor watched in disbelief as *Saladin* turned through a full ninety degrees. She was just far enough abaft *Fearless*'s beam to deny them an "up the kilt" shot through the wide-open after end of her wedge, but Honor couldn't believe how close the battlecruiser's captain had come to giving her that deadly opening. And now he was going to maximum power! Preposterous as it was, Rafe was right—she was breaking off the action!

"Shall we pursue, Ma'am?" Cardones' tone left no doubt as to his own preference, and Honor couldn't blame him. His missile armament was untouched, and he'd outscored his opponent at least six-to-one. But Honor refused to let her own enthusiasm suck her out of her guard position.

"No, Guns. Let her go."

Cardones looked rebellious for a moment, then

nodded. He sat back, calling up his magazine lists and shifting ammunition to equalize his loads, and Ensign Wolcott looked over her shoulder at her captain.

"I'm sorry I missed that one, Ma'am." She sounded miserable. "It took a jog on me at the last minute, and—"

"Carol, you did fine, just fine," Honor told her, and Cardones looked up to nod firmly. The ensign looked back and forth between them for a moment, then smiled briefly and turned back to her own panel, and Honor beckoned to Venizelos. The exec unlocked his shock frame and crossed to her chair.

"Yes, Ma'am?"

"You were right about the way he was fighting. That was pitiful."

"Yes, Ma'am." Venizelos scratched his chin. "It was almost like a simulation—like we were up against just his computers."

"I think we were," Honor said softly, and the exec blinked at her. She unlocked her own shock frame, and he followed her over to the tactical station. She keyed a command into Cardones' panel, and they watched the master tactical display replay the brief battle. The entire engagement had lasted less than ten minutes, and Honor shook her head when it ended.

"I don't think that's a Havenite crew over there at all."

"What?!" Venizelos blushed at the volume of his response and looked quickly around the bridge, then back at her. "You don't really think the Peeps turned a ship like that over to lunatics like the Masadans, do you, Skipper?"

"It sounds crazy," Honor admitted, pulling gently at the tip of her nose as she brooded down on the display, "especially when they kept their own man in command of *Breslau*, but no Peep skipper would've fought his ship that way. He gave us every advantage there was, Andy. Add that to the ham-handed way he came in in the first place, and—"

She shrugged, and Venizelos nodded slowly.

"Haven has to know it's put its hand into a sausage slicer, Ma'am," he said after a moment. "Maybe they just pulled out and left Masada to its own devices?"

"I don't know." Honor turned to walk back to her own chair. "If they did, why didn't they take *Saladin* with them? Unless—" her eye narrowed. "Unless they *couldn't*, for some reason," she murmured, then shook her head.

"Either way, it doesn't change our mission," she said more crisply.

"No, but it may make our job a whole lot easier, Skipper."

"It may, but I wouldn't count on it. If that's a purely Masadan crew over there, God only knows what they'll do. For one thing, they're probably a lot more likely to nuke Grayson if they get the chance. And inexperienced or not, they've got a modern battlecruiser to do it with. That's a lot of ship, Andy, and they made so many mistakes this time they have to have learned at least something from them."

She leaned back in her chair, and her good eye met his gaze.

"If they come back at all, they'll come in smarter," she said.

• CHAPTER THIRTY-THREE

Thunder of God arced her way through a huge outside loop in an effort to cut in behind her opponents, and damage control teams labored furiously. It took time to complete their surveys, but Matthew Simonds listened in weary wonder as their reports flowed into the bridge.

It didn't seem possible. Those hits would have destroyed any Masadan ship, yet for all the gaping wounds in *Thunder*'s flanks, his broadside had lost only one missile tube and a single graser.

Simonds chewed his hate as his enemy executed her own loop inside his, matching him move for move, yet under his hate was a dawning comprehension of why Yu had been so confident he could destroy *Fearless*, for *Thunder* was tougher than the Sword had dreamed. A sense of his own power, his own ponderous ability to destroy, suffused his tired brain . . . and with it came a sour appreciation for how clumsily he'd misused that power.

He checked the plot again. Two hours had passed since he'd broken off action, and the range was back up to sixteen and a half light-minutes. Workman assured him Missile Twenty-One would be back on line in another thirty minutes, but time was ticking away, and he was only too well aware of how he'd allowed Harrington to dictate the conditions of engagement. He had at least two days before anyone from Manticore arrived to help her, but she hovered stubbornly between him and Grayson, and he'd let her burn up precious hours in which he should already have been about God's Work.

No more. He stood and crossed to the tactical

station, and Ash looked up from his conference with his assistants.

"Well, Lieutenant?"

"Sir, we've completed our analysis. I'm sorry we took so long, but—"

"Never mind that, Lieutenant." It came out more brusquely than he'd intended, and Simonds tried to soften it with a smile. He knew Ash and his people were almost as tired as he was, and they'd had to run their analyses with reference manuals almost literally in their laps. That was one reason he'd been willing to waste time trying to outmaneuver Harrington. He'd been fairly certain the attempt would fail, but he'd had no intention of reengaging until Ash had time to digest what he'd learned from the first clash.

"I understand your difficulties," Simonds said more gently. "Just tell me what you've learned."

"Yes, Sir." Ash drew a deep breath and consulted an electronic memo pad. "Sir, despite their missiles' smaller size, their penaids, and especially their penetration ECM, are better than ours. We've programmed our fire control to compensate for all of their EW techniques we've been able to identify. I'm sure they have tricks we haven't seen yet, but we've eliminated most of the ones they've already used.

"Defensively, their decoys and jammers are very good, but their counter missiles and point defense lasers are only a little better than our own, and we've gotten good reads on their decoy emissions and updated our missiles' exclusion files. I think we'll be able to compensate for them to a much larger extent in the next engagement."

"Good, Lieutenant. But what about our own defenses?"

"Sword, we're just not experienced enough with our systems to operate them in command mode. I'm sorry, Sir, but that's the truth." Ash's assistants looked down at their hands or panels, but Simonds simply nodded again, slowly, and the Lieutenant went on.

"As I say, we've updated the threat files and

reworked the software to extrapolate from our analysis of what they've already done. In addition, I've set up packaged jamming and decoy programs to run on a computer-command basis. It won't be as flexible as a fully experienced tactical staff could give you, Sir, but taking the human element out of the decision loop should increase our overall effectiveness."

The Lieutenant didn't like admitting that, but he met Simonds' eyes without flinching.

"I see." The Sword straightened and massaged his aching spine, then looked over his shoulder. "Is your course updated, Astrogation?"

"Yes, Sir."

"Then bring us around." Simonds gave Ash his most fatherly smile. "We'll give you a chance to show us the fruits of your labor, Lieutenant."

"They're coming back in, Skipper."

Honor set her cocoa in the beverage holder on her arm rest, cocked an eyebrow at Cardones, then looked down at her own repeater. *Saladin* had reopened the range to almost three hundred million kilometers, but now she was decelerating towards *Fearless* at four-point-six KPS^2.

"What do you think he's up to this time, Ma'am?"

"I imagine he's spent the last couple of hours thinking over what we did to him, Andy. If he's coming back for more, he must think he's figured out what he did wrong last time."

"You think he'll try to close to energy range, then?"

"I would in his place, but remember the saying about the world's best swordsman." Venizelos looked puzzled, and she smiled crookedly. "The world's best swordsman doesn't fear the second best; he fears the *worst* swordsman, because he can't predict what the idiot will do."

The exec nodded his understanding, and Honor turned to her com link to *Troubadour*. She opened her mouth, but McKeon grinned and shook his head.

"I heard you talking to Andy, Ma'am, and I wish you were wrong. Too bad you're not."

"Even so, he probably learned a lot the last time, Alistair. If he has, he'll concentrate his fire as he closes."

"Yes, Ma'am." McKeon didn't say any more, but they both knew *Saladin*'s logical target. *Troubadour* could take far less damage than *Fearless*, and her destruction would eliminate a quarter of Honor's launchers.

"Stick close. Whatever he's up to, it's going to open with a missile exchange, and I want you inside *Fearless*'s inner point defense perimeter."

"Aye, aye, Skipper."

"Rafe," she turned back to Cardones, "call Lieutenant Harris to relieve you, then you and Carol get some rest. You, too, Chief Killian," she added with a glance at the helmsman. "We've got four or five hours before missile range, and I want all three of you sharp when it happens."

Sword Simonds shoved himself firmly against the command chair's cushioned back.

Part of him wanted to wade right in, get to close grips with his enemies, and destroy them once and for all, yet he dared not. Harrington had handled *Thunder* too roughly in the first engagement. Prudence was indicated until he was certain Ash had made sufficient adjustments to their own defenses, so he'd ordered a turnover to kill their closing velocity and hug the edge of the missile envelope once more rather than get in too deep too quickly.

Harrington had turned away enough to extend his closure time, and he gritted his teeth as the long, exquisite tension tore at his nerves. She'd played her games with him for fourteen hours now, and he'd been on *Thunder*'s bridge continuously for forty-five, broken only by brief, fitful naps. Now his stomach was awash with acid and too much coffee, and he wanted it to *end*.

"He *is* going for another missile engagement."

Rafael Cardones had just come back on watch, relieving Lieutenant Harris, and despite her own tension—or perhaps because of it—Honor felt an almost overpowering urge to giggle at the disgust in his voice.

"Count your blessings, Guns," she said instead. "If he's willing to stay out of energy range, *I* certainly am."

"I know, Skipper. It's just—" Cardones bent over his console, updating himself, and Honor shook her head fondly at his back. "He'll enter range in another ten minutes," Cardones announced after a moment. "Closing velocity will be down to four hundred KPS at that point."

"Close up your missile crews, Lieutenant," Honor said formally.

The range fell to six-point-eight million kilometers, and *Thunder of God* spat missiles towards her foes, their computers crammed with every tactical improvement Ash had been able to think of. This time she went to rapid fire with the first salvo; a second broadside followed fifteen seconds later, then a third, and a fourth. Two hundred and sixteen missiles were in space before the first reached attack range, and Manticoran broadsides raced to meet them.

"They're concentrating on *Troubadour*," Cardones said tautly, and Honor gripped her chair arms.

"Yankee-Three, Alistair."

"Aye, aye, Ma'am. Executing Yankee-Three." McKeon's voice was flat and metallic.

"Chief, take us to Yankee-Two," Honor went on, and *Fearless* slowed and rolled "up" towards *Saladin*. *Troubadour* slid past her, tucking in to hide as much of her emission signature behind the more powerful ship as she could without blocking her own fire. It was a cold-blooded maneuver to place the cruiser's tougher sidewalls between her and the enemy, but *Saladin* had detailed scans on them both. It was unlikely her missiles would be fooled into going for *Fearless*, and they still had plenty of maneuver time on their drives.

"Missile Defense Delta."

"Aye, aye, Ma'am. Initiating Plan Delta." Wolcott

sounded calm and cool this time, and Honor felt a brief
glow of pride in the young woman.

The glow faded as she turned back to her plot and
the sheer density of the Masadan fire. *Saladin* carried
far more ammunition, and she was using it ruthlessly.
Honor longed to reply in kind, for *Fearless* mounted
the new Mod 7b launcher, with a cycle time of only
eleven seconds. She could have pumped out twenty
percent more fire than *Saladin*—but only while her
ammo lasted, and the range was too long for her to
burn through it that way.

Sword Simonds' lip drew back in a canine grin as he
watched Ash's efforts pay off. Harrington's decoys were
less than half as effective this time, and freed from the
effort to coordinate *Thunder's* defenses, Ash and his
staff were adjusting far more rapidly to her other defensive measures, as well.

Missiles tore down on the Manticoran ships, and even
at this range he sensed the pressure they placed on
Harrington's defenses. Seven of the first broadside broke
past her counter missiles, and if her lasers stopped all of
them short of lethal range, the rapidity of Ash's fire gave
her far less engagement time on each salvo.

He tore his eyes from that display to check missile
defense, and his heart rose still higher. Ash's
prerecorded ECM programs were performing much
better than he'd hoped. Ten of the incoming missiles
lost lock and veered away, seeking *Thunder's* own
decoys, and counter missiles and lasers easily burned
down the six that held their course.

Five minutes passed. Then six. Eight. Ten. Somehow,
Carolyn Wolcott stopped every single missile *Saladin*
threw at her, but the enemy was adapting to *Fearless's*
defensive ECM far more quickly. His fire was more
accurate and heavier, and this time he wasn't flinching
away. Cardones hit the battlecruiser once, then again,
and a third time, and still she bored in, pounding back,
shrugging aside her injuries.

* * *

Matthew Simonds mouthed an oath as yet another hit slammed into his ship, but then his bloodshot eyes glowed as a shout of triumph went up from his tactical crew.

HMS *Troubadour* vomited debris and atmosphere as the X-ray laser chewed deep into her unarmored hull. Plating buckled and tore, an entire missile tube and its crew vanished in an eyeblink, and pressure loss alarms screamed. The destroyer raced onward, trailing wreckage and air, and her surviving missile tubes belched back at her massive foe.

Honor winced as the laser ripped into *Troubadour*. *Saladin* had learned even more than she'd feared from that first engagement. Her ECM was far more efficient, her heavier, more numerous point defense stations burned down incoming fire with dismaying efficiency, and each hit *she* scored hurt far worse than the missiles that got through them hurt her.

She should have given Rafe his head earlier. She should have pursued *Saladin* before the big ship's inexperienced crew had time to adjust to their weapons, but she hadn't quite been able to believe her own suspicions then. And, she told herself pitilessly, she'd let herself be dissuaded not just by the need to stay between *Saladin* and Grayson, but by her own desire to live.

She bit her lip as another Masadan missile was picked off less than a second short of *Troubadour*. She'd lost her best chance to kill *Saladin* while she was still clumsy; now too many of her own people were going to die because of her failure.

"Look! *Look!*" someone shouted from the back of *Thunder*'s bridge.

Sword Simonds wrenched around in his chair to scowl at the culprit for breaking discipline, but his heart wasn't in it. He, too, had seen two more missiles break through everything the bitch could throw against them.

* * *

"Direct hits on Missile Nine and Laser Six, Captain!" Lieutenant Cummings reported harshly. "No survivors from either mount, and we've got heavy casualties in Tracking and CIC."

Alistair McKeon shook his head like a punch-drunk fighter. Dust motes hovered in midair, the stink of burning insulation and flesh had leaked into the bridge before the ventilator trunk to CIC slammed shut, and he heard someone retching.

"Beta Fifteen's down, Skipper!" Cummings told him, and he closed his eyes in pain. There was a pause, and then his engineer's voice went flat. "Captain, I'm losing the port sidewall aft of Frame Forty-Two."

"Roll her, Helm!" McKeon barked, and *Troubadour* spun madly, whipping her rent sidewall away from *Saladin.* "Engage with the starboard broadside!"

Thunder of God heaved as another missile got through, but a sense of indestructible power filled Matthew Simonds. His ship had lost two lasers, a radar array, two more tractors, and another missile tube—that was all, and his sensors could see the shattered plating and wreckage trailing from the bitch's destroyer. Another broadside belched out as he watched, the exultation of his bridge crew flamed about him like a fire, and he felt himself pounding the arm of his chair as he urged those missiles on.

Sweat dripped from Rafael Cardones' face onto his panel. *Saladin's* electronic warfare patterns flowed and changed with incredible speed compared to their original, arthritic slowness, and the battlecruiser's point defense seemed to be seeing straight past his own birds' ECM. He could feel Wolcott's anguish beside him as more missiles stabbed through her over-strained defenses to maim and mangle *Troubadour*, but he had no time to spare for that. He had to find a chink in *Saladin's* armor. He *had* to!

* * *

"Jesus C—!"

Lieutenant Cummings' voice died with sickening suddenness. Fusion One went into emergency shutdown a fraction of a second later, and the destroyer faltered as Fusion Two took the full load.

There were no more reports from Damage Control Central. There was no one left to make them.

"Go to rapid fire on all tubes!"

Honor's eye was locked on the com link to *Troubadour*, and the live side of her face was sick as she heard the tidal wave of damage reports washing over Alistair's bridge. Ammunition or no, she had to draw *Saladin*'s fire from *Troubadour* before it was too—

The com link suddenly went dead, and her eye whipped to the visual display in horror as *Troubadour*'s back broke like a stick and the destroyer's entire after third exploded like a sun.

Cheers filled *Thunder*'s bridge, and Matthew Simonds pounded the arms of his chair and bellowed his own thick-voiced triumph.

He glared at his plot and the single godless ship which still stood between him and the Apostate, his face ugly with the need to kill and rend. But even through his bloodlust, he saw the sudden quickening of *Fearless*'s fire. *Thunder* lurched, alarms screaming, as another laser head got through, and this time he snarled in fury, for the hit had cost him two of his own tubes.

"Kill that bitch, Ash!"

It was *Fearless*'s turn now.

Damage alarms screamed like tortured women as the first Masadan broadside lashed her, and Honor tore her mind away from the horror and pain of *Troubadour*'s death. She couldn't think about that, couldn't let herself be paralyzed by the friends who'd just died.

"Hotel-Eight, Helm!" she ordered, and her soprano

voice was a stranger's, untouched by anguish or self-hate.

"We've lost the control runs to the after ring, Skipper!" Commander Higgins reported from Damage Central. "We're down to two-sixty gees!"

"Get those impellers back for me, James."

"I'll try, but we're shot clean through at Frame Three-Twelve, Skipper. It's going to take at least an hour just to run replacement cable."

Fearless twisted again as a fresh laser gouged deep.

"Direct hit on the com section!" Lieutenant Metzinger's voice was ugly with loss. "None of my people got out, Skipper. *None* of them!"

Thunder heaved as two more lasers ripped at him, and Simonds swore. Missiles were coming in so fast and heavy even computer-driven laser clusters couldn't catch them all, but he was pounding Harrington with equal fury, and his ship was far, far tougher. A readout flickered on the edge of his plot as *Fearless's* impeller wedge suddenly faltered, and his eyes flamed.

"Increase acceleration to max!" he barked. "Close the range. We'll finish the bitch with energy fire!"

Fearless staggered yet again as another laser head evaded Ensign Wolcott. The fresh blast of X-rays wiped away two more missile tubes, and Rafael Cardones tasted despair. He was hitting the bastards at least as often as they were hitting *Fearless*, but *Saladin* was so damned tough she didn't even seem to notice, and he was down to nine tubes.

And then he froze, staring at his readouts. That couldn't be true! Only an idiot would run his EW that way—but if the Captain was right about who was in command over there. . . .

The analysis flashed before him, and his lips thinned. *Saladin's* ECM was under computer control. It had to be, and the engagement had lasted long enough for his own sensors to spot the pattern. The battlecruiser was cycling through a complex deception plan that shifted sequence every four hundred seconds—but every time it did, it reset to exactly the same origin point!

There was no time to clear it with the Captain. His flashing hands changed his loading queues, updated his birds' penetration profiles . . . and slammed a lock on all offensive fire. He ignored the consternation around him as his fire ceased. His eyes were glued to his chrono, watching it turn over, and then he pressed the firing key flat.

Simonds frowned as the *Fearless*'s fire suddenly died. Fifteen seconds passed without a single answering shot, then twenty. Twenty-five. He felt his lungs fill with air as he prepared to shout his joy, then swore in savage disappointment as her broadside fired again.

Nine missiles charged through space, and *Thunder of God*'s computers blinked in cybernetic surprise at their unorthodox approach. They came in massed in a tight phalanx, suicidally tight against modern point defense . . . except that the three lead missiles carried nothing but ECM. Their jammers howled, blinding every active and passive sensor system, building a solid wall of interference. Neither *Thunder* nor their fellows could possibly "see" through it, and a human operator might have realized there had to be a reason *Fearless* had voluntarily blinded her own missiles's seekers. But the computers saw only a single jamming source and targeted it with only two counter missiles.

One jammer died, but the other two survived, spreading out, varying the strength and power and shape of the transmissions that baffled *Thunder*'s follow-up counter missiles. They charged onward, and then, suddenly, they arced up and apart to expose the six missiles behind them.

Last-ditch point defense lasers swiveled and struck like snakes, spitting rods of coherent light as the computers finally recognized the threat, but the jammers had covered them to the last possible moment, and the attack missiles knew *exactly* what they were looking for. One of the six died, then another, but the final quartet came on, and an alarm screamed on Lieutenant Ash's panel.

The Lieutenant's head whipped around in horror. He had less than a single second to realize that somehow *these* missiles had been programmed to *use* his EW systems, as if his decoys were homing beacons, not defenses, and then they rammed headlong into their target.

Two of them vanished in sun-bright fireballs that shook *Thunder* to her keel as twin, 78-ton hammers struck her sidewall at .25 *C*. For all their fury, those two were harmless, but their sisters' sidewall penetrators functioned as designed.

Fearless writhed as a fresh hit killed two more missile tubes, but then someone emitted a banshee shriek of triumph, and Honor stared at her repeater. It wasn't possible! No one could get old-fashioned nukes through the very teeth of a modern warship's defenses! Yet Rafe Cardones had done it. Somehow, he'd *done* it!

But he hadn't scored direct hits. *Saladin*'s impeller wedge flickered as she staggered out of the fireballs, clouds of atmosphere and vaporized alloy streamed back from where her port sidewall had died, but she was still there, and even as Honor watched, the maimed battlecruiser was rolling desperately to interpose the roof of her impeller wedge against the follow-up missiles charging down upon her. Her wedge restabilized, and her drive went to maximum power as her vector swung sharply away from *Fearless*.

She accelerated madly, breaking off, fleeing her mangled opponent, and HMS *Fearless* was too badly damaged to pursue.

• CHAPTER THIRTY-FOUR

Two brutally wounded starships swept onward around Yeltsin's Star while their crews fought their damage. Medical staffs fought their own wars against the horror of maimed and broken bodies, and every mind aboard them knew their next clash must be the last.

Honor Harrington listened to the reports and forced the living side of her face to hide her desperation. *Fearless*'s communications section had been blotted away, rendering her deaf and dumb, but there was more than enough internal bad news.

A quarter of her crew was dead or wounded, and Commander Brentworth had found a job at last. The Grayson officer manned the damage control net from the bridge, releasing Lieutenant Allgood, Lieutenant Commander Higgins' senior assistant, for other work, and Higgins needed him badly.

Fearless's entire after impeller ring was down, and her starboard broadside was reduced to a single graser and eight missile tubes. Almost worse, the combination of damaged magazines and seven minutes of maximum-rate fire had reduced her to less than a hundred missiles, and her sensors had been savagely mauled. Half her main radar, both secondary fire control arrays, and two-thirds of her passive sensors were gone. She could still see her enemy, but her best acceleration was barely a third of *Saladin*'s until Higgins' vac-suited engineers restored her after impeller ring (if they could), and even then, she'd lost so many nodes she'd be down to barely two-point-eight KPS^2. If the battlecruiser's captain guessed the truth, he could easily pull out and lose her. He'd already reopened the range to almost ninety-four million kilometers; if he opened it another two light-minutes, Honor wouldn't even be able to *find* him, much less fight him, without *Troubadour* to relay from the recon drones.

Agony struck again at that thought, and she thrust it away. There was no time for it, yet try as she might, she couldn't forget that there'd been three hundred men and women aboard Alistair McKeon's ship; few of them could have survived.

But Rafe had hurt *Saladin* badly, too, she told herself. Maybe even badly enough. If her damage was severe enough, even fanatics might withdraw; if they didn't, it was very unlikely *Fearless* could stop her.

Sword Simonds held himself rigidly still as the medical orderly put the last stitch into the gash in his forehead, then waved aside the offer of a painkiller. The orderly retreated quickly, for he had more than enough to do elsewhere; there were over twelve hundred dead men in *Thunder of God*'s hull, two-thirds of them soldiers who'd brought no vac suits aboard.

Simonds touched his own ugly, sutured wound, and knew he was lucky he'd only been knocked senseless, but he didn't feel that way. His head hurt like hell, and if he couldn't fault his exec's decision to break off, that didn't mean he liked the situation he'd found when he regained consciousness.

He clenched his jaw as the latest damage reports scrolled up his screen. *Thunder*'s armor and the radiation shielding inside his wedge had let him live, but his port broadside had been reduced to five lasers and six tubes, and half of them were in local control. His maximum acceleration had been reduced twenty-one percent, his gravitics and half his other sensors—including *all* of them to port—were gone, and Workman's report on his sidewall generators was grim. *Thunder* wasn't—quite—naked to port, but spreading his remaining generators would weaken his sidewall to less than a third of design strength, and his radiation shields were completely gone. Simonds dared not even contemplate exposing that side of his ship to Harrington's fire . . .

but his starboard armament and fire control were untouched.

He touched the stitches again, and his mind was cold and clear despite his exhaustion. The bitch was still there, still stubbornly defying God's Will, and she'd hurt him. But he'd hurt *her*, too, and he'd checked the Havenite data profile on the *Star Knight* class against her missile expenditures. Even if she hadn't lost a single magazine, she had to be almost dry.

He glanced once more at his plot, his hate like ice at his core as he noted the way she continued to loaf along between him and Grayson. He didn't know how she was monitoring his every move, and he no longer cared. He was God's warrior. His duty was clear, and it was a vast relief to throw aside all distractions and embrace it at last.

"How much longer to restore the port sidewall?"

"I'll have it up in forty minutes, Sir." Workman sounded weary but confident, and the Sword nodded.

"Astrogation, I want a straight-line course for Grayson."

"He's changing course, Skipper."

Honor looked up quickly at Cardones' report, and her blood ran cold. *Saladin*'s captain had made up his mind. He was no longer maneuvering against *Fearless*; instead, he'd shaped his course directly for Grayson, and his challenge was obvious.

She sat very still for a moment, mind racing as she tried to find an answer, but there was none, and she cleared her throat.

"Put me through to Commander Higgins, Mark," she said quietly.

"Yes, Ma'am," Brentworth replied. There was a brief pause, then a strained voice spoke over her intercom.

"Higgins," it said.

"James, this is the Captain. How much longer on those control runs?"

"Another ten minutes, Ma'am. Maybe a bit less."

"I need them *now*," Honor told him flatly. "*Saladin* is coming back."

There was a moment of silence, and the chief engineer's voice was equally flat when he replied. "Understood, Ma'am. I'll do what I can."

Honor turned her chair to face Stephen DuMorne.

"Assume we get our remaining after impellers back in ten minutes. Where can we intercept *Saladin?*"

She felt her bridge crew flinch at the word "intercept," but DuMorne only bent over his console, then looked back up at her.

"On that basis, we can make a zero-range intercept one-five-two million klicks short of the planet in just over one-five-seven minutes, Ma'am. Velocity at intercept will be two-six-zero-six-eight KPS." He cleared his throat. "We'll enter missile range eleven minutes before intercept."

"Understood." Honor pinched the bridge of her nose, and her heart ached for what she was about to do to her people. They deserved far better, but she couldn't give it to them.

"Bring us around to your new course, Steve," she said. "Chief Killian, I want the belly of our wedge held towards *Saladin.*"

"Aye, aye, Ma'am."

Fearless began her turn, and Honor turned to Cardones.

"We should be able to run a fair plot on *Saladin* with our belly radar, Rafe, but tracking missiles through the grav band will be difficult."

Cardones nodded, and his face was very still. Honor saw the understanding in his eyes, but she had to say it.

"I intend to hold the belly of our wedge towards her all the way in. We don't have the ammunition to stop her with missiles, so we're going to close to pointblank range unless she shears off. Set up your fire plan on the assumption that I will roll to bring our port energy broadside to bear at twenty thousand kilometers."

Cardones simply nodded once more, but someone hissed. That wasn't energy weapon range; it was suicide range.

"She won't know exactly when we intend to roll," Honor went on in that same, calm voice. "That should give us the first shot, and at that range, it won't matter how tough her sidewalls are." She held Cardones' gaze with her single eye and spoke very softly. "I'm depending on you, Rafe. Get that first broadside on target, then keep firing, whatever happens."

Matthew Simonds' grin was ugly as his ship accelerated towards Grayson. There were no fancy maneuvers for the bitch now. Harrington was still inside him, still able to intercept, but this time it would be on his terms, not hers, and he watched her projected vector stretch out to cross his own. They met 152 million kilometers short of the planet, but *Fearless* would never survive to reach that point.

"Andy."

"Yes, Ma'am?"

"Go aft to Auxiliary Fire Control. Take Harris with you, and make sure he's completely updated on Rafe's fire plan."

Venizelos' mouth tightened, but he nodded.

"Understood, Skipper." He hesitated a moment, then held out his hand. Honor squeezed it firmly, and he nodded once more and stepped into the lift.

The warships slanted towards one another, and there was a finality in their movements. The challenge had been issued and accepted; they would meet at an invisible point in space, and one of them would die there. There could be no other outcome, and every soul aboard them knew it.

"One hundred minutes to intercept, Sir," the astrogator reported, and Simonds glanced at his tactical officer.

"If she keeps coming in behind her wedge, we won't have very good shots until she rolls down to engage, Sir," Ash said quietly.

"Just do your best, Lieutenant."

Simonds turned back to his own plot and the crimson dot of the enemy ship with an inner sense of total certainty. Harrington wasn't going to roll for a missile duel. She was going to carry straight through and engage him beam to beam, and he felt a grudging, hate-filled respect for her. Her ship would never survive at that range, but if she reached it alive, the damage to *Thunder* would be terrible. He knew it, and he accepted it, for terrible or not, *Thunder* would live to attack Grayson. He knew that, too.

God would not permit any other result.

Neither of the maimed, half-blind ships any longer had the capability to look beyond the other even if they'd wanted to. And because they didn't, neither of them noted the wide-spaced hyper footprints as sixteen battlecruisers and their escorts suddenly emerged from hyper 23.76 light-minutes from Yeltsin's Star.

"That's it, My Lord," Captain Edwards said. "Tracking's got good reads on both impeller signatures. That's the battlecruiser at three-one-four; the one at three-two-four has to be *Fearless*. There's no sign of *Troubadour*."

"Understood." Hamish Alexander tried to keep his own emotions out of his voice as he acknowledged his flag captain's report. If *Reliant* couldn't see *Troubadour*, that meant *Troubadour* was dead, yet all the way here, he'd known they were almost certain to arrive too late, despite the risks he'd run with his hyper generator settings. Now he knew they hadn't, and a sense of elation warred with the blow of the destroyer's loss.

He'd spread his battlecruisers by divisions, spacing four separate formations about Grayson's side of the primary as they translated from hyper to give himself the best possible coverage, and brought them into n-space in a crash translation. He could hear someone still vomiting behind him, but he'd carried the highest possible velocity across the alpha wall with him, and it was as well he had.

Reliant's own division had come in with Grayson directly between them and Yeltsin, covering the most important arc of the half-circle, and the vectors projecting themselves across his plot told their own tale. Alexander's ships were not only ahead of the two warships on his plot but cutting their angle towards Grayson. That gave him an effective closing velocity of almost twenty thousand KPS, and the range to *Saladin* was barely twelve light-minutes, which meant *Reliant* would cross her course five-point-six light-minutes short of Grayson . . . and enter extreme missile range three minutes before that.

They were in time. Despite all the odds, despite *Troubadour's* loss, they were in *time* for Grayson and HMS *Fearless*.

"I don't understand why *Saladin* isn't trying to run," Edwards muttered. "Surely she doesn't think she can fight *all* of us, My Lord!"

"Who knows what religious fanatics think, Captain?" Alexander smiled thinly at *Reliant's* commander, then looked back at his plot and hid a wince.

Fearless's course made Harrington's intentions brutally clear. It was no less than he would have expected of an officer with her record—which made him respect her courage no less—and he thanked God she wouldn't be called upon to make good her determination after all.

He raised his eyes to Alice Truman, and for the first time since she'd come aboard *Reliant*, some of the strain had faded from her face. She'd brought the relief force to Yeltsin two full days before it should have been possible . . . and that meant *Fearless* would live.

But he knew from Truman's report that the cruiser's gravitics were gone, and without *Troubadour*, she had no one to relay from the recon drones for her. That meant Harrington couldn't know his ships had arrived unless he told her, and he turned to his com officer.

"Record for transmission to *Fearless*, Harry. 'Captain

Harrington, this is Admiral White Haven aboard HMS *Reliant*, closing from zero-three-one with BatCruDiv One-Eight, range twelve-point-five light-minutes. I estimate eight-two minutes before I can range on *Saladin*. Break off and leave her to us, Captain. You've done your job. White Haven clear.'"

"On the chip, Admiral!" the Lieutenant said with a huge grin.

"Then send it, Harry—send it!" Alexander said, and leaned back with a matching grin.

The range continued to fall, and Honor knew there could be only one outcome. She'd made herself accept that from the moment *Saladin* started back in. She understood the fear she felt about her, for she, too, wanted to live, and she, too, was afraid. But this was why she'd put on the Queen's uniform, accepted the responsibility and privilege of serving her monarch and her people, and it didn't matter that Grayson was some- one else's planet.

"Joyce."

"Yes, Ma'am?"

"I think I'd like a little music, Joyce." Metzinger blinked at her, and Honor smiled. "Punch up Hammerwell's Seventh on the intercom, please."

"Hammerwell's Seventh?" Metzinger shook herself. "Yes, Ma'am."

Honor had always loved Hammerwell. He, too, had come from Sphinx, and the cold, majestic beauty of her home world was at the heart of everything he'd ever written. Now she leaned back in her chair as the swirl- ing strains of Manticore's greatest composer's masterwork spilled from the com, and people looked at one another, first in surprise and then in pleasure, as the voices of strings and woodwinds flowed over them.

HMS *Fearless* sped towards her foe, and the haunt- ing loveliness of Hammerwell's *Salute to Spring* went with her.

"*Fearless* isn't breaking off, My Lord," Captain

Hunter said, and Alexander frowned. His message must have reached Harrington over five minutes ago, but her course had never wavered.

He checked the time. At this range, it would take another five or six minutes for her reply to reach him, and he made himself sit back.

"She may be afraid *Saladin* will launch against the planet unless she keeps the pressure on," he said to Hunter, but his voice sounded self-convincing even to himself.

"Intercept in seven-five minutes," Simonds' astrogator reported, and the Sword nodded.

Hamish Alexander's frown deepened. *Reliant* had been in Yeltsin space for over thirty minutes, and *still* Harrington's course held steady. She was still boring in for her hopeless fight, and that didn't make any sense at all.

He had four battlecruisers, supported by twelve lighter ships, and there was no way *Saladin* could outrun them with their initial velocity advantage. With that much firepower bearing down on her enemy, there was no sane reason for Harrington to keep coming this way. The separation was still too great for *Saladin* to range on her, but unless she broke off in the next ten minutes, that was going to change.

"Dear God." The hushed whisper came from Alice Truman, and Alexander looked at her. The Commander had gone bone-white, and her lips were bloodless.

"What is it, Commander?"

"She doesn't know we're here." Truman turned to him, her face tight. "She never got your message, My Lord. Her communications are out."

Alexander's eyes went very still, and then he nodded. Of course. Harrington had already lost *Troubadour*, and her own acceleration was barely 2.5 KPS^2. That spelled battle damage, and if her com section had been destroyed as well as her gravitics—

He turned to his chief of staff.

"Time to missile range, Byron?"

"Three-niner-point-six minutes, Sir."

"Time until their vectors merge?"

"Nineteen minutes," Hunter said flatly, and Alexander's jaw clenched in pain all the worse for his earlier elation. Twenty minutes. Less than an eyeblink by the standards of the universe, yet those twenty minutes made all the difference there was, for they hadn't been in time after all.

Grayson would be safe, but they were going to see HMS *Fearless* die before their eyes.

The soaring finale of *Salute to Spring* swept to its climax and faded away, and Honor inhaled deeply. She straightened and looked at Cardones.

"Time to intercept, Guns?" she asked calmly.

"Eighteen minutes, Skipper—missile range in six-point-five."

"Very well." She laid her forearms very precisely along her command chair's arms. "Stand by point defense."

"Captain Edwards!"

"Yes, My Lord?" *Reliant's* captain's voice was hushed, as he, too, watched tragedy unfold before him.

"Bring the division ninety degrees to starboard. I want broadside fire on *Saladin* right now."

"But—" Edwards began in shock, and Alexander cut him off harshly.

"Do it, Captain!"

"At once, My Lord!"

Byron Hunter looked sidelong at his admiral and cleared his throat.

"Sir, the range is over a hundred million klicks. There's no way we can score at—"

"I know the range, Byron," Alexander never turned away from his own display, "but it's all we've got. Maybe Harrington will pick them up on radar—if she still *has* radar—as they close. Or maybe *Saladin's* suffered sensor damage of her own. If she isn't trying to break off because she doesn't know we're here, either, maybe she will if we let her know we are. Hell, maybe we'll actually score on her if she holds her course!"

He looked up at last, and his chief of staff saw the despair in his eyes.

"It's all we've got," he repeated very, very softly as Battlecruiser Division 17 turned to open its broadsides and went to rapid fire.

The first missiles spewed out from *Thunder of God*, and *Fearless*'s crippled sensors couldn't see them above a half million kilometers. That gave Rafe Cardones and Carolyn Wolcott barely seven seconds to engage them, far too brief a window to use counter missiles.

Their damaged jammers and decoys fought to blind and beguile the incoming fire, and they'd learned even more about *Thunder*'s offensive fire control than Lieutenant Ash had learned about theirs. Three-quarters of the first broadside lost lock and veered away, and computer-commanded laser clusters quivered like questing hounds, pitting their minimal prediction time against the surviving laser heads' acquisition time

Rods of coherent light picked off targets with desperate speed, but *Fearless* couldn't possibly stop them all, and she didn't. Most of those which got through wasted their fury against her impenetrable belly band, but a few raced across "above" and "below" her to attack her sidewalls. Damage alarms wailed again, men and women died, weapons were wiped away, but the cruiser shook off the damage and kept closing, and there was only silence on her bridge. Honor Harrington sat immovable in her command chair, shoulders squared, like an eye of calm at the heart of that silence, and watched her plot.

Seven more minutes to intercept.

Matthew Simonds snarled as *Fearless* kept coming through the whirlwind of his fire. Seventy-two missiles per minute slashed out at the cruiser, his magazine levels fell like a sand castle melting in the rain, but she hadn't fired a single shot back at him, and her unflinching approach sent a chill of fear through the heart of his exhaustion-fogged rage. He was hitting her—he *knew* he was hitting her!—but she came on like some nerveless juggernaut only death itself could stop.

He stared at the light bead in his display, watching atmosphere spill from it like blood, and tried to understand. She was an infidel, a *woman*. What kept her *coming* for him this way?

"Intercept in five minutes, Skipper."

"Understood."

Honor's cool soprano was unshadowed by her own fear. They'd already endured *Saladin*'s fire for six minutes and taken nine more hits, two serious, and the battlecruiser's fire would only grow more accurate as they closed.

A massive salvo hurtled through space, eighty-four missiles spawned by four battlecruisers from a base closing velocity of thirty thousand KPS. Another came behind it, and another, but the range was impossibly long.

Their drives had burned out three minutes and twelve-point-three million kilometers after launch, at a terminal velocity of almost a hundred and six thousand KPS. Now they tore onward, riding a purely ballistic course, invisible on Hamish Alexander's plot, and his stomach was a lump of iron. Thirteen minutes since launch. Even at their velocity, they would take another four minutes to enter attack range, and the chance of their scoring a hit raced downward with every second of flight time.

Fearless rocked as a pair of lasers slashed into her port side.

"Missile Six and Laser Eight gone, Captain," Commander Brentworth reported. "Dr. Montoya reports Compartment Two-Forty open to space."

"Acknowledged." Honor closed her eye in pain, for Two-Forty had been converted into an emergency ward when the casualties spilled out of sickbay. She prayed the wounded's emergency environmental slips had saved some of them, but deep inside she knew most of those people had just died.

Her ship bucked again, and fresh tidings of death and injury washed over her, but the time display on her plot ticked steadily downward. Only four more minutes. *Fearless* only had to last another four minutes.

"Intercept in three-point-five minutes," Lieutenant Ash said hoarsely, and Simonds nodded and slid down in his chair, bracing himself for the holocaust about to begin.

"Missiles entering attack range . . . *now!*" Captain Hunter rasped.

A proximity alarm flashed on Lieutenant Ash's panel, a warning buzzer wailed, and a shoal of crimson dots appeared on his radar display.

The Lieutenant gaped at them. They were coming in at incredible speed, and they couldn't be there. They couldn't *be* there!

But they were. They'd come over a hundred million kilometers while *Thunder of God* moved to meet them, and their very lack of drive power had helped them evade all of *Thunder*'s remaining passive sensors. Ash's radar had a maximum range against such small targets of just over a half million kilometers, and that was less than five seconds at their velocity.

"Missiles at three-five-two!" he cried, and Simonds' head jerked towards his secondary plot.

Only five of them were close enough to attack *Thunder*, and they no longer had any power to adjust their trajectories—but *Thunder* had held her undeviating course for over two hours. They raced across her bow and rolled on attitude thrusters, bringing their laser clusters to bear down the unprotected throat of her wedge, and all five of them detonated as one.

Thunder of God bucked like a mad thing as half a dozen lasers ripped into her port beam, and Matthew

Simonds went white with horror as he saw the second incoming broadside racing down upon him.

"Hard a starboard!" he shouted.

The coxswain threw the helm hard over, wrenching *Thunder*'s vulnerable bow away from the new menace, and Simonds felt a rush of relief.

Then he realized what he'd done.

"Belay that helm order!" he screamed.

"He's turning!" Rafe Cardones shouted, and Honor jerked upright in her chair. *It couldn't be!* There was no—

"Roll port! All batteries, *engage!"*

"Engage with forward batteries!" Simonds yelled desperately.

He had no choice. *Thunder* was too slow on the helm, and he'd compounded his original mistake. He should have completed the turn, gotten around as quickly as he could to interpose his wounded port sidewall while he rolled to block with the top or belly of his wedge; instead, his helmsman obeyed the orders he'd been given, checking the turn to come back to port in the same plane, and *Thunder* hung for a few, short seconds bow-on to *Fearless*.

The battlecruiser's forward armament spat fire, two powerful spinal lasers blazing frantically at the target suddenly square across her bow. The first salvo wasted itself against the belly of *Fearless*'s wedge, but the cruiser was rolling like a snake. *Thunder* fired again, pointblank energy fire ripped through her sidewall, and armor was no protection at that range. Air and debris vomited into space, but then her surviving broadside came to bear.

Four lasers and three far more powerful grasers went to continuous rapid fire, and there was no sidewall to stop them.

Matthew Simonds had one flaming instant to know he'd failed his God, and then HMS *Fearless* blew his ship apart around him.

• CHAPTER THIRTY-FIVE

Honor Harrington stepped into a trill of bosun's pipes, and Nimitz stiffened on her shoulder even as her good eye widened in surprise. Admiral White Haven had summoned her for a final, routine meeting before she took *Fearless* home, but Ambassador Langtry waited beside him in *Reliant's* boat bay. That was odd enough, yet no lesser personages than Admiral Wesley Matthews and Benjamin Mayhew himself stood with them, and speculation frothed through her even as her hand rose in automatic salute.

Hamish Alexander waited for Protector Mayhew and Sir Anthony Langtry to find chairs, then sat behind his desk and considered the woman before him.

Her treecat was obviously restive, but she looked calm, despite the surprise she must be feeling, and he remembered the first time he'd seen her. She'd been calm then, too, when she'd come aboard to report her damages and casualties with an indifference which had repelled him. She hadn't even seemed to care, as if people were simply part of a ship's fittings, only weapons to be expended and forgotten.

Her emotionless detachment had appalled him . . . but then the report came in that Commander McKeon had somehow gotten almost a hundred of his crew away in his single surviving pinnace, and the mask had slipped. He'd seen her turn away, trying to hide the tears in her good eye, the way her shoulders shook, and he'd stepped between her and his staff to block their view and guard her secret as he realized this one was special. That her armor of detachment was so thick because the pain and grief behind it were so terrible.

His memory flickered ahead to another day—the day she'd watched in stone-faced silence as the men who'd raped and murdered *Madrigal*'s crew faced a Grayson hangman. She hadn't enjoyed it, but she'd watched as unflinchingly as she'd headed into *Saladin*'s broadside. Not for herself, but for the people who would never see it, and that unyielding determination to see justice done for them had completed his understanding of her.

He envied her. He was twice her age, with a career to make any man proud, including the freshly accomplished conquest of the Endicott System, yet he envied her. Her squadron had been harrowed and riven, its two surviving units battered into wrecks. Nine hundred of her crewmen had died, another three hundred were wounded, and she would never, ever believe—as he would never have believed in her place—that the death toll couldn't have been lower if she'd been better. But she was wrong, as he would have been wrong, and nothing could ever diminish what she and her people had done. What her people had done *for* her because of who and what she was.

He cleared his throat, and as she turned to look at him, he was struck once more by the clean, sharp-edged attractiveness of her. He felt it even with half her face paralyzed and her anachronistic eye patch, and he wondered what her impact must have been like before she was wounded.

"Obviously, Captain Harrington," he said quietly, "I asked you aboard for something besides the traditional pre-departure meeting."

"Indeed, Sir?" Her slurred soprano was no more than politely inquiring, and he smiled slightly and tipped his chair back.

"Indeed. You see, Captain, there've been a lot of dispatches flowing back and forth between Grayson and Manticore. Including," he let his smile fade, "a rather sharp protest from the Honorable Reginald Houseman."

Her steady regard never flickered.

"I regret to inform you, Captain, that the Lords of Admiralty have placed a letter of reprimand in your personnel file. Whatever the provocation, and I grant there *was* provocation, there is no excuse for a Queen's officer's physically attacking a civilian representative of the Crown. I trust it will never be necessary for me to remind you of that again?"

"So do I, My Lord," she said, and her tone meant something very different from his. There was no arrogance in it, no defiance, but neither was there any apology, and he leaned across the desk.

"Understand me, Captain," he said quietly. "No one can dispute your accomplishments here, nor is any officer of the Queen inclined to waste much sympathy on Mr. Houseman. My concern is not for him. It's for you."

Something happened in that cool, brown eye. Her head cocked a bit to one side, and her treecat mimicked the movement, fixing the admiral with his unblinking green gaze.

"You're an outstanding officer." Her sharply carved face blushed, but she didn't look away. "But you have the vices of your virtues, Captain Harrington. Direct action isn't always the best policy, and there are limits. Overstep them too often, whatever the provocation, and your career will end. I would consider that a tragedy, both for you and for the Queen's service. Don't let it happen."

He held her gaze for a moment, and then she bobbed a small nod.

"I understand, My Lord," she said in an entirely different voice.

"Good." Alexander leaned back again. "Now, however, at the risk of undoing my effort to put the fear of God into you, I must inform you that, aside from your tendency to pummel her diplomats, Her Majesty is quite pleased with you, Captain. In fact, I understand she intends to express her thanks to you in person upon your return to Manticore. I imagine that should, um, *offset* any potential consequences of your reprimand."

Her blush turned dark and hot, and for the first time since he'd met her, she looked almost flustered.

"I also have to inform you that a certain Captain Alfredo Yu, lately in the service of the People's

Republic of Haven, was picked up in Endicott. He's requested asylum from the Crown." Harrington straightened in her chair, her eye very intent, and he nodded. "I'll be sending him home aboard your ship, Captain, and I expect you to show him the courtesy due his rank."

She nodded, and he nodded back.

"That completes what *I* needed to say to you, but I believe Protector Benjamin has something to say." Alexander turned politely to Grayson's ruler, and she followed suit.

"I do, indeed, Captain Harrington," Mayhew said with a smile. "My planet can never adequately thank you for what you did for us, but we are keenly aware of our debt, not simply to you but to your crews and your Kingdom, and we desire to express our gratitude in some tangible fashion. Accordingly, with Queen Elizabeth's permission through Sir Anthony, I ask *you* to sign our draft treaty of alliance in her name."

Honor inhaled sharply, and his smile turned sad.

"Had he lived, Admiral Courvosier would have signed. I feel certain there is no one he could have more desired to do so in his place than you, and I ask you to complete his work here for him. Will you do it?"

"I—" Honor had to stop and clear her throat. "I'd be honored to, Sir. Very honored. I—" She broke off and shook her head, unable to continue.

"Thank you," Mayhew said softly, then waved a hand. "There are, however, two other small matters. With the benefits of our new relationship with Manticore, we expect to expand our orbital farms—and population—at a much faster rate, and the Chamber has, at my request, authorized the Grant in Organization of a new steading on our southernmost continent. With your permission, we intend to call it the Steading of Harrington, and I ask you to assume the office of its Steadholder for yourself and your heirs."

Shock jerked Honor so suddenly to her feet that Nimitz swayed for balance, digging his claws deep into her padded shoulder.

"Sir—Protector Benjamin—I can't—I mean, *you* can't—" She floundered, trying desperately to find the words to express her feelings. Her shock and disbelief, and the residual memory of what a freak she'd been treated as when first she arrived here.

"Please, Captain," Mayhew interrupted her. "Sit down." She obeyed numbly, and he smiled at her again. "I'm a pragmatist, Captain. I have more motives than one for asking you to accept this post."

"But I'm a Queen's officer, Sir. I have other duties, other responsibilities."

"I realize that. With your permission, I intend to nominate a regent to see to the day-to-day affairs of your steading, but your title will be very real, Captain, and documents will be forwarded to you from time to time which will require your signature and authorization. Moreover, Yeltsin and Manticore aren't that far apart, and we hope to see you here often, though the Chamber fully realizes it will be impossible for you to personally govern your people. But aside from the income—which will be substantial, in a few years' time, and which the Chamber earnestly wishes you to have— there is a much more pressing reason for you to accept. You see, we need you."

"*Need* me, Sir?"

"Yes. Grayson faces tremendous changes over the next few decades, political and social as well as economic. You'll be the first woman in our history to hold land, but you won't be the last, and we need you as a model—and a challenge—as we bring our women fully into our society. And, if you'll forgive my frankness, your . . . determined personality and the fact that you're a prolong recipient means you'll be a very strong model for a very long time."

"But—" Honor looked at Langtry. "Sir Anthony? Would this even be legal under Manticoran law?"

"Normally, no." The ambassador's eyes gleamed with unmistakable delight. "In this instance, however, Her Majesty has personally authorized it. Moreover, the House of Lords has determined that your dignities as a noblewoman of a sovereign ally of the Kingdom will equate to those of an earl of the realm. Should you accept them—and Her Majesty's Government asks you to consider doing so most seriously—you will become Countess Harrington as well as Steadholder Harrington."

Honor stared at him, unable to believe a word of it yet unable to *dis*believe, either, and felt Nimitz's tail twitch against her spine.

"I—" She paused once more, then shook her head and smiled crookedly. "Are you *sure* about this, Protector Benjamin?"

"I am. All of Grayson is."

"Then I suppose I have to accept. I mean," she blushed hotly, "I would be *honored* to accept."

"I know precisely what you mean, Captain. We've jumped out and bagged you without warning, and you'd really rather we did it to someone else, but you'll accept anyway." Her blush went wine-dark, and his smile became a grin. "On the other hand, this sort of thing sometimes happens to people who hold pistols to a government's head, and I think—" his grin grew positively wicked "—that once you get over the shock, the idea will grow on you."

She laughed. She had to, and he laughed with her.

"I don't deserve it, Sir, but thank you. Really."

"You're welcome—really. And now there's just one more little thing." He rose and gestured to her. "Stand please, Captain Harrington."

Honor obeyed, and the Protector extended his hand to Admiral Matthews, who drew a blood-red ribbon from a small, velvet case and draped it across his palm. An exquisitely wrought, many-rayed star of gold hung from its end, and the Protector shook the ribbon out almost reverently to display it.

"Captain Honor Harrington, it gives me more pleasure than I can possibly say, to present to you, in the name of the people of Grayson, the Star of Grayson, for heroism in the service of our world."

Honor inhaled and came to attention almost automatically, and Mayhew rose on his toes to loop the ribbon about her neck. He adjusted it with care, and the star's bright glory shone like a flame against her space-black tunic.

"This medal is our highest award for valor," he told her quietly. "Over the years, it has been worn by some truly extraordinary men, but never, I think, by one more extraordinary than the woman who has received it today."

A moment of utter silence filled the cabin, and then Langtry cleared his throat.

"And now, Captain," he said, "there's one more formality before you accompany Protector Benjamin and myself back planet-side for the formal treaty signing and your investiture as Steadholder."

Honor simply looked at him, too dazed by all that had happened to do anything else, and he smiled at her. Then he stepped back and opened the door to the admiral's dining cabin, and Alistair McKeon and Alice Truman walked through it, beaming as if to split their faces.

Honor's confusion was complete. She'd thought Alistair was still aboard *Fearless*, waiting with Scotty Tremaine and his other survivors to return to Manticore with her. But here he was in full mess dress—and where he'd gotten it when all his gear had gone up with *Troubadour* she couldn't begin to imagine—and carrying a sheathed sword. Alice was just as formally dressed, and she carried a small silk cushion.

She crossed the cabin and set the cushion on the decksole. Then she held out her hands, and to Honor's utter surprise Nimitz leapt lightly into them. Alice cradled the 'cat in her arms and stood back and came to attention as Alistair stopped at Langtry's elbow.

"Kneel, please, Captain." The ambassador gestured to the cushion, and she obeyed as if in a dream. Steel rasped as he drew the shining blade, and McKeon retired a half-pace behind him with the sheath and came to attention.

"By the authority vested in me as Her Majesty's Ambassador to Haven and by Her express commission, acting for and in Her stead and as Knight Grand Cross of the Order of King Roger," Langtry said in his deep voice, "I bestow upon you the rank, title, prerogatives, and duties of Knight Companion of the Order of King Roger." The glittering steel touched her right shoulder lightly, then her left, then back to her right once more while she stared up at him. Then he smiled and lowered the blade once more.

"Rise, Dame Honor," he said softly, "and may your future actions as faithfully uphold the honor of the Queen as your past."

excerpt from
WAR OF HONOR

available from Baen Books
October 2002
0-7434-3545-1, hardcover, $26.00

CHAPTER ONE

"Steeeee-*riiiiike* onnnnne!"

The small white sphere flew past the young man in the green-trimmed, white uniform and smacked into the flat leather glove of the gray-uniformed man crouching behind him. The third man in the tableau—the one who had issued the shouted proclamation—wore an anachronistic black jacket and cap, as well as a face mask and chest protector like the crouching man wore. A rumble of discontent went up at his announcement, sprinkled with a few catcalls, from the crowd which filled the comfortable seats of the stadium to near capacity, and the man in white lowered his long, slender club to glower at the man in black. It didn't do him any good. The black-clad official only returned his glare, and, finally, he turned back towards the playing field while the man who'd caught the ball threw it back to his teammate, standing on the small, raised mound of earth twenty or so meters away.

"Wait a minute," Commodore Lady Michelle Henke, Countess Gold Peak, said, turning in her own seat in the palatial owner's box to look at her hostess. "That's a strike?"

"Of course it is," Lady Dame Honor Harrington, Duchess and Steadholder Harrington, replied gravely.

"I thought you said a 'strike' was when he swung and missed," Henke complained.

"It is," Honor assured her.

"But he *didn't*—swing, I mean."

"It's a strike whether he swings or not, as long as the pitch is in the strike zone."

For just a moment, Henke's expression matched that which the batter had turned upon the umpire, but Honor only looked back with total innocence. When the countess spoke again, it was with the careful patience of one determined not to allow someone else the satisfaction of a petty triumph.

"And the 'strike zone' is?" she asked.

"Anywhere between the knees and the shoulders, as long as the ball also crosses home plate," Honor told her with the competent air of a longtime afficionado.

"You say that like *you* knew the answer a year ago," Henke replied in a pretension-depressing tone.

"That's just the sort of small-minded attitude I might have expected out of you," Honor observed mournfully, and shook her head. "Really, Mike, it's a very simple game."

"Sure it is. That's why this is the only planet in the known universe where they still play it!"

"That's not true," Honor scolded primly while

the cream-and-gray treecat stretched across the back of her seat raised his head to twitch his whiskers insufferably at his person's guest. "You know perfectly well that they still play baseball on Old Earth and at least five other planets."

"All right, on seven planets out of the—what? Isn't it something like seventeen *hundred* total inhabited worlds now?"

"As a trained astrogator, you should appreciate the need for precision," Honor said with a crooked grin, just as the pitcher uncorked a nasty, sharp-breaking slider. The wooden bat cracked explosively as it made contact and sent the ball slicing back out over the field. It crossed the short, inner perimeter wall which divided the playing field from the rest of the stadium, and Henke jumped to her feet and opened her mouth to cheer. Then she realized that Honor hadn't moved, and she turned to prop her hands on her hips with an expression halfway between martyred and exasperated.

"I take it that there's some reason that *wasn't* a—whatchamacallit? A 'homerun'?"

"It's not a homerun unless it stays between the foul poles when it crosses the outfield wall, Mike," Honor told her, pointing at the yellow and white striped pylons. "That one went foul by at least ten or fifteen feet."

"Feet? *Feet?*" Henke shot back. "My God, woman! Can't you at least keep track of the distances in this silly sport using measurement units civilized people can recognize?"

"*Michelle!*" Honor looked at her with the horror normally reserved for someone who stood up in church to announce she'd decided to take up devil worship and that the entire congregation was invited out to her house for a Black Mass and lemonade.

"What?" Henke demanded in a voice whose severity was only slightly undermined by the twinkle in her eyes.

"I suppose I shouldn't have been as shocked as I was," Honor said, more in sorrow than in anger. "After all, I, too, was once even as you, an infidel lost and unaware of how barren my prebaseball existence had truly been. Fortunately, one who had already seen the truth was there to bring me to the light," she added, and waved to the short, wiry auburn-haired man who stood in his green-on-green uniform directly behind her. "Andrew," she said, "would you be kind enough to tell the Commodore what you said to me when I asked you why it was ninety feet between bases instead of twenty-seven and a half meters?"

"What you actually asked, My Lady," Lieutenant Colonel Andrew LaFollett replied in a gravely meticulous tone, "was why we hadn't converted to meters and rounded up to twenty-eight of them between each pair of bases. Actually, you sounded just a bit put out over it, if I recall correctly."

"Whatever," Honor said with a lordly, dismissive wave. "Just tell her what you told me."

"Of course, My Lady," the commander of her personal security detachment agreed, and turned courteously to Henke. "What I said to the Steadholder, Countess Gold Peak," he said, "was 'This is *baseball*, My Lady!'"

"You see?" Honor said smugly. "There's a perfectly logical reason."

"Somehow, I don't think that adjective means exactly what you think it does," Henke told her with a chuckle. "On the other hand, I have heard it said that Graysons are just a bit on the traditional side, so I suppose there's really no reason to expect them to change anything about a game just because it's over two thousand years old and might need a little updating."

"Updating is only a good idea if it constitutes an improvement, as well, My Lady," LaFollet pointed out. "And it's not quite fair to say we haven't made any changes. If the record books are accurate, there was a time, in at least one league back on Old Earth, when the pitcher didn't even have to bat. Or when a manager could make as many pitching changes in a single game as he wanted to. Saint Austen put an end to that nonsense, at least!"

Henke rolled her eyes and sank back into her seat.

"I hope you won't take this the wrong way, Andrew," she told the colonel, "but somehow the discovery that the founder of your religion was also a baseball fanatic doesn't really surprise me. It certainly explains the careful preservation of some of the . . . archaic aspects of the game, anyway."

"I wouldn't say Saint Austen was a fanatic about baseball, My Lady," LaFollet replied in a considering tone. " 'Fanatic' would probably be much too mild a term, from everything I've ever read."

"I never would have guessed," Henke said dryly, letting her eyes sweep over the stadium once more. The huge sports facility seated at least sixty thousand in its tiers of comfortably upholstered chairs, and she hated to think how much the place must have cost. Especially on a planet like Grayson, where what would normally have been outdoor sports required stadiums with things like air filtration systems just to protect the local population from the heavy metal contents of their own atmosphere.

Not that any expense had been spared on more mundane considerations when James Candless Memorial Field was erected. The immaculately manicured playing field was a green jewel, broken only by white stripes of the traditional powdered lime and the bare, rich brown earth of the base lines. The colors of the field and the even brighter colors of the festively garbed spectators glowed brilliantly in the protective dome's filtered sunlight, and the crowd was liberally festooned with team pennants and banners exhorting the home team to victory. There was even a ventilation system carefully designed to exactly recreate the wind conditions outside the dome, and the Grayson planetary flag, with its crossed swords and open Bible, flew from the top of one of the two foul poles while the Harrington Steading flag flew from the other.

She let her eyes rest balefully on those same foul poles for a moment, then glanced at the huge digital scoreboard projected holographically above the infield, and sighed.

"I know I'm going to regret asking this, but would one of you insufferable know-it-alls care to explain to me where *that*—" she pointed at the scarlet numeral "2" which had appeared in the "STRIKES" column "—came from? I thought it was only strike one."

"That was before the foul ball, Mike," Honor explained brightly.

"But he hit it," Henke protested.

"It doesn't matter. A foul ball counts as a strike."

"But—"

Henke broke off as the pitcher delivered a curveball, which the batter promptly hooked foul over the third base dugout. She looked expectantly at the scoreboard, then drew a deep breath as the count of balls and strikes remained unchanged.

"I thought you said—" she began.

"Foul balls are only strikes until the count has already reached two strikes," Honor said. "After that, they don't count as strikes . . . or balls, either, for that matter. Unless one of them is caught by one of the fielders, of course. Then it counts as an out instead of a dead ball."

Henke regarded her sourly, and Honor grinned back. The countess glowered, then turned an equally disapproving expression upon the armsman.

"'Simple game,'" she snorted. "Right. Sure!"

The Harrington Treecats lost by a score of eleven to two.

Michelle Henke tried valiantly to project an air of proper commiseration as the luxury air car swept up to the owner's box's private slip to collect her and her hostess' party. Alas, her success was less than total.

"It isn't nice to gloat, Mike," Honor informed her with a certain severity.

"Gloat? Me, gloat? Me, a peer of the Star Kingdom, *gloat* just because your team got waxed while you and your friend the Colonel were so busy pointing out my abysmal ignorance to me? How could you possibly suggest that I'd do such a thing?"

"Possibly because I've known you so long."

"And possibly because it's exactly what you'd be doing if our positions were reversed," Henke suggested.

"All things are possible," Honor agreed. "On the other hand, some are less likely than others, and given the strength of my own character, that one's less likely than most."

"Oh, of course. I keep forgetting what a modest, shy and retiring type you are, Honor," Henke said as they climbed into the air limo, followed by LaFollet, carrying Nimitz's mate Samantha, and the rest of Honor's regular three-man detachment.

"Not shy and retiring. Simply a more mature and responsible individual."

"Not so mature and responsible that you didn't name your team after a certain furry, six-footed celery-thief and his friends," Henke shot back, reaching out to rub the treecat on Honor's shoulder between his ears.

"Nimitz and Samantha had nothing to do with my choice," Honor replied. "Mind you, they approved of it, but I actually picked it as the lesser of two evils." She grimaced. "It was that, or the 'Harrington Salamanders.'"

Henke looked up sharply, then spluttered a half-smothered laugh.

"You're joking!"

"I wish I were. As a matter of fact, the Commissioner of Baseball had already assigned the Salamanders name when the Owners' Committee and the Rules Committee agreed to expand the league. I had an awful time changing their minds."

"I think it would've been a marvelous name," Henke told her with an impish grin.

"I'm sure you do," Honor said repressively. "I, on the other hand, don't. Leaving aside the entire question of modesty, can you imagine how High Ridge and his crowd would have reacted? It would have been tailor-made for their op-ed pieces!"

"Um." Henke's grin vanished at the reminder of the unpleasant political realities inherent in the existence of the High Ridge Government. Those realties had become progressively less pleasant and more personal, for Honor at least, over the last three-plus T-years. Which, Henke knew, was the real reason her friend had been so delighted to return briefly to Grayson to attend to her obligations as Steadholder Harrington. It was also one of the reasons Henke herself had shown such alacrity in accepting the invitation to spend her own leave as Honor's guest here.

"You're probably right," she said, after a moment. "Of course, in any properly run universe, High Ridge would never have become Prime Minister in the first place, much less held onto the office for so long. I think I'll complain to the management."

"I do that every Sunday," Honor assured her with very little humor indeed. "And I suspect the Protector has Reverend Sullivan do the same thing, just to put a little more horsepower behind it."

"Horsepower or not, it doesn't seem to be working," Henke observed. She shook her head. "I can't believe they've managed to hang on so long.

I mean, Jesus, Honor, most of them *hate* each other! And as for their ideologies—!"

"Of course they hate each other. Unfortunately, at this particular moment they hate your cousin even more. Or feel sufficiently scared of her to hang together, come what may, in opposition to her, at any rate."

"I know," Henke sighed. "I know." She shook her head again. "Beth always has had a temper. It's too bad she still hasn't learned to keep it muzzled."

"That's not quite fair," Honor disagreed, and Henke arched an eyebrow at her.

Michelle Henke, thanks to the assassination which had killed her father, her older brother, the Duke of Cromarty, and the entire crew of the Queen's royal yacht, stood fifth in the line of succession for the Crown of the Star Kingdom of Manticore. Her mother, Caitrin Winton-Henke, Duchess Winton-Henke and Dowager Countess Gold Peak, was Queen Elizabeth III's aunt, the only sibling of the Queen's father, and now Michelle was her mother's only surviving child. Henke had never expected to stand so high in the succession, or to inherit her father's title, for that matter. But she'd known Elizabeth all of her life, and she was only too familiar with the fiery Winton temper which the Queen had inherited in full measure.

Despite that, she had to admit that Honor had actually spent more time with the Queen over the last three T-years than Michelle herself had. Indeed, the visibility of Duchess Harrington as one of the Crown's staunchest supporters in the Lords (and as one of the inner circle of "kitchen advisers" the Queen turned to for advice instead of the members of her official government) was one reason the pro-Government media had spent so much time trying to discredit Honor in any way it could. The subtle (and sometimes not so subtle) vilification which had come her way had been downright ugly at times. But however that might be, she admitted, Honor had not only spent more time working with Elizabeth but also possessed certain advantages others lacked when it came to evaluating people and their emotions. Still . . .

"Honor, I love Beth as my cousin, and I respect her as my monarch," she said after a moment. "But she has the temper of a hexapuma with a broken tooth when something sets her off, and you and I both know it. If she'd just managed to hang onto it when the High Ridge Government was first being formed, she might have been able to split them up instead of driving them together in opposition to her."

"I didn't say she'd handled things perfectly," Honor pointed out, leaning back while Nimitz arranged himself comfortably across her lap. Samantha wiggled down from LaFollet's arms to join him, and Honor gave the female 'cat's ears a welcoming caress. "In fact," she went on, "Elizabeth would be the first to agree that she blew her best opportunity to hang onto control when she lost her temper with them. But while you've been off having adventures in space, I've been sitting on my posterior in the House of Lords, watching High Ridge in action. And from what I've seen there, I don't think it really mattered, in the long run, how she handled them."

"I beg your pardon?" Henke said just a bit

uncomfortably. She knew Honor hadn't meant it as a criticism, but she couldn't help feeling at least a little guilty. Her mother held a seat of her own in the Lords as a duchess in her own right, so she and Michelle had seen no reason why she shouldn't hold her daughter's proxy and represent them both. Duchess Winton-Henke had always found politics far more absorbing than Michelle ever had, and the deaths of her husband and son had left her looking for a distraction. Michelle had needed a distraction of her own, which she'd found by throwing herself even more completely into her space-going duties as an officer in the Royal Manticoran Navy.

A distraction Honor had been conspicuously denied.

"Even assuming that there were no ideological fissures within the High Ridge Government, there aren't enough Conservatives, Liberals, and Progressives in the Lords to sustain High Ridge's majority without the support of at least some of the Independents," Honor pointed out. "High Ridge has managed to bring Wallace's New Men on board, as well, of course, but even that's not enough to change the dynamics of the major parties significantly. And however much she might have frightened or angered High Ridge and his cronies, she never said anything threatening to the Independents who've decided to support him, now did she?"

"No," Henke admitted, remembering bits and pieces of conversations she'd had with her mother and finding herself wishing she'd paid more attention at the time.

"Of course not. He managed to gain their support without her ever losing her temper with them.

And even if she had, you would have thought something like the Manpower Scandal would have split a lot of those Independents away from the Government."

"As a matter of fact, that's exactly what I expected to happen when Cathy Montaigne dropped her bomb," Henke agreed, and shrugged. "Personally, I always liked Cathy. I thought she was a little dippy before she went off to Old Earth, maybe, but it was obvious she's always believed in her principles. And, damn, but I like her style."

"I've decided I like her, too," Honor confessed. "I never thought I'd say that about any member of the Liberal Party, either. Of course, aside from the Liberals' anti-genetic slavery stance, I don't know how much she really has in common with the rest of 'her' party." Honor's tone remained almost serene, but her eyes narrowed dangerously. Her bred-in-the-bone hatred for the genetic slave trade was as implacable as a Sphinx winter, probably because of her mother. "I don't believe I've ever heard anyone else express herself so, um . . . eloquently on the topic," she added.

"She does have a way with words, and I'd certainly agree that she suffers from a certain tunnel vision on that particular topic," Henke allowed with a smile. "Not to mention a pronounced need to kick the Establishment in the teeth just on general principles. One of my cousins is married to Cathy's brother-in-law George Larabee, Lord Altamont, and she tells me Lady Altamont, George's mother, is absolutely livid over the way Cathy is openly 'living in sin' with a mere commoner. And not just any commoner! A Gryphon highlander who's on half-pay for his offenses against military discipline!"

Henke chuckled, then sobered.

"This time, though, I thought she had the bastards nailed. God knows how she got her hands on those records—and, personally, I'll be just as happy if He never gets around to explaining it all to me. But from what Mom said, and from everything I read in the 'faxes, it certainly sounded like there wasn't much question that they were genuine."

"No question at all." Honor, who, unlike Henke, had a very good notion of how the Countess of the Tor had come into possession of the damning documentation, agreed. For a moment, she considered explaining her suspicions about Captain Zilwicki and his role in the mysterious intelligence windfall to her friend, then decided against it. They weren't really something Mike needed to know . . . just as she didn't need to know some of the other things Andrew LaFollet had discovered about Anton Zilwicki. Like exactly what it was that the half-pay captain's new private security firm was doing with some of the information which the Countess had *not* turned over to the authorities.

"Unfortunately," she went on instead, "the individuals who were specifically named were all relatively small fish. Socially prominent in some cases, perhaps, and politically important enough to be highly visible in others, but not close enough to the seats of power to be really crippling. The fact that so many of them had connections to the Conservatives and—especially!—to certain members of the Liberal Party, as well, was certainly embarrassing. For that matter, the Ministry of Justice has put a couple of dozen of them away for a long, long time. But there were just enough of them in the other parties or among the Independents—even two among the Centrists, I'm sorry to say—for the apologists to argue that 'everyone did it' and keep any one party from being singled out for blame. And the fact that there were no direct links to the party leaders let the Government defuse the worst possible repercussions by shouting louder than anyone else for the prosecution of the individuals who were named. Like Hendricks, when they recalled him from Old Terra and sent out a new ambassador."

"Or Admiral Young," Henke said grimly, and Honor nodded with a carefully neutral expression. The implacable hostility between her and the Young clan went back for over forty T-years, punctuated by bitter hatred and more than one death. Which was one reason she'd taken great pains to maintain her facade of neutrality when the Navy recalled Admiral Edwin Young from Old Terra, convicted him of violation of the Articles of War before a court-martial, and stripped him of his rank. The civilian courts had been equally harsh, even with his family links to the powerful Earl of North Hollow, whose influence at the highest level of the Prime Minister's own Conservative Association was enormous. He'd managed to escape the death penalty, but despite his exalted birth, he would be spending the next several decades as a guest of the Royal Ministry of Justice.

"Or like Young," she agreed after a moment. "In fact, what happened to him is a pretty fair example of just how ruthlessly the leadership was prepared to cut its losses . . . and exactly who they were prepared to jettison in the process. He was a Young, which made him highly visible, and a Navy flag officer, which made his 'isolated criminal actions' even more satisfyingly visceral. But he was only a fourth cousin of North Hollow, and, frankly, he was a nonentity in terms of the Conservative Association's real power structure. So when North Hollow made no move to save him, he became a highly satisfactory sacrifice to the 'principles' of his noble relative and simultaneously served as 'proof' that North Hollow himself and—by extension—all of the Conservative Association's leadership had never been involved in such heinous offenses. Which was precisely why the Government party leaders turned on *all* the minor fish so violently . . . and publicly. After all, they'd not only broken the law; they'd also betrayed the trust those leaders had reposed in them." It was Honor's turn to shrug. "Much as it stuck in my craw, I have to admit it was a brilliant job of political damage control. Which, however, High Ridge and New Kiev only managed to pull off because a majority of the Lords who weren't involved, including the Independents, decided to look the other way and settle for scapegoats."

"But why?" Henke demanded. "Mom said exactly the same thing to me in one of her letters, but I never understood the logic behind it."

"It all comes down to politics and what you might call the historical imperatives of constitutional evolution," Honor told her as two heavily armed stingships in the markings of the Harrington Steadholder's Guard slid into place on either wing.

She and Henke were invited to supper at Protector's Palace, and Honor leaned further back and crossed her legs as the air limo started out on the lengthy flight to Mayhew Steading through a brilliantly blue, cloud-stippled sky, carefully watched over by its escorts.

"Basically," she said, "a majority of the House of Lords are willing to close their eyes to things they don't want to know about, even where something like slavery is concerned, because, however honest they may be themselves, they'd rather have a government like High Ridge's than take a chance on what might replace it. Despite all the corruption and pork barrel vote-buying that involves, they regard High Ridge as a lesser risk than giving Elizabeth and her supporters back control of both houses."

"Mom said something about that—and about how San Martin fitted into the political equation. But she was in a hurry to finish her letter, and I never asked her for a complete explanation," Henke confessed.

"To paraphrase something Admiral Courvoisier once said to me, no captain—or commodore—in the Queen's Navy can afford to be a virgin where politics are concerned, Mike. And especially not when she also stands as close to the Throne as you do."

There was absolutely no condemnation in Honor's tone, but there was a certain sternness in her eyes as her gaze locked ever so briefly with Henke's. The countess looked back almost defiantly for a few heartbeats, but then her eyes fell, and she nodded in unhappy agreement.

"I know," she admitted in a lower voice. "It's just—Well, I suppose when it comes right down to it, I never really liked politics much more than you did. And since Dad and Cal were killed and that slimy bastard managed to steal the premiership from Willie Alexander, the very thought of sitting down in the same chamber as him is enough to turn my stomach."

"And you the one who was just criticizing the Queen for her temper!" Honor scolded gently.

"Guilty as charged," Henke acknowledged. "But you were saying?"

"I was saying that a majority of the House of Lords is backing High Ridge for reasons of its own. Which is probably what your mother meant when she mentioned San Martin. That same majority is afraid of what will happen when the San Martino peers are finally seated."

"Why?" Henke asked with such genuine incomprehension that Honor, despite herself, sighed.

"Mike," she said patiently, "this is basic Political History 101. What's the one thing the Crown has been trying to take away from the Lords ever since there's been a Star Kingdom?"

"The power of the purse," Henke replied.

"Very good," Honor said. "But the Founders, who were otherwise a fairly decent lot, were virtually unanimous in their determination to see to it that they and their descendants hung onto the real political power in the Star Kingdom. That's why the Constitution specifically requires that the Prime Minister come from the House of Lords and specifies that any finance bill must be introduced in the Lords. I happen to think there's something to be said for placing substantial political power in the hands of a legislative chamber which can be . . . insulated from the political and ideological hysteria *du jour*, but the Founders set up too much of a good thing. The fact that they never have to stand for election means that too many of the peers—present company excluded, of course—have . . . questionable contact with reality, let's say. Worse, it's even easier for someone who inherits her title to become an empire builder within the Parliament. Trust me," she added dryly. "I've seen how that works on two different planets now, and with a considerably better vantage point than I ever wanted."

She gazed useeingly out the window at the port escort for several seconds, her long fingers gently caressing both 'cats' soft, silky fur. Nimitz looked up at her speculatively as he tasted her emotions through their empathic link. For a moment, Henke half-expected him to sink his claws, however gently, into Honor's kneecap. He was quite capable of making his displeasure evident when it was time to scold his person for brooding over past events no one could change, anyway. But this time he decided against it, and left Honor alone until she shook herself and turned back to their guest.

"Anyway, I think that over all the Crown would be just as happy to leave the premiership where it is. Much as I like and respect your cousin, honesty compels me to point out that she does have a vested interest in maintaining an hereditary aristocratic system. And I suppose that while I'm in honest mode, I should probably point out that you and I do, too. Now, at least.

"But for generations, the Crown has wanted to see a better balance between the powers of the Commons and the Lords, and the best way to accomplish that would be to give the Commons control of the purse as a counterweight to leaving the premiership permanently lodged in the Lords. Except that the Crown has never been able to assemble the required majority in the Lords to amend the Constitution to transfer that power to the lower house."

"Of course not," Henke snorted with the rich contempt for aristocratic defense of privilege possible only for one born to that same aristocracy. "What? You really think that anyone who has as good a thing going for them as the peers do is going to vote to give half of her power to someone else?"

"Actually," Honor said seriously, "that's exactly what High Ridge is afraid of, and a lot of the Independents agree with him."

"That's what Mom said," Henke said in an exasperated voice, "but I just can't see it happening, somehow."

"High Ridge can. And so can Elizabeth and Willie Alexander. It's all a matter of numbers, Mike, and the San Martino peers could very well shift the balance in the Lords to a point that makes it possible for the Queen to pull it off at last. But the joker in the deck is the combination of the Constitution's limit on the creation of new peerages and the terms of the Act of Annexation which admitted Trevor's Star to the Star Kingdom. The Constitution limits increases in the total membership of the House of Lords to no more than ten percent between any two general elections, and the Act of Annexation specifies that none of the new peers from San Martin will be confirmed or seated until after the *next* general election.

"So what the Government and its supporters in the Lords are trying to do is to postpone that election as long as possible. At the moment, there's not much question that the San Martinos are very solidly behind the Queen and the Centrists. After all, it was our Navy, under Elizabeth and the Cromarty Government, which kicked the Peeps out of the Trevor's Star System and liberated them, and it was Cromarty and your father, as Foreign Secretary, who negotiated the actual terms of their admission to the Star Kingdom. Not only that, but San Martin had no hereditary aristocracy before its annexation, so it's not likely that the San Martinos are going to have the same . . . devoted attachment to the *status quo* in Parliament. Gratitude to the people they see as responsible for their liberation, coupled with that lack of aristocratic tradition, means the new peers would be likely—almost certain, in fact—to support a motion by Lord Alexander, as the leader of the Centrist Party, to transfer that power of the purse to the House of Commons.

"But until they're actually seated, they can't support anything. And what High Ridge and his cronies are up to right now is building a sufficiently strong majority among the members of the existing peerage to resist any such action. According to the latest figures I've seen, the number of current peers opposed to the required constitutional amendment gives them at least a fifteen-percent edge, but that number could erode. And even if it doesn't, two general elections will put enough San Martinos into the Lords to overcome it, assuming their support for the amendment is solid.

"So in addition to trying to increase their own margin of support among the peers, High Ridge and his allies are trying to cut into the Centrist majority in the Commons, as well. Since it's the Commons who vote to confirm the creation of any new peerages, High Ridge hopes that if he can increase his clout in the lower house, he may be able to influence the approval process in a way that confirms peers he figures can be co-opted to support of the continued dominance of the Lords.

"The fact that San Martino MPs are going to be card-carrying Centrists or Crown Loyalists lends that particular concern added point. Technically, San Martin still doesn't have any MPs, either, but their 'special representatives' in the Commons are serving a lot of the same functions, even if they can't actually vote yet. And there's no question where their loyalties lie. Nor have any of the peers failed to take note of that little fact.

"And that, Mike, is why otherwise reasonably decent members of the House of Lords are actively supporting a piece of work like High Ridge and let him get away with his damage control on the Manpower Scandal. None of them really like him, very few of them have any illusions about the 'thoroughness' of his investigation of Countess Tor's charges, and most of them wouldn't trust him or any of his allies to look after their dogs, much less their children. But their general position is that even if the present Constitution is imperfect, the

system it's created has served the Star Kingdom
well, and at the moment, he's the one defending
the *status quo*. I doubt that many of them are blind
to the degree of self-interest inherent in their
opposition to changing it, but that doesn't make
their opposition any less genuine."

"I see." Henke leaned back in her own seat,
facing Honor across the passenger compartment of
the luxurious vehicle. It still startled her whenever
she heard Honor Harrington, of all people, ana-
lyzing politics so clearly and concisely. It shouldn't,
she supposed, given how acutely Honor had always
been able to analyze military problems, but for
almost forty T-years, it had always been Henke who
understood the Star Kingdom's internal politics
better than Honor did. Of course, Henke's understanding had been based on her own family connections. As the Queen's first cousin, she'd absorbed
that understanding almost by osmosis, without ever
really having to think very much about it. Which,
she admitted now, might be part of the reason
Honor saw the current situation so much more
clearly than she did, for Honor hadn't been born
into those rarified circles. She'd come to them with
a lack of instinctive, insider awareness which had
forced her to really think about her new environment.

But the fact that her friend hadn't been born
to power and nurtured within the ranks of the Star
Kingdom's hereditary elite also created some dangerous blind spots, Henke reflected with carefully
hidden anxiety. Blind spots that left her unaware
of dangers someone like Henke herself would have
recognized instantly, despite any distaste for politics.

In spite of all that had happened to place Honor at the very pivot of political power in two separate star nations, she continued to think of herself—and her private life—as the yeoman's daughter she had always been.

Michelle Henke faced her friend and wondered yet again if she should say something to her, remind her of how her private life could and would be used against her by her political foes if she gave them an opening. If she should ask Honor if there were any truth to the rumors beginning to be whispered ever so quietly.

"That sounds like it makes sense," she said instead, after a moment. "It still surprises me to hear it coming from you, though, I guess. May I ask if Lord Alexander shares your analysis?"

"Of course he does. You don't think I haven't discussed it with him—at length—do you?" Honor snorted. "Between my own position in the Lords and my role as Benjamin's friend at court, I've spent more hours than I care to think about in skull sessions with the man who *ought* to be Prime Minister!"

"Yes, I suppose you'd have to," Henke agreed slowly, and cocked her head ever so slightly. "And has Earl White Haven been able to add anything to your perspective, as well?"

"Yes," Honor replied, reaching down to stroke Nimitz's spine. Her eyes, Henke noticed, dropped to watch her own hand on the treecat's silken pelt rather than meet her guest's gaze, and the brevity of her one-word response struck Henke as . . . ominous.

For one moment, the countess considered

pressing further, making the question explicit. After all, if she couldn't ask Honor, who could? But the problem was that she couldn't, and so she only leaned back in her own chair and nodded.

"That tallies with what Mom was saying, too," she said then. "And I guess she figured I should have known enough about what was going on to understand it without her drawing a detailed map for me the way you just did." She shrugged. "Sometimes I think she never realized how much I left all that sort of thing to Cal. I was too busy with the Navy."

A fresh memory of sorrow flowed across her face, but she banished it quickly and produced a lopsided smile.

"Now that you *have* explained it, though, I see what you meant about historical imperatives. I still say Beth's temper didn't help things any, though."

"No, it didn't," Honor agreed, looking up from her lapful of 'cat once more with a slight air of what might have been relief. "If nothing else, it made the stakes personal for High Ridge, New Kiev, and Descroix. But from the moment the Duke of Cromarty and your father were killed, it was almost inevitable that we'd wind up where we are. Except, of course, that no one on either side could have realized what was going to happen in the People's Republic while we were tending to our domestic squabbles."

"You can say that again," Henke agreed somberly, and cocked her head. "Do you think Pritchart and Theisman understand what's happening any better than I did?"

"I certainly hope so," Honor said dryly.

DAVID WEBER

The Honor Harrington series: *(cont.)*

Flag in Exile

Hounded into retirement and disgrace by political enemies, Honor Harrington has retreated to planet Grayson, where powerful men plot to reverse the changes she has brought to their world. And for their plans to succeed, Honor Harrington must die!

Honor Among Enemies

Offered a chance to end her exile and again command a ship, Honor Harrington must use a crew drawn from the dregs of the service to stop pirates who are plundering commerce. Her enemies have chosen the mission carefully, thinking that either she will stop the raiders or they will kill her . . . and either way, her enemies will win. . . .

In Enemy Hands

After being ambushed, Honor finds herself aboard an enemy cruiser, bound for her scheduled execution. But one lesson Honor has never learned is how to give up!

Echoes of Honor

"Brilliant! Brilliant! Brilliant!"—*Anne McCaffrey*

Ashes of Victory

Honor has escaped from the prison planet called Hell and returned to the Manticoran Alliance, to the heart of a furnace of new weapons, new strategies, new tactics, spies, diplomacy, and assassination.

continued ☞

DAVID DRAKE RULES!

When it comes to the best
in science fiction and fantasy,
Baen Books has something for *everyone!*

IF YOU LIKE...
YOU SHOULD ALSO TRY...